Also by Samantha Chase

The Montgomery Brothers
Wait for Me
Trust in Me
Stay with Me
More of Me
Return to You
Meant for You
I'll Be There

The Shaughnessy Brothers
Made for Us
Love Walks In
Always My Girl
This Is Our Song
A Sky Full of Stars
Holiday Spice

Shaughnessy Brothers: Band on the Run
One More Kiss
One More Promise

Holiday Romance
The Christmas Cottage / Ever After
Mistletoe Between Friends / The Snowflake Inn

Life, Love and Babies
The Baby Arrangement
Baby, I'm Yours
Baby, Be Mine

In the EYE of the STORM

······································

CATERING to the CEO

SAMANTHA CHASE

sourcebooks
casablanca

In the Eye of the Storm © 2013, 2018 by Samantha Chase
Catering to the CEO © 2013, 2018 by Samantha Chase
Cover and internal design © 2018 by Sourcebooks, Inc.
Cover design by Dawn Adams/Sourcebooks, Inc.
Cover image © Bruce Ayres/Getty Images

Published by Sourcebooks Casablanca, an imprint of Sourcebooks, Inc.
P.O. Box 4410, Naperville, Illinois 60567-4410
(630) 961-3900
Fax: (630) 961-2168
sourcebooks.com

Printed and bound in Canada.
MBP 10 9 8 7 6 5 4 3 2 1

For Emilie—thank you for encouraging me when I doubted myself and for helping me achieve my dream. I hope to someday be able to return the favor. XOXO

Contents

In the Eye of the Storm
1

Catering to the CEO
185

In the EYE of the STORM

Chapter 1

"I COULD DO WITHOUT THIS RAIN," HOLLY MUMBLED UNDER her breath as she ran from the front door of her home to her little Toyota SUV in the driveway. "Two o'clock in the morning, and he feels the need to call *me* for help.

"I mean, who calls their assistant in the middle of the night to come and pick them up with no explanation? It's unreasonable! It's selfish, it's obnoxious, and it is so going to stop tonight!" Feeling better after her little pep talk, Holly drove off into the stormy night to pick up the man who was persona non grata at the moment.

Stephen Ballinger. Just thinking his name made Holly grind her teeth in agitation.

Checking her GPS and trying to figure out where exactly she was, she continued to stay the course down the highway for another twelve miles until her exit. The sky was illuminated with a steady stream of lightning strikes, and Holly shivered with the fierceness of it.

"I could quit! I have money in savings," she began. "It's not like I'd starve to death or anything. Most companies would love someone like me." Thinking she sounded a little smug didn't stop her from continuing. "I mean, I am a hard worker, I don't take frivolous amounts of time off, I'm never sick, I'm available almost 24/7 because I have no social life, *and...*"

Having worked for Stephen for three years, Holly thought she had seen and done everything humanly possible that could be expected of a personal assistant. She wouldn't mind so much if it didn't all have to be done on top of the twelve-hour day she normally put in with Stephen at the office. But the extra work was becoming a problem. The call tonight had made her suddenly feel as if it were all coming to a head. That phone call—that stupid two a.m. phone call—was the proverbial straw that broke the camel's back.

The man had friends; why not call one of them? He had a personal driver! Why not call him? Why, oh why, had he insisted on dragging Holly out of bed at this ungodly hour—in the pouring rain, no less!—and making her come get him? It made no sense whatsoever.

A strong wind shook the silver SUV, and Holly held the steering wheel a little tighter. The rain seemed to be coming down harder. What had the weatherman said on the news tonight? she wondered. Wasn't this the outer bands of some tropical storm? Great, just what she needed: to be out in the middle of the night in a tropical storm, looking for a place that she was unfamiliar with.

Pulling into the parking lot as directed, she pulled out her cell phone and texted Stephen to alert him to her arrival. Hitting the send button, she sat back and waited. And waited. And waited. With each second that passed, her ire grew. "What in the world?" she yelled to no one, slamming the steering wheel. Picking up her phone once again, she dialed his number and waited to hear his voice. The phone went directly to voicemail. Turning the car off, Holly threw the door open with a huff of frustration, pulled up the hood of her jacket, and hopped out of the car, cursing like a sailor the entire time. A strong wind nearly blew her into the bushes, and she screeched at the closeness of a lightning strike.

Stalking to the heavy wood door of the bar, she yanked it open and stepped inside. She spotted Stephen practically slumped over the bar. Not really caring what kind of shape he was in, she stomped over to him and said his name. Loudly. The place was fairly deserted, but the eighties big-hair metal music coming from the sound system was a bit loud.

"*Stephen!*"

He stirred a little and lifted his head. It seemed to take a minute for things to come into focus. With a grunt of thanks toward the bartender, Stephen stood and threw a twenty down on the bar before walking out the door straight to Holly's car and climbing in on the passenger side. For a minute, Holly was too dumbfounded to move. She glanced at the bartender with raised eyebrows and questions written all over her face.

"He drank. He fought." The man shrugged. "He lost. Thanks for getting him out of here. Now I can close up." With those few short words, the bartender turned his back on her and went about his business.

"Thank you," Holly mumbled and walked out the door. Climbing into the car, she fought off a chill from the rain. While her first instinct was to yell and rant and rave and demand to know what in the world had gone on tonight, her main need was to get the heat going in the car once again.

Stephen's head was turned away from her, and for a moment, Holly thought he was asleep. "Absolutely not," she murmured and summoned all her courage to confront this man who had ruined her night.

"Stephen," she snapped and waited for him to face her. He finally did on the third try. "What went on here tonight?"

"Nothing."

"Really? So I had to come out in a monsoon in the middle of the night to a place I don't know over nothing. Is that what you're telling me?"

He sighed wearily. "Look, if I had any other option, I would have called someone else—"

"There are cabs," Holly interrupted. "Then there's your driver, George. I thought his sole purpose in life was to drive you where you needed to go! Then there's Will and Derek, who probably would have—"

"They were here earlier, and they are the reason I had no ride." His tone was quiet, serious, and sleepy.

"You fought with Will and Derek, and so they *left* you here? You are grown men! Why would they do that?" Her voice was raised, and she noticed Stephen wince at the volume. Clearly her brain was still not fully awake because none of this made any sense, and Stephen *always* made sense.

"I don't want to talk about it, okay? I need to go home and get some sleep."

The man had some nerve! "Oh, you want sleep?" Holly asked sarcastically. "Well, you know what? So did I. As a matter of fact, I wanted it so badly that I already *was* asleep, as is most of the normal population at two o'clock in the morning!" Taking a moment to calm down, she pulled the car out of the bar's parking lot, unsure where they were going. If she could have, Holly would have avoided any more conversation, but she had no other option.

"Um, Stephen, I know this is an odd question, but I have no idea where we're going."

He punched the information into the GPS and then leaned heavily back against the seat, looking away from her again. "My house," he said.

"Well, I figured that much, genius. But you moved last month, and since I was handling all the stuff at the old place, I haven't been to the new one yet. Geez." A small chuckle had Holly turning her head ever so slightly to look at him. "Something funny to you?"

"You're not normally this snippy at the office," he observed.

"That's because it's never two thirty in the morning while we're at work, and I've normally had a full night's sleep. A full night's *uninterrupted* sleep."

"Cute. Sarcasm. That's never been an issue in the office either. This is a side of you I've never seen before." He yawned and settled more comfortably into the passenger seat, clearly not having a problem with all the frustration Holly was feeling.

"Wake me up in the middle of the night again, and you won't have to worry about what is and what isn't an issue in the office because I won't be there," Holly snapped.

"*What?*" That got his attention.

"You heard me, Stephen. You may be my boss Monday through Friday, but you know what? You have no respect for my personal time! Do you have any idea how inconvenient this was for me?" Before he had the chance to answer, Holly went on. "No, of course you don't, because you don't care who is inconvenienced as long as it's not you. I mean, I would *never* call someone in the middle of the night unless it was a dire emergency and—"

"It was," Stephen tried to argue.

Holly silenced him with a hard glare. "No, it wasn't. You could have called a cab. You *chose* not to. Why? Because you didn't think it was any big deal to wake me up in the middle of the night to jump through fiery hoops for you!"

"Holly, it's a drive in the car—"

"It's *two in the morning*, Stephen! And have you noticed the weather? Do *not* try to make it seem like I am wrong to have a problem with this."

"Fine, I'll pay you for the time."

If there could possibly be the number one wrong thing to say in this situation, that was it. Holly jerked the car over to the side of the road, threw it into park, and turned to face Stephen, full of fury. "Seriously?" For a moment, it was a toss-up as to who was more surprised by what she said. "You think it's okay to do something so inconsiderate and then throw money at me? What is *wrong* with you?"

Rubbing his temples and finally snapping out of the stupor of the last few minutes, Stephen turned to face her. "Look, had I known this was going to turn into such a fiasco, believe me, I would have *walked* home!" he growled, full of frustration. "I didn't think calling a friend was going to cause all this, for crying out loud, Holly! Stop being such a drama queen."

Drama queen? She saw red. Everything around her seemed tinged in a bright, fiery red. "How dare you! And friends? *Friends*?" she shrieked. "Since when are you and I friends?"

"We're not?" His voice was instantly calm, and he seemed perplexed by this knowledge.

"*No*, we are *not*! I work for you. I work hard for you. Five days a week, fourteen hours a day at times, and that's not including the weekends when you give me extra projects! We don't pal around, we don't socialize, and we don't hang out outside of the office." Holly realized she had some major anger issues going on and decided to take a moment to calm down. After a few seconds, she looked up, met his eyes, and said quietly, "We work together. You are my boss, and I am your assistant. I don't know how to be friends with you, Stephen."

"Why? What's so hard about being friends with me?"

"Well, for starters, everything we have together at work is all about you. It's *your* company. *You* are in charge. Everything we do is focused around you and your needs or the company's needs. While we're working, we're talking about work. When we stay late and while we eat dinner, we still *only* talk about work and your plans about *more* work. You know nothing about me that wasn't on my résumé, you never ask about me or my life, and you are rather inconsiderate of my personal time. That's not friendship, Stephen, that's being a boss. And an inconsiderate one at that! Do you know where I'm from? Do you know how many siblings I have? What I wanted to be when I grew up? Why I chose the college I did? What's my favorite color? Or my favorite flower? Did you know that I have a fear of water due to a boating accident in high school? *No!* Because you do not *care* about my life. All you care about is Ballinger's."

He stared at Holly for a long moment, barely blinking. When her green eyes had met his minutes ago, something weird happened. It was as if he was seeing Holly for the first time. His brows furrowed as he continued to stare at her. That was the most she had probably ever said to him at any given time, and other than the fact that he would have preferred a nicer tone, Stephen realized that he *liked* this interaction with her. People didn't usually interact with him; they played to him, and they catered to him, even Holly. Until now. This was fascinating.

"What?" she finally asked uncomfortably.

"Nothing, it's that you not only sound different but… look different." He continued to stare at her as if he were seeing or meeting Holly for the very first time.

Self-consciously, Holly ran a hand over her hair. "Well, it is two thirty in the morning. I don't sleep in a suit with my hair pulled back, you know. I threw on sweats and ran out the door when you called. I didn't realize I was expected to be in 'personal assistant' mode all the livelong day!"

Holly knew she wasn't beautiful—men didn't normally give her a second look—but the way Stephen was looking at her right now made her wish they weren't in *this* particular moment, fighting. Why couldn't he look at her like that while they were at work? Or at one of those blasted charity events he was always dragging her to? Goodness, on those occasions Holly went crazy trying to dress in a way that would make Stephen see her as a woman, and apparently there weren't enough makeup and sequins on the planet to do that. But sure, bring her out in the middle of the night in sweats with no makeup, and the man couldn't take his eyes off her! Clearly he'd had too much to drink.

Yes, her chestnut hair was down and longer than he would have thought it was, but there was something else. Studying her face, it finally hit him. "Your glasses. You're not wearing your glasses." Without them, he could see high cheekbones and a silky-smooth, creamy complexion. He stopped his hand from reaching out and touching her.

"Oh, yeah, well…um…I don't really need them," she stammered, uncomfortable with the way he was watching her. "I mean, they have a tiny prescription to them, and I use them more for when I have some eye strain."

"You wear them every day," he stated.

"Yes, well, with the amount of time I spend on the computer, it makes sense to keep them on."

"Oh."

They sat in silence for a minute before Holly finally looked away, put the car back in gear, and headed toward Stephen's house. Glancing at the GPS, she noticed how far away it was. "Thirty miles!" she cried. "Stephen…" Holly whined. She was ready to start arguing again but realized there was no point. She would get him home and get herself home—probably somewhere around five a.m.—but luckily it was Saturday so she could sleep all day if she wanted. Well, as long as *he* didn't call her later with any work-related issues.

"I'm sorry, Holly. Believe me when I tell you that this was *not* the way I saw the night going either."

"Well, I would hope not." She sighed at her own snippy tone and decided to *try* to be pleasant. "So what happened? What did you fight with the guys about? It

had to be pretty intense for them to leave you there."
When he didn't answer, Holly prodded a little bit more.
"I mean, I can't imagine you guys fighting at all. You
seem to always be laughing and having a good time."

Not taking the bait, he simply replied, "Like I said
earlier, I don't want to talk about it."

By silent agreement, they dropped the subject and
drove the rest of the way without speaking another
word. The only sounds came from the rain pelting the
car and the roar of thunder.

When Holly finally turned into his subdivision, she
gasped with surprise. With nothing more than the light
of the street lamps, she could tell that the homes were
beautiful. Large wooded lots gave way to homes that
took her breath away. They passed a sizeable lake on
the right side of the road, and Holly saw a gazebo off
in the distance. At the prodding of the GPS, she turned
into Stephen's driveway, drove up the winding drive,
and had to stifle another gasp. His home was very
rustic-looking with stone facing and cedar shingles. She
couldn't see the colors in the dim light, but Holly knew
they would be stunning. As much as she hated having to
be here at this ungodly hour, suddenly she wanted to get
out and explore—rain and all.

Stopping the car directly in front of his door, she
waited for him to climb out. It seemed that Mother
Nature had decided to wait for that exact moment to
throw more high winds and now hail into the mix.
"Great," Holly mumbled. "More fun for the drive home.
Can't this night end?" Her head slumped forward onto
the steering wheel in defeat.

Without a word, Stephen reached across the car,

turned the key, and shut it off, taking the keys out of the ignition. "Um, excuse me," Holly chimed in a singsong voice. "What do you think you're doing? I can't drive home without my keys."

"You can't drive home at all in this. It's almost three thirty in the morning, and the weather's gotten worse. I may have been an inconsiderate bastard thus far, but I'm hoping to remedy that right now. I have five extra bedrooms, Holly—you can take your pick and sleep here. I've kept you out and awake long enough." With that, he climbed out of the car and went to open the front door of the house.

Holly sat mutely for a minute. Was the man for real? Sleep at Stephen's house? Was that appropriate? Should she protest? It wasn't like she was sleeping *with* Stephen; she was sleeping *in* his house. She could choose whichever bedroom was furthest from his, and it would be fine, right? Chewing her lip, she looked up and saw him leaning in the open doorway, half-asleep and waiting. Sighing with resignation, she pulled up her hood, climbed out, and went to join him.

"Thank you," she grumbled as she walked past him into the house. Stepping inside, Holly immediately kicked off her wet sneakers while she waited in the foyer for him to lead the way. Within minutes she found herself walking up a grand, curved staircase before coming to stand in a bedroom that was almost the size of the first floor of her own condo!

Besides being massive in size, it was beautifully decorated. Holly had decorated Stephen's last home, but he had purchased this one as the model home with all the furnishings. The back wall had a huge picture window with floor-to-ceiling drapes in shades of cream and taupe. The bed, which looked the size of a small continent with four posters, stood along the middle of the right wall and was piled high with pillows in jewel tones. The furniture was large and honey-colored, and Holly wanted to sigh.

"You have your own bathroom through here," Stephen indicated, "and there are fresh towels in the closet. Soap, shampoo, toothbrushes, and toothpaste are all in there as well, and there's a robe hanging on the back of the door." He stopped with hands on hips and glanced around the room as if making sure he wasn't forgetting anything. And then it hit him. "Wait here."

He strode from the room, and Holly peeled off her wet coat and was about to place it on the upholstered lounge chair that sat invitingly in the corner but then thought better of it, fearful of ruining it. Glancing around for a better option, she walked into the bathroom and hung her coat over the shower curtain rod. She came out of the bathroom as Stephen was walking in with a small pile of clothes.

"I figured you might want something other than wet sweats to sleep in. There's a T-shirt here, a flannel shirt, dry sweat pants…I wasn't sure what you would be most comfortable in, so I grabbed a variety." He looked nervously at her as if he were handing her a hand grenade rather than pajamas.

"That was very kind of you, thank you," she said as she took the clothes from him and turned to place them on the bed. Turning back to wish him good night, Holly found him rooted to the spot staring at her. They stood that way for countless seconds with only the ticking of an antique clock that was sitting on top of the dressing table before Holly finally whispered the words to him. It had been a long night, and Stephen staring at her had Holly feeling funny. Surely it must be the exhaustion making her feel so…so…weird. Him, too, she thought, because Stephen *never* stared at her. Ever.

Stephen nodded and pivoted toward the door. With a hand on the handle, he began to walk out and close the door behind him when he stopped. Holly was still standing next to the bed. "The fight was about you," he said quietly and closed the door. There was no malice in the statement, no accusation or blame; he was merely answering her earlier question.

Holly wanted nothing more than to go after him and demand to know what exactly that meant. Why would he fight with his two best friends about her? She got along very well with both Will and Derek. What could they possibly fight about? As much as her curiosity demanded to know, her sleep-deprived body won the battle of wills, and she changed into the T-shirt Stephen had given her. Even though she had gone through her bedtime routine hours earlier, Holly felt the need to wash her face and brush her teeth one more time before taking on the task of moving the mountain of pillows so she could crawl between the cool, silky sheets.

The whole time she moved about, her thoughts stayed on Stephen's last words to her. God, how she hated to be left hanging like that! It wasn't enough that she had trudged all over the place for him tonight? He had to drop a bomb like that and leave? She glanced at the door for what seemed like the tenth time and then resigned herself to the inevitable—answers would have to wait until morning.

Pulling back the plush comforter, she climbed into the bed. As she snuggled into the pillows and into a comfortable position, her final thoughts were of the look of sadness on Stephen's face as he had closed the door tonight.

What had that been about? The man she had dealt with in the last hour was hardly the confident, powerful man she worked with every day. What could possibly have happened tonight to cause such a dramatic change in his demeanor?

If Holly could have stayed awake to analyze it any more, she would have. But the comfort of the bed and her extreme sleepiness took their toll. Before long, sleep claimed her.

Chapter 2

THE NEXT MORNING HOLLY AWOKE WELL RESTED BUT confused about her surroundings. It did not take long, however, for it all to come back to her with blazing clarity, and she groaned with remembrance. Stephen. The rain. The fight. The look.

That stupid, sad look.

Stretching lazily, Holly looked over at the clock and gasped when she realized it was after ten. She couldn't remember the last time she had slept in so late on a Saturday. Well, that was usually because Stephen had her on the phone by eight a.m. with some sort of project idea that he had come up with the night before. Honestly, didn't the man's brain *ever* rest?

Apparently it had this morning because he hadn't bothered her. Okay, maybe his brain hadn't rested, but he was being polite enough to let her sleep in. Was he even awake yet? Holly kicked off the blankets and jumped at the sound of thunder as she padded her way to the bathroom. In her exhaustion the night before, she had not taken in the opulence of it all—a marbled double vanity, a deep and wide garden tub, a shower that looked like it could bathe four people with a double showerhead. It was like staying at a five-star hotel!

Stripping off the T-shirt Stephen had given her to sleep in, she grabbed some towels, stacked them outside the shower, and climbed in. The hot-water spray felt heavenly. The soaps and shampoo were all brand-new and from one of those designer bath shops that Holly never could afford to shop in. Feeling completely decadent, she lathered up from head to toe—twice!—before getting out of the shower and drying off.

She put the soft, fluffy, spa-quality robe on before she brushed her teeth and went in search of a blow dryer to try to do something with her hair. Thick hair past her shoulders would take forever to dry on its own; she most definitely needed more than a towel. Finding a dryer under the sink, she did the best she could without her usual styling products and brushes, and less than thrilled with the results, she put the dryer back where she found it.

With a quick look through her purse, she found a small supply of makeup. Luckily there had been moisturizer in the well-stocked bathroom, so by the time she put last night's sweats back on—which luckily were now dry—she felt almost like her normal self. One last look in the mirror told her what she already knew: under normal circumstances, she would never, ever, go out in public like this. But with no other choice, Holly straightened the room, grabbed her jacket, and headed out the door and down the stairs in search of Stephen.

At the bottom of the curved wooden staircase, Holly heard the sound of plates being moved around. If that hadn't drawn her attention, the enticing smell of food would have helped her find her mark. Silently walking into the kitchen, she expected to find the housekeeper there making the food that was causing her stomach to growl. Instead, she found Stephen. The sight of him dressed casually in flannel pajama pants and a T-shirt, with his jet-black hair still mussed from sleep and a day's worth of stubble on his chin, had Holly's mouth going dry. The normally impeccably dressed-in-a-suit-and-tie Stephen—who, in her opinion, looked like he was born to wear that ensemble—somehow looked even better in his morning attire.

Shaking her head clear of those wayward thoughts, she cleared her throat to get Stephen's attention. "Good morning," she said, and he replied in kind.

"Are you hungry?" he asked as he popped a couple slices of bread into the stainless-steel toaster on the counter. "I didn't want to wake you, but I was ravenous."

"Sure. What are we having?"

"Breakfast is the only meal I can cook, and if I do say so myself, I cook it well. I've got all the makings of any kind of omelet you could want."

Holly raised her eyebrows in surprise. "Really?"

"Really."

"Okay." She walked over to the butcher-block island where he had all his ingredients laid out and took it all in. "I'll have…hmm… I think I'll go with a Western one if it's not too much trouble."

In response, Stephen held up the omelet pan that was already on the stove. "Great minds think alike," he said with a smile, and Holly felt her stomach dip. Had he always had that dimple? "Coffee's already made." He pointed to the coffeemaker at the end of the counter. "Mugs are in the cabinet right above it."

Without a word, Holly helped herself and, as was habit, made his as well. They worked together in silence, and within minutes they were seated at the table over-looking the massive yard through the bay window.

"I cannot believe it's still raining," Holly said after

thanking Stephen for the plate he handed her. "I thought for sure the storm would have moved on by now."

"I watched the weather report this morning, and according to TV5, it's going to be like this all weekend with the worst of it hitting this afternoon."

Nearly choking on her food, Holly said, "Seriously?"

He nodded while sipping his coffee. "'Fraid so. I don't think anyone expected the storm front to stall over us." He nodded toward her plate, which he'd loaded not only with the requested Western omelet but also with home fries and toast. "How's your breakfast?"

"Oh…um, everything's great. Thank you." Sighing, Holly looked out the window, dreading the drive home in this weather. "So why breakfast?" she asked, desperate to keep the conversation neutral and avoid looking at him. For some reason, sitting here in Stephen's kitchen, having him cook for her in his pajamas, seemed way too intimate for comfort. The faster she ate, the faster she could go out into that miserable weather, go home, and stop fantasizing about other intimate activities she'd like to engage in right about now.

"I figured you'd be hungry…"

She laughed. "No, I mean, why can you only cook breakfast? When most people say something like that, it usually means they can make toast or instant oatmeal. But this"—she nodded her head toward all the food on the table—"is clearly more than that. This is a feast! I can't remember the last time I had such a decadent breakfast. But I would have been fine with some instant oatmeal."

"Ah. Gotcha. My mom used to make big breakfasts on the weekends. After my father died, she had to work two jobs all week long, and the only time we really spent together was on the weekends. I used to make sure I got up early with her, and we would make breakfast together, the two of us. She didn't believe in being lazy, so I had to be an active participant in the making of the meal."

"Wow, impressive!"

"Not at first. I thought it was girl stuff to cook, so I'd try to mess up so she would let me sit and watch. But she caught on to my scheme pretty quickly and made me eat whatever I cooked." Holly laughed. "I figured if I wanted to eat something edible, I was going to have to pay attention and get better at it. Burnt pancakes and eggs with shells in them taste as bad as they sound."

"That is a very sweet story," Holly said. She nibbled on her whole-wheat toast. "My family loves to cook. We spend hours in the kitchen concocting things. My parents had their own café for years up on Long Island. I always thought I would do the same, but I enjoy cooking much more when it's not a career." She paused at that thought. "You know, I can't even remember the last time I put an effort into cooking a meal." Shaking her head, she added, "I'm going to have to remedy that."

"What made you stop? I mean, I know it's not as much fun cooking for one, but…" he asked, sincerely curious.

"Oh, no, it's not that, it's…well…" She hesitated. "Our work schedule doesn't allow me to come home and cook. You know, we eat dinner most nights in the office. Why would I come home and cook dinner at nine o'clock at night after already eating with you earlier?"

He had the good sense to look sheepish. "Sorry. What about on the weekends? Why not cook then?"

Placing her fork down, she looked at him pleadingly,

not wanting to say any of this. "You normally call each morning and talk to me all through breakfast, and then I spend the rest of the day trying to do the things I need to do for my life." Stephen paled.

Unfortunately, Holly realized this would be the perfect opening to clear the air of all that was said in the car the night before—or, rather, earlier that morning. She slowly finished chewing her last forkful of home fries, lingered over the last drop of coffee, and even went so far as to play around with her place setting before chancing a glance at her boss and speaking what was on her mind. "Look, Stephen, I think we need to talk about some things."

Taking a last drink from his coffee mug, Stephen set it down and then stood to clear the table. "I know, I know," he said wearily. "I had no idea you were so unhappy working for me, Holly."

"It's not that I'm unhappy. I never said that," she began. "It's just…I need a life outside of work. I didn't realize how much I was resenting it until last night." *And now.* "You made me so mad that I guess everything came to the surface."

"I don't think I've ever told you that you couldn't have a life," he snapped as he put the plates into the sink.

Getting defensive at his tone, she replied, "No, you never *told* me I couldn't have a life, but you sure make it hard to! I don't go out during the week to see friends because I'm too tired from the long day. I don't sleep in on the weekends because you're calling me first thing in the morning. I know your business is very important to you, Stephen, and you are very good at what you do, but it's not *my* company or *my* business, and it certainly isn't *my* life. I want to go out and not worry about staying out too late and being woken up early on my day off. I want to socialize with people. I want to date!" A thought suddenly occurred to her. "What if I hadn't been alone last night?"

"What?"

"What if I had been with a man last night? Do you think I would have left him in bed to come and get you?"

"Were you in bed with a man last night?"

Holly sighed with frustration. "Of course I wasn't in bed with a man last night! I wouldn't be here now if I was! Geez, did you *not* see where I was going with this?" The man was clueless. "What I am trying to say here is what would you have done if I was not available to help you?"

"But you were."

"But what if I wasn't?"

"But you were."

"*Stephen!*" she yelled. "Stop being obtuse for a moment! Why didn't you call a cab? Or George?"

It was as if she had flipped a switch, so fast and so sure was the change in him. Where he had been calm and casual, he now stalked like a caged animal. He ran his hands through his jet-black hair as he prowled the length of the kitchen. In normal circumstances, Stephen was intimidating by his size alone; standing at a little over six feet tall, he was built like an athlete. But seeing him now, clearly angered, he seemed to have doubled in size. "You know, Holly, I think I kind of like it more when you're not so pushy and argumentative," he snapped.

Totally taken aback, Holly opened her mouth to speak, but Stephen held up a hand to silence her. "Oh, no. You have had a *lot* to say in the past twelve hours, and you've been poking and picking and prodding for answers, so here they are!"

He started off telling Holly how Derek and Will had shown up at the office not long after she had left the night before. "I guess you must have missed them because it could not have been more than a matter of minutes after you left," he said. "The plans were to find someplace casual to go and hang out like we used to do when we were younger—nothing fancy."

Stephen stared out the window at the rain pounding the deck as he continued. They had ended up at McGavin's to have a couple beers and maybe shoot a couple games of pool or darts. "I started telling them about the new Gideon project you and I were going to be working on, and Will made the comment that I work you too hard." Stephen turned around abruptly; his eyes bore into the top of Holly's head as she looked at the floor. "You felt comfortable enough to tell Will that I worked you too hard but not me. Why?"

She looked up then. "I didn't tell Will any such thing." She sighed. "Remember last week when he came to the office to have lunch with you and your conference call ran long?

"Well, he sat with me out in the office and asked what my plans were for the weekend, and when I told him, he looked at me like he felt sorry for me."

"Why? What were your plans?"

"Cleaning house. Balancing my checkbook. Basic things that most people do during the week but I do on the weekends because it's the only time that I can." Saying the words out loud made her feel lousy about herself all over again. "He asked me why I wasn't going out on a date or to a movie with friends, and I sort of shrugged. I had no excuse except I was too tired to."

Stephen stalked away and began to pace again as he talked. "Anyway, we were shooting pool, and I argued that I do not work you too hard. Will snorted. Derek laughed. So I asked what his problem was, and he made a snarky comment that maybe if I had a social life, I'd get out of the office once in a while."

Holly looked at him quizzically. "What's the big deal about that?"

"I'm trying not to be crude here, Holly. He didn't word it quite that way…"

"Oh."

"So I told him my sex life—or lack thereof at the moment—was none of his business. But he kept going at it like a dog with a bone. 'You need to get out more.' 'You need to get laid more.' Honestly, sex is Derek's answer to everything." Needing to stop the pacing, Stephen began cleaning up the breakfast mess. "Will told him to back off, and I thought we were through with it, when he looked at me and said that maybe I wasn't interested in getting laid because I had you around."

"*What?*" Holly wheezed. She had always liked Stephen's friends, but of the two, Derek was certainly a little more vulgar and harder on the senses. The fact that he would think such a thing about her hurt her feelings but didn't really surprise her. "Why would he think that?"

"He figured that the only reason I'd not be out screwing around and instead staying around the office with you was because *we* were screwing around."

"Well, that's ridiculous," Holly said, pulling at some imaginary spot on her sweatpants.

"Then Will chimed in that it did seem odd that a woman as attractive as you had no other social life besides the time you spent with me and that it didn't seem to faze you. They agreed and conspired about how it all made sense and then wanted to know how the sex was."

"Oh…my…God…" Holly stammered. She was sure she was blushing form the roots of her hair to the soles of her feet. If Stephen's friends thought this, was it possible other people in the office thought it too? "Oh…my…God…" she repeated as she stood, her heart racing, and then began to pace herself. "This is unbelievable."

"I tried brushing them off, but after a couple of beers, they were a little relentless, and I was a little defensive, and one thing led to another, and the next thing I knew, pool cues were being thrown, and I had Derek on the pool table by the throat. Will pulled me off him, but not before I had pounded his face pretty good."

"Oh, no! You didn't!"

He nodded. "Unfortunately, I did."

"Was he all right?"

Stephen looked away before answering her. He busied himself loading the dishwasher and placing food in the refrigerator. "It didn't end there. It got worse."

Holly rolled her eyes. How could it possibly have gotten any worse? "Why? What happened next?"

"Are you sure you want to know? Because it's not pretty," he snarled. If he was hoping to change her mind, he was sorely mistaken. At this point in the story, Holly had to know everything. "Will pulled me off Derek, and I was about to apologize for what I'd done when he looked at me and said, 'Well, if you're not man enough to'"—Stephen searched his brain for a kinder word for what Derek had said but could find none before continuing—"'then maybe I will.'" He turned and looked at Holly and cringed at the horrified look on her face. "I snapped. I have no excuse. I don't know why it bothered me so much for him to say such a thing. I mean, he's always saying things like that about women we see when we're out, but for some reason, hearing him say it about you, well, it…it made me snap."

He stood there, waiting for her to say something, anything. Minutes passed, and still Holly stood there, her green eyes huge in her pale face. Not knowing what else to do, Stephen did one final sweep of the kitchen, poured himself another cup of coffee, sat back down at the table, and stared at Holly's back. The tiny pit bull that had been relentless in wanting to know what happened the previous night apparently had nothing left to say. He should be smug about silencing her, but thinking about the look in her eyes stopped him.

"Holly?" he whispered. "Say something. Please."

Slowly she turned to face him. "To be honest with you, Stephen, I don't know what to say." She sat down slowly, almost as if being poured into the chair, before standing back up again. "No, that's not true. I do have something to say."

Stephen hid a small smile behind his coffee mug. He wasn't sure what was coming, but at least that devastated look was off her face. He'd welcome anything she had to say as long as he didn't have to see such hurt in her eyes again.

"If this is what your friends think of me, I can only imagine what the rest of the company must be whispering about us. I...I don't think I can work for you anymore. I had no idea people thought this way. I...I..."

Standing abruptly, he walked over to Holly and grabbed her by the shoulders. "You can't make a judgment call on everyone based on the words of a couple of drunken men, Holly! You're being ridiculous!"

For the briefest moment, she wanted to agree with him. She really did, but the reality of it all wouldn't let her. "You have no idea what people think, Stephen, because you don't pay attention to anything around you that doesn't directly pertain to a project that you're working on. I would hate it if after all this time people had such low thoughts of me."

"Sleeping with me would be low?" he asked, taking his hands away from her shoulders.

"For the love of it, would you *focus*? This is not about that, and you know it. I thought your friends truly liked me. I liked them. But after a few beers suddenly they think I'm some sort of...of...slutty secretary or something!"

He knew he shouldn't have laughed, but somehow he couldn't stop himself. "Holly, please! You make it sound like bad porn or something. Those guys were drunk! They were being stupid. I'm sure if I talked to them right now they'd apologize for what they said." Thinking he had it all worked out, Stephen walked over to grab the phone.

"Don't you dare!" she cried. Holly walked over and took the phone out of his hands. "I do *not* want any part of that discussion. And besides, you need to finish the story. None of this explains how it ended up that they left you there at McGavin's. That seems rather juvenile to me."

"Really? That's the only part of this whole scenario that seems juvenile?" His voice dripped with sarcasm as he stared down at her. Had she always been this petite? Looking down, he realized that she was barefoot. Her toenails were painted a bright coral color, and for a moment he was simply fascinated. His conservative little assistant wore a sassy color on her nails, and it had him wondering what other sassy items she might wear under her normally sensible attire.

"Stephen?" she prompted.

"Oh, right." He looked back up at her face. "Well, there was a lot more yelling and shoving, and for a while Will tried to break us apart, and then Derek and I both turned at the same time and sort of swung at Will."

"Oh, no! You didn't!"

"We did."

"Oh, this is all way too much, Stephen. I don't want to be the cause of you fighting with these men who you've been friends with almost your whole life, especially over something that's not even true! Was Will okay?"

"No, we knocked him unconscious."

Holly knew she was beginning to sound like a broken record but could not stop the *oh no* from coming out. "What did you do?"

"I went to get some water and ice from the bartender. In the meantime, Derek threw Will over his shoulder and left. By the time I got what I needed, they were pulling out of the parking lot." He shrugged as if it weren't a big deal. "And that's what happened."

The walk to the kitchen table felt like it was a mile.

How did this weekend go so terribly wrong in such a short amount of time? It didn't seem possible. When she left work last night, Holly had high hopes for a relaxing weekend. It didn't seem right that in a matter of a few short hours she had come to realize that people thought she was sleeping with her boss and now she had to seriously face the possibility of quitting her job. After a good night's sleep, she had come to realize that it was the last thing she wanted to do.

But apparently the choice was made. "You realize, Stephen, that in light of all this, I can't continue to work for you. It would be too awkward. I would feel like from this point on everyone was watching us, and, God forbid, if Will or Derek ever came to the office again, I would die of embarrassment."

"Holly, you have nothing to be embarrassed about! Quitting is a little extreme, don't you think?"

"No, I don't. I said it last night, and this whole thing has snowballed from one bad issue to another, and while I would have preferred that it not come to this, we can't turn back time." Her eyes filled with tears as she looked up at him. She hated herself for wanting to cry. "I have loved working for you, Stephen, but there are too many obstacles now that I can't overcome." She would miss seeing him every day, being challenged by him every day, but the only way to keep her pride intact was to leave Ballinger's.

One lone tear fell, and Stephen felt it all the way to his soul. "Stop, Holly, please. Don't say any more." Once again he placed his hands on her shoulders, but this time he pulled her in close before lowering his arms to wrap her in them. "This will all blow over in a couple of days. I can make sure Derek and Will stay away for a while. I'm sure I'm not high on their list right now either. Chances of them even wanting to come around are probably slim to none. Don't quit!" He said the words with a quiet fierceness that Holly had never heard before. "I can fix this. I swear I can. Give me some time."

Holly pulled back to look at him and smiled sadly. "I appreciate that you wanted to fight this battle for me, I do. No one's ever done anything like that for me. But the truth of the matter is it's not your issue, it's mine. It may very well be only Derek and Will who have this theory, but I'll never be sure of that, and it's not something I can live with. I know I work hard and the work I do is legit. I'm not exchanging sexual favors for job perks."

"So if you know that and I know that, then why let them win? Don't you see, Holly, by leaving you're playing their childish game. Don't do it."

Oh, how she wanted to believe him. Without conscious thought, she let herself be pulled fully back into his embrace and let herself relax into it. It felt nice. It felt better than nice; it felt bone-meltingly good. That thought worried her for the briefest of seconds, but she chased her concern away and let herself enjoy the moment. After all, this could be the first and only time she would ever have the opportunity to feel this closeness with him.

Although she would never admit it to anyone—she could barely admit it to herself—she had always harbored a slight crush on her boss. He seemed like the perfect man; he worked hard and was successful in his field, he was kind to his employees, he was friendly and had a great laugh—not to mention that he wasn't hard on the eyes! Allowing herself to have this moment with him was sort of a fitting ending to this chapter of her life.

Not working with Stephen, not seeing him or speaking to him every day, was going to be really hard. It would probably be one of the hardest things she'd had to do at this point in her twenty-six years of life, but it had to be this way. Holly hugged him back briefly and then went to pull out of his embrace, but Stephen wouldn't allow it.

"Don't do this, Holly," he whispered. One hand was stroking up and down her back while the other kept her anchored to him. "I'll cut back on your hours, I'll stop calling on the weekends. You can go home and cook dinner at a reasonable time. Don't…quit."

She smiled sadly into his chest. Oh, if only it were that easy. She knew what her decision had to be but didn't want to continue this conversation. "I need some time to think about this, okay? I'm going to get the rest of my things and head home, and we'll talk more about this on Monday. Is that all right?" Stephen released Holly and nodded.

He stood back and watched her walk out to the foyer where she had placed her jacket that morning, and put on the sneakers she had taken off when they first got to the house in the wee hours of the morning. He waited quietly, hands in pajama pockets, unsure what to do. Should he force the issue and not let her leave until she agreed to stay on working for him? Should he be arguing his case and pleading and begging until she agreed to stay? No; Stephen Ballinger did not beg! If Holly chose to leave, Stephen knew things would be rough for a while because he hated having to take time out of his schedule to train someone new.

Holly had been a natural from the beginning. It had always seemed as if she had been made for the job, the perfect assistant for him. She had a quick mind and wasn't afraid to ask questions. The fact that she had such an infectious personality was a perk. All his colleagues and associates loved her. Stephen always knew that he could take Holly with him to any meeting or formal event and she would be an asset to him. She had managed to wow some of his more difficult clients and maintained easygoing friendships with the wives of many of his favorite ones.

With deep-down resignation, Stephen knew he could not let her quit. He'd give into any demand she made if it came down to it. He'd be willing to give up his friendship with his two best friends if that's what made Holly stay. He shook his head at his own desperation. Was he insane? Sure, she was an amazing personal assistant, but was she really worth all that?

"I think that's everything," Holly said and snapped him out of his inner dialogue. She looked years younger than she did in the office, wearing sweats and very little makeup. Stephen decided he liked her hair down and found that he wished she'd do that more around the office—if she stayed. "I really do hope you work things out with Will and Derek. I'm sure in the light of day, things will be clearer for everyone."

Stephen merely grunted in response because at that moment, he couldn't care less about what was clear and what wasn't for his friends. *His* life was a damn mess, and as far as he was concerned, it was *their* fault. He walked over and opened the front door for her. The wind was howling, and the rain was coming down in sheets.

"Holly, I don't think this is the best time for you to be on the roads. Maybe you should wait it out for a little while longer."

Hesitating for a heartbeat, Holly knew she had to get out of the house now while she still could. "I'll be fine. I've driven in worse. Besides, you said yourself that the TV5 weatherman predicts it's going to get worse as the day goes on. This is probably the best time for me to go." Pulling her hood up and taking her keys out, she turned and smiled. "Thank you for breakfast. It was wonderful." Clicking the remote to unlock the car door, she stepped out onto the porch. "We'll talk on Monday, okay?"

"No," he said quickly. "I mean, call me when you get home so I know you made it okay." When Holly looked at him with disbelief, he added, "I promise not to try to talk business with you or pressure you into staying. I want to make sure nothing happens to you on the drive home."

"Okay," she said and made a mad dash for her car. Once inside, she felt as if a great weight had been lifted off her shoulders. "Thank God!" She sighed as she started the engine. There was no way she could make the decision she had to make while wrapped in Stephen's embrace.

Three years she had worked for him, and it had taken something like this to make the man notice her as anything more than his assistant! Did that make her pathetic or really, really unlucky? Putting the car in gear, she pulled forward in the circular drive and waved to Stephen, who was still standing in the doorway watching her. At the end of the driveway, she entered her destination into the GPS and turned right.

The drive home was going to be long and slow, to be

sure. The rain was coming down so hard that she could barely see beyond the nose of her car. The wind was fighting her compact little SUV with all its might. For a moment she thought about going back to Stephen's and doing as he suggested and waiting it out. Thinking better of it, Holly decided that what was best for her, both mentally and emotionally, was to take the drive as slowly as possible and resign herself to spending a large portion of the day in the car.

Sighing with her decision, she relaxed into her seat and almost missed what was coming up ahead of her. The road was blocked. In the fierceness of the storm, a tree—or perhaps several—had fallen across the road. She could easily turn around on the street, but there was no way out on the other end.

"This can*not* be happening," she heard herself moan. "For crying out loud, I decided to get the heck out of Dodge, and now I have to go back?" She wanted to cry. She wanted to scream. She wanted to wail. "Why is the universe against me?"

With no alternative, Holly turned the car around and headed back in the direction she had come. She pulled back into the long winding driveway and as close to the front door as humanly possible—this time making sure that the driver's side was facing the front door from the circular drive.

Pulling her blasted hood back over her head, she was about to climb out when she remembered that she had a gym bag in the back seat. It had sat and mocked her for weeks because she never did *get* to the gym, but now she could almost kiss it! She would have clean clothes at least.

Grabbing her bag, she hopped out of the car, ran up to the front door, and rang the bell. Stephen opened the door, one hand on the doorknob, the other holding his phone, his expression shocked.

"Are you up for a roommate for one more night?"

Chapter 3

STEPHEN STOOD ROOTED TO THE SPOT, THINKING THAT clearly he had conjured her up in his imagination. She'd only been gone five minutes, but it seemed much longer. When he noticed her raised eyebrows, he snapped out of his reverie and stepped aside to let her in. "Sure, no problem. What made you change your mind?"

Holly toed off her wet sneakers once again and placed her gym bag beside them. "There are several trees down across the road. I couldn't get out of the subdivision."

"Oh, well," he began as he closed the door, "the storm must have taken a phone line down, too, because I don't have a dial tone." He gestured to the cordless phone in his hand as if he needed to give her a visual aid.

"Have you tried your cell?"

"Not yet. I had just found out about the house phone when you knocked on the door. Come on in." He waved his arm in a sweeping motion as if to gesture for her to precede him farther into the house. Holly headed back toward the kitchen.

Without conscious thought, she started another pot of coffee before sitting down at the table and looking at Stephen like "now what?" He put the cordless phone back on its cradle and then went in search of his cell phone. Holly chuckled because during the day at the office, his cell phone was practically strapped to him or he used his Bluetooth.

Taking the time to look around the place, Holly couldn't believe that she had missed how spectacular the room was. Cherrywood cabinets that went to the high ceiling, glass doors, stainless-steel appliances, granite countertops as far as the eye could see except on the butcher block–covered center island—it was a chef's dream! She smiled at how her family would have loved to have this much space in their kitchen while she was growing up. The view of the property from the bay window was amazing; there was a large, multilevel deck right outside with the largest grill she'd ever seen! One whole wall of the kitchen contained a stone fireplace that separated it from the living room. Walking around the wall, she found that the fireplace opened on both sides. How lovely.

She was about to turn back into the kitchen when Stephen came down the stairs, cell phone in hand. "Any luck?"

"I've got service. Not great service, but at least something. I tried calling Will, and it went directly to voicemail. I'm going to try Derek next. Make yourself at home while I make this call."

Holly cringed. The last thing she wanted to do was hear what was being said about her or perhaps have to bear witness to an argument. Stephen walked away from her and down a short hallway. Holly heard a door close and breathed a sigh of relief. Wandering back to the kitchen, she noticed that the coffee was ready and poured them each a cup.

Taking a quick peek back down the hall, she saw that the door was still closed and decided to investigate the kitchen. If she was going to be here for any extended period of time, she was definitely going to cook something in this kitchen! Holly opened cabinets and was thrilled to find high-quality cookware that included everything a person would need to cook a feast. Turning to the pantry, she was surprised to find it similarly well stocked. If the man couldn't cook anything besides breakfast, why have so much food on hand?

But the most pleasant surprise came when she went to the refrigerator in search of cream for her coffee and found it fully stocked as well—fresh produce and cold cuts, colas, wines…she would have no trouble cooking here. Opening the freezer side, she found a wide variety of meats and quite the stockpile of casserole dishes. She pulled out a few, read the labels, and knew they wouldn't starve.

"My housekeeper does all the shopping and then takes pity on me and cooks so that I have some 'real food,' as she puts it," Stephen said from the doorway, startling her.

"I'm sorry, I was—"

"Being nosy?" he joked. "It's okay. But if you're hungry, please help yourself to anything."

She laughed out loud. "Hungry? You made me a breakfast that could have fed a lumberjack! I don't know if I'll be hungry for the rest of the day!" She let her laughter die off and waited before asking about the phone call. "Any luck with Derek?"

The fact that he started with a sigh could have meant a few things. Holly was hoping it meant that he didn't get through. When he walked across the kitchen, grabbing his coffee that she motioned to along the way, she knew that he had. "Yeah, I talked to Derek."

"Was Will okay?" she asked worriedly.

"Yes, he's fine. He had come to by the time Derek got him to the car. He's got a black eye and possibly a broken nose." He muttered a curse. "What the hell were we thinking?" He looked at Holly and then down at the mug in his hand. "Derek apologized for razzing me and provoking me, and I apologized for being the first to throw a punch." He took a sip of his hot beverage. "How did it get so out of hand? I mean, we're fairly civilized grown men, and we were in a dirty roadside bar, brawling like teenagers!"

Holly stood leaning against the center island, sipping her own coffee and listening. She knew he wasn't really asking her the question; he was truly perplexed about what had transpired and was trying to work it all out.

"Derek and I both agreed that we had no idea what made us behave like that. Apparently Will isn't speaking to either of us, and I can't say I blame him. I'm thirty-two years old, for crying out loud. I haven't been in a brawl since I was seventeen!"

"Maybe you were all a little on edge over different things, and though it does seem a little weird that you'd all blow at the same time, it's not unheard of," Holly offered. "You have been working a lot lately to get the Gideon project prepped and ready. Maybe you're under more stress than you think. You never do take any time off for yourself, and I know for a fact that you have not taken more than a weekend off since I came to work for you."

"It hasn't been that long, has it?" Stephen denied, but it didn't take long before he realized she was right. "Well, I've been working to build this company up. When things get to a level I'm happy with, I'll take time off."

"Will you?" she challenged. "Because I don't believe you. I don't think you'll ever get to that place where you have reached a level that you're happy with. You'll always be striving for something more, one more project, a bigger client, newer technology… Face it, Stephen, you are a workaholic."

He grimaced at the word. His father had been a major workaholic and was never at home. He died young and left Stephen and his mother with nothing much to show for all his work. All the hours that the elder Ballinger spent away from his family had amounted to nothing. For years after his father's death, Stephen's mother had worked day and night to make ends meet.

Stephen swore he would not repeat his father's mistakes. He loved his work, and he was good at it, and so he knew that this was the path his life was to take. That was why Stephen avoided getting too deeply involved with anyone or thinking about marriage. He was married to his work. He grew up witnessing that you could not put energy into having both; his father had shown him that. Stephen knew he was successful at what he did, but it took all his time and energy. He glanced over at Holly and knew that she was a large part of why his company had achieved so much in the past three years.

An idea began to form in his mind. Maybe it was time that he leaned back a little and lived. If he could convince Holly to stay and take his promises seriously and cut her hours, he'd have to cut his own. He simply couldn't work without her.

As much as he still wanted to tackle that discussion, Stephen knew how to negotiate a deal. Holly was going to be there with him for the entire weekend. He'd have to force himself not to bring up work or the Gideon project—though he had a million things to do for it that he had planned to tackle this weekend—and focus on getting to know her. Once he knew what made Holly tick and became that "friend" they'd talked about the previous night, he was confident that he would be able to convince her to stay on as his personal assistant.

He smiled at his own genius.

Sensing that Stephen no longer wanted to talk about last night—and, quite truthfully, neither did she—Holly switched topics as she walked over to the window. "I cannot believe how hard it is raining! I couldn't see beyond the nose of the car. I'm kind of relieved not to be out in this. Who knows how many other trees have fallen between here and my house and how many detours I'd have had to take." She turned and smiled over her shoulder. "You're sure you don't mind if I stay?"

He returned her smile easily. "If memory serves, and I believe it does, I was the one who told you not to leave in the first place. You were the one running for the door. I'm glad you didn't have to be out in this for more than an eighth of a mile!"

Sitting back down across from him at the table, she chatted with him about the weather, current events, nothing of any particular importance. They were comfortable with one another, and Holly told herself that it was nice to talk about something other than work with him.

"Tell me about this house," she prompted. "I mean, from what I've seen of it, it is magnificent. This kitchen is a fantasy!"

"I don't think I've ever heard it described that way." He chuckled. "I'm still getting used to it. It's weird to have bought a place this size already furnished, but everything was made for this house, so I couldn't imagine bringing any of my things from the other house here." Remembering that Holly had decorated the last house, he made sure to explain himself. "The other stuff was beautiful, don't get me wrong…"

"Uh-huh…"

"But you have to admit that the other place was a bit more contemporary than this one." She nodded in agreement, but she didn't like the fact that after all her hard work on making the other house a home, he not only didn't take anything with him, but he purchased this house completely furnished.

"You have excellent taste, Holly, and I loved what you did with the condo, but this house is so…different. This is the house I always dreamed of." He sighed. Holly never thought she'd live to see the day that Mr. Business-Ballinger would sigh when describing something as personal as his home. This was a whole new side to him that was both attractive and a little unnerving. "Care for a tour?"

There wasn't anything else to do, and she was curious, so she agreed. "Sure."

For the next hour, they toured the 10,000-square-foot home. It was much larger on the inside than it looked from the outside. Besides the six bedrooms and eight bathrooms, Stephen had a state-of-the-art office that rivaled the office he had in Raleigh. There was a formal living room plus the more casual one with the stone fireplace she had seen earlier. The dining room had a table that seated twenty without the leaves in it, and she could have parked her car in the laundry room!

"Isn't this all a bit much for one man?" she finally had to ask as they reentered the kitchen. "I mean, it's wonderful and it's gorgeous, but unless you're planning on having, like, a dozen kids, why get such a big house?"

He laughed at her observation. "No, I don't plan on having a dozen kids. I don't plan on having any, as a matter of fact." Holly turned to him in surprise. "I don't plan on getting married either. I wanted a home that has everything I ever wanted."

"So what you always wanted was a big house to live in by yourself?"

Well, when she put it that way, it didn't sound palatable. "No." *Yes.* "I like the location, I love the property. Everything in this house is state-of-the-art. I can entertain here. I can bring clients here and not have them feel like they are in a bachelor pad."

"Ah." He was trying to sell her on the idea. She had a sneaking suspicion that there was more to this than he was saying but decided to stay quiet. "I guess I can understand that. And, hey, if things don't work out for you with the company, you can use this place as an upscale resort and charge for the rooms."

There was amusement in her voice that made him chuckle. "And why would I want to do that?"

"Well, for starters, the bedrooms are larger than any hotel room I've ever stayed at. The bathrooms are spa-quality. You managed to provide everything a stranded traveler could ever need." She thought quietly for a moment before adding, "Well, almost everything."

"Only almost? What did I miss?"

"There were no chocolates on my pillow." With that simple statement, she sat herself down with all the properness of royalty, and Stephen knew he had never seen anything as delightful. He walked over to the pantry, opened the door, and stepped inside. A minute later, he was standing next to Holly with a square of foil-wrapped dark chocolate in his palm and bowing to her butler-style.

"I'll be sure to remedy that tonight, madame," he said in a deep, serious voice that had Holly cracking up.

"Now that's more like it." She smiled as she took the chocolate from his hand. "Can I request one for each pillow?"

"Aren't there, like, forty pillows on that bed?"

Shrugging, she replied, "A girl can get hungry in the night, can't she?"

Placing the bag of chocolate that he had behind his back on the table between them, he sat back down. "So, what do you usually do on a rainy Saturday afternoon?"

"Laundry. Food shopping. Pay the bills. Rain or shine," she answered.

"Sounds exciting. Sorry to disappoint you, but I don't have any laundry that needs to be done. We could watch a movie," he suggested.

Holly remembered the media room he had downstairs in the finished basement. He had a mini-movie theater with deluxe seats that resembled recliners. Yes, she could definitely see herself curled up in one of those buttery-soft leather chairs watching a movie and…

"Okay, I know you'll think I'm crazy, considering my earlier comment, but…"

He arched a dark eyebrow in response.

"Can we make snacks to bring down there with us?"

He laughed out loud. Honestly, Stephen could not

remember the last time he had laughed this much with anyone. Since waking up this morning or, rather, since Holly came back this morning, he felt lighter than he had in a long time. Maybe there was something to be said about relaxing once in a while. "Snacks? Aren't you the one who said she ate as much as a lumberjack at breakfast and wouldn't be hungry again for the rest of the day?"

Blushing, she turned her head away and mumbled, "Maybe."

Pulling her up from her chair, he led her to the pantry and gave her a little shove. "Go ahead, have at it. What should we have?" He watched her inspect each and every shelf and then go to the refrigerator and snoop around there and in the freezer.

"Okay, I'll tell you what," she began. "You go and get the movie and whatnot set up. Give me forty-five minutes, and I'll have everything ready. Deal?"

"It's going to take you forty-five minutes to open some chips?"

She rolled her emerald eyes at his naïveté. "Do I look like the kind of woman who would merely snack on chips?" At that moment, Stephen really looked at her. She was adorable. With her hair loose and wavy, barely a trace of makeup, and dressed in black yoga pants and a blue hooded sweatshirt, she should have looked plain, unappealing. But she didn't. She looked like temptation. Stephen almost found himself telling her to skip the snacks because he wanted to feast on her.

"Hello?" she sang. "Earth to Stephen."

He cleared his throat. "Sorry, my mind wandered for a moment. And to answer your question, I honestly have no idea what you like to snack on, so I'm going to step aside and wait to find out. I think I'll go grab a shower and get changed while you run amok in my kitchen."

"Sounds like a plan." Holly was relieved when he finally left the kitchen because now she could play. This was where she felt most at home. She grabbed ingredients from the pantry, the refrigerator, the freezer, and the cabinets; she pulled out pots, pans, and baking dishes. She had things baking, sautéing, simmering while she chopped and prepared plates.

Right on cue as the timer went off, Stephen walked into the kitchen and stopped dead in his tracks. "What in the world have you done?" There were platters of food of every kind all around him, yet there was no trace of it having been prepared. There were nachos, cheese and crackers, fruit and vegetable platters; there were potato skins piled high with cheese and bacon and sour cream. Stepping closer he noticed mini hot dogs wrapped in pastry and a tiny bowl of popcorn. He looked at her quizzically.

"You can't watch a movie in a theater without popcorn." She shrugged.

"I'm sorry, but is the neighborhood joining us?" he teased.

Holly looked around and suddenly felt self-conscious. "I guess I did get carried away…"

"Ya think?" When she made to apologize, he stopped her and went about finding trays to carry their bounty on.

"Should I grab drinks?" she asked.

"I've got a fully stocked refrigerator downstairs and a bar. I think we're good. Now come on before all this gets cold." They made their way down the stairs and into the theater. "What shall we watch?"

"I don't know…what have you got?"

Stephen flipped a switch, and one wall lit up. He took her by the hand and led her to the back of the room to a flat-screen computer monitor. Steven touched the screen, and it came to life. "You can scan this list of all the movies I can stream for us. Click on the genre you want, and it will prompt you from there."

She looked at him slyly. "This place must be a real babe magnet."

"Well, since you're the first and only 'babe' to see it, you'll have to let me know."

"Seriously?" He nodded. "How can that be? Don't you date?"

"Of course I date. I just don't bring them home." Man, did *that* sound shallow. "Come on, pick a movie while I get everything else set up. You want a beer? Soda? Milk shake?"

The last option piqued her interest, but considering how much food she had prepared, she settled on a Coke. She muttered thanks as she continued to scan the movies. After much deliberation, she found a favorite, *Speed*, with Sandra Bullock and Keanu Reeves. Stephen nodded his approval when she told him. "I figured you for a *Pride and Prejudice* kind of gal."

"Only when I'm alone," she quipped. "Besides, I'd hate for you to fall asleep from boredom and let all this food go to waste."

They laughed; they ate; they shared a running commentary throughout the movie. Stephen was discovering that his assistant was quite intriguing. She was passionate in her conversation, and he couldn't remember ever having such a pointless conversation and enjoying it quite so much.

Holly, on the other hand, wasn't quite so focused on Stephen; she was too busy enjoying the luxury that surrounded her. Snuggling deeper into the buttery softness of the recliner, she was sure than she had never been in a more comfortable chair and found herself thoroughly content. Between them, they did manage to go through quite a bit of the food, and her stomach protested that fact by the end of the movie.

"It's a rare combination of love story and action adventure," she said as the credits rolled. "I'm a sucker for a happy ending." She looked around, and the thought of moving and cleaning up the mess was not appealing at all. Beside her, Stephen's expression told her the same thing.

"How about a double feature?"

With a sigh of relief and giving in to the urge to recline, Holly looked over at him and smiled. "It's like you read my mind. This one's your choice." Within minutes they were watching the intro to Jackie Chan's *Shanghai Noon*. With mindless abandon, Holly reached for several squares of cheese and crackers as Stephen took the mini hot dogs and potato skins and warmed them in the microwave he kept behind the bar.

"I know there's not really a love story here, but it's still a great movie," Stephen said conversationally while he waited for the ding of the microwave.

"That's fine. I enjoy a good comedy, too. But I have to tell you, if I don't stop eating, the only thing I'm going to do after this movie is go across the hall to your mini YMCA and walk on the treadmill until Monday."

Well, at least she wasn't trying to leave anymore, Stephen thought to himself. He removed the food from the microwave and placed the plates between them again, refreshed both of their drinks, and sat back down as Jackie Chan watched the Princess escape in the night. For a minute, he glanced at Holly and watched her nibbling on a cracker, so relaxed, so at ease. She truly looked different from the woman he worked with every day. Was he really that bad to work for that having a day off actually changed her appearance?

Turning to the movie again, he couldn't seem to break that train of thought. He looked at Holly again. Yes, she looked transformed. It was more than the hair or the glasses; her whole face was relaxed. Her posture was relaxed. During the week, she held herself as stiff and upright as a ruler. Sitting here now, curled up with her feet tucked under her, watching a movie, she looked too young to be anyone's personal assistant. She looked like she should be hanging out at a sorority house, not her boss's house. Her *older* boss's house.

He had never thought of himself as old until that moment, and thirty-two wasn't *that* old, but looking at Holly suddenly made him feel that way. Old. And creepy for staring at her. Shaking his head, he put all his effort into watching the movie.

"Do I have something on my face?" That got his attention, and as much as he wanted *not* to look at Holly again, he could not ignore her question.

"Excuse me?" He coughed.

"I said, is there something on my face? You were staring at me."

"Oh, that, well, it struck me how truly different you look today."

She huffed with annoyance. "I thought we covered this last night. Yes, my hair is down. Yes, I'm in sweats,

I don't have my makeup with me… Geez, Stephen, I'm self-conscious enough about it. Thanks for bringing it up." She was mortified. She rested her face in her hand to cover the side of her face that was facing Stephen and went back to watching the movie, hoping that he didn't want to keep talking.

Ninety minutes later, she had to move; she *had* to. The credits were rolling as Holly stood and stretched. Stephen followed suit, and now it was her turn to stare. Earlier, she had been so preoccupied with prepping the food and coming down to watch the movie that she hadn't taken the time to notice that he had showered, shaved, and dressed casually. Twice in one day of seeing Stephen dressed like a normal person was devastating to her senses.

As he stretched, his plain black T-shirt rose up about the waistband of snug, well-worn jeans. The word *yummy* came to mind, and she decided the only thing she could do was start collecting dishes so that she stopped staring before she started to drool. How uncool would *that* be? Stephen joined in, and between the two of them, the theater was back to normal in less than ten minutes.

Holly followed Stephen up the stairs and into the kitchen where they continued to work together in silence, scraping and rinsing the dishes before loading them in the dishwasher. When the task was done, they stood awkwardly facing one another, each unsure what to do next.

"So, um…I don't think either of us is going to want to eat anytime soon, right?" he said for lack of anything else to say.

"Definitely not." A glance at the clock revealed that

it was only six o'clock. What were they supposed to do for the rest of the night? She walked over to the kitchen window and saw that it was almost dark and the rain was still coming down. The theater was soundproof with no windows. The rain could have stopped, but no such luck. "I cannot believe that this storm has not passed yet!"

"Maybe we should turn on the news and see what they have to say. Come on, I'll turn on the TV in the den." Holly followed, and for the next thirty minutes they sat at opposite ends of the sofa and watched the local news. Then, still unsure what to do, Stephen turned on the Weather Channel to verify what the local news had said. By seven o'clock, Holly had had enough of staring at a TV screen and had to get up and move around.

"Okay, I have not sat around so much in my entire life. I can't do it anymore!" Her tone was light, but Stephen knew that she was serious. "I don't know what to do with myself. I'm out of sorts, and I can't help thinking about all the things I'm supposed to be doing at home!" Holly was pacing from pent-up energy.

"I know what you mean. I've got to be honest with you, Holly, I promised myself that I would not bring up work or the Gideon project, and as pleasant as this whole afternoon has been, deep down I am going crazy with the need to go work on it!" He could have kicked himself. Sure, being honest was great, but in that moment Stephen was sure he had blown everything; all the headway he'd made in the friendship category was gone.

"As much as I hate to admit it, I wouldn't mind having something productive to do. As long as we set a time limit, I'll help you. I am not going to stay up all night working, though. Is that okay?"

He could have kissed her right then and there, but Stephen was sure that if he did, the topic of work and friendship would certainly be the furthest thing from his mind. Watching Holly all day, laughing with her, had been mildly arousing. He wasn't used to being attracted to a woman under these circumstances, and he certainly shouldn't be feeling anything toward his assistant. He had to get things back on track fast!

This whole afternoon had been for her, and yet she was still willing to help him out. It took every ounce of willpower not to ask her if this meant that she'd changed her mind about quitting. He wanted an answer! But a good businessman knew when to push and when to bide his time. Right now he had no choice but to wait her out. She was graciously helping him, and that would be enough for now.

Chapter 4

THREE HOURS LATER, HOLLY POLITELY CALLED AN END TO their work session. She had been expecting Stephen to put up a fight, but he simply nodded, closed the folder he was using, and shut down the computer. If only he was this agreeable during the week! She didn't realize she had spoken that out loud until Stephen said, "You never say when you want the day to end, so I keep going."

Unfortunately, he had a point. Proper manners instilled in her from an early age had taught her to respect her employer, and that meant working when she was needed and not complaining about it.

"I really wish you had told me how you felt about working late so much, you know. I'm not such an ogre that you couldn't come talk to me, am I?" He looked so vulnerable. He had run his hands through his hair about a hundred times during the past three hours, and for some inexplicable reason, her hands itched to do the same.

Distance. She needed to put distance between them. It was ten o'clock. She could easily go to bed at this hour and not feel like she was running away. Unfortunately, she knew that Stephen was going to want an answer before he let her go. "No, you're not an ogre. It's like I told you in the car earlier. Last night brought everything to the surface. I didn't realize how much it was bothering me until then. Does that seem weird?"

"I'm not sure that *weird* is the right word, but I guess sometimes we have no control over where our breaking point is on certain things." With his hands in his pockets, Stephen stared at the floor before looking at Holly and saying solemnly, "I really am sorry about working you so hard, keeping you from having a social life, calling you at two a.m....everything."

"How could you know that it was bothering me if I never said anything? I'm as much to blame as you are. Sort of." She looked at him through veiled lashes and grinned. "You are definitely to blame for the two a.m. thing, though."

"Agreed." Seeming satisfied, Holly went about straightening up the office before telling Stephen that she was tired and was going to go to bed.

"I'm going to grab my gym bag so I have a change of clothes for the morning, but if you don't mind, I'd like to borrow another T-shirt to sleep in." He agreed, and they left the office; Holly went down the hall and grabbed her bag while Stephen went upstairs to get a shirt for her. They met at the top of the stairs.

"Here you go. Is there anything else you need?"

"There was the chocolate rumor…" When he turned to go down the stairs, Holly reached out and stopped him.

"Stephen! I was kidding! I'm still full from all our movie food. The last thing I need right now is chocolate!" Her laughter was infectious, and Stephen found himself laughing yet again. "Now, if you'll excuse me, I'm off to bed. I'll see you in the morning—but not too early, okay?"

Agreeing, Stephen watched her walk down the hall

to her room and waited until he heard her door click. It had been a strange day all around. Mostly pleasant, but for the life of him, he couldn't remember the last time he had felt so laid-back and carefree. Descending the stairs, he played over the day in his mind: Holly at breakfast, leaving and coming back, cooking in his kitchen… She *fit* in his home, in his life, and he could not lose her!

Why had he called her last night? She had a point with that one, and luckily she'd let it go after a while, but the truth was that he could have called a cab or he could have called his driver. But after all that Will and Derek had said to him regarding Holly, she was on his mind. Heavily. And he had to prove to himself that they were wrong, that there was nothing there, no attraction, no anything.

But the joke was on him. All he'd managed to accomplish was discovering that she was a fascinating woman who was way more attractive than he had ever noticed, and she'd made him laugh and smile more in one day than he had in years. She made his work easier, she brought happiness to this big house. What was he going to do if she really did quit on him?

Wandering around the main floor of the house—the house that he usually loved—he felt lonely. Growing up poor had made him determined to have the best of everything. When Holly had mentioned the house being too big for one person, Stephen realized that he had never thought of it that way. To his way of thinking, it was a house that represented everything that he had ever wanted. Never again would he wonder if there was enough food to eat or if there was going to be heat or hot water.

He *was* this house. It gave Stephen a sense of pride.

Often he would walk around it and feel satisfaction. Tonight, it seemed like a foolish way of thinking. Damn! It was a lot easier when Holly was his personal assistant who kept her opinions to herself. In less than twenty-four hours, she had turned everything upside down. Walking into the darkened dining room, he went to the bar and poured himself a brandy. He drank it in the dark, which fit his mood.

Deciding that he needed something, anything, to do to get his mind off the woman sleeping upstairs, he headed to his office in search of his cell phone and decided that he had to talk to Will and at least try to mend that situation. They had been friends for far too long and had been through far too much together to let something like last night come between them. Suddenly remembering that the last place he'd had his phone was the kitchen, he headed there, found it on the counter next to the cordless phone, and then decided to make the call from the sofa in the living room rather than the office. Again sitting in the dark, he dialed Will's number. He was surprised when he heard his friend's voice.

"Hey," Will answered.

"Hey," Stephen began, feeling nervous suddenly. "So, um, how are you feeling today?" Will went on to tell him that his left eye was purple, and his nose, while bruised, wasn't broken.

"What the hell happened last night? I mean, Derek was no more obnoxious than usual, so why not ignore him like we normally do?"

"I wish I knew, man. I wish I knew."

"How'd you get home? Did you have to call a cab, or did George come to get you?"

"I called Holly." Stephen sat and waited for Will to respond. He waited several long moments before his friend spoke.

"Seriously? You still want to cling to your story that there's nothing going on between the two of you? Because I've got to tell you, buddy, a normal, unattached guy would have called a cab or his driver, not his beautiful assistant."

Will thought Holly was beautiful? Stephen felt himself getting defensive again and had to take a deep breath before continuing, "I don't even know why I called her, and five minutes after she got there I wished I hadn't."

"Why?"

"She gave me hell for it. She yelled at me most of the way home."

"*Holly?* Sweet, friendly, quiet Holly *yelled* at you? Come on now, you've got to be kidding me."

Stephen went on to tell Will all about their discussion in the car, leaving nothing out. Stephen had always been able to trust Will, and that was why it was so important that they talk right now. Stephen was confused about so many things, and he needed the sounding board of his close friend.

"Unfortunately, no. Listen, man, I need to know if we're cool again. Can you forgive me for being such an ass last night?"

"Yeah, we're cool. I know it wasn't me you were pissed at. I was stupid enough to let myself get in the middle. I should have kicked back and let the two of you pound on each other for a while. If it's any consolation, I lit into Derek pretty good, too, all the way home. He hasn't called today, so I guess he's still sulking. I don't think anyone's ever told Derek what a prick he can be at times." Stephen agreed.

"I…well, I need you to know that I really am sorry. I have no excuses. I'm not going to try to make any. I was wrong, and I'm sorry." He paused. "Listen, now that we've got that squared away, I need your advice."

Will sighed. "Is it about Holly?"

Stephen pulled the phone away from his ear for a moment in disbelief. "How'd you know?"

"A hunch. So what's the problem? You pissed because she yelled at you?"

"I was, but I got over it when I realized how much I deserved it. No, my problem is that she wants to quit." Will stayed silent. "I convinced her to think on it for a little bit longer, and then she stayed the night and…"

"Wait a minute, wait a minute, wait a minute!" Will interrupted. "You slept with Holly?"

"No! It was three thirty in the morning, and it was storming, and I already felt like crap for getting her out of bed in the middle of the night, so I set her up in one of the guest rooms."

"Uh-huh," Will said skeptically. "So she went home today?"

Silence.

"Stephen? Did she go home today?"

"No. There were trees down in the subdivision, and the roads were blocked. She did leave, but she came back five minutes later. We spent the day together, hanging out and talking, and I *swear* to you, I never had a single sexual thought about her before. But now, after spending the day with her…something's different."

"No, it's not. It's always been there, but you never let

yourself think about it because you were so focused on the business." He chuckled. "You have to understand, being your friend and all, I was a third party watching it all from the outside. Man, you watch her."

"Why? Why should I watch her? You don't trust her?"

Will snorted. "No, you idiot, I mean you *watch* her, like when she's not looking, you are looking at her. All. The. Time. It's been rather entertaining to witness. I knew that Derek had no idea what he was talking about last night because I knew if you had slept with Holly, you would have told me. Plus, the look of pure longing on your face wasn't a longing of *I can't wait to have her again* as much as it was *I can't wait to have her*. So what are you gonna do about it?" Stephen was silent for a long time. He was staring out the big picture window into the moonless night. "Stephen?"

"I wish I knew."

"You have to decide what you want. Do you want Holly as your assistant or as a lover? It never works when you try to have it both ways. Trust me. Which relationship is more important to you?" Stephen was silent, thinking. "You know that Holly runs your office like a well-oiled machine. I think because of her, you have far exceeded your projections for Ballinger's. Is that worth losing for the sake of sex, or are you thinking of something more serious?"

Snorting with disgust at the idea, Stephen said, "More serious? You know I have no plans to get serious with anyone. Ballinger's is my life. I don't want to do to a wife and kids what my dad did. It wouldn't be fair. There is too much going on right now for me to put any kind of energy into a serious relationship with anyone."

"Holly doesn't strike me as a casual sex kind of girl."

"Me either." Stephen sighed.

"So I'll ask again. What are you going to do?"

Raking a frustrated hand through his hair, he murmured, "I still don't know."

"Call me tomorrow and let me know what you decided, if you want." With that, Will was gone. Tossing the phone down on the sofa, Stephen went to stand by the window and watched the rain come down. Off in the distance he saw that the wind was bending some of his trees practically in half. He'd be surprised if they all lasted after such punishment.

The sights and sounds of the storm calmed him. The rumble of thunder started up again, and he saw lightning off in the distance. If his mind wasn't racing so much, now would be the perfect time to crawl into bed and sleep. There was something about a storm that always lulled him, but there was no way he could sleep right now. He had to settle this situation in his mind. He ran a hand through his hair and muttered a curse. How was he supposed to know what to do? Either way he was going to lose Holly in some capacity. The businessman in him knew that she was what kept him and his company going. The man in him, the one who'd been in a state of arousal all damn day, wanted what he wanted and to hell with the consequences. It shouldn't be this hard to have it all. If only Holly were the kind of woman who would have a casual affair.

Feeling more confused than ever, Stephen walked back through the house to the dining room for another brandy. Now he watched the storm through a front window for a few minutes before going back to the living room to sit in the dark on one of the sofas. The only light on was in his office; he'd shut off the kitchen light when he grabbed his cell phone earlier. The occasional flash of lightning lit up the place, but Stephen barely noticed.

For how long he sat there, Stephen had no idea. The grandfather clock in the entrance hall was ticking, but it didn't register with him how many times it had chimed. After some time, he noticed a movement out of the corner of his eye. He turned his head and saw Holly tiptoeing toward the kitchen. Not wanting to startle her, he sat quietly and let her get into the kitchen before following her there.

He almost laughed out loud. Holly was sitting at the table, unwrapping a piece of chocolate! He stood in the doorway watching her. She wore a white T-shirt of his. It was huge on her, hitting her mid-thigh when she was standing, he was sure. But now? While sitting at the table? It hugged her bottom and rode high up her thighs, which looked amazing. His mouth watered. His hands twitched. He had to find a way to let her know of his presence without scaring her, and make light of the situation so that he didn't pounce on her.

Treading lightly into the kitchen, Stephen noticed that Holly was watching the storm as he had earlier. A flash of lightning brought his reflection into the window and made her scream out. To try to calm her, he said, "You wanted the chocolates after all." His tone was light but quiet, and he hoped that she wasn't too badly startled.

"Stephen! You scared me half to death! I thought you were back in the office."

"Nope, I'm done for the night like you said I should

be. I'm trying to take your advice and relax a little bit more." He came and sat across from her at the table—a spot that was somehow never going to be the same after she left. "Unfortunately, I have no idea what to do with myself, so I've been wandering around in the dark."

Holly noticed the glass in his hand and nodded toward it. "What are you having?"

"Brandy. I was hoping it would help me fall asleep."

"Any luck?"

"Not yet."

Silence. Holly nibbled on the dark-chocolate square and sighed. "I can't believe I came down here for this. I mean, I ate a *ton* of food today, and yet all I could do was lie in that continent of a bed thinking that I didn't have any chocolate. How insane is that?"

"Continent of a bed?"

She gave a wicked smile, and Stephen's blood stirred. "Silly, I know, but that bed is so darn huge that it reminds me of a small continent. A family of four could sleep in that thing without touching each other!"

An image of Holly sprawled naked across the bed flashed in Stephen's mind with the same brightness as the lightning outside. In his mind, however, it was his bed that she was sprawled across, and he was touching her all over those silky thighs he was trying not to stare at.

Holly finished her chocolate quickly and stood up. "Well, I think that should do it." Looking at the bag, she reached down and grabbed one more piece. "Just in case."

"Sure." He stood and went to stand directly in front of her so that he could see her more clearly in the darkened room as he looked down at her face. Her eyes looked huge, and even in the dark, he could clearly see how the T-shirt did little to hide what was underneath—which promised to be a spectacular body. Her nipples had hardened to tight peaks, and he had to fight the urge to lean forward so they would be touching.

Holly cleared her throat but couldn't make her feet move. "I guess I'll see you in the morning." Looking up at him, she waited for his response. His eyes were intently on hers, and while she should look away, she couldn't.

"I promised myself that I wouldn't ask you this," he began. His voice was low and deep. "But I have to know…have you given any more thought to our work situation and what's going to happen come Monday?"

It was a mild disappointment, she told herself, that he was asking her about work and not about anything of a more…personal nature. "I…I haven't really thought too much more about it. I still think it would be best for me to leave. I don't want to be the topic of office gossip." She nervously chewed on her bottom lip, willing him to stop staring. His eyes were drawing her in, making her want things that she had no right to want, to yearn for things she shouldn't yearn for.

Inhaling deeply and closing his eyes briefly, Stephen knew what needed to be done. It was inevitable, and he knew that the longer he put this off, the worse it would get. Reaching out, he placed his hands on her shoulders, and Holly thought he was going to pull her into his embrace as he had earlier in the day. But he didn't. This time, it was more than mild disappointment.

"Well, I have thought about it, and I think it would be best if you did leave Ballinger's."

It was the very last thing she had expected him to say. All the way to his house last night and all day today she felt as if he was doing everything humanly possible to convince her to stay on as his assistant. Maybe she had overstepped her bounds; maybe he found her to be too pushy or demanding now that she had finally stood up for herself, and had decided that he didn't want to deal with her anymore. Whatever his reasoning, Holly didn't expect it to hurt so much for him not only to accept her resignation but to encourage it and want her to leave. Her heart ached.

"Oh," she whispered and finally looked away, down at her feet, willing them once again to move and get her up to her room as quickly as possible before she lost it and started to cry.

Stephen watched her head bow, chin to her chest, and waited to see if she would say anything else, if she would demand to know why he had so suddenly changed his mind. His hands were still on her shoulders, and if she moved even a tiny bit, he would release her. But she didn't. She stood there, looking fragile and hurt and more beautiful than he had ever noticed before. He'd seen her in suits, he'd seen her in cocktail dresses and evening gowns, but for some reason, the sight of her barefoot and in his basic white T-shirt had him wanting her like he'd never wanted a woman before.

Finally looking back up at him, she seemed about to speak but thought better of it. She licked her lips, and Stephen followed the path of her delicate pink tongue with hungry eyes. She was killing him. He wanted her to speak, to say something. But when, after several moments of silence, she didn't, Stephen did. "Aren't you curious? Don't you want to know why?" Not trusting her voice not to shake, Holly merely shook her head.

Taking his hands from her shoulders, he placed an index finger under her chin to keep her looking at him. "I think you deserve to know."

"Stephen, please," she begged, not wanting to hear his explanation and not sure how much longer she could stand there before the first tear fell. Holly had never considered herself weak or an overly emotional woman, but something about this entire situation had brought out the absolute worst in her. He had her off balance, and for the first time in her life, she had no confidence in herself and was unsure what to do. How was one supposed to stand toe to toe with someone while they told you how much they didn't want you around? She'd borne witness to Stephen declining deals with potential clients or ending relationships with clients; she'd overheard him breaking up with a woman or two, but she had never been on the receiving end, and now that she was, it made her feel ill. It took her a minute before she realized that he was talking again.

"If you were no longer my assistant, then we wouldn't have to worry about office gossip like you mentioned earlier, or what Will or Derek thought of our relationship, or anyone else for that matter. You wouldn't have to be looking over your shoulder wondering if people were whispering about you or questioning how you got the job or what we were doing together while working late or if we were away on a business trip."

He was saying exactly what she had said earlier, and she was confused. She wanted to get mad then and remind him that it was *she* who had been saying this all along. Why was he suddenly agreeing with her and throwing her words back at her? Did he want her to beg? Cry? Funny, she'd never thought Stephen to be cruel, but right now she wasn't so sure.

"You said that didn't matter since there was nothing going on. You said that I was being crazy and dramatic about the whole situation. What…I don't understand. What changed your mind?"

"This." With that, he bent his head and claimed her mouth with his.

Chapter 5

THE MOMENT HIS MOUTH TOUCHED HERS, STEPHEN WAS LOST. He had never craved a woman the way he craved Holly. At this time yesterday, he would have denied it with every fiber of his being. But now, standing here with her in his arms, he knew he could no longer deny anything where she was concerned.

Stephen had no idea when it had happened, but somehow it had. Somehow he had developed feelings for Holly; he wouldn't call it love, hell no. But what he felt for her right now, while wildly sexual, he knew that it went deeper than that and that he needed her like he needed oxygen to breathe.

The feel of Stephen's mouth on hers took Holly by surprise, but it didn't take long for her to join in and give as good as she was getting. His lips were so soft and wonderful, and as his tongue gently invaded her mouth, she touched her own to it shyly. When she felt his body shudder, she grew bold. Chocolate fell to the floor as first her arms wound around his neck and then her fingers raked through his hair as she had itched to do all day, and it felt glorious.

Heads changed angles, bodies shifted, but all Holly knew was that she did not want this to end. All thoughts of Ballinger's and coworkers and friends vanished. There was only this need, this chemistry, this desire to be with this man.

Stephen pulled her closer and sighed at the feel of those stiff and glorious nipples against his chest. His hands ran up and down her back, keeping her close.

He cupped her bottom and felt what had to be the tiniest pair of panties ever created. It was as if she were wearing nothing, and that had him harder than stone. He forced himself to leave her mouth and work his way across her cheek to the shell of her ear and felt her sigh, heard her moan. He kissed her throat up one side and down the other until she was writhing in his arms.

"Stephen, please," she begged, and if he didn't rein himself in quickly, he'd be taking her right there on the kitchen floor. The storm continued to rage outside, but it was nothing compared to what was going on right there in the darkened kitchen.

"Are you sure?" he asked raggedly. He was a little fearful that she had come to her senses, but he had to ask, had to know.

"I don't want to think about work, or people, or even tomorrow. I want you, Stephen. Now. Please." It was all he needed to hear. He knew his bedroom was a mile away, and yet there was no place else that he wanted to be with her for the first time. Scooping her up in his arms, he hugged her in close and kissed her thoroughly.

He kept his eyes on her as much as humanly possible as he carried her across the darkness to the stairs and up to his bedroom. Holly planted kisses along his jaw, his cheek. Her hot breath felt like heaven. At the door to his room, he placed her on her feet and pressed her against the cool wood. He needed to feel her against him fully again.

She reached for him and arched her back away from

the door so that she could be pressed against him where she needed him the most. He was going mad with want for her. His mouth claimed hers once more, and Stephen knew he could kiss her forever and still not have enough. It was a thought that stilled him briefly. To clear his head, he broke the kiss and took her by the hand as he opened the door. He led her into the room and didn't stop until they were next to the bed.

Without words, without asking, he reached for the hem of her T-shirt, pulled it over her head, and stood in awe. That wonderful mane of hair fell about her shoulders, looking tousled and sexy to the point of making him sweat. She truly was perfection—high, firm breasts; a tiny waist; curvy hips; and lean, smooth legs that he could not wait to have wrapped around him.

Reverently, he reached out and cupped her breasts, and she shuddered and purred with pleasure. He almost came from the sound of it. Her head fell back and her hair spilled down her spine. That pose, in nothing but those tiny panties, was the single most erotic picture Stephen had ever seen in his life.

She came around slowly, her eyes slumberous as she reached out and ran a hand up his chest and then down, getting under the hem of his shirt so that she could touch skin. Her hands were so small, so smooth, and they felt so good on him that he almost ripped his own shirt off to give her better access. Holly worked quickly in getting his shirt over his head. Once it was gone, she touched him all over before leaning forward and kissing his chest. She flicked her tongue over each nipple, and when he growled, she smiled.

Feeling satisfied that he was as crazed as she was,

she stepped away from him, lay down on the bed, and reached for him. It was all the invitation he needed. Peeling off his jeans and briefs in record time, he joined her on the bed. He was beside her, kissing her mouth, touching her body at random but everywhere. It was heaven. It was hell. He wanted to be inside her desperately but wanted to take it slow. He wasn't a teenager; they were two adults, and they had all night. There was no reason to rush this, and yet that was exactly what his body was yelling at him to do.

Before he completely lost the ability to think, he reached into his bedside table for a condom. Sheathing himself quickly, he looked down at the sexy picture she made. Holly writhed against him, driving him mad with each movement. "Stephen," she whispered; it was a plea. That one single word had him knowing that if he didn't have her right now, he would be insane in minutes. He peeled her panties away. Moving on top of her, Stephen looked down at her face, flushed with passion, her eyes dazed. "Please."

He was inside her before the word was finished. He groaned at the sheer pleasure of it, the sweet perfection of their bodies fitting together. He wanted to go slowly, knew that if he didn't get some sort of control of himself, it would be over too soon. But as Holly wrapped her legs around his waist and locked her ankles behind him, he was lost. Stephen knew that never before had a woman obsessed him as Holly did, no woman had ever made him crave as Holly did, and certainly no woman brought out this animalistic need in him as Holly did.

As he drove into her fiercely, picking up tempo, she met his every move and purred for more. Shifting his angle ever so slightly, Holly screamed her release, tightening around him in such a way that threw him over the edge with her. Blind with need, teeth grinding, and with a growl that came from the depths of his soul, Stephen spilled all he had into her and then cursed himself that it was over so soon. Too damn soon.

Collapsing on top of her, Stephen could feel Holly's heart racing against his. He liked it. Lifting up so that he could see her face, he was pleased to see that she was smiling and that it was the smile of a very satisfied woman. Dipping his head, he gently kissed her lips. She smiled against his before kissing him back. The first thought to go through his mind was to deepen the kiss and have her again, but then he thought better of it. Rolling to the side, he pulled her in close. Holly's legs twined with his as her hand rested over his heart and her head lay on his shoulder. Stephen played with her hair as he had wanted to all day, only now getting to know its essence, its texture.

"That was amazing," she finally said, afraid to speak and break the spell. So many times she had dreamed of this exact moment—a time where Stephen would finally see her as more than his assistant and not be able to control himself. The reality was way better than the fantasy. Unfortunately, she'd never allowed herself to dream or think beyond this point. Was he going to say that he was sorry this had happened? Did she satisfy him? She knew that Stephen was no saint, and over the years she had seen girlfriends come and go. Would she soon be on that list of those forced to exit? Thanks to the storm that seemed to settle over his home, Holly had no choice but to stay; would Stephen be wishing that she could leave? Was she supposed to get up and go to her own room now?

Oh, it was too soon; she was busy basking in the afterglow of mind-blowing, orgasmic sex to think about being shown the door. As long as there was a storm outside, she was safe. Like it or not, Stephen was stuck with her for as long as the weather continued to rage. If this was what they could do to pass the time waiting out the storm, Holly thought that she could live a hundred lifetimes with the wind and rain!

Finally, Stephen answered her, kissing her forehead lightly. "I don't think amazing even begins to cover it." Holly felt relief at his words and only hoped that her sigh didn't give her away. "How about instant oatmeal for breakfast?" he joked.

She chuckled and settled in comfortably beside him. Stephen hugged her close, and within minutes they both fell asleep, for peace had finally come.

Chapter 6

THE REST OF THE NIGHT WAS A HAZE OF PASSION. HOLLY LOST count of how many times they had awakened and reached for one another. Sometime around dawn, they finally agreed that sleep was necessary. There was something to be said for sleeping in the biggest bed she had ever seen and in the arms of the man who had turned her simple life upside down.

There was no place else she would rather be.

Stephen would have liked to say that it was awkward having someone in his bed, but it wasn't. He'd never brought his former lovers to his home, to his bed, because he'd never wanted them to get the wrong idea and expect more from him than he had been willing to give, especially after seeing the size of his home. Yet again, Holly had proved to be the exception to the rule. Here was another example of her fitting into his life when he least expected it. He wanted to argue it out in his head because he had seriously complicated everything. He should never have touched her; if he had controlled himself, he'd still have his assistant, and his business would go on unaffected. That wasn't the case now. Then again, was now really the time to think about business when he had a sexy naked woman sleeping beside him?

Definitely not.

A glance at the bedside clock told Stephen that it was a little after nine o'clock. He should still be asleep as

Holly was; hell, they should sleep all day after the night they had shared, but old habits die hard, and he found himself wide awake.

Looking at the woman beside him, Stephen knew he should let her sleep. Yet he was filled with a raging desire to wake her and experience her again. Forcing himself from the bed, he walked quietly over to his closet and found a pair of jeans to throw on before leaving the room. He stood for a long while in the doorway looking at Holly sleeping in his bed and finding it oddly soothing knowing that she was there.

Descending the stairs, he headed for the kitchen to put on a pot of coffee and to check on the status of the weather. Not much had changed outside—well, at least nothing except the fact that he had two trees down in the far corner of the yard and there were several others that would most likely soon follow suit. Stephen made a mental note to find the number of his landscaper and alert him to the damage.

The wind continued to whip, and a sudden chill came over him. It was almost as if it were destiny that this weekend played out the way it did, and yet he was still left with no real answers. Yes, Holly was here, and yes, what had happened last night had been amazing, but what did it all mean for the future? He hated himself for even putting Ballinger's into the equation. What kind of bastard did that make him for selfishly thinking about his business before considering Holly and her feelings?

What would Holly be feeling this morning? He knew she had been as eager and giving as he had all through the night, but in the light of day, how was she going to view things? He was dreading the conversation they would need to have. Over the course of the weekend, they had been forced to have more personal discussions than they'd had over the past three years they had worked together, and it was beginning to grate on him.

There had never been a woman in his life in whom he took enough interest to have deep discussions about feelings or the future, and suddenly here was this woman, this amazing woman, who was making him have to have these talks. He was no good at this; how was he supposed to tell Holly what he was thinking without sounding like a world-class ass? *Last night was amazing, and I'd really like for us to do it again, but... could you please stay on working for me? We'll keep the sex part a secret.* Sure, that would go over really well! Dammit, why did he have to let his control slip? Why did it all have to work out this way this weekend? It was as if the universe was plotting against him.

Destiny or plotting? He snorted. Take your pick. All Stephen knew was that he wanted to have his cake and eat it too. Hmm...the thought of cake had his stomach rumbling, and he walked over to the refrigerator to contemplate breakfast. A slow smile crept across his face at the thought of bringing Holly breakfast in bed. She would certainly be surprised and thankful. His smile grew. And if she were thankful, she'd *want* to thank him—preferably in the same manner as they had been together all night long—and then they could put off any discussion of what it all meant and work and everything else for a while longer.

Geez, he really was a bastard—trying to use food *and* sex to distract her. When had he become this kind of man? He was beginning to feel like Derek. Now *there* was a man who was a complete jerk where women were concerned, and Stephen had always sworn that he would never be *that* guy. And now here he was and feeling awful about it. Derek often talked of his conquests and how he manipulated women. He could get what he wanted through sex and when he was done, he could walk away without blinking an eye. Stephen knew it would be hard if and when Holly walked away, but not hard enough that he was thinking of doing anything permanent about it, was he?

Was Holly looking for anything permanent? She knew him better than anybody, and because of that, she also knew that he never took any relationship seriously. Would she think she was the exception to the rule? Did she want to be the exception to the rule? For all he knew, she could be dreaming of the long term after last night and thinking that this meant they were in love and would get married; then what would he do? Holly never talked about wanting to get married, but then again, they'd never had any conversations about her personal life until yesterday. Damn. What if she *was* thinking marriage? Could he go that far to keep her from leaving his life altogether?

It certainly wouldn't be a hardship to be married to Holly. Hell, they were together all the time already. Fourteen-hour days at the office topped off by nights of incredible lovemaking like they'd had last night sounded pretty tempting.

Derek would mock him seriously, and Will would question his sanity. Married? No one would ever believe that confirmed bachelor Stephen Ballinger was considering the idea of marriage. Was it too cold-blooded of him to think of using it as an excuse to keep Holly at his side? Was it better to let her go after this one fantasy-worthy weekend? None of this pondering brought him any closer to knowing what to do. Shaking his head with resignation, Stephen went about gathering food out of the refrigerator and making breakfast for Holly. He wouldn't think about her gratitude or how she would express it; he would do the decent thing and merely focus on feeding the woman who was a guest in his home.

Deciding on French toast, he took out the bread, eggs, and milk and, after another glance around, decided on some bacon as well. He was busily cracking eggs and pouring milk when Holly found him in the kitchen.

She had woken up not long after Stephen had left the room, and that big bed had felt even bigger when she was alone in it. To say that she was relieved to have some time alone would be an understatement. Never in her wildest dreams could she have imagined such a night! The passion that had exploded between them had been amazing. It was hard to comprehend how it had happened, how they had kept their obvious attraction for one another so well guarded that it never had the chance to be explored until now.

But the sky had been dark then, and it was so obviously daytime now. True, there was still a storm outside, and if she were honest, she'd admit that there was still a storm raging inside her. One night with Stephen Ballinger was not enough. She was prepared for the reality that this weekend would probably be all they had. Stephen was not into relationships, and whether she stayed on working for him or not, that wasn't going to change.

A frown came across her face as the thought of work

crossed her mind. No, the decision had been made; there was no way she could go on working with him and pretend this weekend had never happened. Of course, there was the possibility of continuing the physical part of their relationship—something that she had never considered before—but now, after experiencing a night of passion like they'd had, she'd almost be willing to do it.

Of course, she could be getting ahead of herself here. There was a very real possibility that Stephen was regretting their night and looking for a way to get Holly out of there as soon as possible. The man really did care only about business, and what happened, what began here in this very kitchen, could well have been merely something to pass the time. He was probably used to having women come and go—a body to satisfy a need. If that were the case, Holly would be okay with it, at least to his face. She'd wait to cry and scream and wail until she got back home and to her own life. Heck, she'd have a lot of time for that, now that she was essentially unemployed.

She almost groaned out loud in frustration but decided that she had to face whatever was to come. Clearing her throat, she breezed into the kitchen. "I'm going to have to think about building an ark if I'm ever going to get home," she said cheerily, walking directly to the coffeemaker and pouring them both their mugs. She looked over her shoulder at a shirtless Stephen and smiled. "Got any spare wood around?"

Stephen stopped dipping the thick slabs of bread in the egg mixture, placed his hands on the butcher-block counter, and laughed. "I've got a couple of trees down. Maybe you can use them."

Holly walked across the kitchen and handed him his coffee. "I guess a raft might work…plus I wouldn't have to worry about finding stray animals to take with me." With twinkling eyes, she met his and froze. That was all it took; she read the passion in his eyes as clearly as he had read it in hers. But unlike the night before, they were both a bit on the cautious side and decided to fight the temptation and try to maintain some sense of normalcy.

Clearing his throat and resuming the task of preparing the French toast, Stephen said, "Did you sleep okay?" It seemed like such a stupid question. He knew exactly how she'd slept—entangled limbs, sweet sighs, and hot kisses—all right next to him. But, trying to feel her out, he wanted to try to keep things simple.

"Fine," she replied. "And you?"

"Fine. I, uh…I hope I didn't wake you when I got up. I tried to be quiet."

Smiling, she said, "You were fine. I'm not used to sleeping late—especially two mornings in a row." She looked around at what he was doing. "Can I help you with anything?"

Within minutes, they were preparing breakfast together, chatting about the weather and the work they had done on the Gideon project the night before. Stephen kept waiting for the awkward part, but it never came. He waited for the feeling of being suffocated to overtake him, but it didn't. Looking at Holly, he was almost willing her to make some unreasonable demand of marriage, but that never came either!

Sitting there listening to Holly chatter on about a camping trip she had gone on as a teenager where it had rained like this and how she'd had to canoe out of the park should have held his interest. Smiling and nodding when he thought appropriate, Stephen couldn't help but be annoyed. He wasn't sure, however, who he was more annoyed with: her or himself. They were two mature adults, weren't they? The very essence of their relationship had changed last night, and neither one of them seemed to want to discuss it!

With each bite of French toast, his annoyance grew. Honestly, Holly should be the one to be making a fuss this morning about the whole thing. After all, Stephen had, for all intents and purposes, fired her so that he could sleep with her! Shouldn't that bother her? He'd expected that she'd be all freaked out and in *let's discuss this* mode. But was she? No! It seemed that she was content to sit there sharing campfire stories! He'd dealt with hysterical women before, the kind who wept and sobbed and wanted to know *where* the relationship was going or *why* it was ending. Why wasn't Holly demanding? Although, wouldn't it be better if there wasn't any drama? Shouldn't he be relieved that Holly *wasn't* doing any of that?

Dammit, he should be, but he wasn't. Did she think he wasn't good enough to have a relationship with? Placing his napkin down on the table after wiping his mouth, Stephen decided that he'd had enough idle chitchat.

"If it were up to me, I'd be happy never to see it rain again," Holly was saying brightly. She finished the last of her coffee and noticed the seriously intent way that Stephen was watching her. "Is something wrong?"

"Wrong? What could possibly be wrong?" he asked defensively, standing to start clearing the dishes in what eerily resembled the day before. "I mean, we're sitting here having a perfectly normal breakfast together, sharing childhood stories, blah, blah, blah…" He turned his back on her to place his dishes in the dishwasher and then began clearing the food he had left out on the counter.

"Breakfast was wonderful, and I guess I don't understand what the problem is here." Thoroughly confused, Holly began clearing her own dishes, and when she was standing beside him, Stephen took her by the shoulders and forced her to face him. It hit him that she was wearing his robe, and in his quick movement, the front pulled open, revealing that she was naked underneath. His throat went dry.

"The problem is that I'm wondering what in the hell I'm supposed to do!" He practically shoved her away and raked a hand through his hair. "We spent the night together for the first time, and yet we sat here at breakfast and acted like it was an everyday occurrence!"

Well, she had wanted to know where she stood; it looked as if she was about to find out. "You know, it's not as if we were strangers, Stephen. We've had breakfast together almost every day for three years. Granted, we weren't half-naked while we were doing it, but this is hardly a new thing!" She gave a mirthless laugh before continuing, "You know, I should have figured you'd react this way."

"What does that mean?"

"It means that I knew you would resent having me here. I'm sure that normally the women you sleep with are up and gone before you have to make breakfast. Well, I'm sorry. If the weather would clear up, I'd be gone!" She turned to storm out of the room, but he grabbed her by the upper arm and spun her back around.

"You think you know it all, don't you? Well, you don't. For starters, no woman has *ever* spent the night in this house. You're the first. Secondly, I don't mind that you're here, I asked you to stay, and I'm fine with you being here until the storm passes. Hell, I don't even mind making breakfast for you. What I *do* mind is sitting here making mindless conversation when all I can think about is making love with you again!" Not waiting for a response, he pulled her to him again and kissed her, long and hard and thoroughly so she had no doubt in her mind that he wanted her.

There was no hesitation this time. Holly clung to him, running her hands up and down his back, keeping him close. Impatiently, Stephen reached between them and untied the robe that was wrapped around her. Pushing it off her shoulders, he pulled back to look at her. She was staggeringly beautiful.

There was no time to wait, no time to walk up the stairs; it had to be now. He lifted her and placed her on the granite countertop behind her, careful to keep the robe under her to protect her from the coolness of the stone. She gasped at the sudden move but quickly recovered and pulled his mouth back to hers while he pushed away his jeans. In seconds he was there, inside of her. It was heady to know that he could bring out this passion in her; his normally cool and composed assistant was nowhere to be seen.

He kissed her mouth, her neck, her breasts, each caress eliciting different sounds and cries of pleasure from her. She was a feast that he could not get enough of, and if the way she was clawing at his back was any indication, Holly felt the same way. It was all-consuming, blinding, and frantic, and soon Stephen felt her tightening around him, her telltale quickening of breath that made him feel more masculine that anything else in the world. He held back long enough to watch her come hard before allowing himself to do the same.

Breathing ragged, Holly draped over Stephen, her head on his shoulder, like a rag doll. "If we had breakfast together like this every day, we'd never get any work done," she mused. Stephen chuckled lightly and agreed. He helped her down from the countertop and righted the robe that was hanging off her.

"You okay?" he asked. Holly merely hummed a reply and went to lean against him again, her arms wrapping around his middle. He liked it. That one simple move made him feel ten feet tall. He was treading into dangerous territory here. With every little movement, every word, every gesture, Holly was beginning to take hold of a part of his life that was off-limits to everyone. He had to take some action to stop that from happening if for no other reason than to wait until he knew for sure what she was thinking.

Carefully, he turned her so he could put an arm around her shoulders and walk her toward the living room. The sofa was the perfect spot to recover from their explosive encounter. He kept her close as they sat down. He grabbed the remote and turned on the TV to check the forecast again. It seemed as if the storm was finally preparing to move out of the area, and the rain was expected to end within the next couple of hours. He felt Holly tense a little beside him and said, "It won't matter if the rain ends today or not. It's Sunday, and the trees are still down. The roads probably won't be cleared until tomorrow." In his own mind, he was saying the words to Holly, but he knew subconsciously that they were as much for his own benefit.

Watching the remainder of the newscast in silence was oddly soothing. When the house phone rang near the end of the broadcast, both nearly jumped out of their skin. Stephen walked to the kitchen to answer it. "Hello?"

"Mr. Ballinger? It's Margret from personnel," she began.

"Hi, Margret, what can I do for you?" Stephen was a little perplexed as to why his employee was calling him at home and hoped that nothing was seriously wrong.

"Yes, sir, I've been trying to reach Holly Abbot with no luck and figured it would be best to try to get to you myself."

"Is there a problem, Margret?"

"Well, I got a call from the building manager, sir, and it seems like there has been extensive storm damage in the downtown area as well as some to the building."

"Are our offices okay?" He was immediately in "boss" mode, and his brain was scrambling with thoughts of what could possibly be ruined.

"Oh, yes, sir, our offices are fine. The entire first floor and the basement were flooded, but our offices are fine up on the eighth floor. No, the problem is that they won't let anyone into the building until at least Tuesday afternoon, and so I needed to get the phone tree going to notify all employees of this fact. Holly normally assists me with that when we have snow days and such. I guess her phone must be out because I can't reach her."

"Um…yes, probably." A part of Stephen wanted to hand the phone to Holly so that she could do what she normally did to help Margret, but doing that would be to let someone know that Holly was staying in his home, and he was not ready for something like that yet. "Are you able to make the calls, or do you want me to help you?"

Margret was stunned silent for a moment. "Oh, no, Mr. Ballinger, I'll be fine. I have the entire company list here, and we have a system. I need to get Holly's branch of the phone tree going, and then everyone passes a call on to the next person on the list. I thought that you should know what was going on for yourself since I couldn't reach Holly."

After thanking Margret and wishing her a good day, Stephen walked back into the living room where Holly was channel surfing in search of something to watch. "You have, like, a thousand channels. How do you ever find and decide on something to watch?" she asked, looking at the TV and not at him.

"Honestly? I don't even watch TV." Holly stopped surfing and turned to look at him with disbelief. "It's true," he assured her. She shook her head and returned her focus to the TV until she found something that caught her attention. She was laughing when Stephen interrupted her. "That was Margret on the phone from personnel." He went on to explain to Holly all that was going on.

"So the earliest that we can go back to the office is Tuesday?"

It was such a simple question, and yet it held many implications. Did that mean that Holly was coming back to work? Was she going to stay on with him? Stephen truly wished that it were true, but all he could make himself focus on at the moment was that this new development meant extra days that they would have here together in his home. In his bed.

This was insanity. He had to force himself to focus and to get his mind out of the bedroom. "It seems that way," he finally remembered to answer. "I'm glad we found out now rather than on Monday morning when we couldn't have gotten near the place." Holly nodded in agreement. "Do you need to call Margret or do anything?"

She took a minute to answer because she was partially still paying attention to the comedy on the TV. "Um…I'm sure Margret has it all under control. Besides, won't it seem suspicious if I call her after she couldn't get through to me? And from your phone?"

"What about your cell?"

"Dead. I forgot my charger. I'm sure my mom is getting frantic by now, but I'll talk to her when I get home and put her mind at ease." She was being pretty casual about the whole thing even though her insides were jumping around. More time with Stephen. More opportunities to lock themselves away from the rest of the world and live the fantasy for a little bit longer. It was more than she would have dared ask for, but she was so thankful to receive it.

Sensing everything was all right at the moment, Stephen returned to his spot beside Holly on the couch and allowed himself the luxury of relaxing on a Sunday afternoon with a beautiful woman by his side. It was a new sensation—yet another one—and he found it to be very comfortable.

Chapter 7

BY THE TIME HOLLY DROVE AWAY FROM STEPHEN'S HOME on Monday afternoon, they had carefully agreed that she would return to work at Ballinger's the next day. As awkward as it might be, Holly was too dedicated to the company, and to Stephen, to leave him high and dry without an assistant.

That had been an easy decision. How to handle what had happened over the weekend had been a little trickier. Holly had been the first to address it.

"You realize that I'm more than willing to stay on at Ballinger's, Stephen, on a temporary basis, right?" He had nodded and let her continue. "I know I'm going to be a little more paranoid than normal because I'm going to be looking for someone to say something off-color or to look at me weird. I'm not quite sure how I'm going to handle it."

"You may be worrying for nothing, Holly. I mean, Derek making a comment doesn't mean anything. Derek thinks everyone is having sex. He sleeps with most of his assistants. He can't imagine why I haven't."

"But you have," she said quietly.

He studied her. They were having this discussion lying in his bed, and she was on her side facing him. One breast was exposed as the sheet had draped over her, and he had to fight the urge to trace its roundness with his fingers. But now was not the time. This was a serious discussion that had to be finished before she left his house.

"I know I have, Holly. I'm not sure where we're supposed to go from here." His voice was raw with honesty, and he was leaving the choice to Holly where they went from here.

The urge to throw caution to the wind was almost more than she could bear. But Holly was a sensible woman who knew she had more of a future as Stephen's assistant than she did as his lover. The revolving door of women she'd seen over the years had proven that. With a lump the size of a grapefruit in her throat, she voiced her decision hesitantly. "I think…it would be best if we left this weekend as that—the weekend. This has been wonderful, Stephen, but I think it would be best if we went back to our previous relationship and let this…go."

While he knew he should be relieved, even thankful, that she was making this easy for him, Stephen wasn't so sure they could go back to the way things were before. How was he supposed to work with her every day knowing what she looked like in the throes of passion? How could he sit at his desk and watch her take dictation and not imagine what she was wearing under her clothes?

Could he possibly go back to asking her to handle making dinner arrangements for him and another woman without feeling guilty? On the flip side, how would he feel watching Holly date another man now that he was promising her that they'd cut back on their work schedule so she could have a social life? Maybe a clean break would be best for them both all the way around.

Glancing over at her as she stretched beside him

made the decision for him; he'd rather see her every day and torture himself than not see her at all.

As Holly made her way home, she was shocked by the damage left behind by the storm. Trees were down; parking lots were flooded. Fortunately the route she took home did not require too many detours, and when she pulled into the driveway of her condo, she was relieved to be there. The weekend was over, and it was time to get back to real life.

The weekend had been a fantasy, a lovely escape. She could never regret it, but she had to put it behind her and regain her focus so she could continue to work at Ballinger's. Maybe Stephen was right and that opinion was merely Derek's. After all, in three years, if people in the office had truly suspected anything, wouldn't someone have said something by now? Holly was friendly and knew almost everyone who worked at Ballinger's; surely if people thought she was sleeping with Stephen, it would have come up in conversation by now.

Feeling confident about what lay ahead of her tomorrow, Holly climbed out of her car, and with a grateful look around to see that her building had no structural damage, she went inside to make calls, do laundry, and return to the role of Holly Abbot, single woman, personal assistant.

Her home seemed tiny after her time at Stephen's, and the walls started to push in on her, but she reminded herself that this had been her home for years and one weekend away should not have her feeling any differently toward her place. When her laundry was going, she placed her much-needed phone call to her parents to let them know she was all right.

"Where have you been?" her mother cried at the sound of Holly's voice. "Dad and I have been worried sick! We couldn't get through to you, and the news reports were showing the devastation around you, and all we could think was that something had happened to you!"

Her mother had always had a flair for the dramatic. "Relax, Mom. The lines were down all over the place, and I was without power so my cell phone couldn't be charged. I'm sorry you worried, but as you can hear, I'm fine." She decided it would be best to leave out any details of being stranded at Stephen's place for the weekend. That was so *not* a discussion she was ready to have. Besides, her parents already had issues with Stephen because he worked her so hard that she hardly had time to visit home.

With a promise to call over the weekend and to think about coming home for a brief Thanksgiving visit, Holly hung up the phone an hour later. Once her mother got her on the phone, sometimes Holly had a hard time getting off. Holly felt thoroughly up-to-date on every friend, neighbor, and family member now and was sure that if she never went home again, she wouldn't be missing anything!

Next on her to-do list was to go food shopping. She looked at her tiny kitchen and once again had to stop herself from comparing it to Stephen's. The good news was that she could look forward to doing some cooking again now that she would be getting home earlier; the bad news was that she was still going to be doing that cooking for only one person.

Later that night as she lay in bed, the enormity of it all hit her. What was that phrase—"'Tis better to have loved and lost than never to have loved at all"? Well, screw that! The first tear fell, and she was helpless to stop the rest. Her bed was too small, her kitchen was too small, her home was too small, and it was all Stephen Ballinger's fault! If she hadn't answered his call Friday night, none of this would have been an issue.

How did she expect to go back to the way things were with all this emotion inside her? Holly was not like Stephen; she felt things. Relationships *meant* something to her, and no matter how she looked at it, she and Stephen had a relationship. They seemed to have a multilevel one, and forgetting about the physical side was going to be a battle. She cried for all she had in that short weekend and for all that would never be. She cried in confusion about what she wanted for her own life and how she was going to make things work.

Kicking the blankets off, Holly walked to the bathroom for a tissue and took a long look at her reddened face in the mirror. "You are a fool," she said to herself. "You *had* to sleep with him, didn't you? You couldn't stay in bed that night, could you? You had to have a piece of chocolate…" Disgust covered her face. Chocolate. All of this happened because she had a sweet tooth. She was pretty certain they would have controlled themselves if they had not seen each other in that moment Saturday night.

Turning on the faucet, she splashed cold water on her face, dried it, and gave herself one last look of deprecation before turning out the light and heading back to bed. Lying in the dark, she waited a long time before her mind shut down enough to let her sleep.

The parking garage was filling quickly at noon on Tuesday. There were still many puddles, and the day was cold and damp, but for the most part it seemed as if the worst was over. Holly climbed out of her car and met up with some of the girls from the accounting department, and they headed across the street to Ballinger's, each telling her harried tale of the weekend storm and how it had taken them all by surprise.

Oh, if only they knew!

Once up on the eighth floor, Holly found Stephen already in his office and on the phone. She went about her normal routine, brewing the coffee while her computer warmed up and then listening to the voicemails that had piled up over the long weekend. Weeding out the important messages, she organized them all and headed back to the small kitchenette where the coffee was now steaming and ready. Fixing Stephen's mug, she came back through to her desk, scooped up the messages, and went into his office.

If she had been expecting awkwardness, she needn't have bothered. Stephen was fully immersed in work mode; he barely acknowledged her presence at first as he talked on the phone to a client in Texas who was having problems with a security system due to a storm that had blown through the area. She placed Stephen's coffee on his desk, laid out his phone messages, and went back to her own desk, relieved that their first encounter held no drama.

Two hours later, Stephen was finally off the phone and called Holly into his office to tell her how to handle each of the messages she had left on his desk, plus what needed to be done to fix the problem with the client in Texas. His tone was impersonal, as if he were addressing a practical stranger. He never once even looked at her. Holly wrote everything down, and as she was making her final notation, Stephen stepped around the desk to inform her that he was heading out to a meeting with Frank Gideon and that he probably would be out for the rest of the day. He reminded her to call it quits at five o'clock, and before she could comment, he was gone.

Okay, fine; this was a *lot* less personal than what she had been expecting, but at least she knew that for today they were fine and more than capable of working with one another.

That pattern of business and behavior continued through the end of the week. By Friday afternoon, Holly had come to the conclusion that their weekend together had clearly meant more to her than it had to Stephen because there had not even been a *hint* of anything personal between them. If anything, the man treated her as if she had the plague. There were no times that they were alone when the door wasn't open or someone wasn't on speakerphone with him; they had barely made eye contact. Well, if that's the way it was, then so be it. Holly could move on just as easily.

At five o'clock on Friday afternoon, Holly walked into Stephen's office, handed him the contracts she had spent the day working on, and wished him a good weekend as she quickly turned back toward the door. As usual, he was on the phone and merely waved a hand without looking at her.

If she slammed her desk drawer with a little more force than usual, nobody seemed to notice. If she scowled a bit on the elevator ride down to the lobby, people chose to say nothing. She was muttering under her breath as she made her way out the main door onto the sidewalk about how rude and inconsiderate a man she worked for and what a completely self-absorbed bastard he was when she walked directly into someone. At the moment of impact, two strong hands gently grasped her upper arms to steady her. She looked up and saw that it was Will.

Great.

"Hey," he said, chuckling, "are you okay?" He had a great smile and brown eyes that twinkled and lit up his whole face. Holly had always liked Will, and she hated that her first reaction to seeing him was to feel her stomach pitch and roll with unease.

"Oh, hey, Will," she said with forced cheeriness. "I'm fine. I guess I wasn't paying attention to where I was going. Sorry for slamming into you."

Will left his hands on her arms for longer than was really necessary and examined her face. She looked about as happy as Stephen had sounded on the phone earlier. He hadn't heard back from Stephen after their phone conversation on Saturday night, but since Holly was still working for him, he could only imagine how the rest of the weekend had gone.

If they hadn't slept together, that would explain why Holly was still here; Stephen must have put his sexual feelings for her aside in favor of the company's needs. That would make a man miserable for sure, especially if it meant not getting involved with a woman as beautiful as Holly. However, the misery on her face was a mystery. And if there was one thing Will knew for certain, it was to butt out of this situation before anything like last weekend happened again.

Deciding that he was staring for an inappropriate amount of time, he remembered to speak. "Kind of early for you to be getting out, isn't it?" He finally released her arms too.

"What?" she asked, mildly confused, and then remembered her new hours. "Oh, yes, well…we're trying something new. I've been leaving at five o'clock with everyone else." She looked at him, and his eyebrows were raised as if he was waiting for her to continue.

"It still feels weird. Like my day isn't done quite yet, but it's nice to be able to go home and cook for myself and relax a little before having to come back here in the morning."

That made him laugh. "Well, I hear that you put the boss in his place last weekend. Good for you! It's about time someone reminded Mr. Workaholic that some of us enjoy having personal lives. I'm proud of you, Holly."

"Thanks."

They stood there for a moment with nothing to say before Holly felt the need to escape. "Well, I guess I should be going. Have a nice weekend, Will." She went to walk around him when he placed a hand on her arm, gently, one more time.

"Is everything okay, Holly?" His forehead was creased with concern, and the question was asked softly so that no one walking by would hear. But one look in his eyes, and Holly knew that his concern was sincere. She only hoped that Stephen had not shared any intimate details of their weekend together. He watched her chew on her bottom lip nervously. "I'm not trying to pry or anything, it's just that…well, I like you. I think you are an amazing woman. I also know that you and Stephen fought a lot last weekend, and yet you're still here. I wanted to make sure that you were okay. That he's treating you all right…"

"I'm fine, Will. Thanks." She sighed. "It's a little awkward right now. I kind of wish I hadn't opened my mouth to begin with. I know Stephen is trying to make everything okay between us. Honestly, I'm glad this week is finally over. I feel like I can relax at last."

He smiled sympathetically at her, and she returned the expression. "Give him time, Holly. Stephen's not used to anyone standing up to him, but he's smart enough to know that he couldn't run this place without you. He's built this company up from nothing, and he's had no one to rely on except himself. It's probably a new experience for him to have to take someone else's feelings into consideration where business is concerned."

"I know," she said softly, the wind starting to whip up, leaves blown off trees over the weekend swirling around them. "I never thought it would be this…weird, you know?"

He nodded in agreement, wished her a good weekend, and watched her walk away. Will wasn't the only one watching, however. Up on the eighth floor, from his wall of windows in his office, Stephen had witnessed the entire scene, his emotions running wild. He had said goodbye to Holly and then stood by the window in hopes of getting one last glance at her before she disappeared into the parking garage. He had not expected to see Will. Stephen had watched their whole exchange down on the sidewalk and wanted to bang on the windows and demand that Will take his hands off Holly. It wasn't right that his friend could casually touch her while he was having to practically sit on his own hands, day after day, since returning to the office on Tuesday.

The week had been pure hell. In his attempt to keep things as professional as possible, all Stephen had accomplished was making himself more miserable than he'd ever been in his life. Holly was the only one being professional around here; she still came in with a smile and asked all her usual questions regarding any project he handed her. He was the one who couldn't bring a smile or even a polite word to his mouth. Damn. He had no trouble running into ex-lovers and being cordial, polite, and downright witty. Why, then, was this so damn difficult? Sure, he never had to see his ex-lovers on an everyday basis, but there was a difference between them and Holly; he and Holly had already had a strong relationship.

Every time she was within his range of vision he would watch her, but as soon as she turned his way, he made himself look busy. She wasn't playing any games, wasn't trying to get his attention, and that was making him crazy. Honestly, Stephen had expected Holly at least to *mention* their weekend together. But she hadn't. He had expected to have to be the one to remind her that they were only working associates, but she hadn't given him any reason to. For four long days, Stephen had had to sit back and watch her go on with her life and her job as if nothing had ever happened—which was what he had wanted. Until he had it.

He hated watching Will make Holly smile and have her meet his eyes when he had done his best barely to look at her, lest she see the heat and longing in his own eyes. It was madness! It was torture. Stalking away from the windows, he walked out to the kitchenette to grab himself a drink while waiting for Will's arrival. He had not been expecting a visit from his friend, but why else would Will have been out on the sidewalk if he was not there to see him?

Trying to seem casual and as if he had no idea his friend was there, Stephen walked back into his office, took a seat behind his desk, flipped open the file of contracts Holly had placed there earlier, and pretended to read until he heard Will's knock on his office door.

"Oh, hey!" Stephen said, feigning surprise. "Come on in. What are you doing here?"

Will walked inside, shook Stephen's hand, and had a seat in the leather chair facing the desk. "Well, I know it sounds cliché, but I was in the neighborhood and thought I'd stop by and check on you. I haven't heard from you since our phone conversation Saturday night, and I've got to be honest with you, buddy, the curiosity was killing me."

Stephen nodded and took a drink from the can of cola he was holding. "Is that right? What's got you so curious?" If Will noticed the slight snarl in Stephen's words, he chose to ignore it.

"I ran into Holly outside, so I take it she didn't quit," Will began, leaning back in the chair and crossing his legs at the ankles, making himself more comfortable. His smirk was irritating Stephen, he could tell, and he decided that if he did not tread carefully, there would be a repeat of last Friday night.

"No, she didn't quit," Stephen said. "We talked about it and decided that the whole situation had gotten out of hand and so there was no reason for her to leave Ballinger's. Of course, it would be helpful if Derek didn't come around for a while."

"Helpful to you or to Holly?" Will asked, and Stephen's eyes narrowed.

"Something on your mind, Will?" Stephen said with a calmness he did not feel. It really was last Friday all over again because suddenly he found himself wanting to lunge over the desk, tell his friend to take the smug smile off his face, and then pound him until he promised to never, *never* lay a hand on Holly again. Instead of raging, however, he merely took another sip of cola and waited for Will's response.

Sensing Stephen's barely concealed rage, something that only came from years of friendship, Will thought it best to clear the air and be done with it. "So you told Holly about Derek's theory, and she's probably embarrassed, am I right?" Stephen nodded. "I don't know about you, but he won't return any of my calls."

"I haven't even tried to call him again. We spoke, cleared the air a bit, and I'm not interested in talking to him right now. I'm interested in not having Holly upset."

"Because you don't want to lose her as an assistant, right?" It would have been an innocent enough question if it had come from anybody else. Because the query came from Will, Stephen knew what his friend was fishing for.

"You want to know if I slept with her?" he snarled. "Fine, yes, we slept together. It was great, it was amazing. It was quite possibly the greatest sex of my life. But at the end of the weekend, we decided that was all it was going to be—a weekend. Holly knows that the company always has and always will come first and that I'm not looking for a relationship, so we agreed that she'd return to work and see how things go, and if she feels that people are gossiping about her or us, then she'd give me suitable notice. There, are you satisfied?" Stephen jumped up from his chair and kicked it aside, turning his back on Will, placing his palms on the window behind him, and glaring down at the street and beyond.

He muttered a curse under his breath and raked a hand through his hair before turning back to his friend. Where had this raging beast come from where Holly was concerned? His life was slowly spinning out of control, and he had no idea how to rein it all back in. The only thing Stephen did know right now with any certainty was that for the first time in his life, he was uncertain of his future and how to go about putting everything back into perspective where it belonged.

Will took pity on Stephen from his relaxed position in the chair. "I take it, though, that you're *not* okay with it, and that's what has you in such a foul mood?"

Stephen wanted to deny it but couldn't. "Damned if I know. I thought I knew exactly what I wanted or at least exactly how it was going to be once we came back to work. But the thing is, she's been the model employee. I can't complain about anything. She's acting as if the weekend never happened—like we didn't have mind-blowing sex all over the damn house! She's done her work as impeccably as she always has, she hasn't made any demands of me or cried or pleaded for a relationship, and dammit, I wish she would! How twisted is that?"

"Extremely." Will laughed. "What would you do if she *did* make demands on you and wanted a relationship with you? How would you handle that?" Before Stephen had a chance to answer, Will added, "And remember, she knows you pretty well and knows how you feel about relationships."

"I should be happy, right? I should be relieved and doing a jig that she has made this so easy on me, and yet I can't let myself be happy! Every time she comes through that door, I want to say to hell with it all and *try*. I've never wanted to try with anyone, but I wouldn't mind trying my hand at a relationship with Holly."

"And when it ends?" Will asked.

Glaring, Stephen hesitated. "What if it didn't end?" He left that thought hanging, wanting to know what Will thought of it. If anyone could help him make sense of this, Will could, and right now, Stephen was desperate for help.

Scratching his chin in consideration, Will shifted in the chair and got more comfortable before answering. "Well, if it didn't end, I'd have to venture a guess and say that you were talking about marriage." He arched an eyebrow and waited for a response. He didn't get one. "Is that what you're considering? Marriage?" Still no answer. "I never thought I'd live to see the day that Stephen Ballinger would consider taking the plunge. But let me ask you this, are you considering this because you *love* this woman and want to spend the rest of your life with her, or are you considering it because it guarantees that you can have Holly exactly where you want and not inconvenience yourself in any way, shape, or form? Sort of like having your cake and eating it too?"

Stephen cringed at Will's choice of words. Hadn't he had the same argument with himself last weekend? It sounded crude when Will said it out loud. Was he considering something so cold and calculated?

"Stephen?" Will prompted. "Tell me that you're not thinking of marriage as a way of not inconveniencing yourself…"

Sitting back down in his chair behind the desk, Stephen put his head in his hands and murmured, "I wish I could." They sat there like that for several long, silent minutes before Will finally stood up.

"Holly deserves better than that," Will said cautiously, afraid to risk Stephen's rage again.

There was nothing but hopelessness written all over Stephen's face. "I know," he replied softly.

"Look, it sounds like you've had a bitch of a week. Let's get out of here and go grab some dinner. Nothing major, but nothing like that bar last weekend, okay?" Stephen agreed, mainly because he needed a distraction. He must have voiced that thought out loud because Will added, "There will be no more talk of Holly, relationships, marriage, or Ballinger's. Okay?"

For the first time all week, Stephen felt his spirits rise. He had been spending too much time obsessing over this situation with Holly. Luckily, he had many irons in the fire with Ballinger's, so it was easy to keep himself busy. It was obvious that he'd think about her during the day because she was always there, but when he went home at night, it was worse. Every room he went into he remembered Holly being there, laughing there, and making him want things that he had never wanted before. This night out with Will promised to take him away from all thoughts of his life of late and help him to clear his mind for a little while.

Will drove them to their favorite steak house, and to both of their surprise, Derek was standing at the bar when they walked in. The three men stood silently looking at one another, unsure what to do. Derek broke the silence. "Well, well, well…how'd you know I'd be here?" he said smugly. Will and Stephen looked at each other and then at Derek, unwilling to believe his conceit.

"We had no idea you'd be here," Will began. "We figured you'd still be at home crying over how we all did you wrong." Derek laughed out loud at that statement and grabbed Will in a bear hug.

"God, I missed you guys this week! C'mon, let's get a table and eat and drink and leave this miserable week behind." They all readily agreed and when the hostess led them to their usual table in the back corner, all seemed right with the world.

It was as if nothing had ever been wrong between them; they talked, they ate, and they laughed. There was no mention of Holly; there seemed to be a silent agreement that that topic was off-limits. Stephen found himself having a better time than he'd thought possible. Maybe it wasn't going to be so hard to move on and get his life back on track.

He wasn't in love with Holly. He knew that was impossible. Soon the haze of lust would fade, and last weekend would be nothing more than a memory. Stephen made a quick sweep of the interior of the restaurant for women with hopes of someone catching his eye. For the first time in memory, it seemed there were none.

Ordering another round of beers, the three friends talked of plans for Thanksgiving, which was a month away. None of them were big on family gatherings, and they tended to do something together like skiing or heading off to an island for a long weekend. This year it looked like they were all up for skiing. Stephen didn't mind; anything was better than staying at home alone.

Derek had a condo in Vail, and so by the end of the

night it was decided that they would fly in the day before Thanksgiving and stay through the weekend. It felt good to have plans. Yes, this could be exactly what Stephen needed; who knew, maybe he would even meet someone up there who would take his mind off Holly.

While Will and Derek talked about slopes and who was the better skier, Stephen tried to picture the scenario in his head. This was the lodge where they normally went, and where he'd met women before. He imagined himself coming in after a long day on the slopes and seeing a beautiful woman—a snow bunny of sorts— sitting by the large stone fireplace nursing a mug of hot chocolate. He smiled at the thought.

Getting deeper into the fantasy while Will and Derek were almost getting violent in their need to prove who the more skilled sportsman was, Stephen leaned back in the booth and closed his eyes. He would walk up to this beautiful woman who, up until now, had been cast in shadows, and ask her if he could buy her another drink. She'd turn to face him, her long chestnut hair spinning over her shoulders, big green eyes staring at him…*Holly*.

He muttered a curse that silenced Derek and Will's arguing. "Something the matter?" Derek asked.

Stephen was stunned and couldn't believe that he was stupid enough to speak out loud. He recovered quickly. "Um, no… I forgot to take some contracts home with me that I need to review this weekend. That means I'll have to go back to the office, and I really was looking forward to *not* going back there all weekend."

"Ah…" his friends both said in unison, totally understanding.

Not long after, it was time to go. Will took Stephen

back to Ballinger's where his car was. He walked Stephen into the office where he watched him grab the contract folder, and then they walked back out to the parking garage together, making idle talk along the way.

"He may be a pain in the ass, but it was good to see Derek tonight," Will commented.

"Absolutely," Stephen agreed. "I think Vail is a good idea. It will be good to get away for a couple of days. It's been too long." Now it was Will's turn to nod in agreement.

"Now if only we could make it a guys-only thing and not have to deal with the pressure of meeting anyone and hearing of Derek's expertise with the ladies the whole damn time, it would be a great weekend," Will said.

Stephen stopped next to his car and looked at Will oddly. "Are you telling me that you are not interested in meeting anyone for a mindless weekend of female companionship? What's up with that?" Stephen had been so wrapped up in his own female troubles that he had not even given anyone else's life a thought. "What's going on?"

Will shrugged nonchalantly, unwilling to talk about his life. Besides, Stephen had enough on his mind without adding his problems. "Look, it was good getting together with you tonight. Go home and try to have a good weekend. I'll talk to you next week." With that, he turned and walked away, the shadows of the parking garage swallowing him up before Stephen had a chance to respond.

The drive home was pleasant for the first time that week mainly because for the first time in days, Stephen had something else to focus on—Will. He couldn't remember Will mentioning being involved with anyone. Why would his friend keep his relationship a secret? Why? Probably for the same reason Stephen had wished to hell he'd kept his and Holly's a secret—once it was out there, everyone would be privy to their business.

Once at home, he went into his office, and, as was becoming a habit, he sat down behind his desk, turned on the computer, and settled in for another sleepless night of work.

———

Sitting on her couch eating Chinese takeout and trying to get into the movie she was streaming on Netflix, Holly wondered why she had made such a fuss about having this extra time at home. At least before she had something to *do*. She was busy, she was moving, and she was having a conversation while eating dinner! Now, she sat here pitifully alone and bored out of her mind. Maybe she should get a cat. That thought made her throw down her fork and plate in disgust. "Is this what it's come to?" she thought. "One doomed relationship and I'm ready to become a cat person?" The thought sent a shiver down her spine.

The movie couldn't hold her attention, so she grabbed the TV remote and turned it off, opting to channel surf for something else. After a while, she settled on the evening news and got caught up on current events.

"This is ridiculous," she chided herself. "I am a grown woman with friends—friends I have not seen in a while." Rising from the couch, Holly walked to kitchen, found her address book, and began furiously flipping through it to start calling people. It was only seven thirty on a Friday night, for crying out loud! What was she doing home? Didn't single people go out on the weekends? Wasn't that what all those beer commercials were about? Hell, *she* could be in a beer commercial if she wanted to! Holly gave herself a pep talk as she picked up the phone and dialed her friend Linda's number. "I am a young, attractive woman," she murmured. "There is no reason for me to be at home on a Friday night." At the sound of her friend's voice, she said cheerily, "Are you up for a girls' night out?"

Thirty minutes later, Holly was walking out the door with a swing in her denim-clad hips and a little bounce in her stiletto-booted step. Climbing into her car, she congratulated herself on taking that all-important first step in having a life outside work. With any luck, this would be the first of many nights out, and eventually, she wouldn't remember her wild weekend with Stephen or feel that pull of desire every time she looked at him in the office.

Yes, a girls' night out was *exactly* what she needed to find out who Holly Abbott *could* be.

Chapter 8

So much for big plans.

The big girls' night out had been a *major* disappointment. She had met up with her friend Linda at a local restaurant-slash-bar, and while she enjoyed talking with her friend, there were no single men hanging around. After noshing on a shared appetizer and nursing screwdrivers, they headed to a bar in downtown Raleigh. That held a few more options, but Holly found she wasn't as interested in finding a man as she'd thought she was at the beginning of the evening.

Once she let go of the notion of finding a man, Holly let herself relax and enjoy this time with the girls. It turned out that Linda had chosen this particular bar because they had other friends who hung out there, and after a couple of drinks, they were all out on the dance floor laughing, dancing, singing, and having a great time.

At the end of the night, Holly was shocked to see that half the women in their group were leaving with men they had met, while Linda and another gal had gotten phone numbers from men. To say that she was a little disappointed would be an understatement. As if reading her mind, Linda had said, "What did you expect? You've got this giant 'back off' thing going on that has scared most of these guys off. I figured if you wanted to talk about it, you would have brought it up. I was just glad to have you out with us for once!"

"Was it that obvious?" Holly asked, totally dismayed.

Not one to hold back, Linda answered, "Unfortunately, yes." They drove back to the restaurant where they had first met up to get Holly's car, the whole while talking about the night's events and how they were going to have to do it again.

Linda made Holly promise to come out with her again soon and to do it without the obvious attitude. "I make no promises," Holly quipped, but she knew that she was going to have to make more of an effort on their next outing. With a sigh of frustration, Holly knew she'd probably enjoy herself more if she relaxed and let her brain go blank for a couple of hours.

That was all the excitement she allowed herself for her first weekend. The remainder of it she stuck to her usual routine of laundry and food shopping, but she did roll up her sleeves to do some cooking. It wasn't as much fun cooking for one person, but she refused to let that stop her. Food shopping was fun because for the first time in what seemed like forever she was *shopping*! She pored over fresh produce and gourmet cuts of meat. It was going to be a great week, food-wise. But now the weekend was over, and it was time to get back to reality. The "Stephen weekend"—as she called it in the recesses of her mind—seemed a million years away at this point.

~~~

Holly pulled into the parking garage at work early Monday morning. Stephen had a big meeting planned for tomorrow with the Gideon people that involved a catered luncheon and dinner with the company president out at the Angus Barn—the most expensive restaurant in Raleigh. Today would be full of last-minute preparations to make sure everything ran smoothly.

Holly had full confidence that both she and Stephen were well prepared. No doubt Stephen had a list of things that needed to be fine-tuned. She was used to it—was already expecting it. She would make her calls to the caterers, the florist, and the Angus Barn to make sure everything was in place and was ready to meet all their specifications.

Tomorrow would also be the first time she and Stephen would have to interact outside the office since their weekend together. For meetings such as these, when he was entertaining an out-of-town client, Holly acted as hostess. She would be there for all the meetings tomorrow, not only speaking on behalf of Ballinger's with her own portion of the presentation, but also at dinner with him to entertain and be company for any of the spouses who came along on the trip.

By this point in the Gideon project, Holly had come to know this particular group of people very well. A contract with Gideon was going to put Ballinger's Security Systems in countries it had never been before. It was a huge coup for Stephen, and Holly was so proud and excited to be working on this project with him. The Gideon group had offices all over the world but was based out of Los Angeles, and so Holly had taken several trips with Stephen out west and knew that by the time everything was in place in all Gideon's locations she would have to travel with him again. Yikes, that was going to be awkward.

She refused to go there right now. For the time being, she was going to focus on getting through today and all that needed to be done. There were gifts to be delivered to the hotel for the president of Gideon and his wife, as well as making sure that the limousine picking them up at the airport was stocked with their favorite champagne.

Riding up in the elevator, Holly kept running a mental checklist in her head even though she knew Stephen would already have the list ready and waiting for her. Sure enough, as she walked to her desk and put her purse down, she saw it propped against her computer screen. The man was meticulous, that was for sure.

Going about her morning routine, she heard Stephen already on the phone in his office. Last week's pattern of behavior seemed to be continuing. Oh, joy. Coffee was brewing, her computer was warming up, she retrieved voicemails, and within minutes Holly was walking toward Stephen's office with the pile of messages that demanded immediate attention.

Predictability and stability were things that most people would love in a job, weren't they? Holly used to think so. Now, she would almost kill for a little spontaneity. The act of merely existing in this job was starting to grate on her nerves. Stephen sat in profile to her as she walked in, and her mouth watered. His hair was a mess already from running his hands through it in frustration, and he was clean-shaven. For a moment, she allowed herself to remember what he looked like with a day's growth on his chin and how it had felt against her cheek, her throat, her thighs. She stifled a sigh, walked up to his desk, and put the mug and messages down.

For the first time in a week, Stephen looked up, met her eyes, and smiled. Holly smiled back at him, and for a moment, it felt as if everything was going to be okay. They were going to have to make things work—especially for the meetings tomorrow. If he couldn't even look at her, someone was going to pick up on that. These people with Gideon had been around them long enough that they would notice if suddenly Holly and Stephen weren't coming within ten feet of each other and acted completely awkward with each other.

That could spell disaster. So for the sake of the deal, Holly vowed to let the awkwardness of last week go and do all she could to restore them to their previous relationship. She'd have to talk to Stephen about that when he was off the phone…or maybe after lunch…or maybe…

"Holly?" She jumped at the sound of Stephen's voice. "Are you okay? You sort of zoned out right there."

Well, it seemed that he was on the same page; gone was the sullen man of last week, and here before her was her old boss. Okay, things were going to be fine. "Sorry, I guess I've got a running tally going in my mind of everything that has to happen in order for tomorrow to be a success."

"Ah." He nodded and reached for his coffee.

"Speaking of which, I've got calls to make to the caterer and whatnot," she began as she slowly made her retreat to the door. She kept her tone friendly and light and remembered to keep casual eye contact the entire time. "I got your list, and if there's anything else you can think of, let me know, okay?" Stephen nodded, and she walked out of his office and shut the door with a sigh of relief.

This was *not* going to be an easy day, she told herself, but Holly was determined to get through it all and do it cheerfully. By lunchtime, all her calls had been placed; the limo was confirmed and stocked as she had requested with Cristal chilling and Godiva chocolates. The caterer was delivering gourmet fruit-and-cheese baskets to the hotel to the top executives and had confirmed the menu for lunch the following day down to the letter. It was everything that Holly needed to hear, and she felt as if a great weight had been lifted in one respect but still had another giant one weighing her down in respect to herself, personally, for tomorrow.

After lunch, she met with Stephen to go over the agenda for the next day and to do a run-through of their presentation. Stephen was impressed with what Holly had put together and knew that, between the two of them, the contracts would be signed and they would be in business with Gideon by the end of the next day.

As Holly rolled up some of the posters they were going to use for the meeting, Stephen watched her and smiled. "I think we've got this one, Holly," he said happily. Nothing made Stephen happier than a job well done and ready to be signed and sealed. "I can't imagine anyone having a problem with anything we present." She turned to him, nodded in agreement, and smiled.

"If it's all right with you, Stephen, I think I'm going to get the conference room set up with easels and everything today so there will be little for me to do tomorrow and I can focus on the caterer and getting the food laid out so that it won't be too crowded in there."

"We are going to have a few more people than usual in there, aren't we?" he asked, suddenly concerned that there was a fly in the ointment.

"We'll be fine, Stephen," she assured him. "We have

had more people in there, and with the right amount of planning and preparation, we'll all be comfortable." Holly turned and walked out of the office with the rolled-up posters under her arm and confidence in her step, and Stephen couldn't help but admire her.

Stephen was about to sit back down behind his desk but decided to follow Holly to the conference room to help her set up. They were so well prepared, there wasn't really much else for him to do except wait for the meetings tomorrow. Anything he did right now would only be nitpicking with perfection.

Holly was surprised when Stephen came into the conference room. As if of one mind, they began moving chairs, clearing off tables, and setting up easels. Within thirty wordless minutes, the room was as ready as it would ever be. Everything else that needed to be done would be handled once the caterers arrived the next morning—they were bringing tablecloths along with the food. Holly could picture how it was all going to look and was pleased.

They spent the remainder of the day separately—Stephen making phone calls, Holly making sure that the assistant she was going to have for the day knew where everything was and showing her what would need to be done during the conference. At five, Holly popped her head into Stephen's office to tell him that she was leaving, and he was sitting behind his desk rubbing his temples.

"Everything okay?"

He dropped his hands and looked at her. "I know we can't possibly be more prepared than we already are. There is nothing that Gideon is going to throw at us that we won't be able to handle and have an answer for, but until it's a done deal, I won't be able to relax."

Holly was about to offer to stay and "run lines," so to speak, but had to stop and think about it before opening her mouth. By staying and working late, she would be breaking the rule that they had set in place in what was a huge point of contention with getting her to stay on at Ballinger's. Stephen was the type who might not see this as a one-time deal and suddenly start expecting her to stay late every night again. Tomorrow night, while not technically working, she would be out late with him and their clients. That would be two nights of her time that she was giving up for the sake of his company. Still, looking at him, she could see that he did truly look worried. This was the biggest contract in Ballinger's history, and while it would not break the company if Gideon decided to pass, it would certainly help skyrocket it if they accepted.

With a sigh of resignation, Holly walked farther into Stephen's office and asked, "Do you want me to stay for a little while so we can go over everything again?" The look on Stephen's face was so hopeful, so full of gratitude, that Holly was sure she had made the right decision. But the look vanished from Stephen's face quickly.

"Thank you, but no," he said politely. "I don't think we need to go over everything again. It's my issue, not yours. Go enjoy your evening, and I will see you here in the morning." He paused and looked at his desk as if searching for something to do and then grabbed his phone and began to dial.

A more stubborn man Holly did not know. Not willing to argue with him—he had made his choice—Holly bid him a good night and walked out of the office. With a stiff spine, she walked to the elevator and waited. Once it arrived, she stepped inside, thankful to be alone, and leaned heavily against the back wall. There was no going back, she guessed. Their relationship was irreparably damaged, and she either had to learn to deal with the distance that was now between them and not let it upset her or she would have to move on.

That was a thought that she did not want to take root right now. This week was too important. Ever the professional, Holly knew that she would stay on until the Gideon project was completed—whether it was the end of the week or the end of next year. She had invested a lot of time and effort into this project herself, and if being cold and impersonal with her boss was what was required to see it through to the end, then so be it. There were worse situations, she imagined, that she could find herself working in.

Once at ground level, Holly headed out of the building and across the street to the parking garage. When she climbed in her car, she sat there and stared off into space. Like it would have killed him to let her stay? She thought, "I mean, there I was, offering my help to the man! This was nothing like it was in the past where it was expected of me to stay. I offered!" Snapping out of her reverie, she drove home while carrying on quite the animated conversation with herself.

"And, you know," she began to herself out loud, "I don't know why I thought it was such a big deal to be home at five thirty every damn night. It's boring! Sure, it's been nice eating real food instead of takeout, but, really, Stephen always brought in whatever I wanted. It wasn't like he was forcing me to eat Burger King every night, for crying out loud. Why did I have to make such a fuss and screw everything up?"

That was a bitter pill to swallow. As much as she'd like to blame it all on Stephen, the truth was that it was her words that had set the ball in motion; Stephen was honoring her wishes, and now Holly had to pay the price. If anyone knew all the things that had happened between the two of them, Holly was sure there would be fingers pointing and mocking voices of "Careful what you wish for."

Pulling into her driveway, she sighed with frustration and climbed from the car. She waved to some neighbors who were out and about in their yards—what were their names?—before heading into the tomb-like silence of her home.

At seven thirty the next morning, Holly was entering the impressive building that housed Ballinger's and found Stephen waiting for the elevator. After saying good morning, they boarded the elevator and rode up to the eighth floor in silence. As they exited, Stephen went straight to his office and Holly went about her thing. When the coffee was done and she headed into Stephen's office as she had done almost every morning for three years, she decided that she'd had enough.

Walking through his door, her hands loaded with mugs and messages, she kicked the door closed behind her. Stephen's head snapped up at the sound. "Is there a problem?" he asked.

Holly carefully put the hot mug of coffee down and placed his messages on the large mahogany desk before straightening and answering. "As a matter of fact, there is."

He raised an eyebrow at her. "Did Gideon and his people get in okay? Was there a problem with the car or the accommodations? Dammit, why didn't anyone call me?" he snapped, frantically searching his desk for...anything.

"This isn't about Gideon, Stephen, it's about us. Here. Work. Everything!" Holly didn't consider herself to be a particularly emotional woman, but in the past few weeks that was exactly how Stephen had made her feel—what he had brought out in her.

Taking a deep breath, she started over. "I appreciate that you have been more than considerate of my time. I have left here at five o'clock on the dot every night with the rest of the staff. And, I'll admit, it has been nice to have some free time. But dammit, Stephen, I cannot work with someone who treats me like a complete stranger! We have worked together for three years, and in the past week I feel like we regressed all that time, and I hate it! At least in the beginning while it was awkward, you were still friendly! But now...now you treat me as if I were someone you would rather not have around, and I have to be honest with you, that's not going to work for me." Holly turned and paced a bit before speaking again.

"I came to a conclusion last night that I wanted to stay on here with Ballinger's until the Gideon project is completed. I worked long and hard on this project with you, and I'd like to see it to fruition. But I cannot do it under these conditions. I can't." She collapsed into one of the chairs facing Stephen's desk and rested her head in her right hand. And waited.

She didn't have to wait long. "You know, Holly, I don't

know what the hell it is that you expect from me," he began very softly, very calmly. "You didn't want to have to stay late, and I made sure that you didn't stay late. You didn't want me bothering you on the weekends, and I haven't called. You don't want people thinking that there is anything going on between us, and so I have made sure that my behavior is above reproach." With each word, his voice grew louder and Holly could see him becoming more and more agitated. "But I will not be controlled like a puppet on a damn string because *now* you don't like everything that you asked for! I will not jump through fiery hoops to keep you from being uncomfortable." He stood.

"Have you given any thought to how I have felt this past week?" He didn't wait for a response. "I've been here until midnight most nights trying to finish everything up on this project. You think you put a lot of time and effort into it? Well, let me tell you, I've put *all* my time and effort into it. And you know what? This last week was freakin' critical in some of its details, and I really could have used your help, but I would've rather swallowed broken glass than ask you to give up any of your precious time because I didn't want to disturb the precarious balance and truce we made.

"You have made my life damn difficult here, Holly, and I can't keep tiptoeing around you. You wanted things to stay impersonal to keep the gossip hounds at bay. I gave it to you. Time off? It's yours! But with everything else that I am trying to do here, like *build* my business, I have to tell you, your timing really sucks!"

Holly had never seen him quite so angry or passionate before—even during their weekend together. She could tell that he was being brutally honest with her and that she had, in fact, hurt him. Yet another bitter pill to swallow.

She was ashamed of herself.

"You're right, Stephen," she said softly, her eyes closed. "There is no excuse for my behavior. I guess I hoped that things could go back to the way they used to be."

"They can't, Holly," he said, equally quietly. "I appreciate that you are willing to stay on here and help me and keep working for me, but last weekend changed everything, and we can't go back."

She nodded and willed the tears that were building behind her eyelids to remain there and not fall. "I know." It took a few moments for her to get herself together and open her eyes to look at him. If it were possible, he looked as miserable as she felt. She managed a feeble smile before slowly rising to her feet and walking out of his office, quietly closing the door behind her.

What she wanted most was to sit at her desk and be left alone. What she got was the caterer and her six assistants walking toward her and giving orders and instructions.

With a sigh of resignation, she plastered what she hoped was a believable smile on her face and began what promised to be a very long, very full, and very emotional day.

The morning session of their meeting went well. The catered breakfast buffet was perfect—tons of fresh fruit, pastries, and muffins along with a gourmet coffee bar. For lunch, Holly had the caterers set up in a different room so that people would feel free to get up and stretch and not feel like they were being held captive in the conference room. As Holly sat with one of Gideon's assistants while nibbling on a slice of quiche, she looked around and felt pride in what she had accomplished. The lunch reception had something for everyone without seeming to be trying too hard. There was a salad bar, a sandwich buffet, and an assortment of soups and quiches all spread out on individual stations in different corners of the room. Tables had been moved into the room and covered in snowy-white tablecloths with a lovely yet simple floral arrangement on each one.

All the plates were plain china, and they utilized simple yet sturdy silverware and linen napkins. All in all, the basic multipurpose room had been transformed, and judging by the looks on everyone's faces, no one was disappointed about not leaving the building for lunch.

After the ninety-minute break, they all headed back into the conference room where a light dessert buffet had been set up for anyone who still had an appetite or who had a sweet tooth as the afternoon wore on. Holly did her portion of the presentation, and by four o'clock things looked as if they were heading toward a positive conclusion.

Everyone stood and seemed to talk at once, and while Holly made the rounds throughout the room thanking everyone, she saw that Stephen and Mr. Gideon were deep in discussion. It didn't take long for the room to clear down to the three of them, and instead of attempting to join their conversation or move it to Stephen's office, Holly began the silent task of cleaning up. The caterers had been instructed to come back after four thirty to clean up, but Holly didn't mind getting started; she hated to see a mess sitting there.

Sure enough, at four thirty, the caterer and her staff

arrived in the conference room to gather their belongings. Holly felt that a sufficient amount of time had passed that she could go over, gently interrupt the men's conversation, ask them if they'd be more comfortable in Stephen's office, and offer to make them coffee.

"That won't be necessary," Mr. Gideon said with a smile as he turned to face Holly. "My wife is expecting me back at the hotel. We have a massage booked before dinner, and I fully intend to enjoy it." He turned back to Stephen, shook his hand, thanked him, and told him that they were all looking forward to dinner at seven thirty.

Stephen walked to his office while Holly oversaw the final stages of cleanup. She paid the caterer, looked at the clock, and saw that it was five thirty. She had brought a change of clothes with her so that she would not have to drive all the way home to Wake Forest and then back to Raleigh for dinner. Stephen had provided a very lovely executive ladies' room for her, and so except for taking a shower, she would be able to get ready for this important dinner without feeling cramped in a public bathroom stall. She was about to walk down to her car to get her things but stopped to tell Stephen where she was going first.

"I think it all went extremely well, don't you?" he asked when she stepped into his office.

"Absolutely! I don't know what the two of you were discussing there at the end, but he looked like a man who was ready to sign on the dotted line." She waited to see if Stephen was going to fill her in on any of the details, but he didn't. Instead he got up and walked around his desk to the door of his office. He shut it. He locked it.

His walk was like that of a predator as he closed in on Holly, took her in his arms, and kissed her.

She was too stunned to speak, to move. It didn't take long for her to kiss him back. It was wonderful. It was glorious. It was exactly what she had been wanting for more than a week! His hands ran up and down Holly's back while hers snaked around his neck and threaded through his hair.

When his mouth finally released hers, it was only to find other places to kiss her. Holly arched her neck to give him better access, and when he walked her backward toward his desk, she was as mindless with need as he was. Her thighs hit the desk, and Stephen leaned over her to once again revel in the feel of her body beneath his.

"This is crazy," Holly whispered against his throat, kissing him, biting him, wanting him more than she'd thought possible. Where had this all come from? They'd been fine an hour ago—not a hint of sexual tension. But now? Oh, now it was too late to turn back, too late to stop.

Stephen's hand ran up her thigh and under her skirt, hooked onto her panties, and yanked them away. Holly gasped in both surprise and excitement, and before either had the chance to think about what they were doing, Stephen was unbuttoning his trousers and inside her. Holly very nearly came from the sensations. Never before had she felt so desired, so necessary.

Stephen made her feel that way. Items went flying off his desk as they moved to accommodate themselves. It was fast and furious, hard and exciting. Holly felt herself on the verge of release and wanted to will her body to wait longer so that she could enjoy being one with him again, but Stephen would have none of that.

He touched her where their bodies were joined with the pad of his thumb, and she went up in flames. She bit into his shoulder to keep from screaming out as she wanted to. Seconds later, it was his turn to bite her as he came inside her.

Their breaths were ragged; their bodies shone with sweat. Stephen lifted off her and gently kissed her lips, which were now red and swollen from their kisses earlier. "Are you okay?"

Holly laughed nervously. "I think so." Doing his best to stand and fix his clothes, he got one last look at her sprawled across his desk. Her blouse was open to reveal a black lacy bra, and her charcoal-colored skirt was pushed up so that nothing was hidden from him. Damn, he'd either have to bronze this desk or burn it, but there was no way he was ever going to be able to work at it again and not remember this image.

There were too many places etched with the memory of Holly. His home and now his office. There was no excuse for what happened except that he still wanted her. Hell, he wanted her again right now. Putting his own needs aside, he helped Holly up from the desk and watched as she straightened her clothes.

"I…um…I have to go down to my car and get my stuff still," she said as she buttoned her blouse.

"Give me your keys," Stephen said. "I'll go get it. You can use my bathroom; it has a shower. You can freshen up in there, and I'll be back with your things in no time, okay?"

Too afraid to risk looking at him, Holly merely nodded, walked directly to his en suite bathroom, closed the door behind her, and locked it. A little late for that, she realized, but she needed a few minutes to wrap her mind around what in the world had happened.

After their argument this morning, Holly had assumed he would still be ticked off at her. The last thing she could have imagined was him wanting to make love to her! Well, didn't this complicate things even more! Who was she kidding, complications or not, there was no way she could regret their wild coupling. It was a bit of an ego boost to know that he had needed her so desperately that there was no time to prepare for it.

Remembering where she was, Holly quickly undressed, twisted her hair up, and stepped under the shower to wash off before Stephen got back. Secretly she hoped that he would come back to the office and join her in the shower but then remembered that she had locked the door. *Stupid, stupid move, Holly*, she chided herself.

With a little squeal as the cold air hit her, Holly stepped out of the shower and quickly unlocked the door.

Just in case.

While she was getting all soapy and lathering up under the steamy water, Stephen ran across the street to the parking garage and grabbed Holly's dress and bag. Luckily the place was deserted, or he might have found himself answering some awkward questions about why he was fetching her clothes and where exactly she was.

He called himself every vile name he could think of. Stephen had no idea what had come over him minutes before. He'd been sitting in his office, basking in the afterglow of an enormously successful meeting and mentally making plans for which of Gideon's offices he was going to travel to and when, when all of a sudden there Holly was in his office. The only thought to enter his mind was that for one minute, one short minute, he wanted to have it all—the contract, the successful business, *and* the girl. Hell if he could regret it. The building could have burned down around them, and Stephen wouldn't have been able to stop himself from making love to her. He had a cocky grin on his face as he rode the elevator back up to the eighth floor.

It was worth it.

That was the only way to describe it. She could hate him; she could damn him to hell for all eternity, but for those few brief minutes, Stephen Ballinger knew what it was like to have everything he had ever wanted. Walking through the door of his office, he noticed that the bathroom door was open, and only one thing came to his mind…

He wanted it all again.

Chapter 9

PULLING UP TO THE RESTAURANT TOGETHER IN STEPHEN'S car, Holly wished they could have skipped the dinner and gone back to either her house or Stephen's. Sitting around talking business for the next three hours while her body was still tingly was so *not* what she had in mind for tonight.

When Stephen had come back into the office after getting her things, he had joined her in the bathroom, and they had spent the better part of an hour pleasuring each other mindlessly. Holly was thankful for the darkness in the interior of the car because she knew that she was blushing. Stephen pulled up to the valet, got out of the car, and walked around to help Holly out.

They arrived before the Gideons, which was perfect for Holly. She needed to compose herself a little more and find a way to block the last few hours out of her mind. Stephen escorted her to the bar while they waited for their table and ordered each of them a drink. Not sure when the Gideons were going to arrive, he had to fight off every urge to take Holly to a corner table, pull her close, nuzzle her neck, and have the freedom to touch her the way he longed to do. But this was a business dinner, and recalling their arrangement of a week ago, for the remainder of this time, she was off-limits and back to being his assistant only.

They made small talk about the presentation and all

the things she knew Mrs. Gideon had wanted to do today so that Stephen might be able to talk to her about her day and involve her in the conversation. Holly always made sure Stephen was coached in such things when they dined with spouses of clients because she knew it made the wives feel like part of the negotiations.

The Gideons arrived within ten minutes, and they were seated not five minutes after that. With no prompting from Holly, Stephen asked Mrs. Gideon about her day touring the museums and shopping at the Streets at Southpoint. He knew she was an avid collector of Lladró figurines and asked her if she had found anything new to add to her collection. The woman positively beamed at him, and after that, dinner flew by in a flurry of conversation that never lulled.

As the evening was coming to an end and Stephen was waiting for the check, Mr. Gideon leaned back in his chair and smiled at Holly and then at Stephen. He seemed to approve of something in his own mind because he nodded his head and then spoke. "You know, Ballinger, I like you. I really do. I think our companies are going to work wonderfully together."

Stephen had to stop himself before he yelled "yippee!" or something else completely inappropriate. "I couldn't agree more," he said simply.

"I look forward to seeing you out on the West Coast and being able to treat you and Holly to the same wonderful hospitality that you have shown me and my wife." Rising from the table, he assisted his wife, taking her hand and then placing his arm around her waist. "I'll be in your office tomorrow morning around ten to sign the contracts." Stephen rose, shook Mr. Gideon's hand,

and leaned in to kiss Mrs. Gideon on the cheek. They all laughed and said good night, and Stephen stood at his seat watching them leave the restaurant.

"Is it too soon to let out the victory cheer?" Holly asked, glancing up at Stephen, who looked like a kid on Christmas morning, grinning from ear to ear.

He chuckled, looked down at her, and felt as if all the oxygen had been sucked from the room. She was breathtaking. Her smile was radiant, and he saw as much excitement over the deal that they had sealed in her eyes as he knew shone in his. She was truly his partner. Could she be more? Could he allow himself to let her be more?

"Not yet," he whispered, remembering that she had asked him a question. Sitting himself back down in his chair and finishing off his glass of wine, Stephen felt more content than he ever had—even more so than earlier in his office. Why was he fighting this thing with Holly? Surely after what they had shared earlier, she might be more open to them exploring a relationship— perhaps a permanent one. If she truly cared for him, as he suspected she might, all the gossip in the world wouldn't stop her from wanting them to be together, right?

Their waiter appeared with the check, and after taking care of the bill, Stephen rose and helped Holly to her feet. They walked out of the restaurant and over to the valet where Stephen handed the driver his ticket. While waiting, Holly stared at the star-filled sky. What was in store for them for the rest of the night? Her car was still back at the parking garage at Ballinger's, so there was a very real possibility that Stephen would take her back there to get it. But what about after that? Would he ask her to follow him home? Would he follow her home? She did not have the guts to ask—her mouth had gotten her into enough trouble lately, it seemed, so she would leave the decision up to him. If Stephen wanted to spend the night with her, she would not turn him down or deny him. All that she had managed to accomplish by demanding that they leave the weekend at the weekend was making them both miserable. *And for goodness' sake*, she thought, *we deserve to be happy*!

Feeling confident that, one way or another, in two cars or one, she would be spending the night with Stephen put a relaxed and confident smile on Holly's face as she climbed into his car. Stephen shut her door after making sure she was settled, walked around to the driver's side, and tipped the valet. Climbing in, he sat and put on his seat belt, then turned to look at Holly and noticed the smile on her face. It made him smile, but he wasn't sure they were smiling at the same thing.

"Care to share what's put that smile on your face?"

She sighed happily. "It's been a good night, that's all. Everything went well, everyone's happy. Who couldn't smile at that?" she asked, turning her head to look at him. Their eyes met in the darkened interior, but even without the benefit of light, Stephen could tell that her big green eyes were pulling him in. And he wasn't fighting it one little bit!

After they pulled away from the restaurant, the twenty-minute drive back to Ballinger's was mostly spent talking business and what they would need to have prepared for tomorrow's meeting. Stephen would have the legal department draw up the final draft of the contract and be at the meeting, and Holly made a mental note to have some sort of mini celebratory buffet put out, with champagne for them to toast to their new venture before Mr. Gideon left to return to California.

Before she knew it, they were back at the garage and parked next to her car. She was a little disappointed that Stephen hadn't mentioned taking the night any further, but she supposed it was for the best. Holly placed her hand on the door handle and turned to give Stephen a final smile.

"I'm so happy for you," she said. "I know that this contract is what you've been working toward for years, and I am thrilled to see that it finally happened." Without thinking, she leaned over, placed her hand on his cheek, and kissed him on the other one. "Good night."

She climbed from the car, and Stephen watched as she walked over to her own vehicle in those skinny heels and a black cocktail dress he itched to peel off her.

He made sure she was safely in her car and followed her out of the garage. It had been his plan to take her back to his house and present her with the idea of continuing their relationship, but somewhere along the way, as they were discussing business, he decided that perhaps it would be best to seduce her slowly into the idea. Perhaps he could make her see that they could be together without putting a full-page ad in the newspaper. They could simply be together.

Of course, Stephen was not a patient man, and the thought of taking this slowly when all he wanted to do was have her back in his bed was not making him too happy. When they had made love this afternoon, it had been explosive. He wanted that. Again. Tonight.

Now.

She couldn't be more than five minutes ahead of him,

the perfect amount of time for him to follow her home without her knowing he was following her home. He grew hard thinking of the look on her face as he pulled in the driveway behind her. Luckily Stephen had been to her house a couple of times, so he knew where he was going. He found himself pushing down on the accelerator harder than he should and had to rein himself in—a speeding ticket would surely slow down his plans to get to her.

It didn't take long to pull into her neighborhood-slash-subdivision, but by the time Stephen pulled up in front of her house, Holly had already gone inside. This was perfect, he mused to himself. The look on her face when she opened the front door would be priceless. Turning off the headlights so as not to alert her to his arrival, he pulled in, turned off the engine, quietly got out of his car, and shut the door cautiously.

Walking up to the front door of Holly's condo had him almost feeling giddy. It was close to midnight on a Tuesday night. Deep down, Stephen knew that he probably shouldn't be here. He should let her be and get some sleep before coming in to work tomorrow.

Work. For the first time since…well, since their weekend together, he couldn't give a damn about work. Hell, if Holly wanted to call in sick tomorrow to recover from all the ways that Stephen planned to please her tonight, he wouldn't mind it at all.

He was about to raise his hand to knock on the door when he stopped himself and allowed his mind to wander for one more minute. True, the longer he waited to get inside, the greater the chance that she'd be out of that black cocktail dress that he so desperately wanted to take off her himself. Stephen needed time to think about how he was going to handle this situation once she opened the door. The beast in him that Holly had unleashed wanted her to open the door so he could make his way inside and have her right there in the hallway. *Been there, done that earlier in the office*, he thought. No, maybe this time they would go slowly and he would seduce her all the way to her bedroom where he would take his time in exploring her and pleasing her and make her as crazy as she'd made him this past week.

Yeah, that was the one.

Raising his hand finally to knock, he was surprised when the door opened and Holly stood seductively in the doorway, leaning against the doorjamb, her head tilted, her lips wet, and her hair spilling wildly over her shoulders.

"What took you so long?" she said as she grabbed his tie and pulled him into the house.

—⁓—

The next morning came too soon as far as Stephen was concerned. Holly's alarm went off at five a.m., and all he knew was that they hadn't finally slept until sometime after three. Last night he'd had the opportunity to live out both fantasies. Holly completely seduced him in the foyer, and it was as wild and as exciting as he had hoped. Afterward, he had carried her up the stairs to her bedroom—she was still in her cocktail dress and heels, a heady combination—and slowly made love to her for hours.

Stephen reluctantly kissed Holly goodbye at six thirty and drove to the office where he had a shower and kept a change of clothes. By the time Holly arrived at eight thirty, it looked like business as usual.

They had to quickly get all the specifics out of the way for Stephen's ten o'clock meeting with Mr. Gideon. Stephen spent the better part of an hour on the phone with legal while Holly went about setting up the conference room—this time for a much smaller group of people.

By lunchtime, contracts were signed, champagne was served, and the Gideon group was on its way to Raleigh-Durham International Airport to fly back to California. While Holly was relieved to have the process over with, a whole new phase of life at Ballinger's had started.

As she went down to the company cafeteria to meet some of the girls from accounting for lunch, she had to wonder if she was entering a new phase of life with Stephen. It was clear that they had moved on to another plane of their relationship, but how long would it last? Was Stephen expecting her to be the type of woman he usually dated who would be satisfied with a week or so of his time and then okay with being dumped with some sort of door prize picked out by…well, Holly normally picked out the parting gift-slash-door prize. Who would Stephen get to pick out hers?

That thought did *not* settle well in her heart or her stomach. The whole thing was making her sick. Luckily, the group of gals she was eating with were all chatty, and it helped divert her mind to simpler things—other people's lives!

Until they were preparing to clear off their tables.

"So, Holly," Donna from accounts payable began, "how can you work for such a good-looking man and get any work done?" All the girls nodded in agreement and looked to Holly expectantly. "I mean, I think I would plant myself in his office all the livelong day and stare! Honestly, the man is beautiful." This was followed by more agreement from the group. Holly felt a little bit trapped.

"You know, I guess I don't even notice it anymore." They all looked at her with disbelief. "It's true," she lied. "When I first came to work for Stephen, I did have a major crush on him, but it didn't take long to realize that he only cared about one thing—his company. He never looked at me twice." Feeling confident and that she'd thrown them off her scent with her small admittance to having a crush way back when, Holly felt as if the topic were over.

She was wrong.

"Oh, come on," Sherry from accounts receivable said, placing her hands on the table as if ready to rise and make a speech. "You mean to tell me all those late nights and all those business trips and the man has not once made a move on you?"

This was so *not* the way lunch was supposed to go. Especially not today. Holly knew she was going to rot in hell for all the lies she was telling. Looking Sherry right in the eye, she said, "Not once. I'm telling you, the only thing that Stephen Ballinger is interested in is his company."

"Now that's not true," Donna chimed back in. "He's had girlfriends; you've said yourself that you've purchased breakup gifts and whatnot. Clearly he occasionally has other interests."

With a shrug and a look of utter dejection, Holly simply said, "Then I guess it's me he finds unattractive."

Bingo! That was the golden phrase that had everyone going from attack mode to sympathy mode. All the way back to her office, she was comforted with offers of blind dates and "Don't worry, honey, he doesn't deserve someone as good as you." Holly had to hold her breath to keep from laughing out loud. Oh, if only they knew!

The rest of the day flew by without incident, and at five o'clock Holly went into Stephen's office to see if there was anything else he needed before she left. It seemed weird to be asking that; it was what she asked him every night, but now, suddenly, it seemed like all she wanted to hear was that he needed *her*.

"Can I take you to dinner tonight?" he asked from behind his desk, looking hopeful.

"You took me to dinner last night," Holly replied, playing coy.

He chuckled. "Well, that was a business dinner. I was thinking of something a bit more casual and a lot more relaxing." Stephen stood and walked around his desk to stand in front of her. His office door was open, so he was trying to be mindful of anyone who might walk by or walk in.

"I'll tell you what. I already have dinner plans. Why don't you join me?" she asked softly.

Plans? She had plans? Who the hell did she have plans with? Stephen had to stop himself; there was that rage again—the same one he felt that Friday night at the bar toward Derek and later in the week toward Will when he saw his friend talking with Holly down on the sidewalk. What the hell was *that* about?

"Stephen?" she prompted when he hadn't replied to her suggestion.

"Oh, right, sorry. Join you, huh? What kind of plans did you have?" God, he only hoped he sounded as casual as he thought he did and not like he was accusing her of anything inappropriate.

"Well, I already set some salmon out that I was going to grill. It's not really enough for two, but I can improvise with some side dishes. My kitchen isn't as well stocked as yours, but I think I can make do. What do you say?"

He'd be a fool to pass up this opportunity, and if there was one thing he was beginning to pride himself on of late, it was not being a fool. "That sounds like a plan," he said, keeping his tone light and casual.

They decided that Holly would head home to get things started while Stephen finished up what he needed to at the office. They'd meet at her house at six thirty. Looking and sounding every bit the personal assistant lest anyone be within earshot, she wished him a good night and said that she would see him in the morning.

On the way to Holly's house, Stephen stopped to buy a bottle of wine. As he walked out of the liquor store, he had the thought that flowers might be a nice touch as well. Feeling like a man on a mission, he drove to a nearby florist and purchased a large mixed bouquet for Holly. Roses would be predictable, and Stephen was trying to show Holly that there was another side to him—a side that could be involved with a woman without the assistance of his…assistant.

Stephen arrived right on time, and Holly was truly pleasantly surprised with his gift of both the flowers and the wine. Normally Holly took care of ordering flowers for his dates and having them delivered. This was completely new territory. Nice, but definitely strange.

They enjoyed the dinner Holly had prepared—salmon and risotto, Caesar salad, and asparagus. The wine Stephen had chosen was perfect, and once the meal was over, Holly quickly cleaned the kitchen while Stephen asked her what her plans were for the holidays.

"I normally head up to Long Island to see my family. For Thanksgiving I do a quick weekend—leave Wednesday night and I'm home on Saturday morning. It's short and sweet."

"Do you want to stay longer? Have I kept you from staying longer?" He almost cringed while waiting for the answer.

Holly laughed—a full, all-out throaty laugh. "Oh, Stephen, you should see the look on your face right now!" She wiped at a tear that was rolling down her cheek from laughing before adding, "No, you do not keep me from spending more time with my family for Thanksgiving. The long weekend is more than enough. I enjoy living six hundred miles away from them for a reason!"

Though her answer had eased his guilt, all Stephen could think about was that he suddenly didn't want to go to Vail for Thanksgiving with Derek and Will; he wanted to meet Holly's family. He took a large swallow of his wine and did his best to block *that* thought from settling itself too firmly in his mind. It was like he didn't even know himself anymore.

First he was thinking about trying out a serious relationship with Holly, and now he was imagining himself meeting her family over a holiday visit! If he didn't know better, Stephen might be starting to see himself and Holly settling down together.

That wasn't possible. Sure, he knew it had been

an internal dialogue in his head ever since that fateful Friday night, but Stephen refused to take it too seriously. After all, he was Stephen Ballinger, a man who had always known he would never get married and settle down. Unfortunately, as of late, that seemed to be *all* he could think about. He glanced at Holly as she finished cleaning up the kitchen. She looked at him over her shoulder and smiled.

He couldn't help but smile at her in return and knew that right now, that very moment, he had to make at least a partial decision about where this was all going. He would ask Holly tonight if she would consider taking on a relationship with him that didn't involve things like sex on his desk because they had been too busy trying to fight having a relationship. He wanted more than a personal assistant-slash-boss relationship with her; Stephen needed it to be personal and intimate. He wanted to spend time with Holly outside the office and take her places.

Settling more comfortably into the kitchen chair, Stephen imagined Holly spending weekends at his home. They would go to movies together and dinners out; they could come here to her place and have casual, intimate meals. Maybe he would bring some of his clothes here, a shaving kit perhaps, and Holly would leave some of her things at his place so that neither of them would ever be inconvenienced.

A smile spread across his face because it all sounded perfect. Stephen couldn't believe that he had avoided all these things, and yet he knew, deep down, that he probably had avoided them for so long because none of the other women he dated were Holly. It felt perfect because she was perfect for him.

Holly wiped her wet hands on a dish towel, topped off her wine, and turned to face Stephen. Whatever he was thinking about had put a relaxed smile on his face. For a moment, she allowed herself the luxury of looking at him. It was rare to see him so relaxed *and* smiling that she had to give herself a moment. He must have sensed her stare because suddenly he snapped out of his trance.

"Let's go into the den," Holly suggested as she walked past him and grabbed his hand. Stephen followed obediently. They settled in front of the TV where they channel surfed a bit. Finding nothing appealing on, Holly shut the set off and turned on the stereo system, left it on low, and sat herself back down next to him.

"This is much better than going out after a long day," she said.

"Thank you for including me in your dinner plans."

Holly smiled. "Thank you for joining me. This was a nice surprise." She took a sip of her wine. "The wine, the flowers, dinner…some would call this a date." She sounded playful, and she hoped Stephen wouldn't be scared by her teasing tone.

"Would they?" he asked quizzically.

Nodding, she answered, "Yes, I believe this is what people would call a date. What's up with that?"

Stephen slowly sipped his wine before giving Holly an answer. "Would that be so terrible? If this was a date, I mean?"

"No, I don't think it would be."

"Good," Stephen said before reaching a hand out to cup Holly's nape gently and pull her close so he could kiss her. It was tender at first—he wanted to taste her and show her that he was sincere—but it didn't take long for it to deepen and become hotter until Holly was strad-dling his lap with Stephen holding her so close that their hearts beat against one another's.

"Bedroom?" he murmured as he trailed kisses down her throat and pulled her blouse aside so that he could nuzzle the roundness of her breasts.

"Absolutely." She sighed, unsure if she wanted to wait that long to have him. She squeaked when he lifted her, and before Holly knew it, she was on her bed, on her back with Stephen looking down at her.

"I think I'm going to enjoy dating you," he said as he pulled off his shirt, a sensuous grin on his face.

Chapter 10

MUCH LATER, THEY LAY SPOON-STYLE IN HOLLY'S BED WITH a sheet lightly draped over them. Stephen's chin was resting on the top of Holly's head. She wiggled a bit to align their bodies even more intimately and sighed with contentment. She peeked at her bedside clock and saw that it was after midnight. As much as she hated to speak and risk ruining the moment, she had to tell Stephen what an amazing night this was but that she needed sleep. To have shared two such passionate nights in a row with him had been wonderful, but she was completely exhausted.

She told him as much, and he didn't say anything. She waited, wondering if he was already asleep. "Stephen?" she whispered. "Are you awake?"

"Yes," he replied softly. He kissed the top of her head. "Can I ask you something?"

Holly nodded, a lump forming in her throat because he sounded so serious. The last time they had had a discussion like this, they were similarly in bed, and it was decided that something like *this* could not happen again. She fervently hoped that Stephen was not going to suggest such a thing again.

"I know that we sort of made light of it all earlier," he began, "about this being a date and all, but...I was sort of wondering if you...I mean, if we could maybe try... you know..." God, he was making a mess of this. He held business meetings with wealthy heads of major corporations and did it without once stuttering, and now here he was talking to one woman, and he couldn't seem to form a complete sentence! He cleared his throat and started again. "I think we sold ourselves short after that weekend. I think we've proven in the last two days that we have something here that deserves to be explored. Would you consider—"

"Are you asking me to be your girlfriend?" Right after she said it, Holly wished that she could take it back because it sounded so…high school!

Stephen must have agreed because she felt and heard him chuckle before he turned her around to face him. "Gee, Holly, do you want to wear my letterman's jacket too?" He burst out laughing, and Holly swatted him on the chest but couldn't stop herself from laughing too.

Though they never finished their discussion, it seemed they were both in agreement that they wanted to continue. Stephen made love to Holly slowly after that, and later, much, much later, they finally slept.

Things fell into a comfortable pattern after that. They maintained a very professional relationship at the office, but the nights and weekends were passionately hot and wild. They divided their time between their two residences, as Stephen had hoped, and as Thanksgiving week approached, there seemed an air of uncertainty as to what they should do.

Holly wanted to spend the long weekend with him; to bring him home with her to meet her family would have been her number one wish. She knew that Stephen had plans with Will and Derek, and although they hadn't discussed it, Holly had a sneaking suspicion that he had not told his friends about their relationship.

That thought bothered her. She had readily agreed to get involved with Stephen, and if she were brutally honest with herself, it was working wonderfully and she should never have thought otherwise. Maybe it was time for them to stop hiding. What was the worst that could happen? Stephen wasn't spending a lot of time with his friends, and Holly had a feeling that, if anything, the girls in the office would almost welcome the news.

Since lunch that one day where they all questioned her relationship with Stephen and she said that he must not find her attractive, they had all at different times encouraged her to try to get his attention. So, really, how the office people viewed her was a nonissue as well. Sitting at her desk, Holly noticed that Stephen was off the phone, and went in to go over his afternoon schedule with him. She made a mental note to bring up the topic of Thanksgiving with him tonight over dinner and then, if that went well, talk about bringing their relationship out into the open. They went out a bit now—not spending time at his house or hers—so it wasn't as if he were truly trying to keep their relationship hidden. True, Stephen always picked the places they would go. Maybe he was doing that to make sure that they wouldn't run into any common acquaintances. Deciding not to go looking for trouble, Holly walked into Stephen's office and went about business as usual.

The plan for that night was to go to Holly's. It was a Wednesday night, and the agreement had been to grab some takeout on the way home and enjoy a night in. She had no reason to change that but felt anxious to be out of the office and to discuss what she had on her mind. As usual, Holly left the office first, and Stephen was to meet up with her at six thirty; that gave him enough time to finish up his work without any distractions.

On the drive home, Holly rehearsed in her mind how she was going to broach the subject of their relationship with Stephen. She was scared of how he was going to respond. If he was not ready to go public with their dating, what was her response going to be? Would she make demands on him? Would she cry? Pout? Hell if she knew.

Once at the house, she straightened up and poured herself a glass of wine. At six o'clock, her phone rang. Figuring it was probably Stephen with a question about their Chinese food, Holly answered.

"Hello?"

"Hey, Holly, it's Derek. I'm looking for Stephen. Is he there?"

She was momentarily stunned. So much for thinking that he hadn't told his friends about the two of them. "Um…no. I think he's still at the office. Have you tried him there?" For a brief moment, she had wanted to play dumb and ask *why* he thought that Stephen would be at her house but decided against it.

"Actually, no, I assumed he would be there with you." He paused, waiting for her to say something. When she didn't, he continued, "Do me a favor and tell him that we have a seven a.m. flight on Tuesday out of RDU. The condo is booked, the caterer is set, and I have seen to the…um…entertainment." His words made Holly cringe a little.

"You're not going to be around for Thanksgiving, right?" Derek asked, his tone sickly smooth, and Holly wanted to hang up the phone and not hear another moment's worth.

"No," she replied calmly. "I'll be visiting my family up on Long Island."

"That's good," Derek said, "because it's been a long time since the boys have prowled together, and we're all looking forward to it. Stephen deserves this time away, and I wanted to make sure that nothing…gets in the way." Holly said nothing. "I've known Stephen a long time, and I know when he gets antsy, you know? Personally, the smartest thing to have happen here is for you to go your way for the holiday and for Stephen to go his. He's too nice to bring this up himself, but I figured you would understand. Are we on the same page here, Holly?"

She wasn't sure why he was being this way, but she merely nodded her head, and then, remembering that he couldn't see her, she said, "Yes, I believe we are." He wished her an early happy Thanksgiving, and then he was gone.

What a bizarre conversation! What in the world had brought that on? Why hadn't Stephen mentioned that he had talked to his friends about her? There shouldn't be a secret like this between them if they were serious, she thought. If Stephen was serious about her, he would have broken it to her gently that he had talked to his friends; and knowing how she felt about the two of them, wouldn't he have left it up to her to see if she was okay with it all? Why, oh why, hadn't he mentioned anything? This put a whole new spin on what she was going to say to him tonight.

If what Derek said was true, could she really bring up the subject of taking their relationship into the open when he clearly already had—and with these kinds of results? It all seemed to make sense: the way he only took her to certain places, the way their whole relationship was kept secretive…Stephen was doing what she'd feared he would do. He was not comfortable in this type of relationship, and now he was trapped and didn't know how to get out of it.

Numbly, Holly walked into her den and collapsed on the sofa. This was so not the way the night was supposed to go. If she was going to salvage her heart—which she knew without a doubt belonged to Stephen Ballinger— she was going to have to be the one to end things, to let him off the hook.

Not much later, Stephen was there, a bag of Chinese food in one hand, a bottle of wine in the other. Holly hoped her emotions weren't showing too much and tried to act as if everything were normal. They discussed the news and the progress on the Gideon project, and after dinner was cleared, when Stephen made a move to take her up and into bed, for the first time in their relationship, Holly faked a headache.

"Are you okay?" he asked, concern written all over his face. "What can I get you?"

"Nothing," she lied. "I think I need to take some Advil or something and go to sleep, if you don't mind." If she hadn't talked to Derek earlier and found out how Stephen *really* felt, she'd say that he was genuinely concerned about her. As he went to walk with her up the stairs, she turned and stopped him. "If you don't mind, Stephen, I think it would be best if you went back to your place tonight. I'm so tired, and I don't think I'll be able to relax fully with you in the bed with me."

The look on his face was so tortured, so torn, that Holly almost took her words back. Of course there was a possibility that Derek was wrong, but why would he lie? If anything, Derek was the brutally honest one of the bunch, and while he didn't seem to care if he hurt anyone's feelings, Holly had never known him to lie. "You want me to leave?" he asked softly.

Unable to speak due to the lump in her throat, Holly nodded, turned, walked up the steps to her bedroom, and closed the door. Stephen stood on the stairs for a solid ten minutes before he could force himself to move. When he did, he walked to the den and sat down on the sofa, wondering what the hell had happened.

He racked his brain and went over the entire day in his mind, and for the life of him, nothing seemed to stand out that would make Holly send him away. True, it was possible that she really didn't feel well, but it didn't *feel* right. Sighing, he gathered up his belongings and locked the house on his way out. Sitting in his car out in the driveway, he looked up at Holly's bedroom window and saw that her light was already off.

The drive home was long and lonely. It had been weeks since he'd slept alone, and he wasn't looking forward to it at all. He liked sleeping with her, even when they slept. Tonight he had hoped that they would discuss the possibility of him going up to Long Island with her and meeting her family, but once he'd arrived at her house with dinner, Stephen sensed that something was wrong.

Once at home and in his own bed, he forced any negative thoughts from his mind. Holly was entitled to not feel well and want to be alone. Tomorrow was another day, and once she felt better, Stephen was sure everything would be all right and they would have their holiday discussion. That thought made him smile, and he finally drifted off to sleep.

Unfortunately, things did not get better. Holly arrived at work Thursday morning and still seemed out of sorts. When he inquired about their plans for that night while she was in his office going over a new client contract, Holly impersonally told him that she had plans with friends she hadn't seen in a while, and before he could ask about the next night, she let him know that she needed the weekend alone to get ready for her trip to see her family.

It was on the tip of Stephen's tongue to demand to know what was going on and talk to Holly about him going with her on her trip. To hell with respecting whatever she was going through; he wanted answers, dammit!

Holly was placing the last page of the documents on his desk when he grabbed her wrist. "What's going on, Holly? Did I do something wrong?"

She pulled free; Stephen didn't put up much of a fight. "I don't know what you're talking about," she lied.

"I know you weren't feeling well last night, but you're pretty much giving me the brush-off, and I want to know why."

"Brush-off? Why? Because I need some time to myself?" she said a bit snappishly. "Am I not entitled to some time alone? I'm here every day, and we're together every night and every weekend!"

He saw red. He knew what this was. Hell, he'd practically given this speech word for word himself a time or two before. Holly was ending things, and for the life of him, he didn't know why. It was an uncomfortable feeling to be on the receiving end of a relationship ending.

For the briefest moment, Stephen thought of begging her to change her mind, to give him another chance… but there was no way he could do it. A man like him did not beg. She wanted space? She could have it. No relationship was worth all this.

Ever since that blasted Friday night his emotions had been all over the place, and Stephen found that he did not like it one bit. Life was simple before, and now, since becoming involved with Holly, he felt crazy and out of control. If she wanted to dump him, then fine. He would handle it; he would move on and never think of it again. They'd work together, and now that he knew the real Holly, it would be easy not to dream about all that he might have had.

If the woman could toss him aside so easily, then she wasn't the woman he thought her to be, and he wasn't going to spend another minute agonizing over the future he had wanted with her. Good riddance!

Friday was even tenser. Stephen hadn't slept well alone for a second night. His anger had not allowed him to relax. When he went to the office the next morning, he treated her as indifferently as she was treating him. He avoided asking her for anything except for what was vitally essential to get him through the day.

He noticed dark circles under her eyes and assumed they were due to Holly being out late with her friends. The thought almost made him growl. At five o'clock when Holly came into the office with a file he requested containing final details on the Gideon project, she handed him a couple of phone messages. She didn't ask if he needed her for anything else; she simply placed the file on his desk and walked out.

Holly's spine was stiff, and she couldn't wait to be out of the building and back in her own home where she could begin the process of mending her broken heart.

It was near midnight when Stephen finally rose from behind his office desk. He was nearly cross-eyed from reading over contracts and travel and installation plans for the Gideon project. He finally picked up the phone messages that Holly had left on his desk—most of them could wait until Monday—and he noticed one from Derek.

"Plane set for seven a.m. Tuesday…" Stephen read out loud. "Caterer…blah, blah, blah…entertainment taken care of…"

Stephen threw down the message in disgust. The last thing that he wanted now was to go skiing with Will and Derek. He'd back out, but at the last moment so he would not have to deal with any bullshit from either one of them. He'd fake a business emergency or something and stay behind and work. Besides, he was due to leave for Texas the Wednesday after Thanksgiving to do an upgrade for a client and then head off to California to begin his work with the Gideon Corporation.

With a much needed full-body stretch, Stephen turned and looked out the window at the city below. He really should head out, but the thought of driving home at this hour was completely unappealing. The sofa would do again. Since Holly wasn't sharing his bed, he found that he didn't sleep well. It didn't matter where he slept now; he didn't stay asleep for long anyway. Removing his tie and kicking off his shoes, Stephen made himself as comfortable as humanly possible on his large leather sofa.

In order to keep himself from thinking about Holly

and what she was doing right now, he forced himself to think about what he was going to need for his travels and how he was going to convince this particular client of doing the upgrade for all his offices…and it didn't take long to fall asleep.

Holly, on the other hand, went to bed early each night and tossed and turned through most of the night. The last two days had been hellacious, and luckily she knew she'd only have to deal with one more day with Stephen and then they'd both be gone for several days. She could do one more day, couldn't she? Apparently not.

Deciding early on Saturday morning that she could not take another day, Holly decided she was going to change her plans. Instead of flying home to Long Island, she was going to drive and leave as soon as possible. Luckily she had opted to add the flight insurance so she wasn't penalized for the cancellation. Besides, the time alone in the car would be a good way to clear her head a little.

She called Judy, the temp who normally took her place whenever she was out of the office sick or away on business with Stephen, and told her of her plans. It was probably improper protocol, and Holly knew she should call Stephen and let him know of her change of plans, but she decided against doing so.

Sunday afternoon, Holly was driving north, heading home. With any luck, a full week away from Stephen Ballinger would be enough to ease her pain.

Chapter 11

STEPHEN STEPPED OUT OF HIS OFFICE EARLY MONDAY morning and froze. What was Judy doing here? He had slept in his office all weekend, and although he had already showered and changed, he hadn't shaved since Friday.

"Oh, good morning, Mr. Ballinger," Judy said. "Coffee will be ready in a few minutes. I'll bring it to you with your messages as soon as it's ready." She smiled and was about to walk away when Stephen spoke.

"Where's Holly?" he demanded, a little more harshly than he had intended.

"Oh, she said she decided to leave early for her Thanksgiving holiday and asked if I would mind covering for her. I assumed that you knew." She stood there, unsure what to do.

Stephen was dumbfounded. He couldn't believe Holly had changed her plans without talking to him first. He had counted on having her here today to help him get his things organized!

This was beyond unprofessional. She could be mad at him, personally, all she wanted, but when she screwed with his business, it made Stephen see red. He glared at Judy as if she was an intruder. He didn't want her here. He wanted Holly here! Hell, if she didn't want to share his bed, he'd live with that, but he was unwilling to let her get away with this kind of childish behavior around the office, screwing with his business.

Stephen spent most of the day taking out all his anger and frustration on Judy. He criticized her dictation, her coffee, anything and everything that she did. By the end of the day, he was sure that the woman had tears in her eyes, and he wouldn't be surprised if she quit. At five o'clock, she walked in with a file he requested and gently asked him if there was anything else he needed for the evening or before he left on his trip in the morning.

"I'm not going on any damn trip!" he snapped. "You'll be needed here again tomorrow and Wednesday." He lifted his head and glared at her. "Will that be a problem?"

Judy visibly swallowed. "No, sir," she said quietly. "No problem at all." She was about to turn for the door when she turned back to him and bravely asked, "Do you need me to cancel any of your reservations?"

"No, I'll take care of it," he sneered. Judy walked out and closed the door behind her. Stephen was glad to see her go. At least she was being professional, he said to himself. She didn't go off and take an early holiday like his *real* assistant did. No, Judy might end up being his new assistant. That thought flitted around in the back of his mind as he worked well into the night once again.

At six the next morning, Stephen woke and called Will.

"Hey, man," Will said, cheerily. "You ready for some downhill competition?"

"I'm not going," Stephen said sternly and waited for Will's response.

"What do you mean you're not going? What's going on? I thought we all agreed to take the time off for this!"

"I've hit a complication with this new client, and I

can't afford to leave. I'm due on the coast next week, and I'm not ready for it. I've been practically living at the office as it is, going over everything with a fine-tooth comb, and I've still got a lot of work ahead of me."

"So delegate some of it, for crying out loud," Will snapped. "You're the president of the company; let someone else do some of the grunt work. What does Holly have to say about that? Can't she help pick up some of the slack?"

"What difference does it make what Holly has to say? She's not in charge here, I am, dammit!"

The situation was beginning to make sense to Will, but he was smart enough not to comment on it. "Fine, stay home. But you're going to have to tell Derek because I'm not doing it for you."

"Who asked you to?"

"Right, you happened to call me to keep me in the loop," Will said sarcastically. "I'm not an idiot, Stephen. You called me so that I would have to break the news to Derek and deal with the backlash. Well, forget it. You want to wuss out of this trip for whatever reason, fine, but man up and do your own dirty work."

Stephen didn't think he was that transparent, but apparently he was. "Fine, I don't need you to talk to Derek for me. There's nothing he can say or do that I can't handle. I kicked his ass once, and I can do it again." With that, Stephen hung up the phone and dialed Derek's number.

"Hey, brother" were Derek's first words. "You almost here? The plane is warming up, and we are going to have beautiful flying weather."

"I'm not going," Stephen said defiantly. Derek was silent. "Did you hear me?"

"Yeah, I heard you," Derek snapped. "Why the hell not? I've got everything freakin' planned and waiting. What the hell's wrong with you?"

Stephen's back went ramrod straight. He hated having to explain himself to anyone, and he knew that if Derek were here right now, they'd be exchanging blows. "Nothing's wrong with me," Stephen snapped. "I happen to have a business to run, and something's come up. No one's telling you that you can't go, so get off my back!" He hung up without waiting for Derek's reply.

Throwing his cell phone down, Stephen went into his bathroom, showered, changed, and got ready for the day. By the time he came out thirty minutes later, there had been more than a dozen missed calls on his cell— most of them were from Derek, but there were a few from Will.

"Screw them," he mumbled and went about starting his day. When Judy arrived, he instructed her that if either Derek or Will called, she was to tell them that he was tied up. He didn't want to speak to either of them and had long since shut off his cell phone.

His mood stayed black all day long, and by the time Judy came in to say good night, her frustration with him was evident. "I'll need those Texas files on my desk by noon on Friday, Judy," he said without looking up at her.

"I won't be here on Friday, Mr. Ballinger," she said, barely concealing her disgruntlement.

"What?"

"The company is closed on Friday for the holiday, and I'm sorry, but I cannot change my plans to be here," she said it firmly, but upon closer inspection, Stephen could see that she trembled a little bit.

"Fine," he sneered. "Leave me high and dry, like Holly. Pretty soon maybe we'll all be without a job because no one wanted to be bothered *doing* their job!" Judy walked out and shut the door loudly behind her.

Stephen wanted to feel guilty about treating her so poorly, but he couldn't bring himself to care. Dammit, why was he the only one who was concerned with this company?

Early Monday morning, Will and Derek arrived at the office, sure that they were arriving before any of Stephen's employees. They had seen that his car was in the parking garage, so they were confident they would find him in his office.

Without knocking, they walked in and found him asleep on his office couch in wrinkled clothes. "What the hell?" Will said, noting the takeout containers littering the office and the trash and dirty clothes lying about.

"This contract must be brutally important for him to be freakin' living here," Derek murmured, kicking a pile of clothes aside as he walked over to the sofa. He said Stephen's name, and when he didn't immediately wake up, Derek gave him a slight shake.

"What the…?" Stephen said as he sat up. It took him a moment to realize that he wasn't alone, and he was shocked to see who his company was. "What do you want?" he snapped, standing up and walking to the bathroom without waiting for an answer.

Taking pity on him, Will started to pick up the trash and place it all in the office kitchen's large pail. He found Derek sitting behind Stephen's desk with his fingers laced behind his head when he walked back into the office at the same time Stephen exited the bathroom.

"So what is going on with this project that you have to skip a vacation and freakin' sleep in your office?" Derek asked. "You missed one hell of a weekend, by the way." Stephen didn't respond. Derek went on to talk about the twins he had slept with and the waitress who had "serviced" him in the men's room of his favorite restaurant.

Stephen felt sick but noticed that Will was leaning against a bookcase taking it all in, not sharing any stories of his own. "No, seriously, man, what's going on here?" Derek asked.

There was a noise in the outer office, and Stephen about tripped over his own two feet running out, hoping that it was Holly. "Judy?" he roared. "Where the hell is Holly? Why isn't she back?" His friends sat silently and looked from one another to Stephen and back again as Stephen ranted and raved about Holly not being there.

Mumbling to himself and forgetting that he wasn't alone, Stephen said, "This is beyond childish. All I wanted to do was spend some time with her, and now she's going to be spiteful and screw with my business? I don't think so. I cannot believe that I thought about marrying her!"

"Whoa, whoa, whoa…wait a minute," Will said, breaking off Stephen's tirade. "What did you say?"

Stephen quickly turned toward Will, his eyes a little crazed. "What?"

"You said that you were thinking about marrying Holly!"

"I knew it, I freakin' knew it," Derek said snidely.

"You've been screwing her all along, and you had the audacity to lie to me and deck me in a bar over it? What the hell's wrong with you?"

Will stood in front of Derek to block Stephen's view of him because he could tell that Stephen was ready to deck him again. "Stephen, what is going on?"

As much as Stephen wanted to howl and wail for them to get out, he needed to be honest with them. All the solitude he had experienced in the past week was making him crazy. He was slowly going insane, sick of his own company and finally beginning to see it.

Within minutes he spilled out the whole story, from the weekend of their fight at the bar until the day Holly left for her trip early. "The thing is I don't know what happened," he said miserably. "I mean, we had plans for dinner, and sometime between when she left the office and I got to her house, her whole attitude changed. There was no warning—one minute she was mine, the next she wasn't." He sat down on the couch, leaned his head back, and closed his eyes. It felt good to say it all to someone other than himself.

"What are you going to do?" Will asked.

"What can I do? She won't come in. I have a feeling that Judy is going to end up being my assistant by default—if I haven't scared her away by now with my ranting and raving like a lunatic for the past week." He sighed angrily. "I don't know if she's even back from visiting her parents, but it doesn't matter. I'm not going to go to her and beg. If she wants to end things, then that's fine. She could have had the decency to tell me to my face rather than running away and leaving me hanging—both personally and with the business." He knew it was a lie and was pretty sure his friends saw through him too.

Without warning, Derek stood and walked out. Stephen shrugged, but Will stared at the office door curiously. "He doesn't understand," he tried to say in defense of their friend.

"It doesn't matter," Stephen said. "I don't give a damn about Derek and his opinion. This isn't about him, anyway, no matter how much he likes to make every-thing about himself. I'm pissed, and I'm disappointed, and I guess I always knew going in that this wasn't going to work. A man can't have a successful career and run a business and have a relationship, a marriage. It doesn't work."

Then Derek walked back in holding a bag of ice. "What are you doing?" Will asked.

Derek went and stood right in front of Stephen.

"Hit me," he said flatly.

"What? Why?"

"Trust me, hit me."

Stephen looked at Derek and then at Will. "Do you have any idea what he's talking about?" Will shook his head.

Derek sighed loudly. "Look, I'm the reason Holly broke things off. I called her house that day and told her that you were looking to cool things down and that it would be best for everyone if you came on this vacation where I was handling the entertainment."

Suddenly, everything made sense. Stephen could pic-ture it all and realized why Holly had reacted the way she did. But why wouldn't she say something to him about it? Why didn't she discuss it with him first?

He didn't know, and he didn't care. If Holly had truly cared about him, she would have fought for him a little more. They had never had a serious conversation about where this was all leading, and he knew now that had been a mistake. Then he looked at Derek and realized the reason he never got to have that serious discussion with Holly. Before he could even begin to reconsider, he swung and had Derek lying on the floor at his feet.

"Feel better?" the man wheezed from the floor. Stephen didn't bother with an answer; he stepped over Derek as he walked to his desk and sat down like a man defeated. Derek stood as Will held out the bag of ice for him. Placing it on his chin, he walked toward Stephen's desk. "For what it's worth, I'm sorry. I had no idea you were serious about her. I wanted the type of guys' week-end that we used to have."

"We're not frat boys anymore," Stephen mumbled. "It's time to grow up." When Derek made to speak again, Stephen held up a hand to stop him. "Just go. Please." He turned his chair around and stared out the window long after his friends had left.

When had life gotten so complicated?

Chapter 12

HOLLY KNEW THERE WOULD BE REPERCUSSIONS FOR HER actions and yet couldn't find it within herself to get back into the swing of things yet. If she played her cards right and still had a job to return to, she'd go back to the office when Stephen left for Texas. He was to be gone for two weeks between the two jobs, and perhaps by the time he got back they would be able to be in the same room without it being too terribly awkward.

Who was she kidding? It would forever be awkward because she was in love with him, and even with a week away at home with her family and everything that was familiar and dear, she had not been able to stop thinking about him and wondering if he was off making love to some slutty snow bunny he'd met on his trip. That was an image that refused to leave her brain as she'd lain in her childhood bed.

By Holly's third day at home, her mother had figured out that something was amiss, and Holly had had no choice but to confess. While her mother had listened without judgment, she did advise Holly to go home, straighten things out with Stephen, and perhaps think about finding a new job.

That was the last thing Holly wanted to do, but since she couldn't make herself get in the car and drive to the office or pick up the phone because the sound of

Stephen's voice was too overwhelming for her, she knew that she didn't have much of a choice.

Looking at the clock and seeing that it was only nine thirty, she rationalized that it was too late to go in to the office anyway; Judy would already be there hard at work. Glancing around her home, she decided she would do her food shopping for the week and run some errands, safe and boring tasks that would keep her mind off her troubles.

Dressed in faded blue jeans and a thick navy-blue hooded sweatshirt, Holly pulled on her sneakers and grabbed her purse as she headed for the door. Keys in hand, she opened it and found Will and Derek standing on the other side, Will's hand raised as if prepared to knock.

It was hard to tell who was more surprised at that moment, but after a brief silence, Holly spoke. "Will. Derek. What can I do for you?" Her tone was cool and steady even though her insides were shaking uncontrollably. Thank goodness for the bulky sweatshirt!

"Can we come in?" Will asked.

Holly glanced at her watch, unsure that she wanted to know what Stephen's two friends were here for at this hour. "Um—"

"We won't take too much of your time, I promise," Will said quickly, sensing her indecision. Derek remained blessedly quiet, but Holly noted the purple bruise on his chin. She was a little envious of whomever put that mark there because she certainly had entertained the thought of doing it herself after his smug phone call that fateful night.

She silently stepped aside, and the men walked in. Holly led them to her living room and sat. Her hospitality skills decided to stay hidden; the quicker they said what they had to say, the quicker they'd leave.

Will cleared his throat as he watched Derek sit in an overstuffed chair opposite Holly. "Obviously we're here to talk to you about Stephen," he blurted out.

"What about him?" She was trying for blasé but had a feeling she asked a little too quickly to pull that off.

"He's in pretty bad shape. He's been sleeping in the office—something about this new contract or something—and he's not prepared to go to Texas. Can you cut him some slack, Holly, and give him a hand? He's a complete mess."

Holly looked at Will for a moment as if he'd spoken Greek. This certainly wasn't the news she had wanted to hear. There was no reason for Stephen not to be prepared for this business trip. Everything had been settled and secured before she left—before she'd sent him away. For the minutest of moments, she had allowed herself to hope that Stephen was a mess because he missed *her*. But as usual, it was the business. It was always going to be the business.

Holly's brows furrowed. "I don't understand," she looked from one man to the other. "Everything was set before I left for New York. Unless something changed after I left, this Texas trip is a no-brainer. As for the second leg of the trip in California, any kinks that had to be worked out would be nothing for Stephen."

"I'll be honest with you, Holly," Will began. "I couldn't even begin to tell you exactly what the problem is business-wise, but the reality is that he is missing you."

"As his assistant," she said flatly, her disappointment evident.

"No," Derek finally chimed in and made Holly's head snap up. "It's *you* he misses. He's been a mess since you…well, since I called here that night."

"Why would he be a mess over that?" she asked, clearly confused. "I did exactly what you told me he wanted."

Derek shifted uncomfortably in his seat and looked to Will for assistance, but Will crossed his arms over his chest and stared him down. "Fine," Derek mumbled. "The thing is, Holly, Stephen never said anything to me, to us, to anyone about the two of you. I sort of found out by accident, and…"

"How?" she asked.

"I stopped by the office one night as Stephen was pulling away. I was planning to see if he wanted to go for a drink and figured I'd follow him home. But he didn't go home, he came here." Running a hand nervously through his hair, he continued, "I really didn't think much of it. I figured he was coming by to drop something off. But I watched the lights go off downstairs and go on upstairs."

Holly blushed, not believing someone had been sitting outside watching all that, especially Derek.

"He stopped coming out, he stopped taking calls. I put two and two together and knew he would end up backing out of our ski trip, and selfishly, I didn't want that to happen. So I called you. I lied. You did exactly what I knew you'd do." He sighed. "I didn't realize how Stephen would react. I didn't see it coming."

She was dumbfounded. There was no way to describe which emotion was running higher right now—anger or sadness. She stared from one man to the other as she sat stiff as a board. "Let me get this straight—*you* decided that I should end things with Stephen without ever talking to him about it?" Derek nodded, unable to look at Holly. "I see. So when Stephen showed up that night and I did what you asked me to do, he had no idea why?" Again, Derek nodded. "Uh-huh," she mumbled.

Holly stood up, stalked across to where Derek sat, and waited for him to look at her. "So basically because you are a spoiled, selfish bastard, my personal relationship with Stephen is over, my job is essentially lost, and my Thanksgiving was ruined. Did I forget anything?"

Derek stood, determined to reason with her. "Holly, listen…I—"

She never gave him a chance to finish. With every ounce of strength she possessed, she swung and hit him square on the jaw where Stephen had earlier. "Geez!" Derek roared. "What the hell?"

"I'll tell you what the hell," Holly began as she jabbed him in the chest with a stiff pointer finger. "How dare you! How dare you play with people's lives! I never did anything to you that would deserve such horrible treatment. *Ever!*" She enjoyed the fact that he winced at her words. "And as for Stephen, he's supposed to be one of your best friends, and yet you care *nothing* about his happiness! What kind of person does that make you?"

Derek sidestepped Holly and looked to Will for assistance, but noticed that his friend was merely standing by, grinning like a loon. "Holly, I'm sorry. You have no idea how much," he stammered, hoping that he'd find the right words to calm her down and keep her from inflicting any more pain. "You're right, I'm spoiled and selfish, but I swear to you that I am through getting involved in other people's relationships. All I know is that Stephen is a miserable mess right now and needs you. Please, Holly, please go to him."

His words sounded sincere, and as far as she could tell, he was speaking the truth. His actions, his recent actions, however, were too fresh on her mind, and Holly couldn't imagine trusting this man yet. She turned to Will, the question in her eyes.

"In all the years that I've known him, Holly, I've never seen him like this. Will you go to him?" It was asked softly, a plea, and she was torn. How could she fix this situation? Was it possible to go back to the way things were before and trust one another again? Or had Derek ruined everything?

Holly refused to let that creep win. This was *her* life, and she was going to take control; she was done running. She sat back down and quietly contemplated her course of action. Within minutes, she had her plan. "Can you possibly get him out of the office at lunchtime?" she asked Will, unwilling to solicit Derek's help.

"He'll have a million and one excuses why he can't leave, but tell me where to deliver him, and he'll be there," Will said as his grin widened. His friend wasn't going to have any idea what hit him, but he envied the fact that Stephen had found such a strong woman who was willing to fight for him.

"Mr. Ballinger?" Judy asked tentatively as she slipped into his office. His back was to her as he sat in his chair behind the desk, staring at the city below. She walked farther into the office and stood beside him before speaking again. "Sir, your meeting this afternoon with the Jordan group has been canceled. I've rescheduled it for when you get back from California."

Stephen nodded. *Great*, he thought. Now he'd have the whole afternoon free to focus on what Derek had done and whether Holly was ever going to come back to work. Life sucked. He turned his head and saw that Judy was still standing there. "Was there anything else, Judy?"

She took a fortifying breath and then rushed forward. "Sir, I think maybe, since your afternoon is now free, that you should get out of the office for a little while. You've been here for days and, well, to be honest, it's a little weird and I'm worried about you."

Stephen raised an eyebrow as she spoke. It was the first time she had talked to him on a personal level, and he had to give her credit for it. He had been miserable and mean and nasty to her for the better part of a week, and yet she'd never backed down. With a weary sigh, he came to realize that if he couldn't have Holly back as his assistant, then maybe having Judy wouldn't be quite so bad.

He gave her a weak smile. "I appreciate your concern, and you're right, I probably should get out of the office for a little while. Hell, I should probably get out of here for a long while. Maybe I'll…"

"Hey, buddy," Will said cheerfully as he strolled into the office. He held his arms up in mock surrender as he advanced into the room. "I come in peace. How about some lunch that doesn't come from a Styrofoam container?"

Stephen chuckled. "Judy and I were just discussing that, and I think that sounds good." He stood, straightened his clothes, and walked to his en suite to make sure he looked presentable. He didn't see the knowing glance between Will and Judy.

"You've probably been in those clothes for a couple of days," Will observed. "We'll swing by your house so you can get a fresh change of clothes and we'll go from there. What do you say?"

Stephen hated the thought of going back to his house because it made him think of Holly. Unfortunately, Will was right, and he could no longer put off the inevitable. "Yeah, sure." The response lacked enthusiasm, but Will pretended not to notice.

"Have a good lunch, Mr. Ballinger," Judy said as he walked out of his office. "Everything is quiet and under control here, so don't rush back."

Her comment struck him as odd as he and Will walked to the elevator, but he decided to let it slide—he was near delirious from lack of sleep and fresh air, so for all he knew her comment was purely innocent.

Without question, Stephen climbed into Will's car, almost sorry to be out of the fresh, chilled air. They made small talk on the way to the house, and when they pulled up in front, Will told Stephen that he had a call to make and that he'd wait in the car. Again without question, Stephen climbed out and let himself into the home he had not seen in almost two weeks.

And stopped cold.

There was a fire burning in the stone fireplace, and there was the wonderful aroma of food cooking in the kitchen. He turned around in time to see Will's car speed off down the driveway. "What the hell?"

Cautiously he walked toward the kitchen, and felt like he had been sucker-punched. There stood Holly at the stove, stirring something. She looked over her shoulder at him and smiled, and for the first time in what seemed like forever, Stephen felt all right. Without moving from her spot in front of the stove, she said, "Go on up and have a shower and a shave. Lunch will be ready in thirty minutes."

He wanted to argue; he wanted to know where she'd been and why she was here, but he was also aware of how he looked and how desperately he needed a shower and a shave. With a curt nod, he strode from the kitchen and took the stairs two at a time to get to his own room.

When he stepped inside, he saw that it had been cleaned; the last he had seen it he had left clothes strewn all over the place and had torn the sheets from the bed. Now, he saw a freshly made bed that had been turned down. There were clean clothes piled on the corner of the bed for him to change into. Glancing around, he noticed the fresh flowers in a crystal vase on his dresser and that every surface was clear of dust and clutter. Upon walking into his bathroom, he saw that fresh towels were waiting for him and that this room, too, had been cleaned.

It felt good to be home. Stephen showered and changed and was back in the kitchen in twenty-seven minutes. Holly was putting the finishing touches on the table and turned to greet him shyly.

"How was your shower?" she asked as she sat down.

"It felt great, thank you." His eyes feasted on her, not quite believing she was really here. Briefly he glanced at the table and took note of the food: some sort of soup, crusty French bread, and spinach salad. "Everything looks wonderful."

She nodded her thanks and began to eat. They sat silently and enjoyed the meal, neither quite sure what to say or where to begin. When it began to feel awkward, Holly spoke. "Will said you were having trouble with the Texas deal and with Gideon. Have you gotten it straightened out?"

The sound of her voice was so soothing that Stephen felt all the tension leave his body. "Everything is fine; it always was, I guess. I panicked. No big deal." He was going for light and breezy, but Holly looked at him with disbelief.

"You slept in the office for a week, Stephen. In all the years I've worked with you, you've never slept in the office for more than a random night. What's going on?" She reached across the table and gently laid her hand on top of his, her voice laced with concern.

The simple gesture, the gentle touch of her hand, gave Stephen the courage to say what had been on his mind since she'd sent him away. "Why did you leave like that? Why didn't you talk to me about Derek's phone call?" His tone lacked accusation, and for that Holly was grateful.

"I had no idea what to say, Stephen," she began. "He caught me off guard, and I figured that he knew you better than I did and maybe you just didn't know how to end things with us." She looked down at their now-joined hands and then back at him. "You know, you're not the greatest at breaking up with women, and I should know; you used to leave it to me to clean up after your breakups." She laughed softly, and it didn't take long for him to join her.

"Fair enough, but still…you left. No phone call,

no explanation…you were gone. I thought if nothing else we still had a decent working relationship, decent enough that you should have been able to come to me and tell me that you were going away for a while and leaving me with Judy."

"I talked to her several times while I was gone. You didn't have to take it out on her, you know," she softly chided. "I know I handled this badly, but I was so hurt. How could I explain to my boss that I'd had to get out of town because the man I was involved with had hurt me? Especially when those two men were one and the same?" She looked up at him as her eyes filled with tears. "I know now that I should have confronted you, but…honestly, I was too hurt."

"Why? Why were you so upset, Holly?"

Was the man dense, or was he going to punish her by making her say out loud what she didn't want to? Stephen looked at her expectantly. Holly pulled her hand from his, rose from the table with her plate and glass, and took them over to the sink. She had a strong urge to smash them into a million pieces in the sink because he'd put her in this position. Turning abruptly back to him, she spoke. "Because I love you, Stephen! There. Are you satisfied?"

He rose slowly, walked over to her, and placed his hands on her shoulders to turn her toward him. Stephen studied her face intently before pulling her close and crushing his mouth over hers. It had been too long since he'd held her, since he'd felt her heart beating against his own. His mouth left hers briefly as he looked down at her upturned face. Holly's eyes slowly opened. "I was devastated when you left, Holly, and not because of any stupid contract or client but because I love you." His voice was thick with emotion, and he loved the way her eyes went soft at his words. "I wanted to believe that I was upset from a business angle, but the truth is that nothing felt right, nothing worked without you. I missed you."

He kissed her again, deeply, and then carried her into the living room where he lay down beside her on the sofa. Their bodies aligned, they kissed. Stephen's hands trailed up and down the length of her as if to reassure himself that she was really there.

"I missed you," she whispered between kisses. "I'm so sorry for leaving, for not trusting you…"

Stephen held her face in his hands, reveling in the softness of her skin. "I didn't give you any reason to trust me, did I?" It was more a statement than a question. "You were only responding to what you knew, and I am so sorry for all that happened and for what Derek did. I did get to hit him again, and that made me feel a little bit better." He kissed her nose, and she giggled.

"So that's where he got the bruise from," she said and then confessed, "I hit him, too. Right on the same bruise."

Stephen couldn't help it; he let out a hearty laugh. How he loved this woman! "You hit Derek?" Holly nodded and joined in his laughter. "What did he do?"

"He wasn't happy, I can tell you that!" He pulled her close and sighed as the laughter subsided. Holly snuggled in close and felt content for the first time since…ever.

She lost track of how long they lay there together like that. A part of her wanted to encourage Stephen to take her upstairs, but then she thought of all the nights he had slept on the sofa in his office and knew that, if anything, the man needed sleep. Carefully, she rose from the sofa and held out her hands to him. Wordlessly he rose and followed her up the stairs to his bedroom.

It had seemed a lifetime since they'd last been in this room together. Holly came to stand in front of him and silently lifted his shirt above his head. Gently she pushed him down on the mattress and went about getting him undressed. If Stephen noticed that she was doing this without the slightest hint of seduction, he chose to say nothing. When he was down to his briefs, Holly pulled the blankets up to cover him. "Sleep, Stephen," she whispered. "You need to get some sleep in your own bed." She leaned over and switched off the small bedside lamp.

Stephen reached out and touched Holly's arm. "Stay with me." That had been her plan, but it pleased her to hear him ask. With a smile, she walked over to his dresser, tugged open a drawer, and pulled out a T-shirt before heading into the bathroom with a promise to be right back. "Spoilsport," he mumbled as he settled comfortably into the bed he'd abandoned for so long.

Holly had been gone no longer than three minutes, and yet when she approached the bed, she found Stephen sound asleep. She ran a hand gently through his hair and kissed his cheek before walking around to the other side of the bed and crawling in beside him. She hadn't slept well either since she had sent him away that night. Even back home in the bed she'd had her entire life, she'd been unable to get a good night's sleep.

Pulling the blankets up over herself, Holly snuggled in next to Stephen and was quietly thrilled when he reached for her and pulled her close. Sighing with deep relaxation, Holly didn't take long to join Stephen in sleep.

Chapter 13

IT WAS THE NUZZLING THAT CAUSED HOLLY TO SMILE AND open her eyes. Stephen was placing whisper-soft kisses on her cheek and neck. The room was pitch-black as she turned toward him and wrapped herself around him, pulling him close. "I missed you," he murmured between kisses.

"Show me," Holly replied and then gloried in the wonder of it all as he did just that.

The next time Holly opened her eyes, the room was sunlit. A quick glance at the bedside clock showed it to be seven fifteen. If things were on the original Ballinger's schedule, Stephen would need to get his files and paperwork in order so he could fly out tomorrow. She had no idea how much he had changed his plans, and so with business in mind, she quietly called his name and shook his shoulder to wake him up.

"Do you need to get into the office and prep for the trip tomorrow?" she asked when he finally opened his eyes.

Stephen stretched and pulled himself up into a semi-sitting position before he answered. "I postponed the trip until Friday." He scrubbed a hand over his face, still fighting for alertness. "I couldn't seem to work up the enthusiasm to go and do the job. That puts me behind getting to Gideon as well, but…" His voice trailed off.

Needing to get up and stretch, Holly kicked away the

blankets and rose from the bed. "Okay, so that only puts you a couple of days behind. Last I checked everything was ready to go. Why don't you take a few days to get caught up on some sleep, and by the time you leave on Friday, I'll have had time to go over everything with Judy and take care of things here."

The blank expression on his face sent a wave of panic through her. True, they never did discuss their working relationship last night; Holly assumed that Stephen would want her back as his assistant. The only sound she heard other that the beating of her heart was that of the antique bedside clock.

Uneasy with the silence, Holly began to ramble. "I mean, I know that you're probably still mad about my taking off like I did, and I'm sure that Judy has done fine… if you want her to stay on as your assistant, I'd completely understand. I'd be disappointed, but I'd understand."

Why wouldn't he say anything?

Holly stared at Stephen expectantly and hoped that he couldn't see her tremble. This was it. It was go time, all or nothing. As if he had all the time in the world, Stephen rose from the bed and walked over to her. Wrapping his arms around her, he pulled Holly close and gently rocked back and forth for a moment before pulling back to look at her.

"So you're telling me that you want your job back, the same job that you abandoned without notice."

Holly swallowed the lump in her throat and nodded. "Yes, please."

Stephen released her, walked to the bathroom, and shut the door. Holly wasn't sure what his response would be, but she certainly didn't expect him to walk away!

When he stepped back out, he walked over to the bed and sat back down, seeming to enjoy her nervousness.

"Well," he began, "Judy seems to have things under control, and she was a real trooper with all that I threw at her this past week or so. Would it really be *fair* to send her on her way? I mean, how do I know that you won't run off again when things get rough?" His tone was light, and deep down, Holly figured he was playing with her, but she was willing to go along for the time being.

Walking over to the bed and sitting beside him, she gave the impression of thinking over his concerns. "I suppose it wouldn't be right. After all, she jumped into a sticky situation and seemed to thrive." She ran a hand through her hair and faced him. "I guess it wouldn't be fair. I'll have to call Will and see if he has any positions available for me. You know he's been trying to steal me away from Ballinger's for a while now."

Holly had no idea Stephen could move that fast. She squealed with delight as they rolled around on the bed until he was on top of her, looking down into her face, his eyes piercing hers. "You will *not* be going to work for anyone," he growled and gave her a heated kiss. "Judy will be more than happy not to have to deal with me anymore. If you want to come back to work, I would love that. However…" He stopped and kissed her again. "I was kind of hoping you'd want to take on another position."

Holly pulled back as far as space would allow and looked at him quizzically. "Another position? Doing what?"

"For starters, I'd like for you to come on this trip

with me. I know you've done that in the past, and I'm sure Judy won't mind staying on, as long as I'm out of the building." He chuckled at the thought. "I think between the two clients, with the two of us working on them, we can get done a lot quicker. And then…" He kissed her again. "Maybe we can take a couple of days for ourselves."

"Well, that definitely sounds like a plan, but it still doesn't explain what position in the company you had in mind for me."

"Company?" he asked. "I never said that the position was with the company."

Holly rolled her eyes. "Stephen Ballinger, if that whole 'position' thing was a sexual innuendo, then I don't find you funny!" She lightly slapped at his chest and laughed but noticed that he didn't join her. "Stephen?"

"Holly," he began seriously, "I think it's past time that we had this discussion." He rolled off her and climbed off the bed, extending a hand to help her up. He paced back and forth twice before facing her fully again. "I don't want you as my assistant, not anymore. I love you, and I want… I mean, I need…damn." Stephen had thought of this moment several times since their relationship began, and now that it was here, he couldn't find the right words.

"Will you marry me, Holly?" She collapsed onto the bed, and Stephen knelt before her, taking her hands in his. "We make a great team, you and I, and I think we can make this work. I need you in my life, not as my assistant or someone to help with the business, but in my life for *me*. So will you? Will you marry me?"

Her eyes filled with tears. In her wildest dreams, she

never could have imagined a more beautiful moment. This was what she had been hoping for before Thanksgiving, only now it seemed to mean so much more.

"Don't cry, sweetheart," Stephen said as he wiped away the first tears that trailed down her cheeks. "I didn't mean to make you cry."

Holly leaned down, placed her hands on his face, and kissed him. "I was hoping you wanted me for something other than my organizational skills," she said lightly. "Yes, Stephen. Yes, I will marry you."

He pulled her close and kissed her again.

Later, much later, Stephen called the office, offered Judy the position as his assistant, and happily explained how she was coming about the position. When she didn't seem all that surprised, Stephen asked, "You were in on it yesterday, weren't you? Did Will talk to you?"

"No," she said cheerily, giddy with the thought of a happily ever after. "Holly called and told me what was going on. I was hoping this would be the outcome. I'm so happy for the both of you."

"Thank you, Judy," he said. "Oh, and Judy?"

"Yes, sir?"

"Thanks for putting up with me during all this. I really am sorry for my behavior."

"It all makes sense now," she said. "All is forgiven."

Stephen hung up the phone and turned to face his fiancée as she lay curled up in the bed. "Everything okay?" she asked.

He leaned down and kissed her before stretching out beside her and pulling her close. "Everything's perfect."

Epilogue

THE SUN WAS SHINING BRIGHT AND HOT AS STEPHEN WALKED through the glass doors of the Gideon Corporation. He held the door for Holly and saw that their car was waiting.

The driver held the door open for Holly, and Stephen climbed in behind her. They settled in, and as they pulled away, Stephen spoke. "I was thinking…"

"Could be dangerous," Holly joked, and he rewarded her with a smile.

"Anyway, I was thinking that maybe we could hit Vegas instead of staying here in California."

"Vegas, huh? Any particular reason? I never knew you to want to gamble."

He grabbed her hand in his and kissed it, pleased to see his ring on her finger. "No, I'm not much of a gambler, but I was thinking that maybe…I mean, it *is* Vegas, and people go there to do other things…you know, other than gamble."

He was adorable when he stammered, she thought. "What kind of things?"

Stephen knew she was baiting him but was willing to play along. After all, it wasn't that long ago that he had done the same to her. "Well, there are fabulous shows, I'm told, and great restaurants…"

"Hmm…"

"There are chapels and such that we might find interesting…"

"Stephen Ballinger, are you trying to get out of the big church wedding I've been planning since I was nine?" She was trying to go for haughty but found herself laughing.

Luckily Stephen was quick on the uptake and knew she was joking. "I'm not trying to get out of anything," he said as he pulled her so close that she was almost in his lap. "I was thinking that I want you to be my wife *now,* not six months from now." When she made to protest, he stopped her with a searing kiss.

Sighing, she pulled on his jacket and went nose to nose with him. "My parents would kill me if I eloped to Vegas, you realize that, don't you?" It was an argument, but she didn't put much behind it, and Stephen knew that if he really wanted to push the subject, they'd be married by midnight.

"I don't want to do anything to upset my future in-laws. If you want to wait, then we'll wait."

"How did I get so lucky?" she asked, truly amazed at the changes in him. A month ago, Stephen was a workaholic with no interest in marriage or relationships, and now, he was asking her to move up their wedding date and elope to a Vegas chapel.

"I'm the lucky one, Holly," he said solemnly. "I can't believe that a brawl in a bar gave me everything I wanted and needed. I love you."

She sighed. Life was good. "I still think we need to make him sweat a little bit longer, but eventually we are going to have to thank Derek for his role in all this."

"Thank him? Why should we thank him? If you remember correctly, he's the reason why you left me!"

Holly stroked his cheek and nodded. "I know that,

but if he had never pushed you in that bar that night, I never would have come out in the rain to get you. I never would have been stranded in that storm with you, and we might never have looked beyond our working relationship. So yes, we'll thank him."

Her kindness and her willingness to forgive never ceased to amaze him. Hugging her to him, he relaxed and said, "Someday...maybe..."

CATERING
to the CEO

Chapter 1

"CONSIDER THIS OUR FINAL MEETING. I'M *DONE*." AS THE words hung in the air, Cassie Jacobs watched Adam Lawrence's face turn to stone. She was used to his demands, his tirades, his cold and brutal treatment of people around him, but today she'd had enough.

Adam stood and walked around the antique mahogany desk that overpowered his dark and masculine office. "We will be done when *I* say we are done, Cassandra." Irritation cracked the facade as she turned to pack her briefcase.

Her heart was racing and her hands were shaking, and Cassie was determined to compose herself before turning around. Luckily she had plenty of paperwork to keep her busy, but she could feel Adam's presence behind her, tension rolling off his Armani-clad body.

It wasn't as if today's meeting was any different from the dozen or so before; as LSS International's preferred caterer and event planner, Cassie had dealt with Adam—and his attitude—on multiple occasions. After all, this was *his* company. But as she sat opposite him today, listening to his condescending tone as he changed the menu for the eighth time—and *after* she had already begun placing orders with her distributors—she'd snapped. If Adam wanted to fire her, he was welcome to. Sure, she needed this account, but not at the expense of her sanity.

Slowly, Cassie collected her briefcase and turned to face Adam. She smoothed her long chestnut hair and kept her expression cool. "I'd say we are done, Mr. Lawrence." She was proud of the fact that her voice sounded steady and that she had her temper under control. "CJ's has enjoyed providing our service for all your events for the past two years, but this is one time that I simply cannot meet your request. It's unreasonable to ask that we change the entire menu on such short notice. If you'd like to find another event planner and caterer, that is your prerogative."

Adam stared into Cassie's face. It wasn't hard to do; he towered over most people.

"I don't want another event planner, Cassandra. We have a contract, one that states that changes can be made—"

"Up to two weeks before," she cut in with frustration.

"The LSS fall retreat is two weeks away," he replied mildly, clearly believing he had the upper hand. His confidence tipped a bit when he noticed Cassie had her own triumphant smile as she reached into her leather briefcase.

Pulling out her planner, Cassie opened to September's calendar and turned it to face Adam. "Today is the twelfth; your retreat is on the twenty-third. That is eleven days, not two weeks." For emphasis, she snapped the planner closed and placed it in her case before facing Adam with her shoulders squared, ready for the consequences of going up against him.

Losing this account would put a big dent in her five-year plan of paying off the loans she took to start the business. Cassie would have no choice but to start cold calling on other companies in the Raleigh, North Carolina, area for business, which she hadn't had to do yet. She could only hope that the man wasn't going to be spiteful and try to ruin her reputation and kill her business.

One eyebrow arched as Adam continued to stare at her as if he could read her mind. That thought unsettled her for a bit. She needed to be confident. She needed not to appear needy or desperate. She needed him to say *something*!

With more bravado than she actually felt, Cassie stepped around Adam. "I believe that settles it, then. If you have any other questions or concerns, your assistant can call me at my office. Otherwise, I will see you on the twenty-third."

She almost made it to the door.

"If you leave this office, Cassandra, consider your contract with LSS finished." Adam let his words hang there for a moment, and Cassie knew he was confident that she would fall in line and do what he wanted. But Cassie didn't turn; she simply stopped. For a second, she considered acquiescing to his latest demand.

But she didn't. Before Adam knew it, Cassie had walked out the door and closed it quietly behind her. She had to stop herself from looking over her shoulder as she walked away from his office to make sure that Adam hadn't called security to chase after her like an angry mob, banishing her for all eternity. The thought made her chuckle but did nothing to put her mind at ease. What had she done? She could not afford to throw away her biggest client. Maybe a couple of years down the road she could have that privilege, but not right now.

Riding down in the elevator, Cassie had to talk herself

out of a panic attack; all was not lost yet. Maybe Adam would calm down. Maybe he would have his assistant call, and they would pretend the whole nasty encounter had never happened.

Maybe she would sprout wings and fly home.

Not knowing what else to do, she pulled her phone from her case and dialed her office. "Hey, Kate, it's me," she said when her sister answered.

"How's it going, Boss? Are all the plans finalized for Satan's retreat?"

Her first instinct was to laugh at her sister's nickname for Adam, but Cassie couldn't sum up the energy to do so. With a sigh of regret, she related the details of her meeting. The good thing about having your younger sister as an assistant was that she was attuned to your needs, Cassie thought.

"Just come to the office, Cass. We'll work it all out, okay?"

Hanging up the phone, she wished she had the first clue how to turn this mess around. Sure, she could cave in to Adam's unreasonable demands and eat the profits on this job to make him happy, but it wasn't right. It was high time somebody stood up to the mighty Adam Lawrence. Not that he'd care; he probably had another caterer on the phone right now drooling over the opportunity to do this job for him on such short notice and swoop in to save the day. *Dammit.*

Climbing into her sporty Honda Accord, she tried her best to wipe all ugly thoughts of replacement caterers aside and focus on getting home and finding something to eat. She had been so nervous this morning before meeting with Adam that she'd skipped breakfast; now all she wanted to do was draw the shades and curl up on her sofa with a large pizza and some ice cream and forget the rest of the world for a while.

The music chiming in from her cell phone broke into her pizza-pity-party fantasy. "Hello?"

"Hey, pumpkin! How's my favorite chef today?"

"Hey, Dad," she said, feeling a sense of comfort from hearing Stephen Jacobs's voice.

Knowing his daughter well, he asked, "What's wrong?"

"I just came from the worst meeting with my biggest client, and I think, *I think*, I might have quit." She waited for the reprimand or the unwanted parental advice but instead got an invitation to dinner. "Tonight? What's the occasion?"

"Does a dad need an occasion to see his daughter?"

"No," she said, feeling lighter than she had in hours. "What time and what am I making?" She knew her dad well, and even though he was inviting her to his house, the man couldn't cook to save his life.

"You know I'm not partial to any one thing, sweetheart. You decide, but…make enough for, say…seven people."

"Seven people? Who's coming?"

"Well, your sisters will be there and your brother, of course. Oh, and I've invited some friends I'd like you to meet. Will six o'clock work for you, Cass?"

Honestly, she hated to say no to her dad for anything. The man had been a rock for his family after Cassie's mom had died of ovarian cancer ten years before, and there wasn't anything he wouldn't do for his kids. Unfortunately, after the morning she'd had, the last thing she felt like was a family dinner with the added perk of entertaining strangers.

"Sure," she lied. "Six will work. Maybe I'll do some of that Greek chicken that you like so much. How does that sound?"

"Like a treat," he said. "I'll see you later, sweetheart." And then he was gone, and Cassie was alone to agonize over something other than Adam and her soon-to-be-doomed business.

Within minutes, she pulled up in front of the building that housed the CJ's Delights office, kitchen, and showroom. She gave herself a glance in the vanity mirror to make sure that she didn't look like a fright after her hellish morning. Luckily, her hair was still in place, and since she'd refused to give in to tears, she did not have raccoon eyes. Locking the car with the remote, she walked in through the front door and smiled at what her sister had done.

Dressed in her best server's attire, Katie stood next to one of their mock-up tables set with some of their best china and crystal. Candles were lit, and there was a beautiful bouquet of silk wildflowers in the middle in shades of pinks and purples. In the background came the strains of classical music. Cassie took a seat where her sister instructed, and in front of her was a large silver-covered plate. With great fanfare, Katie placed a cloth napkin in Cassie's lap and reached for the lid.

And revealed a tuna sandwich.

"It's all in the presentation," Katie deadpanned and then pulled up a chair for herself after grabbing her own sandwich from a nearby table. "So," she began, "family dinner tonight. Won't that be fun?"

Cassie finished chewing and nodded. "Oh, sure. Nothing says relaxing after a really bad day than cooking for seven people and getting grilled on why I did what I did wrong and how I am going to fix it. And who are these friends Dad invited?"

"What are you talking about?"

"Dad said that we were going to be seven for dinner—all of us and two friends."

"I have no idea. He hasn't mentioned anyone to me."

"I guess we'll find out soon enough," Cassie sighed. "I told him we'd do Greek tonight. Do we have everything here, or do I need to take a trip to the supermarket?" Once dinner plans were discussed and lists were made, Katie ran to the store while Cassie sat in her office trying to figure out how she was going to make her world right again.

The phone ringing was a wonderful distraction some minutes later. "CJ's Delights, this is Cassie, how can I help you?"

"Cassie? It's Grace Clark, Adam's assistant. How are you?"

She cringed. There were so many different ways this whole situation could play out that Cassie was afraid to get too far ahead of herself and dare to hope that Grace was calling with good news. Sitting up straight in her chair, she finally found her voice to answer.

"I'm fine, Grace. Thanks. How are you?"

"Oh, Cassie, please!" Grace began, her Southern drawl becoming more pronounced. "You ran out of here as if your skirt was on fire, and I didn't know what to do. I wanted to stop you and talk to you, but then Adam barked for me to come into his office."

"Barked?" Cassie laughed. The image of Adam as a wolf came to mind and had her sympathizing with his assistant.

"You know what I mean." She lowered her voice, as if afraid for anyone to overhear her. "Are you okay, Cass? I'm so sorry it's all worked out this way. I have loved working with you, and I consider you a friend. Is there any way we can make this right?"

While Cassie appreciated the offer, deep down she knew she had to stick to her guns; otherwise her word would be useless. "Honestly, Grace, maybe it's all for the better. Adam was unreasonable. The contract clearly states—"

"I know, I know," she interrupted. "Believe me, I deal with him every day, and I know how unreasonable he can be. He's had me calling caterers ever since you left, and no one is willing to take on an event of this magnitude on such short notice. He is having a fit!"

"Enough of a fit that he'd apologize?" Cassie asked hopefully. That would solve her problem. If Adam were the one to call her and restore the event with CJ's, then Cassie would have her dignity.

"Please, the great Adam Lawrence does not apologize to anyone. It's never going to happen."

"I was afraid you'd say that," Cassie murmured. Kicking off her shoes under her desk, she slouched dejectedly.

"But, seriously, are you going to be okay? I don't mean to pry, but it's that…well, I know that you're still building up your business and the LSS account was a big one for you."

"It sure was. *Was* being the operative word."

"Oh, Cass…"

"It'll be okay, Grace. I've always had a hard time working with Adam, having to listen to him yell and talk down to everyone. You deserve a medal for putting up with him every day. Don't worry about me. I'll be fine." She wished she believed it herself.

"Well, I've got your business cards, and you can believe that I will pass them along."

"I appreciate that, Grace. Really." With not much left to say, they made promises to meet for lunch and to keep in touch before hanging up. Cassie was going to miss working with Grace. What had started as a work relationship had grown into a friendship, and Cassie had come to look forward to events with LSS for the opportunity to work with Grace. She'd often teased that if Adam ever fired her, she'd give Grace a position with CJ's.

Unfortunately, there was no one offering her a replacement job. She heard Katie in the kitchen and pulled herself up, put her shoes on, and went to help with the groceries and prep work for their dinner.

By five o'clock, Katie was packing up. "I gotta run, Cass. I have to pick up Ella from the sitter's." Ella was Katie's three-month-old daughter, a baby who had drawn the Jacobs family closer together after Katie's boyfriend had taken off, never to be heard from again.

"I'll see you at the house in a little while," Cassie called after her as she packed up the supplies she would need to cook at her father's house. Stephen Jacobs still lived in the house he and his wife had raised their children in. Though it had a fully stocked kitchen, Cassie had a couple of favorite pots and pans that she preferred to cook with. By five thirty, she had changed into more casual clothes and was heading to her childhood home.

Her brother Matt was the first one out of the house to help her. He met her at the trunk of her car and picked her up in a bear hug as if she weighed nothing. "Hey! There's my cooking angel of mercy!" He gave her a smacking kiss on the cheek before putting her down. Of course, it helped that he was well over six feet tall and built like a linebacker and took his police training seriously. Reaching into the trunk, he took most of what Cassie had brought with her and headed toward the two-story Colonial.

Cassie stood in the driveway for a moment taking in the grand house and realized that it still looked the same. Her dad kept it clean and well manicured, and it always said "home" to her. It was a nice feeling to know that some things were sacred and stable and never changed. Grabbing the grocery bags, she closed the trunk just as a car pulled in behind her.

Waving to Lauren, she stopped and waited for the middle sister to get out of the car. "How goes law school? Ready to sue anyone yet?" she teased.

Making a face at the lame joke, Lauren grabbed her satchel and walked with Cassie to the door. "Very funny. Unfortunately, they don't let you sue anyone until after graduation. It's wrong." They laughed and made their way to the kitchen. Matt was already setting up his sister's supplies, and Katie was getting Ella settled into her baby swing.

—⁓—

Stephen Jacobs smiled as his family came into view. His kids were his whole life, and seeing them all in his kitchen, grown up and happy, always made him beam with pride. They were a close-knit group, and he'd always thought that it would be that way forever. With a quick prayer, he hoped that by the end of the night it would still be that way.

Life had not changed much in the ten years since he'd lost his wife. Stephen had tried to keep things as normal as possible for the sake of the kids. Cassie and Matt had had to take on a bit more responsibility to help out with Katie and Lauren, but, if anything, it seemed to make them all closer. They were a pretty unshakeable bunch, he thought to himself. Heck, even Katie's unplanned pregnancy hadn't been able to shake their bond. Somehow, he feared, tonight's dinner might be big enough to cause a tremor or two.

Walking into the kitchen, he heard Cassie telling the story of her difficult client whose account she'd lost today. *Bastard.* As a father, he hated to think of anyone hurting or upsetting any of his children, and although Cassie was a grown woman of twenty-six, he still wanted to fight her battles for her.

"Basically, it's a breach of contract on his part," Lauren was saying, anxious to use her legal knowledge around the house to prove that she was taking law school seriously. "You could probably sue him for the total amount of the contract. It might not get you future work with his company, but it would cover your butt until you can get another client or two to replace him."

It was funny to listen to Lauren talking so seriously when she was wearing sweats, her hair pulled up in a ponytail; she looked more high school than law school, Stephen thought. He was so proud of all his kids, and listening as they were pulling together to help one another told him that he'd done a good job raising them.

"That would not endear me to any future clients, I think," Cassie said as she cleaned and chopped fresh spinach to use in her Greek chicken. She was dressed casually like her sister, in faded blue jeans, a white T-shirt, and a black apron tied around her waist. She moved around the kitchen multitasking and was definitely at home here; cooking had always been a joy for her, and she had been fortunate to turn her passion into a successful career.

"Why would future clients have to know?" Katie asked, joining the conversation after getting Ella settled.

"If he decides to be spiteful, he'll let it be known to all the local businesses that I would not do what he asked and then sued. I'm telling you, he's that kind of person." From all that she'd said before, Stephen knew Adam Lawrence did not let anyone get the better of him, and if he failed to get a new caterer, she could kiss her business reputation goodbye.

Conversation veered away from her and her miserable day and went on to make the rounds of all the Jacobs siblings. With everyone laughing and smiling, Stephen thought now was a good time to talk about what was new in his life. "I sure am glad y'all came over tonight. It seems we don't get to do this often enough." All four of his children turned to look at him and smile. "The thing is, I've invited someone over tonight for you to meet, and I hope you'll like her."

"Her?" all four voices said at once.

Stephen had to smile. Their shocked tone matched the confusion on their faces. "Yes, her. Her name is

Beverly, she likes to be called Bev, and we've been dating for a couple of months now."

"A couple of *months*?" Matt asked incredulously. "How come you never mentioned this to any of us before?"

Stephen knew there'd be questions; he was glad they'd decided to ask before Bev arrived. "Well, when Bev and I first met, Katie was in her ninth month, and as you remember, she was having a rough time." They all nodded. "Then Ella arrived, and we were all caught up in celebrating and getting them both settled. Well, it wasn't the time to introduce any of you to somebody new. That was Katie's time. She deserved to be the center of attention."

Turning to look at his youngest daughter, he noticed her blue eyes shining with unshed tears. "I didn't want to take anything away from you, peanut. Besides, I had no idea if this relationship with Bev was going anywhere. After all, I'd been out of the dating world for quite some time."

"I guess it's going somewhere then," Lauren stated, not looking up from slicing a cucumber lest her father see the pain in her eyes.

"It is. This whole thing took the both of us by surprise, but after almost four months we figured it was time for everyone to meet. So I invited her tonight for a casual gathering. She has only one son, and he is coming with her, and if it's any comfort to you, he is learning about this today as well."

"I guess that's something," Lauren mumbled. Cassie elbowed her in the ribs.

"Geez," she whispered, "lighten up. This is new territory for all of us." With that, chatter returned to the kitchen, and they finished prepping the meal. Cassie put the chicken into the oven and then pulled the tzatziki from the refrigerator along with fresh vegetables and hummus for the appetizer. She was arranging a basket of toasted pita chips when the doorbell rang.

"That must be them!" Katie said, giddy with excitement. "Can you believe it? Dad has a girlfriend!" This caused the girls to giggle, even Lauren, while Matt stood back, arms crossed over his chest, ready to observe the whole scene before he decided whether he was happy about this new development in his family.

Cringing, Cassie could only hope that her brother lightened up quickly or this night could be a disaster. Remembering the tray of olives that she had forgotten to take out of the refrigerator, she turned, her back to the door when everyone walked in. "Everyone, this is Bev." He gestured to the room as a whole and then added, "And this is her son Adam. He's—"

Cassie nearly dropped the olive tray as she turned; her whole body had gone rigid. "The jackass who fired me today."

Chapter 2

YOU COULD HAVE HEARD A PIN DROP IN THE KITCHEN before all hell broke loose. Cassie slammed the tray of olives on the counter and stood there shooting daggers at Adam before she noticed that her siblings had surrounded her and were doing the same.

Bev looked stricken, and Stephen put his arm around her and silently begged his children with his eyes to knock it off. With a nervous laugh, he said, "Well, small world. Um…Bev, these are my kids, Matt, Katie, Lauren, and, uh, Cassie." Remembering their manners, they each shook Bev's hand and welcomed her, but their gazes soon returned to Adam. Cassie was enjoying watching him squirm. And he was indeed squirming.

"Um, maybe I should leave," he murmured, clearly looking for an escape.

"That won't be necessary, Adam. Please, you are our guest, and my children will remember themselves and stop trying to intimidate you." He shot them all a glare guaranteed to get them to do what he said, and within seconds, they were all scurrying around the kitchen, pouring drinks, setting out plates, and chatting with Bev as if she were an old friend.

Except for Adam and Cassie. Each stood where they were as if in a standoff. It took only minutes for Stephen to notice, and when he did he summoned them to follow him into his office on the other side of the house. "Listen, this is a big night for Bev and me, and I will not have the two of you ruining it. I understand that you have a business relationship and some issues with one another right now, but that is about business and tonight is not. So say whatever it is that you need to say to each other to clear the air so we can have a nice dinner." His tone left no room for argument, and with that, he turned and shut the door.

Arms folded, Cassie turned, leaned against her father's desk, and stared, daring Adam to speak first.

He looked uncomfortable enough to cave. "I did not appreciate being called a *jackass* in front of my mother and your family."

"Really? I did not appreciate being fired for sticking to a legally binding contract."

She heard his sharp intake of breath and knew she had hit her mark. "I guess we'll have to agree to disagree on that point for right now. As it stands, I am here purely to appease my mother. I thought we were meeting with potential business clients; I had no idea she was bringing me to meet her *boyfriend* and his family. I mean, seriously," he said with disgust, "a boyfriend. At her age. What the hell is she thinking?"

"Oh, maybe that she met a wonderful man?"

"Of course you'd say that; you're his daughter. Don't you think it's a bit ridiculous for them to be dating at their age?"

"I think they're in love."

"Love? Please." If his snort of derision didn't get the point across that Adam did not believe in love, the look of disgust on his face certainly did.

"You are a sad, sad human being, you know that?"

Pushing off from the desk, Cassie crossed to the door. "I don't know what your problem is, but I think it's sweet and wonderful that they've found each other. As for tonight, we have no choice but to be civil. Remember, you're on my turf, and right now no one here is impressed by you."

--~~~--

It was a glorious exit; he had to give her that. Rubbing a hand across his chin, he closed his eyes and tried to think of a believable excuse to get the hell out of Dodge. Unfortunately, nothing came to him. The sound of laughter and the tempting aroma he was sure was Cassie's cooking wafted toward him. His stomach knew a good thing when it presented itself because it suddenly let out a very loud protest at the idea of not staying. With a growl of frustration, Adam left the safety of Stephen's office and returned to the kitchen.

Conversation stopped briefly, but Stephen pulled out the chair beside him and offered it to Adam. Grateful not to have to speak, Adam sat quietly, and soon the conversation was lively again.

"Cassie, this dip is fabulous!" Bev gushed. "Adam sent me on vacation to Greece a couple of years ago, and I have to tell you, this is as good as anything I ate while I was there! You're a genius!"

Stephen broke in to talk about how Cassie had come to start her own business: from cooking with her mother and grandmother when she was a little girl to hosting a business dinner or two for him when she was in her teens. "She has a knack for it," he said. "She doesn't need any recipes—you tell her what you want, and she can create it!"

"Dad, please," she murmured.

Adam sensed more than saw Matt sit next to him. He didn't turn to acknowledge him; he was too wrapped up in watching as Cassie tossed the rice in a large skillet one-handed without spilling any of it.

"Lauren, grab me that lemon, please," she said and in a flash had the pan on the stove and the lemon cut and was squeezing the fresh juice over the salad greens. Like a well-choreographed dance, the three sisters were moving about the kitchen, each knowing what to do without speaking, and soon there was a complete dinner set before them at the large kitchen table.

"Well, well, well," Bev said with a bright smile. "What have you made for us, Cassie?"

Cassie cast a glance at Katie, who took over. "We've got boneless chicken breasts stuffed with spinach and feta cheese and drizzled with a balsamic glaze, rice pilaf, and, of course, a Greek salad." She smiled at her sister. "This is one of Dad's favorites."

"Oh, I can see why. Everything is fabulous, girls, thank you for preparing such a treat." She took a small bite of her chicken, and when she had finished chewing, she looked at her son and said, "Isn't it wonderful, Adam?"

He nodded and grunted in agreement, afraid to say too much around this crowd. "Adam has always said that Cassie is an amazing chef. After every event he has, he's always praised your cooking," Bev said, glancing between Cassie and Adam, hoping to ease some of the tension.

"Really?" Cassie asked. "Funny, I don't remember hearing that hell had frozen over—"

"*Cassandra!*" Stephen hissed. "That is enough! I

could see if you were twelve and you were behaving like this, but you are a grown woman, and Adam is our guest. I know this has been a rough day for you both, but…"

"Please, Mr. Jacobs," Adam began, "there's no need to intercede on my behalf. I'm afraid I handled things poorly this afternoon. I don't see that three days make that much of a difference, and…"

That was it! It seemed as if everyone started talking at once.

"Three days *do* make a difference…"

"*You* were the one who broke the contract!"

"Do you have any idea how much planning and ordering go into an event like this?"

"You'll never get anyone to do this job on such short notice…"

"*Enough!*"

All heads turned to look at Stephen. He reached for Bev's hand, and they held on tightly to one another. "You should all be ashamed of yourselves. There will be no more talk of this contract here tonight. The two of you can talk it out to your heart's content tomorrow, but as of right now, you are done. Am I clear?"

Everyone nodded. "Good. Now pass me the rice."

For an hour, there was peace. To Adam's way of thinking, the Jacobs family was sneaky in their attack. No one said anything directly to him, but the conversation did seem continually to find its way to Cassie and her business. With each comment in her favor, the speaking sibling would give him an accusing glare. Fine, if they wanted to believe him to be Jack the Ripper, Scrooge, and an ogre rolled into one, then so be it. Maybe after dinner he'd find some puppies to kick to prove their point.

Cassie's laughter broke through his train of thought and caused a slight clench in his stomach. Why had he never noticed what a great laugh she had? Probably because he never gave her a reason to laugh when they were working together. Come to think of it, no one laughed around him. This was the first time in he couldn't remember how long that he was surrounded by people having a good time. When had his life become such a misery?

Matt slapped his hands together, startling everyone into silence. "What's for dessert, Cass?"

All eyes turned expectantly to Cassie as she cried out, "Oh, no!"

"What? What's the matter?"

"I had some lovely pies and pastries, and I left them at the shop." Standing, Cassie began clearing the table, quickly followed by her sisters. Once again, Adam couldn't help but admire the way the siblings worked together, enjoying the domestic tasks.

He held in the shudder that wanted to overtake his body at the thought.

"Cass, go get the dessert. We'll do the cleanup, right, Kate?" Lauren suggested. Katie nodded and continued to clear the table, all the while answering Bev's question about baby Ella.

Untying the apron that she'd forgotten to take off before sitting down to eat, Cassie tossed it into the laundry room and walked through the kitchen, telling everyone she'd be right back. Grabbing her purse from the living room sofa, she called to Lauren that she was taking her car since it was behind Cassie's, and walked out the door. It was pitch-black outside, and it wasn't until she stepped around to the driver's side of the car that she saw Adam.

If there was a single thought prevalent in her mind as she was heading out it was that it would be good to have a reprieve from Adam. Apparently, it was to be a short-lived one.

"What are you doing out here?"

"I thought I'd ride with you so maybe we can clear the air a little and try to salvage this night."

A mirthless laugh came out before Cassie could stop it. "You mean you want to make me fall in line like one of your employees so my family will stop shooting daggers at you, don't you?"

With a shrug, Adam stepped aside as she came around the car to climb into the driver's seat. Leaving him standing there, Cassie started the car and buckled herself in before rolling the window down. "It'll be mighty hard for you to ride with me while you're standing in the driveway…"

With that, he walked around to the passenger side and climbed in.

Cassie's shop was only ten minutes away, and they spent nine of them in silence. "I've never been to your facility before," Adam said, noting its proximity to her family home as well as downtown Raleigh. "How long have you been here?"

Parking the car right in front, Cassie turned it off before answering him. "It's been almost three years, although it took a few months of renovating the place before I could use it to its full potential." She climbed out, and Adam followed.

From the outside, the building didn't look like much;

it was a brick facade with a large window display and a pretty wood door with a stained-glass design. Walking inside, however, Adam was impressed. The showroom was designed to present the available table settings, each table done in a different color scheme with coordinating china and flowers. Around the room were shelves holding displays of baskets, silk flowers, and an assortment of pictures from what he guessed to be events that Cassie had done.

Walking farther in, he passed under an archway that led into a smaller room with pocket doors that felt open and inviting. There was a large desk to the left sitting at an angle, and in front of it were two large upholstered chairs, presumably for clients. This must be her office. Very clever, he thought to himself. Bring the customers through the showroom before sitting with them.

Adam heard Cassie moving around in the room behind her office. The door to it was wide and swung as one would find in a restaurant leading to the kitchen, and once he stepped through, he realized that was exactly where he was.

There was glimmering stainless steel everywhere, and the smell of bleach was strong enough to prove the place was clean but not enough to be overpowering. He saw Cassie stepping out of what he saw to be a walk-in refrigerator. There was a row of stoves, four of them, on the right-hand wall. In the center of the room were work islands, to the left were cabinets and shelves, and toward the rear were the sinks. Adam found himself quite impressed with the efficiency of the overall layout.

Cassie had several pink cake boxes in her hands, and she placed them on the nearest island before turning to shut the refrigerator door. Rubbing her hands together, she moved to one of the cabinets to find a bag for easier transport.

"You've got a great setup here, Cassandra, truly impressive."

She had to stop herself from turning and giving him a snarky remark. After all, he sounded sincere, and if what he'd said earlier about wanting to clear the air was true, this was not the time for sarcasm.

"Thank you. It took a while to get it right so we can all work without bumping into one another, but I finally ironed out all the kinks, and I'm pleased with it."

"You should be. I guess I never put much thought into *where* you worked." Looking around the kitchen, he noticed two doors in the corner; one led to the outside, and the other to an alcove. Cassie saw where he was looking.

"We load everything from here. Our truck is kept in a small parking lot. There's also a storage shed for extra tables, chairs, and whatnot. The other door leads to my apartment upstairs."

"You *live* here?"

His tone put her back up; he sounded a bit appalled at the prospect. "I don't live here in the kitchen, Adam. My apartment is separate and soundproofed, and it makes things easier for me when we have to pull a late night."

She continued packing the desserts. "I can drive the truck here, have the staff help me unload, and then walk up the stairs and be done with the day. Don't tell me you don't have something similar in your building because I happen to know for a fact that you do."

"True enough, but this is such a…a commercial

space. I spend the occasional night at the office when I'm dealing with overseas accounts, but I wouldn't want to live there full time."

"Well," she replied tartly, "lucky for you that you have the kind of income that you can afford both. Most of us in the real world only have one place of residence." She scooped up the bag with the dessert in it and was walking past Adam when he reached out and gently touched her arm to stop her.

"Okay, okay, truce. I was out of line," he said wearily. He had no idea why he had to explain himself to this woman, but things would be easier when they got back to the house if they were playing nice. "Look, everything got out of hand today at the office."

"You think?" She liked the fact that her tone had him arching an eyebrow at her.

"Yes, I think," he said with equal sarcasm. "The thing is, you were right." *Dammit.* "If the tables were turned, I would not break the terms of my contract for any client, and that was what I was expecting you to do."

Cassie stood in stunned silence.

"Your company has done nothing but a good job for mine, Cassandra, and I respect you as a business associate. I think you are a fine cook; nothing you've made for any of my events has ever disappointed, and I would very much like it if you would continue with the fall retreat plan and maybe…forget what happened earlier today."

Adam stood and waited—somewhat patiently—for Cassie to say something. He became quickly irritated when she, as she had earlier, did not immediately respond. Taking a deep breath, he was ready to speak when—

"All right, Adam, I'll continue with this project." He released the breath. "But there are some things that need to be said if we're going to move forward and work together again beyond this event."

When he nodded, she continued. "For starters, I can't speak for your staff, but I can tell you that I, personally, do not appreciate being spoken to like I'm an idiot."

"I've never—"

She held up a hand to silence him. "You do. All the time. To everyone. As you can see here, I own my own business, and I know how to run it. I'm not operating out of the back of a van, so clearly I know what I am doing. I would trust you if I hired you for security because that's what you do for a living. As an act of simple courtesy, I expect you to trust me when it comes to event planning and catering because this is what I do for a living."

"Now wait a minute—"

"I'm not done!" she snapped, pleased to see his mouth snap shut. "I am damn good at what I do, Adam, you've said so yourself. I appreciate you wanting to give your input, I honestly do, but I expect it to be given in a respectful tone. I'm a grown woman, not a child."

She stood tall, crossed her arms over her chest, and heaved a sigh of completion. "Now, do you have something to say?"

Oh, man, did he! Adam's first instinct was to blast her for speaking to him that way, and then he reined himself in. Mentally counting to ten, he leaned on the island in front of her. "I did not realize that the way I spoke was so offensive. No one's ever said anything to me before about it."

"That's because you would fire them," she said blandly.

He gave her a look that showed she was grating on his patience. "I was not allowed to interrupt you. I'd expect the same courtesy." Cassie nodded and let him go on. "In my line of work, in my position, that is the way that it's done. I demand perfection from the people around me because it is my reputation on the line, not theirs. I realize that although you are not a full-time employee of mine, maybe I have been equally demanding of you. For that, I apologize."

Cassie nearly fell where she stood.

"I would like us to continue to work together, Cassandra, and maybe now that we've talked this through and know where we're each coming from, we can do so with no hard feelings." Adam held out his hand to seal the deal and watched as Cassie eyed him warily. He hated having to apologize. But if he told the truth, he really did need her to finish the event. Their meeting tonight had been serendipitous and allowed him to save face, actually. It would have been much worse if he'd had to call her in a few days and grovel to get his damn event catered.

When Cassie finally reached out her hand to his and shook, Adam was temporarily stunned. There was a jolt that had never been there before. He looked at her and saw that she felt it too, as she snatched her hand away. "Thank you, Adam."

"I'm looking forward to this event, and I know it will be perfect as we discussed." Adam scooped up the bag with the dessert and followed Cassie out of the kitchen. He watched the sway of her hips in faded jeans and smiled in the darkness with pure male appreciation as she turned out the lights.

While Adam couldn't deny that Cassie Jacobs was an attractive woman, he also couldn't deny that she had crossed a line with him, one he didn't allow anyone to cross. Unfortunately, in this particular situation, he had to bide his time to meet a deadline. With the event in eleven days, his hands were tied. Once this retreat was over, however, so was his business with Cassie.

Permanently.

Chapter 3

ADAM WALKED OUT BEHIND CASSIE AND WAITED BESIDE her as she set the alarm and locked up. They climbed into the car, and he could see that some of the tension had left her. Excellent. That meant she believed what he had said and that the dogs should be called off when they arrived at her father's house with dessert.

It didn't take long, however, to note that something was wrong. Cassie had a white-knuckled grip on the steering wheel, and she was breathing deeply, as if trying to get through something. "Are you all right?" he asked, genuinely concerned.

"Fine," she said tightly, fumbling slightly as she reached for her cell phone. Adam wanted to offer to dial for her or at least remind her to keep her eye on the road while she dialed, but in a flash, she had the phone to her ear and was speaking.

"It's me…we're on the way home…no, no, I'm not. Thanks." Tossing the phone into her purse with some irritation, Cassie resumed her death grip on the wheel.

"Cassandra, what's going on?" Adam demanded.

"It's nothing," she managed through clenched teeth. "I would appreciate it if you wouldn't speak right now."

Before he could argue any further, they were pulling into the driveway—practically on two wheels—as her entire family piled out the front door. Within seconds,

Cassie's sisters were helping her out of the car while her brother grabbed her bag. Her father stood at the door with Bev as Cassie was essentially carried into the house and out of sight. Adam stood by the passenger side door, wondering what had just happened.

Taking the dessert with him, he slammed the car door and stalked to the house. Stephen and his mother were waiting for him. He stopped in front of them, expecting an explanation.

"I'll take that in" was all Stephen said as he took the bag from Adam and went into the house. Adam looked to his mother for answers.

"Well?" he demanded of his mother. "What was that all about?"

Stepping away from the door and out onto the porch, Bev let the door close and stood next to Adam. "Cassie has a condition. It flares up occasionally, and apparently it did so tonight. She'll be okay in a little while. No worries."

"No worries?" he snapped. "She damn well nearly passed out in the car! Then we get here, and the whole family carries her inside! That doesn't sound like a 'condition,' Mother. What's wrong with her?"

"Adam, trust me. It's all okay, and Cassie will be fine. Her family is concerned about her, but that's because they love her and don't want her to be in any pain. I think it's sweet." Bev turned and surveyed the house. She sighed and looked at her son, who didn't seem the least bit appeased by her explanation.

"They're a wonderful family, aren't they?" she asked.

Wanting more of an explanation than his mother was willing to give, Adam couldn't help but be annoyed.

"Yeah, sure, they're great. You're not the one they were giving the evil eye to all night. That doesn't seem so wonderful to me."

"You had it coming. You hurt Cassie, and in turn, they wanted to hurt you because of it. They stick together. You have to respect that."

"Respect what?"

"Their loyalty."

"Whatever," he mumbled and saw Lauren and Matt heading for the kitchen and Katie not far behind them. "I guess we should head in." Nodding, Bev waited as Adam held the door for her, and then went inside.

On the way to the kitchen, Adam couldn't help but look around to see where Cassie had gone to. He found the rest of the family setting dessert plates on the table and pouring coffee, but no sign of Cassie. With a sigh of frustration, he sat in the same chair he'd used during dinner. Lauren slammed a plate in front of him and sat across from him. And glared.

"At least you apologized," she said with a sour look and waited for Adam to respond.

"I know when to admit I was wrong." There was confidence in his words, but one look at Lauren showed him that she wasn't buying it.

"I guess it's a good thing that I'm not doing business with you, isn't it?" he said, not liking her mild intimidation. He mocked her pose and was relieved when she turned away and returned to setting out their dessert.

Without appearing to care, Adam looked around to see if Cassie was going to join them or at least to get a clue to her whereabouts. Conversation kicked up around him while dessert was served, and within moments he got caught up in listening to the story of how his mother and Stephen had met.

Rolling his eyes would have been completely inappropriate, and so would checking his watch; there was no choice but to listen to Bev and Stephen take turns talking about their awkward blind date arranged by friends. Bev's eyes shone brightly as she talked about the point when they knew they were in love.

It didn't take long to see where this was going. Shifting in his seat, Adam could only pray that his instincts were wrong. He wasn't used to his mother dating as it was; she used to date quite often when he was younger, but after one particularly nasty situation, she'd stopped. It had been easily ten years since she'd been serious with anyone.

"I know this might be something of a shock to all of you," Stephen was saying when Adam tuned back in, "but I've asked Bev to marry me."

The room erupted in congratulations so raucous that baby Ella was startled and started to cry. Katie rushed to pick up her daughter and soothed her as she went over to hug her father. Adam observed the rush before offering his own reserved congratulations to their parents.

"Thank you, Adam," Stephen said as he shook his hand. "I know we all got off to a rocky start this evening, but it seems you and Cassie have managed to work things out, and we don't hold grudges around here. I want you to know that your mother means the world to me." To reinforce his point, he put an arm around his fiancée and pulled her close before kissing her.

Bev beamed, and Adam could not deny that his

mother believed herself to be in love. But why did it have to be with the patriarch of this particular family? How was he supposed to keep his promise to himself to fire Cassie as his event planner and coordinator after the fall retreat when they were practically family?

By the time dessert was finished and he and Bev were getting ready to leave, he still didn't have the answer to what to do about Cassie, nor had she returned to the festivities. As much as he tried to tell himself that he wasn't concerned or didn't care about her, he couldn't deny being curious.

Once he was in the car with Bev and heading to her house, Adam couldn't wait any longer to find out what was going on. "Okay," he began cautiously, "I know you said that Cassie has some mystery 'condition,' but seriously, what's wrong with her? Does this secret ailment have a name?"

With a sigh of defeat, Bev said. "You know, Adam, sometimes I wish you'd learn to leave things alone. Some things don't need to be discussed."

"Mom…"

"Cassie has endometriosis. It's a gynecological problem. It's very painful when it flares up. Apparently, that's what happened tonight. According to Stephen, it doesn't happen often, but when it does, she has a rough time of it." She tsked with pity. "Poor girl."

"So why doesn't she do something about it?"

"Gee, it's no wonder you're the CEO of a big corporation. I wonder why Cassie hasn't thought of that. 'Do something'! Why don't I call her right now and tell her that you've solved yet another of the world's problems!"

"Sarcasm doesn't suit you, Mother," he said wearily.

"I'm not trying to make light of this. I'm saying maybe something can be done to help her, that's all."

Bev turned and looked at her son. "She takes medication and she's done everything the doctors have said. The next option is surgery, and she doesn't want that."

"Why not?"

She looked at her son with disbelief. "Not everyone is excited about getting cut open, you know."

"But if it would cure this problem…"

"There is no real 'cure' for this. It's manageable but not curable. Even with the surgery, there is a possibility it will return. She's learned to live with it and has these occasional setbacks. She's lucky she wasn't out at an event or anything and could be comforted by her family."

Adam made a noncommittal sound and continued to drive. He didn't want to talk about Cassie. He'd had enough of Cassandra Jacobs for one day. He was about to broach the subject of the engagement when his mother spoke again.

"You know I don't like to pry into your business, dear, but I have to tell you I was a little embarrassed when I heard about your behavior today."

So much for not talking about Cassie.

"It's none of your business—"

"I know, I know," she said, placating him. "It's just that I can't imagine you being so hard on anyone, especially a woman."

Adam rolled his eyes at his mother's naïveté. "Mother, please," he began. "Cassie is a businesswoman; she doesn't expect preferential treatment, and how I conduct myself at work is none of your concern."

"It's just that—"

"You don't seem to mind reaping the benefits of how I do my business," he snapped.

By seven the next evening, Adam was mentally exhausted. He'd spent a brutal day dealing with a difficult client, and all he wanted to do was go home and enjoy the silence. As he walked through his building, he noticed that everyone else was long gone, and to hear only the sound of his own footsteps was a godsend.

Out of the building, wishing the security team a good night, he almost felt his spirits lifting. It had been a long time since a client had frustrated him so. Adam was the security expert; why wasn't that good enough? His conversation with Cassie from the night before came to mind. He could see her point now that he was deeply entrenched in a situation that frustrated him as much as she must have been frustrated.

It had almost been twenty-four hours since he'd given her a thought. As he pulled his car out of the parking garage, he tried to shake her image from his mind. It didn't work. He could see the conservative businesswoman he'd always dealt with, and then more firmly in his mind was the woman in jeans from last night, with her loose, wavy hair framing her face and her big blue eyes twinkling with laughter when she was with her family.

He sighed with frustration and then with disgust when he realized he was driving not toward his house but toward her shop. Her business. Her home. What the hell was wrong with him? He'd known Cassie for two years! He'd been doing business with her all this time and never managed to give her a second thought, and now, for some ungodly reason, he was driving past her house like he was some teenager hoping to get a glimpse of her.

The light was on in the showroom, and he slowed to see if he could spot her. God, he was pathetic! As he neared a stop, he did, in fact, see her walking toward the kitchen. Not giving himself time to question his actions, Adam turned the car around and parked by the rear door.

Climbing out of his car, Adam began to question himself. What was he going to say? Why was he here? Maybe he was concerned because of what had happened last night? Maybe he was checking up on her to make sure she was okay? That was plausible, right? He knocked and waited.

"Adam?" Cassie said as she pulled open the door, unable to hide her surprise. "What are you doing here?"

"Can I come in?"

Cassie stepped aside as he came through the door. He stood only a few feet away and watched as she closed the door and led him into the kitchen. She stared, waiting for an answer. "Adam?"

"You never did come back to the table. Are you feeling okay?" If he didn't know himself any better, he'd swear he was actually concerned.

"Well, that's nice of you." She smiled. "Come on in. I'm cooking." Without waiting to see if he'd follow, Cassie walked over to her workstation and finished tossing ingredients into a bowl.

"Do you have a client tonight?"

"What? Oh, you mean this?" When he nodded, she continued. "Well, normally I make enough for two or three when I'm concocting, you know, so I can get a second or third opinion. Katie is usually my guinea pig, but she left early tonight. So she'll have to taste it as leftovers."

"What are you making?"

"I'm not exactly sure yet," she said with a grin. "I've got chicken and artichoke hearts, roasted peppers, fresh mozzarella…I think I'll use some penne and maybe some vodka sauce." At this point, she'd stopped talking directly to him and was mumbling more to herself as she walked around the kitchen grabbing ingredients. She was putting a pot of water on the stove to boil when she remembered he was there.

"Sorry, I get distracted easily when I'm cooking. Why exactly did you stop by?" She began heating olive oil in a large skillet as Adam walked closer.

"As I said, I wanted to make sure you were feeling all right."

"Oh, right, yes. I'm fine. No big deal. I took some Advil and rested for a little while and drove myself home around eleven. I'm fine today."

"That's good," he said, watching as she threw all sorts of things into the pan and tossed them around with abundant seasonings. "That smells amazing." The words were out before he could stop himself.

She flashed him one of those smiles that he was really starting to like, never stopping the pan-flipping action she had going on. "Thanks. I love it, the creating and the experimenting. Sometimes it works, sometimes it doesn't, but a girl's gotta eat, right?"

Adam nodded. "You cook for yourself every night?"

"Absolutely!" She lowered the flame on the stove and went to grab the pasta to add to the boiling water. "Do you cook?"

"Does hitting 'cook' on the microwave count?" he asked, hating how pathetic he sounded. While standing here watching her cook, smelling the wonderful aroma of whatever this was that Cassie was throwing together, his microwave dinner had lost more of its appeal than usual.

"Well, I'll tell you what, grab two plates from that cabinet over there, and we'll discuss our soon-to-be-merged family over dinner. How does that sound?"

Like a treat, he thought.

It amazed Adam, but within minutes they were sitting up in Cassie's apartment eating a meal that was…well, it was even better than the one she'd cooked for her family the night before.

"I wish I could have seen everyone's faces when Dad made the announcement," Cassie said as she lifted her glass of wine. "I'm sure I would have been equally shocked. None of us had any idea he was dating. Did you know about your mom?"

"Not a clue, but then again, I don't spend a whole lot of time with Mom talking about her social life." After the words were out, he realized how cold and callous they sounded. "I mean, with my schedule, we don't…"

Cassie shook her head and smiled. "No need to explain. I completely understand. Not many families spend as much time together as mine, and honestly, even we didn't know."

"Why would your dad not want you to know?" Adam tasted his wine and nodded with approval. Not only could the woman cook, but she had good taste in wine.

"I don't know. I mean, we're all adults with our own lives, and we want him to be happy. My mom's been gone for more than ten years, so he's mourned enough.

We've often talked about wanting him to find someone and start living again. I guess he wasn't sure how we'd react." Reaching for a napkin, she gently wiped her mouth. "We talk about everything in my house, and he never talked to us about this."

"Are you upset?"

Cassie shook her head. "Not at all. It's so obvious that they're crazy about each other, and I think it's wonderful. All I want is for Dad to be happy. He's sacrificed so much for us, and now we're all grown up and creating lives for ourselves, and I want him to be selfish now and focus on what makes him happy."

"Maybe being a dad made him happy."

Cassie put her fork down and looked at Adam, tears glistening in her eyes. "That was quite possibly the nicest thing you've ever said." She reached over and touched his hand. "Thank you."

Before Cassie could remove her hand, Adam turned his over, linked his fingers through hers, and gave a gentle squeeze. This wasn't supposed to be happening, Cassie thought. She wasn't supposed to be enjoying herself with Adam; she still didn't fully trust him. The fact that they were going to be "family" soon didn't help matters. But sitting here next to him, enjoying a meal, talking like two regular people—not adversarial business associates—had her seeing him as if for the first time.

That wasn't to say that she'd never taken notice of Adam. A woman would have to be blind not to notice him. Dark brown hair trimmed in that sexy-executive style. A strong jaw, eyes such a deep brown they were almost black, and he had an athletic physique that looked amazing encased in Armani. Adam was the stuff most fantasies were made of—until he opened his mouth. That was a deal breaker, for sure.

Realizing that she was staring, Cassie casually pulled her hand free and returned to her meal. Clearing her throat, she said, "I guess he could have been satisfied with being a father to four kids, but now that we're all grown, I want him to do something for himself. He's raised us all, and as much as I know he wants to help with Ella, he needs your mom."

"I think Bev needs him too. I guess I didn't realize how much or how lonely she was until I saw them together last night. It was a bit eye-opening."

"Um, Adam," she said cautiously and blushed. He didn't think women blushed anymore. "As long as we're honest, you have to know I don't normally…argue with clients. I mean, I can usually get what I want without having to be…bitchy." If possible, her blush deepened at her description of herself.

"If it means anything," he replied, "I seriously provoked you." An inner voice told Adam he was going to have to kick his own ass soon if he didn't stop apologizing and getting sappy with this woman. In one day's time, he had fired her and then pretty much begged, groveled, and put himself down to make her feel better.

As wonderful as dinner was, he had to get out of here. There was no way for him to hang onto who he was and what he was planning while he was getting all "in touch with his emotions" here in Cassie's home. He had to get out quick.

Tossing aside his napkin, he stood. "Let me help you clear these dishes, and then I have to get going. I've got a midnight conference call." He didn't, but it sounded plausible. "I'm hoping to catch an hour's sleep before it starts."

Cassie shooed his hands away from the plates. "Not to worry, I've got this. You go and do what you do." To prove it, she began clearing the table and placing dishes in the sink. When everything was cleared, she noticed him standing next to the table watching her, his brows creased. It was both exciting and unnerving. Leaning against the counter, she folded her arms across her chest and observed him right back—only with a smile. "This was a surprise, Adam."

He nodded, almost mesmerized by the sight of her. He had to get out. Now. "Thank you for dinner. That too was unexpected. And delicious. Thanks for sharing." He turned to go down the stairs, and Cassie followed him.

"Oh, wait one minute," she said and walked over to the walk-in refrigerator. When she came out, she had a round foil takeout container. "Here," she said. "Take the leftovers for yourself for dinner another night. I know you'll still have to nuke them, but at least they're homemade." She handed the container to him with a smile, and Adam felt like he'd been kicked in the solar plexus.

With a gruff "good night," he was out the door, in his car, and pulling away. He had no idea what had happened tonight, but it made him uncomfortable, and if there was one thing he knew for sure about himself, it was that he hated to be uncomfortable.

Speeding off into the night, he looked at the takeout container as if it were plutonium. It was a simple gesture, one that showed her kindness. Switching his focus between the container and the road, Adam had a feeling that he'd left Cassie's tonight with more than another meal.

He might have left there with the ice around his heart starting to melt.

Chapter 4

THE ROOM WAS DONE IN GREENS AND GOLDS, AND WHEN Cassie was finished with it, the guests would feel as if they'd wandered through the mountains of North Carolina amid the fall foliage. It was magical to look at. Though Cassie had not seen Adam since their impromptu dinner the week before, she knew he was going to be pleased with the results.

With one last look around, she noticed Katie coming toward her. "Any problems?"

"None," Katie said with a smile.

"That's what I like to hear." Feeling confident, she walked the room one final time and felt satisfied that she had done all she could for the day. Taking the elevator up to the tenth floor, she found Grace sitting at her desk and smiled and waved as she approached.

"Are we ready?" Grace asked giddily.

"As we'll ever be," Cassie confirmed. "I did a final survey, and the room looks amazing."

"You are impressive. I bow to the master." With great fanfare, Grace did an over-the-top bow, and both women started to laugh.

And instantly stopped when Adam stepped out of his office.

Grace immediately sat in her seat and got to work, straightening stacks of paper for effect and saying in a clipped, professional tone, "Thank you for the update,

Miss Jacobs." Cassie thanked her for her time and turned to leave.

"Cassandra?" Adam called after her. "May I speak with you for a moment?" He was careful to stay respectful and courteous as he'd told her he would.

Cassie followed him into his office and immediately gave him an update on the event status. He smiled with pleasure. Adam never doubted she would pull it all together and make it look beautiful and professional. That's what he paid her for. No, what he wanted right now wasn't so much an update on the retreat as much as to talk with her.

But in the end, he had to remember his initial plan. Cassie had crossed a line with him, and while he couldn't outright fire her like he'd wanted to—not with their parents' newly announced engagement—he had to find a way to end their business arrangement that didn't have him looking like the bad guy. He wasn't sure yet how exactly he was going to accomplish that.

"If you'd like to come to the ballroom, I'd be happy to give you the tour."

"I trust you," he replied smoothly. "I'm sure it will look exactly as you promised and my staff will be thoroughly impressed. I have every confidence in you."

His words shouldn't have made her feel all gushy inside, and yet they did. The man never praised anyone, and lately, he'd been doing that a lot to her.

"I…um…I tweaked the menu a bit," she began nervously, almost afraid to broach the subject that had nearly ended their working relationship. "I added—"

Adam cut her off. Holding up his hand to stop her words, he said, "I'm sure whatever it is, it'll be wonderful."

She stood there in front of his desk, taking in the sight

of the man in the perfectly fitted Italian suit, not a hair out of place, his deep-brown eyes serious, and longed for the more carefree, relaxed man she'd dined with.

Oh, well; another time, another place. He was the CEO of a major international security corporation; this was the image most fitting for him. With the upcoming wedding of their parents, Cassie was sure she'd get to see him looking a lot more relaxed and at ease, but right now all she wanted to do was to lean over the desk, rip off his tie, run her fingers through his hair, and mess it up.

What the…?

As if reading her mind, Adam gave her an equally thorough look and smiled a truly sexy smile that had Cassie stammering and wishing him a good night as she walked out the door, telling him she was needed downstairs. Maybe he believed her, maybe he didn't, but right now all she knew was that this new footing they were on was way more confusing and arousing than their previous working relationship had been.

With a quick wave to Grace, Cassie raced for the elevator and didn't breathe with any ease until the doors closed and she was safely on her way to the main floor and headed for the doors that would take her outside. She needed fresh air; she needed to be out of this building and to focus on the job, not the man.

Easier said than done.

By the time five o'clock rolled around on Friday evening, Cassie was in full-blown work mode. The room looked stunning, and guests were beginning to arrive. She spotted Adam and Grace by the door greeting everyone as they came in.

Within fifteen minutes, hors d'oeuvres were being

passed butler-style by tuxedoed servers, along with champagne. The bar was serving mixed drinks, and by five thirty, bread and a field greens salad were placed at all one hundred seats. Cassie stood in the kitchen and watched every tray that left for the ballroom to make sure it met her standards. Her staff worked quietly and efficiently, and by the time Adam took the stage at seven thirty, tables were cleared, the kitchen was being cleaned and packed up from dessert, and fresh coffee was making the rounds.

It was only then that Cassie allowed herself to sit for five minutes to catch her breath. Katie put a plate of food in front of her, but she merely picked at it. She felt the twinge that she had hoped wouldn't hit tonight and quietly made her way to the storage closet where she'd placed her purse earlier. Knowing her sister well, Katie followed.

"Are you okay?"

Cassie took a deep breath. "Hopefully, I will be in a few minutes." She swallowed a pill with some water and went to the kitchen to try to eat a bit more. The painkiller seemed to work better on a full stomach.

"Look, we've got this under control. I know the breakdown and setup routine as well as you. Go home and rest, please, Cass," Katie said.

Shaking her head, she refused to leave. This was an important event and one that she had fought with Adam over, and she was determined to see it through to the end. An hour later, Cassie heard the round of applause and knew that the presentation was over, the music would resume playing, and the guests would mingle and socialize for the next ninety minutes before she could begin to clear them out and start the setup for the breakfast portion of the retreat.

There was a lot of movement and talking; the kitchen was a hot spot for activity. Cassie didn't think anyone would notice when she slumped against the wall and fought the wave of pain that hit.

Strong arms came around her before she could comprehend that she was going down. "Cassandra? Are you all right?"

"Adam? What are you doing in the kitchen?" Even in her weakened state, she felt panicked at the thought that something was so wrong out in the ballroom that he felt the need to come to the kitchen. "Is everything all right? The food—"

"Don't worry about the damn party. What's going on with you?" By this point, Katie had noticed what was happening and rushed over.

"Damn it, Cass!"

"How long has she been feeling like this?" he snapped at Katie.

"About an hour." Katie sighed. "I told her to leave, but she refused."

"Don't talk about me as if I'm not here," Cassie hissed. She looked up at Adam, her eyes ablaze. "You hired me to do a job, and I am here to make sure it gets done to both our satisfaction."

"At the risk of your own health?" The sight of her nearly fainting had sent him racing across the room. In truth, he had come to the kitchen, something he never did, to congratulate her on a job well done and to thank her for managing to add some of the items he had requested to the menu. The food had been superb, and the service was top-notch. Overall, he had been very pleased. Now all he felt was concern for Cassie's health and disgust with himself because he knew it was his fault she was working herself so hard.

"You know nothing about my health, so please spare me the dramatics, Adam."

"Cassie, please," Katie interrupted, "go home. I've got this covered. Take my car...I'll pick it up when we bring the van to the shop later."

"She can't possibly drive like this!" Adam turned to look at Katie as if she'd lost her mind. "I'll drive her home."

"Just a minute," Cassie said, suddenly snapping out of her wave of pain long enough to be annoyed with Adam's tone. "I don't need you making arrangements for me, and you can't leave! This is your event!"

"And as such, I can leave whenever I want. My presentation is done, and if I stay, all I'll have to deal with is people kissing up to me about my words. Believe me, I can live without the accolades." With that he had Cassie bundled into her coat and tucked against his side as they exited the kitchen. He'd left Katie in charge of getting a message to Grace about where he was going. Within minutes he had Cassie in his car and they were heading to her apartment.

He could tell even in the dim light that she was battling between being angry at him for making her leave and true pain from her condition. Whatever she was feeling, however, she was keeping to herself, refusing to look at him.

In fact, she didn't utter a single word until he opened the door that led to the stairs to her apartment. "Thank you for getting me home. Good night." She didn't have enough strength to fight him when she went to shut the door in his face. He merely stepped around her, locked the door, and helped her up the stairs. Cassie wanted to scream at him to leave, but she knew there was no way she could find the energy to do so.

Once up the stairs, Cassie kicked off her shoes as Adam took her coat from her and hung it up. Without looking at him, she walked to her bedroom, grabbed a pair of pajamas, and went into the bathroom to change. Adam kept himself busy in her kitchen making Cassie a cup of tea and wondered what the hell he was supposed to do now. He had no idea how to take care of anyone, and really, he didn't want to know. He had no idea what he could do to help Cassie right now.

She came out of the bathroom in a pair of pink flannel pajama pants and a white tank top. Maybe she'd hoped that he'd be gone by now, but he wasn't, and he wasn't going to leave until he knew she was all right. "I made you some tea," he said feebly.

Cassie stopped and looked at him suspiciously. "Why?"

He shrugged. "It seemed like the thing to do." When she made no attempt to take the mug he'd indicated, he said, "Is there something I can get you? Something to eat? A painkiller? A heating pad?"

Cassie sighed wearily as she headed toward her bedroom. "Actually, yes, the heating pad…it's in the linen closet." Adam found it and followed her into the bedroom, where she curled up in the fetal position on the bed.

He wanted to scold her and tell her how foolish she

was to stay at work when she was clearly in pain, but he knew that while he'd feel better getting in a rant, it wouldn't help Cassie any. Finding an outlet, he plugged in the pad, turned it to high, and then left the room to grab the cup of tea he'd made. Adam gently placed the mug on the table next to her bed and heard a faint "thank you."

Walking around to the opposite side of the bed, he flicked off the lamp and managed to pull the blankets around her with minimal shifting. Next, he picked up the now-warm heating pad, knelt on the bed, reached over her trim form, and placed the pad over her belly. She purred with relief.

Cassie took the pad from him to position it better and finally let herself relax. She was home and in her own bed, and with the help of the heating pad, she would be okay. She snuggled in deeper as Adam pulled the blanket over her ever so gently. His consideration brought tears to her eyes that, if anyone asked, she'd say were from the pain; she most certainly didn't want to cry in front of him.

And yet she couldn't stop herself from turning her head to look at him. "I don't know what to say," she whispered. "I wanted to be mad at you for taking over and making me leave, but now that I'm here, I know it's what I needed." Even with only the light coming through the doorway from the kitchen, she could see that the expression on his face was new.

It wasn't full of anger or arrogance, it was compassionate. It was tender. "Rest, Cassandra."

"But…" Cassie wasn't sure what she was going to say, but she watched Adam walk out the door and felt oddly saddened. It wouldn't be appropriate for him to stay, and yet she knew she didn't want to be alone.

The kitchen went black, and she heard the lock on her door catch. The first tear fell without warning, and Cassie curled a little tighter around the heating pad. Normally she didn't mind being alone when she was in pain like this, but tonight…tonight it would have been nice to have someone stay with her until she fell asleep.

The mattress dipped, and before she could turn, she felt Adam's full length behind her. "What are you…?"

"Shh…rest, Cassandra. Try to sleep. If you need anything, I'll be right here." He placed a strong hand on top of the heating pad and held it close to her so she could relax her own tired grip on it and get more comfortable.

His body was warm against her back as much as the heating pad was against her front. Cassie wiggled slightly and aligned their bodies better until she found she could barely hold her eyes open any longer. She felt secure for the first time in what seemed like forever. "Thank you…"

Her words were barely a whisper, but Adam found that they packed a powerful punch.

Chapter 5

CASSIE SLEPT DEEPLY THROUGH THE NIGHT AND ONLY awoke to remove the heating pad that was getting uncomfortable. As soon as the pad was gone, Adam's hand returned to take its place. The illuminated clock next to the bed told her it was nearing five thirty. Adam was stirring behind her, moving carefully.

Wanting to turn around and thank him once again, she blinked but heard Adam leave the room and go into the bathroom. Maybe it would be better to let this be. It was an awkward situation to be sure, and the more Cassie thought about it, the more she realized she needed to let it settle in her mind before talking to Adam about it, even if that talk would only be to say thank you again.

Adam splashed some cold water on his face to wake himself up. He was due back at the office at nine for breakfast and to start the next session of his corporate retreat. Cassie was due to cater both breakfast and lunch, and he was unsure whether to wake her up or let her sleep. Stepping out of the bathroom, he looked into her room and saw she hadn't moved. Surely her staff could handle the breakfast. He had great confidence that Cassie'd return for the lunch service; he grabbed his shoes and coat and walked quietly to the door.

There was an almost inexplicable pull to return to the bedroom, but Adam thought better of it. This could be the situation he needed to end this working relationship and reclaim his peace. There was a very real possibility that Cassie was going to be embarrassed that he'd stayed the night. If she was uncomfortable enough, maybe she'd want to end their working relationship, and Adam could go about finding a new event planner and caterer who didn't argue with him or speak to him in a way that, even now, had his temper flaring.

Out of the corner of his eye, he saw movement on the bed, and the temper faded. Cassie hadn't done anything *that* bad; Adam did not appreciate people speaking their minds to him and disobeying his wishes, that's all. If he were completely honest with himself, he'd agree that the event had gone perfectly the night before without all his changes and that Cassie had done the job to his needs and expectations. How could he stay angry about that?

Opening the door quietly, he slipped out and walked down the stairs, realizing that he had no answers, and at the bottom nearly collided with Katie.

"Adam! What are you doing here?"

"Your sister was, um…in pretty bad shape. I fell asleep on the couch, you know, in case she needed anything." This was worse than coming in past curfew and getting caught by your parents.

"How is she this morning?"

Adam wished he'd gotten the hell out of here last night. It was bad enough he'd spent the night; he didn't feel like getting the third degree from anyone, especially not a twenty-year-old! "She's still sleeping. I didn't want to wake her." Making his excuses about needing to get home and get ready for this morning's session, Adam got in his car and pulled away from the shop as if his life depended on it.

Last night he was supposed to go home and tweak his speech for today and get a good night's sleep. Instead, he'd slept in a strange bed, fully clothed, while holding a very stiff and miserable Cassie. He'd have to avoid her today, that's all. Blow her off and pretend he hadn't shared her bed.

A quick shower and shave had Adam feeling refreshed. He'd rehearsed his speech during the whole process and was confident in the day to come. The point of this retreat was to energize his staff for the upcoming year. The plan was to branch out into several more countries, and to do that, his staff had to be as excited about the company's new products and services as he was. They needed to understand how he created the systems and how to use them. He planned on doubling his fortune.

He was prepared for the leeches to come out of the woodwork when that happened. Like his father had all those years ago. Adam looked in the mirror and straightened his tie as he frowned at the thought of the man who had deserted him and his mother and then showed up when Adam had first made a name for himself in the business world. The old man had walked away from his wife and ten-year-old son in the hopes of climbing the corporate ladder unhindered. It must have worked because for years, William Lawrence had led a very good, very pampered existence. Unfortunately, like most corporate stooges, he had gotten greedy, made some bad investments, and lost it all. When Adam was twenty-five and made his first million with the LSS 3.0 security system, his father had come calling.

And begging. The man had groveled and begged to

have his family back, claiming he'd been a shell of a man without them and that he'd made a terrible mistake. When both Adam and Bev had hesitated in opening their hearts to him, he'd turned bitter and flat-out asked for money. Adam had kicked him out and made it abundantly clear that he was never to contact them again. Bev had been devastated; Adam had learned that love didn't exist. It was all about the money. Well, he had money—lots of it. He didn't need love.

Sure, his mother loved him, and that relationship was never in doubt, but other than Bev, he didn't have anyone else in his life, and Adam doubted that real love existed out there. Even knowing that Bev was claiming to be in love with Stephen Jacobs, he had his doubts. Maybe they were both lonely and looking for companionship. At least have the guts to call it what it was! As long as Stephen didn't come to him for any loans or investments, Adam approved of the situation.

Wiping the Jacobs family from his mind, Adam strode into the ballroom, which was now set up to serve breakfast. Most of last night's decorations were still set up around the room, but the tables were clear of flowers and candles and now held information packets for the day's seminars.

Spotting Grace, Adam called her over to their table next to the stage and went over last-minute details. Within minutes, employees began to file in. The smell of coffee and pastries filled the air, and although breakfast was going to be done buffet-style, there were still a handful of servers walking around assisting Adam's staff. A quick glance at his watch showed that it was eight forty-five, and he was about to stand and get a plate of food for himself when he saw her.

Cassie.

She was smiling and talking to two of his sales staff, and both men seemed to be enthralled with whatever she was saying. Adam had to stop himself from going over to them, demanding they find their seats, and telling Cassie he wasn't paying her to talk to his people. Even in his head that sounded unreasonable and over the top.

Adam frowned. He never minded thinking himself to be forceful with his people; it was how he had achieved the level of success he had. Somehow, acting like that in front of Cassie seemed mean. His mother's words from their ride home came to him. "*I can't imagine you being so hard on anyone, especially a woman.*" Apparently, his mother didn't know the real Adam.

Waiting until Cassie finished her conversation with her two admirers and walked into the kitchen, Adam quickly made it across the room to grab himself something to eat before he had to begin this morning's session. Back at the table, Grace was already eating.

"I know Cassie doesn't do all the baked goods herself, but she chose a fabulous assortment, don't you think?"

Adam merely grumbled a reply and didn't notice the smug look on his assistant's face. "Everyone is still talking about how wonderful everything was."

Adam still wasn't taking the bait as he finished his cinnamon Danish. "I think it's time to get started." He drank his coffee and headed to the stage. Straightening his folder of paperwork, Adam looked into the crowd and saw her again. Dammit. Why the sight of her flustered him, he wasn't sure. All he knew was that right now he wanted to skip his introduction to his staff and ask how Cassie was feeling.

Not exactly the actions of a man trying to get rid of a woman.

Shaking his head as if to clear it, Adam began, "Good morning. I want to tell you all about my plans for LSS's expansion in the next three years…"

Cassie listened to the man speak and smiled to herself. Here, in this environment, Adam Lawrence was a man in charge. Last night, however, while dealing with a woman in pain, he'd looked anything but confident. She still couldn't believe Adam had actually left his conference and stayed the night to take care of her. That was a side of him she wasn't sure what to do with. The more she saw it, the more attracted she became.

It would have been easy this morning to turn over in his arms and see if he was interested, but the bedhead look was never her strong point. No, it would be better to pick a time when she didn't have morning breath or looked as if she'd had a cat do her hair. True, Adam had never really given off any vibe that he was interested, but that didn't mean anything. He was definitely a man whose focus was on one thing: business. Should she tempt that balance they'd found by testing his interest? Especially if they were going to be related through their parents' marriage?

Walking into the kitchen to check on the progress of the lunch preparations, Cassie scolded herself. Why on earth would she look for more complications where Adam was concerned? Clearly, she'd seen the real him over the past two years; a man did not suddenly change in a little over a week. Besides, it would be awkward with their parents getting married. What if she and Adam did get involved and then things didn't work out?

She'd be stuck seeing him at every holiday and family get-together, and she would cringe at the thought that he'd seen her naked.

By four o'clock, Cassie and her crew were loading their supplies into her van. She did a final review of the kitchen and then headed out to the ballroom, where she ran into Grace.

"Another great job, Cassie," Grace said with a smile as she walked across the room. "Everyone loved the food, and I think between you and Adam you pulled off the perfect event!"

Smiling with pleasure, Cassie didn't want to think of Adam having as much to do with people's pleasure from the weekend. "I'm glad there were no problems. I had my doubts a couple of weeks ago."

"Oh, don't get me started on that. I wanted to choke Adam for the way he behaved." Grace looked around the room to make sure they were alone. "To be honest, I was surprised when he told me you were staying on and doing the event. I mean, he had me calling people that afternoon to try to find a replacement. How did you manage to change his mind?"

Her first reaction was to be annoyed all over again about being fired, but then she remembered it had all worked out in her favor and it didn't do her any good to hold a grudge. Cassie told Grace of their soon-to-be-merging families, and the other woman about doubled over with laughter.

"Oh, what I would have given to be a fly on the wall when the great Adam Lawrence found himself face-to-face with your family! Did they all gang up on him?"

"Pretty much." The memory had Cassie smiling. "It

was a silent attack for most of the evening, but then… Adam and I sat and talked and cleared the air. I'm kind of glad we did."

Grace frowned. "Wait, so you spoke to him and told him you didn't like the way he treated you and…"

"Lauren even told him he was the one in breach of contract…"

"And he still asked you to do the event? That doesn't make sense. That's not like Adam at all."

"Why?"

"I have yet to see, in the six years I've worked here, anyone speak their mind or disagree with Adam and continue on here. It doesn't happen." She pulled an envelope from her purse and handed it to Cassie. "I'd be on guard if I were you. This doesn't seem right."

"Maybe he's mellowing because we're going to be family."

Grace shook her head. "Please…he hardly ever spends time with Bev, and she's the only family he has. No, I'm telling you, Cass, something's not right with this whole situation… Be careful, okay?"

Agreeing but not convinced, Cassie hugged her friend and finished her final inspection of the facility before walking out to her van and driving to the shop. Grace's words bothered her mainly because they made sense.

"So how are you feeling today?" Katie asked as Cassie walked into the kitchen. "Any lingering effects?"

"Thankfully, no, but I have to face the facts. I'm going to call Dr. Jackson first thing Monday morning and make the appointment."

"You're going to have the surgery?"

"I don't see a choice. I've had a flare-up twice in two

weeks, and while I don't mind when it hits at home, having nearly passed out in the kitchen of an event was not an experience I ever want to repeat."

"Adam about freaked out."

"Well, he hates when things don't go his way."

"No, it was more than that," Katie said, her voice soft with contemplation. "It was more like he was concerned about you. It was nice of him to bring you home and stay the night to take care of you."

"He told you about that?"

"I saw him when he was leaving this morning."

"Oh."

Katie started to giggle. "I have to admit, for a minute, I thought he was sneaking out after maybe the two of you…you know…did the deed!"

"*What?* Me and Adam? Are you crazy?"

"Well, that's what it looked like! If I hadn't known you were in such bad shape last night, I would have totally believed that he was doing the walk of shame!"

"Thanks for the vote of confidence." She hated the sarcastic tone in her own voice, but somehow thinking of anyone slinking away in the wee morning hours because they were ashamed to have had sex with her rubbed her the wrong way.

"That's not what I meant, and you know it. Gosh, don't be such a drama queen." Katie turned and finished unloading the van. When everything was put away, she wiped all the kitchen surfaces down and grabbed her coat. "I guess I should get home and relieve Dad and Bev from babysitting. Besides, I miss my girl."

Cassie envied her little sister and knew that someday she wanted a baby of her own. That was another reason to call Dr. Jackson and schedule the surgery. Infertility was a big concern for someone with endometriosis, and now that she was twenty-six, thoughts of getting married and having children were becoming more and more important to her. Her business was thriving, and by the time she did meet Mr. Right, Cassie didn't want any obstacles to keep her from having everything she wanted.

The thought of surgery scared her. Her own mother had died of ovarian cancer, and deep down, Cassie was afraid this surgery, even though it was an outpatient procedure, would have the doctors finding more than she was willing to deal with. So far, ignorance had been bliss, but Cassie was no fool. The pain from the endometriosis was getting worse and couldn't be ignored any longer, and if they did find something, Cassie would rather catch it early. And considering how her mother had died of ovarian cancer, it was important for her to be as proactive as possible where her health was concerned.

She knew it was the responsible thing to do, and she knew that she would feel better both mentally and physically when it was all over. But that didn't mean she still wasn't scared to death.

And there was nobody there to hold her.

Chapter 6

LAUREN WAS BUSY FLUFFING PILLOWS AND MAKING PROMISES of Chinese food as Cassie slowly crossed the room Wednesday afternoon. The laparoscopic procedure had been done that morning because Dr. Jackson had had a cancellation and was anxious to get Cassie in as soon as possible before she could change her mind. As she climbed into the bed, Cassie appreciated her doctor's efficiency; it hadn't given her too much time to dwell on the whole thing, and now that she was home and in her bed, she had to admit she was relieved it was over.

"That was a lot faster than I thought it would be. Dr. Jackson seems pleased that she got everything." Pulling the window blinds closed as she spoke over her shoulder, Lauren continued, "You have to take it easy for a week. Kate's got your weekend event covered, so you can relax."

"By Sunday, I should be fine," Cassie mumbled. Her stomach was sore from the tiny incisions, and the last thing she wanted to think about right now was work.

"Doctor's orders. Don't make me stick around here and lock you in your room."

"Okay, okay, geez…"

"Get some sleep. I'm going to be in the living room studying for a test. If you need me, call out, okay?" Cassie nodded, and her eyes were closed before Lauren had shut the door.

Getting settled on the sofa, Lauren had set up several textbooks in front of her on the coffee table when she heard Cassie's cell phone ring. Not hesitating, she walked over and answered. "Hello?"

"Hey, Cassie, it's Grace."

"Hey, Grace, this is Lauren, Cassie's sister."

"Oh, hi! Is Cassie available?"

"Actually, she is sound asleep. Can I take a message?"

"Is she okay?"

Lauren told her about the surgery, remembering that Grace was Adam's assistant.

"Oh my! Is there anything I can do? Does she need anything?"

"She seems okay right now. We got home a little while ago. The doctor said she should be normal within a week. She's on some serious painkillers for now, but by this time next week, she'll be as good as new. Do you want me to leave her a message?"

"No, no…I was calling to tell her how much everyone enjoyed the event this weekend. She was a hit as usual." Lauren could hear Grace's smile. "Please tell her I'm thinking of her and I'll give her a call in a few days."

"No problem."

"Thanks, Lauren. Bye!"

—◈—

As soon as she hung up the phone, Grace immediately called her florist and arranged for a large bouquet to be sent to Cassie from the company. "That's right, I want the card to say 'Wishing you a speedy recovery,' and sign it from 'Your friends at LSS.'" She paused and listened. "Yes, that's perfect. I'd like them delivered today." Another pause. "Yes, please put it on our account. Thank you!"

She hung up and nearly fell off her chair when she turned and saw Adam leaning on her desk and looking thoroughly annoyed. "Who's ill?"

"What? Oh, Cassie is. She had surgery today, and I wanted to send her some flowers."

"On the company's account?"

Uh-oh.

"Well, um…she does work for us quite a bit, and while I realize I should have checked with you first, I didn't think you would mind. I mean, with Cassie almost family and all, I thought it would be okay. Plus, you were on a call, and I wanted to place the order in time for it to be delivered today. So…"

"You're babbling, Grace."

Darn it, he was right, but she knew that look on his face and that if she didn't distract him and plead her case quickly, he could get nasty. Fast. "I could call and cancel the order if you'd prefer. Or I could change it to put it on my credit card…" Turning her back on him, she picked up the phone and began to dial. Adam reached across the desk, snatched the phone out of her hand, and hung it up.

"That won't be necessary," he snapped. He took a deep breath and had to force himself to speak calmly. "It's a very nice gesture, and I thank you for doing it. Now, if I could get you to find me the Cairo contract, I need to make some amendments." He turned and walked into his office.

———

Once at his desk, he had the urge to pick up the phone and call Cassie to see if she was okay. She hadn't mentioned the surgery, but then again, when would she have had the time? He didn't speak to her at all on Saturday, and that was the last he'd seen of her. Adam looked at his calendar and saw that his schedule was pretty full, but maybe he could find time to stop by her place tomorrow after work. He'd have to call his mother and try to find out if anyone was staying with her; he hated to have to play twenty questions with another family member like he had with Katie on Saturday morning.

To say his mother was surprised when she heard his voice on the phone was an understatement. "Adam! How are you, sweetheart? This is a wonderful surprise!" Adam rolled his eyes.

"I'm fine, Mother, fine. I was calling to…um, see how you were? I realize we left things…well, things were a little awkward when I dropped you off that night after dinner, and I wanted to make sure you were doing okay. How's Stephen?"

"Oh, he's fine, thank you for asking. We've been having a wonderful time. We babysat for Ella last weekend while Katie was working that event that Cassie did for you. We had such a time! I had forgotten how exhausting babies can be, but I loved every second of it!"

Great, pretty soon she'd be hounding him about getting married and having kids. Just what he needed. "Sounds like fun." His words lacked enthusiasm, and he knew he'd hurt her feelings by the way her tone changed.

"Yes, well, anyway, how's business?"

Adam pinched the bridge of his nose, closed his eyes,

and counted to ten. Dammit, it shouldn't be this hard to have a conversation with his own mother! "Business is fine, Mom. The retreat went well, and I think we're going to have another great year ahead of us. Listen, I was wondering…Grace mentioned that Cassie had surgery today. Is everything all right?"

Pleasant Mom was back. "Lauren's with her right now, and the doctor is very pleased with how it went. They found a couple of small cysts and took care of several lesions, but they believe they got everything, and Cassie will be up and around in no time."

"So Lauren's staying with her?"

"Only for tonight. She had to force Cassie to let her stay. We've all offered to go in shifts, but she wouldn't have it. Tomorrow Lauren's got some big test, so Katie and Ella are going to go over for lunch and spend some time with Cassie. Stephen and I were going to go for dinner, but he's got a late meeting."

"So are you going to go alone?"

"No, no…I guess I still feel a little new to all of this, and I don't want to overwhelm her."

Adam was baffled. How could his mother overwhelm anyone? "Why would you say that?"

"I don't want Cassie, or any of the kids for that matter, to think I'm swooping in and trying to be their mom. I know I'm marrying their dad, but this is still new to all of them, and it's been a long time since their mom passed, and I'm sure they're trying to…see what my role is going to be. I want to give them time to get to know me."

This was all a little too emotional for him. "I don't think you have anything to worry about."

Bev sighed. "I'm sure you're right. Anyway, Cassie's going to be fine. She's a little sore, but really we're all concerned she's going to overdo it somehow and hinder her own recovery. She hates to sit still."

"Well, then maybe someone should be with her," he suggested.

"Adam…she is a grown woman. She's well beyond the age of being babysat. For the next twenty-four hours, she'll have people with her, and after that, she's capable of taking care of herself."

He knew his mother was right, but he would make the time to stop over and see Cassie tomorrow night after work. Maybe he'd return the favor and bring her dinner. Just as the thought of flowers entered his head, Adam cut himself off with disgust. "Yeah, sure, she's a trouper."

Why the hell was he thinking of going over to Cassie's? They were done! She had finished the event, and that was all he needed her for. If he never hired her again, she'd have to deal with it.

There would be no harm, however, to see her socially, as if they were family already, right? He'd never had to deal with anyone on a family level other than Bev, and, well, outside of business, he found he actually liked Cassie, so it wouldn't be a hardship to stop by and visit her. Like family.

"Adam? Are you still there?" He realized his mother had been talking the whole time his mind had wandered.

"What? Yes, sorry, I got distracted for a minute. So, what else is new?"

It didn't take a rocket scientist to realize that one simple question had done wonders for his mother. Was he that much of a bastard that he'd never engaged in social niceties or chitchat with his own mother? And why all of a sudden was he?

Ten minutes later, he was off the phone and felt his spirits had lifted a bit. Maybe he had been too deeply entrenched in the business and had forgotten how to relax and talk with people. Like he had at Cassie's that night.

Adam had no idea why he was having this change of heart and then the ensuing tug of war over what he was doing with his life. He was in control of it all, dammit! He could do whatever he wanted, talk to whomever he wanted whenever he wanted! Right now, with the confidence he was legendary for, Adam made the decision that his business association with Cassie was over, which freed him up to see her socially—since she was going to be family.

Grace walked in with the file he'd requested. Adam noted the slight tension in her shoulders ease as if she noticed that he seemed a bit more relaxed. Adam reviewed the contract, made his notes, picked up the phone, and went on with his day.

By three o'clock on Thursday afternoon, Adam was ahead of schedule. His calls were completed, and Grace had typed up everything he'd asked her to. To pass the time, he straightened his desk and made a list of possible new clients he'd like to make contact with by the end of the month.

Throwing his pen down in disgust, he knew what he was doing: busy work. God, he was feeling pathetic. Did he purposefully do work at home the night before to lighten his load today? Maybe. Did he deliberately cut a couple of chatty clients short in hopes of getting done quicker? Perhaps. The truth was he was feeling caged in his office and wanted to leave.

He paced. He talked to himself. He picked up the phone a half-dozen times and realized there was no one he needed to call. By four o'clock, he gave up the pretense of trying to work and gave himself a pep talk.

"I'm not leaving because of Cassie," he said out loud, "I'm leaving because I want to. I own the damn company, and I can leave whenever I want to!" Picking up his briefcase and keys, Adam strode across the office and yanked open his door. Grace looked up and he gave her a searing look that almost dared her to question what he was doing.

"Have a nice night," she said cheerily, unwilling to engage in a discussion over the fact that in six years the man had never left the office before seven.

Adam gave her a curt nod as he walked past her desk and to the elevator. He didn't notice the shocked looks of his employees as he strode with purpose. He didn't notice the people who merely stepped aside and let him pass. By the time the doors on the elevator closed and he was safely inside, Adam found himself to be feeling something he hadn't in a very long time.

Nervous.

Why on earth should I be nervous? he thought to himself. He was stopping by to see a friend. A family friend. A family friend who happened to be an attractive woman.

Adam loosened his tie as he stepped off the elevator and made his way out to the parking garage and his car. He hadn't felt this nervous or ridiculous since he was a teen.

He pulled up in front of one of his favorite Italian restaurants and went in to place his order. Making small talk with the manager, he bided his time, trying not to be obvious by checking his watch often.

Figuring Cassie may still be on pain medication, Adam bypassed the liquor store and opted for something a little less traditional that he thought would cheer her up.

Pulling into the parking lot, he figured she'd be by herself and then felt bad that he'd be making her walk down the stairs to open the door. "Dammit," he grumbled as he pulled dinner out of the car and walked to the door. He hit the doorbell and waited.

He hadn't noticed the intercom before, but suddenly he heard Cassie's voice. "Hello?"

"Um…hello, Cassandra, it's Adam. Can I come up?" She didn't answer right away, and he had a brief moment of uncertainty and fear that she'd send him away. A solid minute passed that had him feeling more and more foolish for coming.

A buzzer sounded, and Adam heard the lock click. "It's a friendly dinner," he mumbled to himself as he climbed the stairs. "No big deal."

Cassie met him at the top of the stairs wearing a similar ensemble to what she'd worn Saturday night: flannel pajama pants, this time in red, with a dark-red tank top. "Adam, this is a surprise." The words were out before she fully saw him, and then the items in his hands caught her attention. "Pizza? You brought me pizza?" Her smile widened to pure delight as she stepped aside and let him in.

"I figured I owed you a meal since you sent me home with leftovers last time. I hope you like pepperoni." Placing the pizza on the table, he then placed a bag in the freezer.

"What was that?"

He gave her a wicked smile. "Milk shakes. Chocolate milk shakes."

Cassie's smile lit up the room, and in that moment Adam understood what the Grinch must have felt on that fateful Christmas morning when his heart grew three sizes. "Wow! This is quite a treat! You came at the perfect time. I was trying to decide what to have for dinner, and I didn't want to cook. You are my hero."

At that moment, Adam truly believed her. Most women would say that to get something from him, but he was finding out bit by bit that Cassie wasn't like any woman he'd ever met before. The occasional women he'd dated casually would never have been happy with pizza and milk shakes; they'd want lobster and champagne. This was definitely new territory for him, and as he shed his jacket and tie, Adam realized he liked it.

Cassie was getting plates and napkins and carrying them into the living room. "What are you doing?" Adam asked, clearly confused that she wasn't setting the kitchen table.

"I thought we'd eat over here. Katie downloaded a couple of movies for me, and we could watch one while we eat. Is that okay?"

Probably a chick flick, he thought. "Um…sure. I'm right behind you with the pizza."

"Don't forget the milk shakes…"

Adam chuckled, grabbed the bag from the freezer, and walked into the living room. Opening the pizza box, he was about to take a slice, waiting for the girly music to start, when he looked up and saw Robert DeNiro's name on the screen. "DeNiro?"

"Oh, it's *Midnight Run*. Robert DeNiro, Charles Grodin? It's one of my favorites."

Placing a slice of pizza on Cassie's plate, he turned,

pulled the milk shakes out of the bag, put a straw in each of them, and handed one to Cassie. This woman was becoming more and more intriguing by the minute. She was sitting cross-legged on the couch, a plate of pizza in her lap, her milk shake on the floor in front of her. The mass of chestnut hair was wavier than he'd ever seen it, and she didn't have on a scrap of makeup, yet she looked more appealing than he'd ever seen her.

Taking a bite of his dinner, Adam turned his attention to the movie and away from the woman, and he waited a full five minutes before he spoke and asked how she was feeling.

"Much better today, thanks." She took a sip of her milk shake. "Oh, that is perfect," she purred. "I'm actually much sorer than I was yesterday, but that's to be expected. Katie was here all day and took care of me. This is way better than being mothered."

"Mothered?"

"You know, fussing about, fluffing pillows, asking if I need anything… It was sweet of her, and I appreciate every minute of her time, but I didn't have a limb amputated or anything. She had Ella with her, and I loved getting to spend time with them, but by the time they left, I was more exhausted than relaxed."

Adam chuckled. "Well, you have my promise not to fluff pillows or to fuss."

Cassie let out a laugh of her own. "Thanks."

They resumed watching the movie with minimal conversation and shared laughs. It was the most pleasant time she'd had in a long time. By the time the credits rolled, Cassie had eaten way more pizza than she should have and had polished off the milk shake. Her head rested on the couch, and she felt completely relaxed. With a sigh of contentment, she turned toward Adam. "At the risk of being redundant, thank you."

He turned and smiled. "And at the risk of answering with redundancy, you are welcome." They sat like that for long moments, smiling. Adam started to feel a pull toward her and knew that he had to do or say something to break the hypnotic spell. "You know, I'm still hearing buzz from people about the food at the retreat. Everything was a big hit." It was on the tip of his tongue to say that she was right about not changing the menu choices, but he wasn't ready for that kind of admission.

"I'm so glad. How did the training go? Are you getting the feedback you want from it?" *Another first*, Adam thought. No woman besides his mother ever asked about his business with any interest, and the look on Cassie's face as she spoke told him she was truly interested.

"Well, I've had a couple of smaller meetings with a select group of programmers and salesmen. I have some executives from three smaller companies in Europe coming over in a few weeks to talk about having LSS rebuild their computer systems."

"Wow, that's impressive. So you'll be entertaining them at the office?"

"That's the plan. I was thinking of moving the meetings off-site since their spouses are coming, but I couldn't think of anything to do that would include everyone and yet give us the uninterrupted time I'd like to have."

Cassie nodded with understanding. "You mean maybe like an actual *retreat* type of environment?" It was Adam's turn to nod. "Well, if I could make a suggestion…"

At any other time, Adam would have resented her insinuating herself into his business, but he was relaxed and genuinely curious about what she could come up with.

"If you want an environment where the spouses could be included and you'd have time to get to know them without interruptions, I would suggest a house either in the mountains or at the beach." She stopped and studied Adam for a moment. "I'm betting that you at least have a beach house, am I right?"

He nodded. "Indeed you are. Now tell me why I want to take them to the beach?"

"For starters, it's more personal. It shows that you are interested in them on more than a business level, and you won't have all the distractions of being in your own office. Since they're business executives, they've seen offices. Plus, their spouses will be bored hanging out at a hotel in Raleigh all day.

"At the beach, you're all in the house together, you have the great scenery, and the spouses can go shopping or enjoy the water while the execs are inside talking business. You can bring in a maid and a cook, and no one has to worry about anything."

Standing, Cassie went to the kitchen to get something to drink and asked Adam if he wanted anything. When he declined, she grabbed some water and returned to the couch. "You could book spa treatments or have a car pick the spouses up and take them shopping… I'm telling you, you'd come across as the best guy to do business with."

"At least from the spousal point of view," he quipped with a smile. "Actually, it's a great idea." It almost pained him to admit it while at the same time his mind was spinning with possibilities. It all seemed so simple that he couldn't believe he hadn't thought of it himself! "They could fly to Raleigh on Thursday, tour the offices, and meet with our people, and then I could have a car drive them to the beach on Friday where lunch would be waiting. We would have the afternoon to get settled in and relax, talk a little business, have dinner together, and start with negotiations on Saturday morning after breakfast while the spouses do their thing. Interesting, Cassandra. It has possibilities."

That made her smile. "I am known to have a good idea or two." She wanted to ask Adam to hire her to do the job, to hire her to be at the beach house to do all the cooking and planning and whatnot, but she knew that the request would be way out of line, and that if she'd learned anything about Adam, it was that the idea had to be his or he didn't like it.

Well, except for this beach idea. He seemed to take well to that, and she didn't want to push her luck. Right now, Cassie didn't want to do or say anything that was going to put an end to the relationship they seemed to be building. It felt good to be here with him. It was comfortable, and if she wasn't recovering from that damn surgery, she'd probably be playing at seduction right now. But knowing that she was no raving beauty on her best days, there was no way a man like Adam would find her attractive in her pajamas with bed hair and no makeup.

Again.

Well, wasn't that a bucket of cold water in the face? *Okay, back to reality*, she told herself and sighed. "With the right amount of planning, you'd be a big hit. After all, if the spouses or significant others are happy…well, you would witness the trickle-down effect."

Adam nodded. She was intelligent and considerate, and even without makeup she was stunning. Leaning in a bit closer and lowering his voice a notch, he asked, "Know anyone who would be willing to take on such a task?"

The corners of Cassie's lips twitched with the urge to smile, but she kept her response low-key. "Well, I'm sure you could call some temp agency for someone familiar with the area who would be willing to come in and cook and clean for a few days. You could get references…"

She almost had him, but he noticed the twitch and decided to play along. "True, true…I mean, how hard could it be to cook a couple meals for seven people? I'm sure they have temps for that sort of easy work." There was no way he could look at her as he finished the statement. Adam was sure she was seething at the direct jibe at her livelihood.

And she was. Mildly. She stood and began cleaning up their dinner mess. "I suppose," she began. "I guess you could take them out for every meal, you know, to play it safe and make sure no one gets food poisoning. Or you could take your chances and hope that your European guests like casseroles and chicken pot pie…" She left that thought hanging as she walked into the kitchen. The smile tugging at her lips couldn't be helped; this teasing and bantering with Adam was making her feel light and happy. After placing her water glass in the sink, Cassie nearly screeched when she turned around and found Adam directly behind her.

He placed his hands on the counter on either side

of her, effectively caging her in and keeping her close. "You sound like a bit of a food snob, Cassandra. I never knew that about you." Adam looked into her face and saw, for the first time, how blue her eyes were. He scanned her face and noticed the freckles, faint though they were, that were scattered across the bridge of her nose, and how long her lashes were without the help of mascara. All in all she made a very fetching picture.

"Who's to say that they don't enjoy a good casserole?" His tone was deep and husky, and Cassie felt his breath on her face and found herself focusing on his mouth.

She swayed slightly and closed her eyes to break the spell but found that she enjoyed looking at him way too much. Clearing her throat, she said, "I guess that's always a possibility."

After that, they moved as if of one mind toward one another. When Adam's lips touched Cassie's, all thought of food and Europeans drained from her mind. She was still caged in close against his body, and she slowly lifted her arms to twine them around Adam's neck and pull him closer. In turn, Adam took his hands from the countertop and first placed them on her waist and then let them travel slowly up and down her spine.

When his tongue reached out and touched Cassie's bottom lip, she tilted her head and gave him entry, her tongue dueling with his in an erotic dance that had her straining against him. For a mouth that always seemed so hard and firm, his was quite soft and thrilling, Cassie thought, as Adam began to work his way from her mouth to her cheek to her throat.

His hands came up and cupped her face and then

moved into her hair and lightly gripped. In turn, Cassie mimicked the move as she purred with satisfaction. Adam leaned into her, his hardness to her softness, and she let out a gasp that wasn't of pleasure but of pain. He backed off immediately.

"Are you all right?"

Placing her hand on her stomach, she merely nodded and took a deep breath. "I managed to forget that I had surgery yesterday." Her voice was laced with pain, and in that instant, Adam felt like the world's biggest heel.

Placing an arm around her waist, he guided Cassie to the sofa and helped her sit down. With a sense of needing to fix what he'd done, he strode to the kitchen, fetched her another glass of water, and found her pain medication next to the sink.

They communicated without words. Handing Cassie the prescription bottle and drink, Adam went in search of the heating pad she'd used the last time he was here. Within minutes he had her settled and comfortable while he felt anything but. "Should I call anyone? Your sisters? Your dad?"

Cassie shook her head. "Really, I'm fine. It was kind of amazing that I hadn't had a whole lot of pain tonight, so I guess I was due." She tried to smile but failed. The pain was ebbing but not completely gone. "Thank you for helping me out, Adam. I appreciate it."

When she looked at him, he was no longer the sexy man who had been in her kitchen but the hard CEO she normally worked with. The transformation was swift, and Cassie had known Adam long enough to know that he was not pleased with the situation. "I'm sorry that you had to take care of me. Again."

He could only stare. She had scared the life out of him, again, made him lose his own head, again, and she was apologizing! "Damn it, Cassandra, I'm the one who's sorry. I knew that you had surgery, and there I was nearly attacking you in your kitchen!" Adam raked a hand through his hair in frustration and started to pace. "Is there anything else I can get you?"

The tone of his voice wasn't quite as clipped as it had been moments before, and Cassie could tell by the look on his face that while he wasn't pleased, it had nothing to do with anger and everything to do with concern. She wanted to smile at the thought, but the pain was still too intense to ignore.

"No, I'll be fine in a little while. The doctor told me that I'd feel pretty bad for a couple days but that by next week I'd be back to my old self." Adam didn't look convinced. "Actually, I think I've had all the excitement I can take for one day, so if you don't mind, I think it's time for me to go to bed."

Brows furrowed, Adam stepped forward and helped Cassie get up; as he had earlier, he placed his arm around her and walked her to her room, where he said good night.

"Thank you again for dinner, Adam. It was a very nice surprise." Her tone was soft, almost sleepy. As Cassie watched him standing next to her bed, her mind immediately played back their kiss and the night he'd spent with her when she'd been in pain the previous weekend. She was sorely tempted to ask him to do the same for her again right now, but Adam took a step away.

—∿∿—

"Dinner was my pleasure. Get some rest, Cassandra, and thank you for the input on my upcoming meetings. I'm going to explore that option." For a man who was normally so confident in everything he did, Adam was unsure what his next move should be. Did he dare kiss her good night the way he longed to do, or would it be best to go?

Seeing Cassie wince as she moved around her room gave Adam his answer. "Good night," he said firmly. "Get some rest." With that he was gone.

Once Adam had left Cassie's apartment and was in his car, he simply sat. What exactly was he doing? This was a relationship that was supposed to be at an end, and yet here he was starting a new aspect to it. It made no sense! And to a man who made sure that he always made sense, it was maddening!

As he drove into the night, his mind raced. Sure, the whole "parents getting married" thing prolonged the relationship that he and Cassie had, but he'd intended their working relationship to be over. So why was he considering hiring her to handle a beach house retreat?

In business, Adam was not known to change his mind; when he made a decision about someone or something, he stuck to it. Why wasn't that the case with Cassie?

With a low growl of frustration, both with himself and, on some level, with Cassie, Adam didn't relax until his home came into view—a large home that, in this frame of mind, seemed ridiculously large for one man.

He thought about the Jacobs family home and realized that he could fit at least four of it in this house with room to spare; at one time, they had had six people living there. Slamming the car door, Adam strode toward the house, calling himself every kind of idiot because no matter what he seemed to do lately, it had him thinking about his soon-to-be family.

Family had never meant much to him; his father had seen to that. Deep down, Adam knew that he would never be able to forgive his mother for being weak with his father. The man had been nothing but a loser looking for an easy ride at Adam's expense. Couldn't Bev see that love and relationships were not to be trusted? No one truly loved anyone. It was all an illusion. If only his mother could learn to be satisfied with being…alone? No, that term did not sit well. Independent? Yes, that sounded better. Why did she need to tie herself down with someone when everyone knew it was going to end—and end badly?

The frustration wasn't ebbing; if anything, Adam felt ready to explode. Tossing his keys down on the nearest surface, he sprinted up the curved staircase to his suite on the second floor, changed into a pair of swim trunks, and then dashed downstairs to the indoor pool. With any luck, he could burn off some of this tension and energy and be able to sleep tonight.

And not dream about the woman he'd kissed earlier or about how it would be to hold her again all night long.

Chapter 7

Adam had arrived at the office before dawn on Friday in hopes of getting things done without his mind wandering to how Cassie was doing. By the time Grace arrived at eight, Adam knew that the day was going nowhere. He was caught up on every project that he had going, and the only thing that needed his attention was the retreat he had spoken to Cassie about. Within an hour, Adam had concluded that the idea would work; he packed up his briefcase and strode to the outer office where Grace sat.

"Going somewhere?" she asked.

"I'll be gone for the weekend. Call the cleaning service we use on the Outer Banks. I need someone to open up the house immediately."

Grace could not hide the look of stupefaction on her face. "Immediately? As in right now?"

"Is that a problem?"

"No, no, of course not. I didn't realize that you… um…it wasn't on your schedule." She fumbled through her Rolodex as she spoke, feeling as if she were all thumbs.

Adam had to stifle a chuckle. It took a lot to unnerve Grace, and clearly the thought of him taking an unscheduled trip to the beach did it. "Ask them to purchase some basic supplies for me as well. Milk, eggs, that sort of thing."

Grace merely nodded as she began to dial the number. "Will you be in on Monday?"

"I believe so, but that could change. I'm thinking of holding a retreat there in a couple of weeks."

The phone slid from her shoulder, and she fumbled to catch it and put it right. Holding up a finger for him to wait, Grace spoke to the agency and made the arrangements Adam had requested. When she hung up, she faced him full-on and asked what was going on.

"This deal is very important to the company, Grace, and I thought I'd try something new. Something that will include the spouses. Why? Do you think it's a bad idea?"

"No, actually, it's a brilliant idea. I can call around and find you an agency to handle the cooking and cleaning and that sort of thing if you'd like. I'm sure the team on their way could help and—"

"That won't be necessary," he interrupted. "I've already made arrangements. Have a good weekend, Grace." The look on her face was nearly comical as he walked away.

Adam threw his briefcase into the car and sped toward his house to pack, and within an hour he was on his way. Pulling into the parking lot of Cassie's shop, he hopped out and knocked on the door.

"Adam?" she said as she pulled open the door. Wearing yoga pants and a T-shirt, Cassie fidgeted with her ponytail as she stood there ogling Adam in his faded blue jeans and sweater. He looked completely relaxed and excited about something. "Wow, twice in one week," she said with a smile. "Come in."

Adam walked through the door and into the kitchen

and waited for her to close the door. "How are you feeling?"

"Much better, thanks. I'm getting a little antsy to return to work, but Katie has our event for this weekend covered, so I promised I'd behave and stay out of the way." She fidgeted some more with her shirt before adding, "It's about killing me."

"I can relate to that." He smiled and felt it broaden as Cassie smiled back. "Actually, I think I can help."

"Really?"

"I'm taking your advice, and I'm going to host that retreat at my place on the Outer Banks. I'm on my way there now for the weekend and thought you might want to come along with me."

"Um…"

Adam walked toward Cassie and fought the urge to take her hands in his. He could tell that her mind was racing with all kinds of questions—he was good at reading people—and knew that he should explain himself.

"This was your brainchild, so I thought maybe you could come with me and help me plan it all out. Plus, the beach is a great place to recuperate, and you'll be able to relax and not be tempted by your kitchen. What do you say?"

"Oh…I don't know, Adam. I mean—"

"There's nothing to know," he said smoothly, ready to cut down all her objections. "This was your creative idea, and I would appreciate your help."

He was being vague, Cassie thought. Was he going to pick her brain for the weekend and then hire somebody else? She wanted to stamp her foot and demand to know but decided to be casual and act as if it didn't matter.

"Well," she began, "I guess it would be nice to get out of here for a few days."

"Good girl."

"I'll need about fifteen minutes to pack and get ready." Cassie turned and headed for the stairs to her apartment, not waiting to see if Adam would follow. She knew he would. Once upstairs, she made a beeline for her bedroom, pulled a small suitcase from her closet, and began filling it with clothes. In minutes she was done. Pulling up the handle, she rolled the suitcase to the door and then turned to grab a sweatshirt to wear for the ride. "I'm all ready," she said as she walked around and made sure that windows were locked and lights were turned off. "I'll call Kate from the road and let her know where I'll be."

With disbelief, Adam looked at his watch. Only ten minutes had passed. "Are you sure you have everything?" He stared at her lone piece of luggage and then looked at Cassie, one dark eyebrow arched.

"Sure. It's only a weekend. I'm guessing we'll be home sometime on Sunday, right?" Adam nodded. "Then I've got all I need."

They each reached for her suitcase at the same time, their hands grazing. Cassie pulled back, but not before she felt the heat of his touch, looked up, and met his dark gaze. "I'll get that," he said, his tone deep and rich, like velvet brushing her skin. Their faces were mere inches apart, and Cassie almost gave in to the need to lean into him and kiss him again.

Instead, reason returned, and she stepped aside for him to precede her down the stairs and joined him in the car.

The conversation flowed effortlessly during the three-hour drive, with Adam asking how she envisioned the retreat. She was an intelligent businesswoman, he already knew that, but it was the way she passionately spoke about her work and her vision that intrigued him.

While Cassie was definitely career-oriented and seemed to have big plans for the expansion of her business, she came off as warm and engaging. Her ideas sparked his own imagination, and she had a way of talking that wrapped around him and made it easy to visualize whatever she was saying. Her only flaw was that one brief meeting in his office.

He shrugged that thought aside, enjoying himself too much to let it get him down. Maybe she'd had a bad day. Hell, he had them occasionally. For this weekend, however, that lone meeting, the only blemish on her impeccable record, was going to be forgotten. Adam had big plans for this weekend, and only some of them were business-related.

"So I'm thinking that, weather permitting, you can make the deck a fabulous dining venue. We can add twinkly lights and rent some extra tables and chairs, use some real linen table coverings…you know, move what's inside to the outside so your guests can enjoy the sounds and smells of the ocean. What do you think?"

In that moment, Adam realized she had been talking the whole time he'd been thinking. Cassie had not even seen his house, and yet she was already making plans as if she'd been there, and what she had planned, from the little he'd heard, sounded lovely.

"I don't think we'll have to rent too much—after all, there'll only be eight of us."

Cassie did the math in her head, and she knew it was three couples and Adam. She was wondering who that eighth person was going to be. "Okay, that makes things a little easier and more intimate. You can do a large table for eight so that everyone is not crammed together and it can still be covered in linen. We'll do seat covers so the guests won't feel like they're sitting on folding chairs. We can decorate the table with tea lights and larger candles and pull together a centerpiece themed with seashells and sand... Oh, it's going to look lovely."

Adam's head snapped toward hers at the use of the word *lovely*, a word he'd used in his mind earlier. Cassie was describing everything that he'd had in his mind for this weekend without him prompting her in any way. Grace was the only other person who thought like him, and even that had taken time. She had worked for Adam for more than a year before she finally stopped asking him how he liked things and simply presented what he liked.

"What about the menu? What are your plans for that?"

Cassie glanced at him out of the corner of her eye and with a wicked grin on her face. "I thought you'd never ask." She rubbed her hands together.

"Okay, you said that they would arrive on Friday for lunch, right?" He nodded. "So you'll want to greet them with something light to eat, some cocktails. We can do some salads and sandwiches, and perhaps some fresh fruit.

"For dinner, we'll keep it casual. After all, they'll have been on the road for several hours after traveling the previous days, so we don't want to command a formal environment that will have everyone fussing about getting ready. We can grill some steaks, get some fresh lobster… I do a fabulous seafood bar."

She stopped and thought some more. "We'll have grilled vegetables, a field greens salad, and lots of wine, fresh-baked bread…" Cassie turned and looked at Adam, whose face looked grim. "Uh-oh," she mumbled. "You don't like any of that, do you?"

On the contrary, she'd nailed it again.

"No, no, what you've outlined sounds wonderful."

"Are you sure? Because you look pretty intense. Did you have something else in mind?"

Yes, telling you that you got it all wrong! he thought to himself. "Actually, you described the perfect meal." Adam stopped and inhaled, releasing it slowly. "What about dessert?"

"Well, in staying with a more casual mode, I think a variety of desserts would be preferable. Something light and fun…finger foods, that sort of thing."

He frowned. "Such as?"

"Oh, assorted cookies, gourmet chocolates, and fresh fruit again, maybe some chocolate-covered strawberries, and cupcakes."

"Cupcakes? Seriously?"

"Cupcakes are all the rage right now."

That disbelieving look returned, and Cassie was beginning to find it endearing. "It's true. Cupcakes are a big thing. They are taking the place of wedding cakes. You can decorate them any way you like, and they are easier to serve."

"But you still have to eat it with your hands," he said with disgust.

"So? You'll be eating the fruit and cookies with your hands—"

"It's a…looking professional thing. You cannot possibly look like an intelligent or articulate person while eating a cupcake."

Cassie refused to argue further. She knew when to drop a cause. "Okay, fine, no cupcakes. How about the rest of it? Does it sound okay?"

Adam nodded, and when Cassie turned forward in her seat, she saw that they were pulling into a long winding driveway. She sat up a little straighter, not wanting to miss a thing. Adam had forgotten how long it had been since he'd been here. Now, pulling into the drive, knowing that he had Cassie to himself all weekend had Adam feeling none of the tension from moments before but pure anticipation.

Cassie gasped when the sprawling house came into view, overlooking a cliff. "Is that the ocean, like, right there?" She cringed at her own words. What else would it be?

"Yes, that's the Atlantic, and the sunrise on it is spectacular." Adam drove the car around to the front of the house, pulled down his visor, and hit a remote button that opened one of the garage doors. There were multiple levels to the house, and between Cassie being in recovery mode and their luggage, it would be easier to use the elevator.

When Adam told Cassie as much, she merely gaped at him. "An elevator? You have an elevator?"

"Of course." He found her naïveté to be adorable and watched her like she was a kid in a candy store as they waited for the elevator to open.

———

Cassie was practically bouncing on her toes in excitement to get up and into the house. From the outside, it was magnificent; she was sure her opinion would not change once she saw the inside.

As the elevator doors slid open on the main floor, her jaw dropped. They walked out into the living area, and Cassie stopped and turned in a full circle to take it all in. Whoever Adam had hired to decorate was a genius. There were light-oak hardwood floors polished to a high-gloss finish. In the different seating areas, plush area rugs were used to define the spaces. The walls were painted in tones of golds and yellows, and everything was so open.

Forcing herself to move, Cassie was immediately drawn to the large kitchen area. She lovingly ran her hands along the granite countertops, marveled at the stainless-steel appliances, and had to hold in a near-orgasmic groan. This kitchen was her dream. It had two refrigerators and an eight-burner stove, and she knew that cooking here for Adam's clients would not be a hardship of any kind.

She was pulling open cabinets and inspecting the restaurant-quality cookware when she finally took notice of the ceramic tile under her feet. Cleanup would be a breeze, too, she thought.

———

All the while Cassie was lost in her own world, Adam observed her. The grin that was slowly creeping across his face couldn't be contained.

It took a moment for Adam to realize that Cassie was talking to herself. "I can fit appetizer platters in here and use the one over there for the steaks to marinate in before grilling… I'll keep all the fresh vegetables and salad ingredients in this one…" She cut herself off and went to a cabinet that contained several pots and pans. "I won't have to bring my skillet… I wonder what's in the pantry…"

With a soft chuckle, Adam left her to her explorations, grabbed their luggage, and climbed the stairs that let up to the second floor, where he considered which bedroom to give Cassie. Most of the bedrooms had incredible views of the ocean as well as their own bathrooms and French doors that led out to the deck, but if he were honest with himself, Adam wanted to have Cassie up on the top floor with him in the master suite.

He was a bastard to consider that for this weekend, as Cassie was still technically recovering from surgery. Still, a man could hope. Choosing a corner bedroom— one of the largest—Adam placed Cassie's suitcase on the bed and opened the doors to the deck to air the room out. Glancing around, he noted that the room would suit her with its cream walls and ivory bedding. The furniture in this house was masterfully crafted, and the mahogany four-poster king bed fit here perfectly.

Adam allowed himself a brief moment to think of Cassie alone in the giant bed before turning on his heel and walking out of the room and up the last flight of stairs to his suite. Taking up the entire top floor, the room was magnificent. The deck was private, there were windows spanning the entire back wall, and the bathroom was a spa dream. A vision of Cassie in the marble tub came to mind, but Adam quickly swept it away.

This weekend was about seduction, no doubt, but not one he was going to act on quite yet. Anticipation was only part of the whole scenario. By the time they were in Raleigh Sunday night, he would know for sure if Cassie were willing to be with him, on his terms, and then maybe, maybe, he'd be on his way to having her out of his system.

Placing his own suitcase in the closet, Adam strode from the room and headed to the kitchen. At the bottom of the stairs, he noticed that Cassie was no longer in the kitchen but found her on the multilevel deck. She was still talking to herself, and Adam wondered if she was aware of the habit.

"If we use these two tables together with the right linens, no one will notice that it's not one table…add some torches and twinkly lights…floating candles in the pool…" She turned and noticed Adam standing in the doorway to the kitchen and smiling.

She liked to see him smile. He didn't do it often enough.

"This is spectacular, Adam." She briefly outlined her plans and hoped that he would be pleased. "What do you think?" Cassie looked at him anxiously. He'd been silent the whole time, and while Adam was known for many things, keeping quiet wasn't one of them. She nervously chewed her bottom lip and waited.

He knew that she was waiting for high praise and that she wanted him to be as excited about the plans as she was. "I think it sounds wonderful, Cassandra. You've truly outdone yourself." She positively beamed. "I do have one suggestion…"

Of course he did, she begrudgingly thought to herself.

"I want to hire a server. This is all too much for one

person. I think you are competent to handle the prep work and presentation, but for the larger meals, I'd like you to have help." He paused for a moment, choosing his words carefully. "Besides, you will be acting as hostess for the weekend, so…"

"Hostess?"

He nodded. "For something like what you're describing, I think it's only fitting that you act as our hostess. I'm sure you'll make everyone feel more comfortable if you interact with them and not serve them."

Cassie considered what he was saying, though she was conflicted. She knew how to be the caterer, the server, the event planner. She was used to dealing with gatherings of any size but going unseen. What Adam was suggesting would put her smack-dab in the middle of the action in a more personal role, and Cassie wasn't sure if she could do that comfortably.

"Do you have a problem with that?" Adam finally asked after watching the play of emotions on Cassie's face.

"I'm not used to being seen at events," she said slowly. "I mean, I'm used to having staff that interacts with the guests while I supervise… I'd feel a little self-conscious sitting down to dinner with your clients—"

"You'll be fine. You'll have a server to help you."

"I guess I can bring one of my girls—"

"No. We'll hire someone from here since it will only be for two meals, tops. There's no need to pay one of your staff for a full weekend when the server will only be needed for a few hours."

While she agreed, Cassie was not comfortable working with someone she'd never met before. As if reading her mind, Adam said, "Tomorrow we'll contact a local agency, and maybe we can interview someone before we leave."

He hadn't said the words that she was hired, and considering their history, she needed to hear him say that. "So you are agreeing with my plan and therefore hiring me to cater this event. Do I have that right?" Her grin was cocky, and while he wanted to be annoyed with…well, he wasn't sure what; he just knew that he should be annoyed.

"Yes, Cassandra. I approve of your plans, and I wouldn't dare imagine someone else carrying them out. You are hired."

She did a little happy dance in place and was tempted to hug Adam and thank him, but she refrained. This was business, and even though they had kissed and clearly there was an attraction between them, she had to remain professional when dealing with the business end of their relationship.

"You won't be sorry, Adam."

"I never thought I would be."

But actually, Adam had a feeling that he was going to end up being sorry for pursuing this relationship. While he was okay with having a brief affair and moving on, it was going to be awkward for that to happen with their combined families. He'd never had to be involved in any capacity with former lovers once the relationship ended, and this was going to be new territory.

And he was sure that there were going to be a lot of people with a lot to say when things ended.

Watching Cassie explore the house further, Adam was pretty sure that he didn't give a damn what anyone had to say. He had to have her, and he wouldn't be satisfied until he did.

Chapter 8

SATURDAY MORNING'S SUNRISE WAS SPECTACULAR, AS ADAM had assured her it would be. Cassie thought she'd sleep in, but the wide windows in her room and the thought of seeing the sunrise had her up with it.

The previous night had been so pleasant and relaxing that Cassie felt as if she'd stepped into another dimension. Not wanting her to exert herself, Adam had herded Cassie to the car, and they'd driven into town for a scrumptious seafood dinner right on the water. The restaurant was nothing spectacular to look at, but the food had been amazing.

They'd spoken with their waitress and the owner of the restaurant about the best places to get fresh food and rent party supplies. When the manager had left, their waitress, Debbie, had slipped them her information and told them that she was always looking for extra work and would love to help them out if they needed a server. Considering that she'd taken excellent care of them throughout their meal, they agreed to call her.

After dinner, Adam drove them through town, pointing out spots of interest, and then they went back to the house where he led Cassie to the sand to walk in the moonlight along the beach. It was hard to believe that they'd known each other for more than two years yet they knew so little about one another.

By the time they'd gotten home, Cassie was exhausted.

She knew she'd overdone it with all the walking, and her body was protesting a little bit. Wishing Adam a good night and thanking him for dinner, she went up the stairs to her luxurious bedroom and indulged in a little bathroom spa time to relax her sore and tired body.

Adam had sat out on the deck listening to the sounds of the waves crashing on the shore for a long time while he drank a snifter of brandy. The night had been most pleasant, and no one was more surprised than him.

Their conversations ran from light and carefree to debates on current events. She made him laugh, she made him think, and she made him hard. He took a drink and looked at the windows of her room. If he were less of a gentleman, he'd be up there right now and to hell with recoveries and consequences. He didn't want to be alone; he wanted to be with her.

Staring intently, Adam saw her shadow go from the bathroom to the bedroom, and he held his breath for a moment until the lights went out. She would be stretching out across the king-size bed. Alone. He wanted to be with her. He wanted to see if she needed anything.

Mainly, him.

Adam continued to stare until his eyes hurt, and then he returned his attention to the shore. He couldn't will her to come back out, and he shouldn't want her to. He'd promised her a weekend away to recuperate, and she'd done everything but relax since they'd arrived. Tomorrow he'd make sure that she didn't tax herself as much. They'd explore around town some more and shop for a dinner to make at home so Cassie could familiarize herself with the kitchen space.

Finishing his brandy, Adam rose, stretched, and

headed inside. Closing the door firmly behind him, he headed up to his own room and, not for the first time in several weeks, found that being alone wasn't all it was cracked up to be.

They met in the kitchen at eight; it wasn't a planned thing, but it worked out that way. Cassie rummaged through the pantry, found the makings for pancakes, and went to work without being asked. Within thirty minutes, they were seated at the breakfast bar, sipping coffee and enjoying pancakes with warm maple syrup. Cassie looked longingly outside and would have preferred to eat out on the deck, but it was a little too chilly for her taste. She had scoped out the formal dining room, which seated ten, and while she knew they'd get great use out of it during Adam's retreat weekend, it was ridiculously big for the two of them. Cassie figured they could easily do breakfast and lunch here at the breakfast bar and then have dinner, weather permitting, on the deck.

Once breakfast was finished, Adam helped Cassie with the cleanup, and they agreed to leave the house at ten to go on their exploration of the town in search of all they would need for their upcoming event.

Cassie felt deliciously relaxed as they drove, enjoying the scenery and the pleasure of not having to keep the conversation going. They were both content to drive and simply enjoy the view. Going on what the restaurant owner had told them the night before, Adam found the party-supply store and escorted Cassie inside. He merely stood back and observed because this was Cassie's terrain.

Within minutes, she had a staff of employees setting up displays and running around to get what she inquired about. He saw tables being set, linens being chosen, and an assortment of chairs to choose from. Cassie walked around and inspected it all, and when she finally had the arrangement exactly as she wanted, she asked for Adam's opinion.

Going with classic elegance, the white on white was tasteful. Picturing it set up on the deck with the proper lighting and centerpieces, he knew that she'd made the right choice. With a simple nod of his head, he gave Cassie approval and she told the manager to write up the order.

Once the rentals were taken care of, they drove on to the local farmers' market and began talking to vendors about what was in season and asking for recommendations. Cassie had a way about her that Adam admired. She was at ease talking to everyone, and in turn, they were at ease with her. She had a rather crotchety produce vendor eating out of the palm of her hand within minutes when he had merely welcomed them with a scowl earlier.

They sampled fruits and vegetables, and when Cassie was satisfied with what she'd seen and tasted, she walked the entire market again in search of ingredients for their meal that evening. It felt odd, but Adam realized he was completely content to follow her around and simply pay for whatever she wanted. Cassie had argued that point at first, but after he made it abundantly clear that he was not going to be swayed, she agreed to let him cover the cost of their purchases.

When she'd exhausted the farmers' market, they drove to the local butcher for steaks. Adam knew good food when he tasted it but had no idea how to go about

choosing things on his own. For this he was thankful
that Cassie was with him. In minutes, she had two truly
fabulous-looking porterhouse steaks in her hand and was
talking to the butcher about their order for the retreat.

And in a move Adam never saw coming, the butcher
walked around the counter, shook both his and Cassie's
hands, and gave them the steaks on the house to
"sample" before placing their extensive order with him.
Adam was dumbfounded for a moment. How had she
done it? He looked over at Cassie, and she was smiling
and being herself, but Adam realized that she, in being
herself, was dazzling.

They thanked the butcher and waved on their way
out. "Does that sort of thing happen often?"

"What? The complimentary steaks?" Adam nodded.
"Not really. I have a couple of vendors who have given
me a couple of freebies in hopes of enticing me to buy
more, and honestly, it doesn't sway me one way or the
other. I don't stock much inventory because I like to
buy everything fresh. So while I appreciate the occasional 'complimentary' item, it doesn't always pan out
for the supplier."

They were standing out on the sidewalk, and Cassie
was looking around as if trying to find something. Her
brow furrowed, she turned to Adam. "Do you think we
could run this stuff back to the house and then grab
some lunch?"

"Why don't we grab something now?"

"I want to keep the food refrigerated, and even though
it is far from hot, I don't want to take any chances with
these steaks."

Agreeing, they took the twenty-minute drive to the

house and unloaded the groceries quickly. Then Cassie went to her bedroom to freshen up and rejoined Adam in the kitchen.

"I wish it was warmer," she began. "It would have been great to pack a picnic basket with sandwiches and salads and eat on the beach."

"We still could…"

She smiled and shook her head. "Too cold for me. You have those great heat lamps out on the deck, so dinner there is great, but I prefer to be a little bit warmer if I'm going to suffer through the sand while I eat."

"Suffer through the sand?" he asked, chuckling.

"I'm not a huge fan of the beach because I hate having sand all over me. It's pretty to look at, not so much fun to get rid of."

"Ah." He nodded with understanding and had to admit he wasn't a fan of sand either. "Okay, so if it's not a picnic on the beach, where to?"

Cassie stopped and considered the possibilities, and then looked at Adam with an impish grin. "Let's get in the car and drive, and we'll know when we get there!" She turned, walked toward the front door, and opened it. With a glance over her shoulder, she asked, "Are you coming?"

Adam watched her walk out the door, clearly excited by all the possibilities. He wasn't so sure. He liked to have a plan, to know what was going on and all the possible variables. Adam didn't cruise around searching for something to do. He was a man with a plan at all times.

The sound of the car horn blasting brought him out of his reverie, and with a slight growl of frustration, he headed out to join Cassie. With resignation, he climbed in and drove toward town. His first inclination was to ask exactly what she wanted to eat so he could find a place that fit the bill immediately and be done with the aimless driving. However, turning and looking at Cassie, he saw that she looked relaxed and happy and he figured she hadn't been wrong in any of the other things she'd asked to do. How bad could this be?

Thirty minutes later, Cassie pointed to what could only be described as a shack on the beach side of the road. The sign out front boasted lobster clubs, and Adam cringed at the thought of getting out of his car and eating there.

"Here!" she cried. "Let's check this place out!"

Glaring, he replied, "Here? Really? I mean, we could go Dumpster diving and get the same kind of atmosphere."

"Oh, look who suddenly let his sense of humor come out and play!" She grinned as Adam pulled the car into one of the three parking spots in front of the shack. Cassie was climbing out of the car before he had it turned off. She walked around to his side of the car and practically pulled him out of his seat.

"Don't be such a snob, Adam. Some of the best places to eat are holes in the wall." She had his large hand in hers and pulled him toward the counter where they could place their orders.

"I thought you said you didn't want to do a picnic in the sand?" he asked, stalling in hopes that she would change her mind and they'd go someplace civilized to eat.

"We have tables around back, buddy," a large man with multiple neck tattoos said. Adam held in the cringe that wanted to wrack his body. "Thanks," he mumbled.

Cassie scanned the menu and ordered. She did not ask for Adam's input; she was willing to deal with the hissy fit he was sure to have if she let him have a good look at what was behind the counter. The Board of Health rating stated an "A," but Cassie had her own doubts about that. "Go grab us a table," she told Adam and shooed him away while she paid and waited for the food.

"Why? I don't see a big crowd here."

Rolling her eyes, Cassie gave him a soft shove and sent him in the direction of the beach. "Nothing too sandy!" she called out playfully as he stomped away. He was quite cute when he was pouting, she thought with a smile.

Within minutes, she had a tray filled with two lobster club sandwiches, French fries, coleslaw, and sweet tea. Walking around to the rear of the building, she found Adam facing the ocean and talking on his cell phone. She let him finish his call while she set the table and seated herself.

Nervous anticipation filled her as Adam finished his call, went to pick up his sandwich, and looked up at her. "What?"

"No, nothing, I was waiting for you to finish your call before starting," she rambled. "Everything all right?" She motioned toward the phone.

"Checking messages." Adam picked up the sandwich, hesitantly took a bite, and let out an unmanly groan of delight. Cassie caught the expression on his face and hid a smile behind her own sandwich as she took a bite. The sweetness of the lobster combined with the perfect amount of spices and mayo made for a wonderful sandwich. The bread was freshly baked sourdough with a crispness that added the right amount of texture to the mix.

They ate in silence for several minutes, with Adam finishing his sandwich first before touching the fries and slaw. Cassie was halfway through her own sandwich and put it down and took a sip of her tea before putting all her attention on Adam.

"What now?" he snapped.

Cassie merely picked up her sandwich and smiled. "Told you so."

They finished their lunches, and Adam cleared the table. It made Cassie smile to see that he genuinely didn't mind helping out with menial tasks. He could have been a total snob and treated her like hired help, but he didn't, and she greatly appreciated that.

Once in the car, Adam suggested they scope out the local shopping and spas so they could prepare a package to offer the spouses. Cassie readily agreed, and she relaxed in her seat, happy to let Adam be in control.

By the time they arrived at Adam's palatial estate, it was after six and Cassie was beat. They had not only found great places to shop and some wonderful salons, they had spoken to what felt like a hundred people as they arranged packages at many of the local businesses. Adam saw her lean against the wall of the elevator on their way up to the main floor and felt concern.

"We could order in tonight if you'd rather not cook," he suggested.

"No, really, I'm fine. I want to kick off my shoes and maybe change into some sweats or something before I get started." Adam got off the elevator on the main level while Cassie indulged and took it up to the next floor.

Once inside her bedroom, she stripped out of the capris, sandals, and sweater, and pulled out a pair of silky pajama pants. She would have preferred the sweats, but she had forgotten to pack them. Walking into the bathroom in nothing but black lacy underwear, she freshened up after splashing some cold water on her face. A quick glance in the mirror showed her hair to be a wild mass of waves and curls that looked completely out of control.

Frowning, she searched through her toiletries and found a clip that she used to put her hair up. A quick change to the silky pants and a cami and an application of lip gloss, and she felt ready to tackle dinner.

Her bare feet felt wonderful after having shoes on all day, and the plush carpet in her bedroom, the hallway, and the stairs felt decadent. The coolness of the ceramic tile in the kitchen gave her a bit of a jolt, but she quickly adjusted. With a look around, Cassie found herself to be alone, and she wondered for a moment where Adam was but took advantage of the uninterrupted time to prep their dinner.

Adam found her standing in the kitchen. The steaks were seasoned and on a platter, a large bowl held salad greens, and she was whisking something in a smaller bowl. It was one of the first times that he could observe her without her knowing he was there. She wasn't talking to him, her staff, or herself, and she looked very serene, very at peace and happy with what she was doing.

Something was cooking on the stovetop, and it smelled wonderful. Adam had not known that she had come back down to start dinner until he smelled whatever it was that was cooking and it had brought him up from his office to investigate.

Cassie put the bowl down and lifted the lid on the pan that was steaming. She gave it a little shake, replaced the lid, then pivoted, went to the spice cabinet, and began sifting through until she found what she wanted. As she put a dash of one thing in the bowl and a sprinkle of something else in the pan, Adam couldn't help but compare her to a dancer as she moved about. Every movement had purpose and was executed with such grace that it was hard to look away.

She finally caught sight of him and merely smiled and went about her task. "I think the grill is ready for these," she said as she walked over, picked up the platter, and headed out to the large grill on the deck. Adam followed.

"I can do that if you have to keep an eye on what you've got going on inside."

Smiling, she shook her head, lifted the lid from the grill, and placed the steaks on it. "These will be quick," she stated, knowing that they both preferred their steaks rare. Pulling a small timer from her pocket, she set it and went back to the kitchen.

He felt like an idiot, but Adam couldn't help but follow. He had nothing else to do. When Cassie turned and nearly ran into him, he knew he had to get out of her way. Walking toward the stairs, Adam went to the lower level and found what he was looking for. Sprinting up to the kitchen, he found a corkscrew and poured them both a glass of wine.

He held one out to Cassie, and she grabbed it on her way to flip the steaks. "Thanks."

Ten minutes later, Adam was sitting down and enjoying a meal that had no rival. He knew that Cassie was an exceptional cook; he never had the time to sit and savor what she created. He told her so and watched a delicate blush creep up her cheeks.

"I think that is the sweetest thing you've ever said to me. Thank you." Cassie took a sip of her wine and sighed. A girl could get used to living like this, that was for sure. "So tell me what your favorite meal is."

"I think I'm eating it right now," he replied as he cut into the tender steak. "I definitely want to use this butcher again, and the produce guy was right on the money, too." After much deliberation, the menu ended up consisting of the steaks, a baby field greens salad with a lemon balsamic vinaigrette dressing, roasted new potatoes with herbed butter, baby carrots, and toasted French bread.

For Cassie, the meal itself did not present that much of a challenge, but it was nice to be appreciated. While cooking was second nature to her, Cassie rarely had the opportunity to cook for someone personally. Sure, there was her family, but they were biased. It had been a long time since she'd been involved with anyone, and back then, she never had the desire to cook for him.

She wanted to cook for Adam. She enjoyed his praise of what she had done. Cassie found herself wanting to be with him more and more, and it had nothing to do with a working relationship and everything to do with a personal one.

What bothered her most was that here they were, in a romantic setting, and he had not made any attempt to touch her or kiss her. Was that kiss in her apartment on

Thursday merely a fluke? Maybe he didn't enjoy kissing her! Maybe Adam had thought about it and realized that it would be awkward for them to get involved. Of all the times for her father to fall in love, it had to be with this man's mother! Talk about bad timing.

She must have sighed because Adam put his fork down and looked at her. "Are you okay? Do you feel all right?"

Great, he was concerned for her health. That should have been a sweet thing, but right now it fed her frustration. What was wrong with her, for crying out loud? Why didn't he enjoy kissing her? Cassie knew she wasn't a supermodel, but men did find her attractive. Maybe Adam was used to more sophisticated women. Well, if that was the case, he could have at them! There was nothing wrong with her, and she had it on the tip of her tongue to tell him so!

"Cassandra?" He interrupted her thoughts. "Seriously, are you all right? You look like you're in pain."

Damn straight she was in pain. Emotional pain. Psychological pain. How dare he kiss her and then never try to do it again! Here she was fawning all over him, trying to get his praise and approval, and for what? So he could ignore the fact that they'd kissed? Cassie realized Adam was staring at her and waiting for an answer.

"What? Oh, no, I'm fine. My mind wandered. Sorry." She stood abruptly and began clearing the dishes. All this thinking about Adam killing her self-esteem had Cassie missing out on the brilliance of the starry night. She had been looking forward to enjoying it over their dinner outdoors, but she felt too ill to sit still any longer.

Adam followed her into the kitchen. "Did I do something wrong?" he asked, confusion sparking his words. "You seem angry."

Cassie turned to him, her eyes ablaze. "Do I? Do I seem angry to you?" she demanded. When Adam stood there, dumbfounded at her tone of voice, she went on. "I'll tell you what's wrong. I am a decent person. I may not be in your league, but I am a damn fine human being who cares about people. I am good at what I do, and you know what? Plenty of people appreciate that and find me attractive!"

Geez, how much wine had she had, she thought to herself, wishing more and more that she could stop the verbal assault that seemed like a runaway train. "I mean, here we are in this fabulous place, having a great time, and you…you are treating me like a damn sister. We're not related yet, you know!"

If she hadn't been so angry, Cassie would have laughed at the expression on Adam's face. He was clearly confused and wanted to speak, but all he could do was sputter. That was fine with her because she had more to say; only now, she was pacing from the deck to the kitchen with the remnants of their dinner.

"You come to my home, bring me pizza, watch TV with me, and then you kiss me and run. What the hell was that about? I know I'm not pinup material, but seriously, you are the first guy to sprint from the building!" She slammed the dishes into the sink and thanked God that nothing shattered.

"So I have no idea what is going on here. Maybe you do this kind of thing all the time where you go around kissing people and then pretending like it didn't happen, but I've got to tell you, Adam, it's weird. It's wrong, and it's weird, and it's—"

She never got to finish because Adam had had enough and had walked up to her and cut off her words with his mouth. It was hot, hard, and hungry on hers, and it took Cassie less than a second to jump on board and open for him. Adam's hands immediately went to her hair to pull it free from its clip while Cassie's arms twined around his neck to keep him close.

This is glorious madness was all Cassie could think as Adam continued to kiss her more intimately than she'd ever been kissed before. His tongue stroked her, and she tasted the wine, the sweetness, and wanted to drink him in. Too soon he moved his mouth from hers and trailed kisses to her cheek and her throat and up to her earlobe before scooping her up in his arms and carrying her over to one of the oversized sofas in the living room.

Settling her down and sliding down next to her, Adam's hands began a journey of familiarizing himself with Cassie's body, and his mouth found his way to hers. Cassie whimpered with need and wrapped one leg around Adam's to give them full-body contact. In the next instant, she found herself pinned beneath him and staring up into his heated gaze.

"Dammit, Cassandra, I was trying to be a gentleman," he said, breath ragged. "I knew you were recovering, and I knew that if I touched you, if I kissed you, that I'd want to make love to you, and I don't think you're feeling up to that yet." Adam rested his forehead on hers. "For once I was trying to be the good guy." He placed a gentle kiss where his head had rested and positioned himself more comfortably between her legs, enjoying the sight of her gasping for breath.

"Really?" Her voice was wispy and soft, and it made him groan.

"Yes, really." He rained tiny kisses all over her face before settling on her mouth. She purred with delight to have him where she most wanted him. Winding her fingers in Adam's hair, all Cassie could think was that she wanted to make love with him. It probably wasn't the smartest thing to do, but right now, with his aroused body pressed so intimately against hers, she couldn't find it in her to care.

"Adam?" she whispered against his mouth. He raised his head, his eyes glazed with passion. "Can we take this upstairs? Please?" She was crazed and desperate to be with him, and as much as she should have been questioning why it had to be this man, all Cassie could think about was getting naked with him and spending the night locked in Adam's arms.

There was a brief hesitation in his gaze before he stood and held out a hand to her. "Are you sure?" He needed her to be sure. He needed her to want him as much as he wanted her. When Cassie smiled and nodded, Adam scooped her up into his arms and considered the possibilities. He strode to the elevator doors and slapped the button on the wall. Once the doors were opened and they were inside, he set Cassie on her feet and pinned her to the wall with his body as he feasted on her mouth once again.

By the time they arrived at the top floor, Adam was nearly ready to lose control. It wasn't supposed to be like this. She wasn't supposed to make him this crazed or want this much. The doors opened, and Adam took Cassie's hand and pulled her into his room. The moonlight pouring through all the glass on the far wall lit the room in a more romantic way than anyone could have asked for.

He didn't stop until they were next to the bed, and without asking, without waiting, Adam reached down to the hem of the tiny white cami Cassie was wearing and pulled it over her head, tossing it to the floor. She let out a small gasp that turned to a sigh as his hands reached up and cupped her full breasts.

She was beautiful. That was all Adam could think. Her skin was milky-white and smooth as silk, and touching her with his hands wasn't enough. Lowering his head, he took one pink tightened nipple into his mouth and suckled. Cassie's knees gave away, and Adam gently helped her to stretch out on the bed and followed her down, immediately returning to the task of laving her with his tongue.

Cassie cried out his name and hugged his head closer, unwilling to let him slip away. She wanted to touch him and be touched by him. Adam's hands continued to roam her body, and it wasn't long before he tugged at the waistband of her silky pants and found his way inside. With unerring precision, he found where she wanted his touch most. She was wet with anticipation, and Adam growled his approval.

Before he allowed himself the pleasure of feeling Cassie more intimately, he sprang off the bed and removed his shirt and then his shoes, socks, and belt. The sight of her dark hair spread across his white comforter and her body sprawled out for his eyes only had Adam barely hanging onto the thread of his control.

They weren't supposed to get to this point this weekend. He had planned on kissing her tonight, but in a much less frantic way. Adam had thought that he'd have to coax her, persuade her; how was he to know that she was as needy and frantic as he was? Unfastening his trousers, he stopped and reached for Cassie. Reaching for the waistband of her pants, he carefully slipped them over her hips and down the incredible length of her legs. Wearing no more than a tiny piece of lace, Cassie squirmed slightly under Adam's heated inspection.

"Please…" Her voice trembled slightly, and Adam's resistance broke. He wanted her; he had to have her. Now. To hell with the consequences. He was already going to burn for many of his life's decisions; this simply added one more to the list.

Stripping away his trousers and briefs, Adam joined Cassie on the bed and settled into her open arms and opened legs. He felt the heat of her, the dampness of her panties, and nearly came from the sensation.

Cassie pulled his head to hers and kissed him as if her life depended on it. She had never known such want, but she was spiraling out of control and needed Adam's hands on her, needed him to feel what he did to her.

Anxious to return to what he had started, Adam slipped a hand between them and let it skim the outside of the lace she wore. Taking his mouth from Cassie's, he trailed kisses along her throat to her breast while his hand teased and tormented the very core of her.

Arching off the bed, Cassie silently pleaded for Adam to touch her more; she felt her body starting to tingle with sensations that had been long missing from her life. With her breast fully pressed against his mouth, she told him exactly what she wanted him to do, and for once, Adam took someone else's command and was happy to oblige.

Tearing the lace from her body, Adam found her— her folds, her wetness—and dove in with first one finger and then two. Cassie bucked off the mattress, but Adam settled her with his body. She loved the sensations he was creating in her, and it didn't take long for her release to hit.

Seeing millions of colors, gasping for air, Cassie cried out Adam's name over and over. Even with her eyes closed, Cassie could tell that he was watching her, and it thrilled her all the more. She wanted Adam to see and feel what he did to her. She wanted to be his.

As her world began to right itself, Adam leaned over and gently kissed her. Cassie could feel his impressive erection pressing against her thigh, and right now all she wanted was to feel it inside of her. She lowered her arms, which had been thrown above her head in reckless abandon, and reached down to touch him.

In the madness that they had created, Cassie had not taken the opportunity to simply touch. She ran her hands over his chest, toying with his flat nipples before letting her hand trail lower to glide and stroke over him. Adam hissed out a breath and pulsed in her hand.

"Cassandra…" She loved that he was the only person to use the formal version of her name, and right now, said in such a husky tone, she loved it even more.

She moaned slightly as she leaned forward and kissed his chest. She wanted to explore all of him as he had her when suddenly pleasure turned to pain. She gasped and let go of him before crying out in agony.

Adam cursed under his breath and sat upright. Dammit, he knew it was too soon for this, and she had made him lose control.

"Cass? What can I do? What's going on?" He was so worried. Cassie was curled up tightly next to him, clutching her stomach.

"I didn't bother to listen to what the doctor said about the timeline for sex because I wasn't expecting to have any," she said through clenched teeth. "But once that orgasm settled, my insides sort of felt like they were being attacked with a rusty razor blade."

Adam stood and walked into his bathroom, hit the lights, and then started the water in the Jacuzzi tub. He went into his medicine cabinet and found some ibuprofen and retrieved a bottle of water from the mini fridge he kept in his walk-in closet. Dimming the lights in the bathroom on the way out, he went to the bed and sat next to Cassie.

"I don't know if you have your pain pills with you, but these should help take the edge off." She mumbled a thank you and took the pills and the water from him. Before she knew it, Adam had her in his arms and was walking toward the bathroom.

"What are you doing?" she asked weakly.

"We're going to take a nice bath to relax you, and then we're going to go to sleep." Cassie was in too much pain to admit that she liked the fact that Adam had taken control and was helping her and that he was using *we* to describe what was going on. It comforted Cassie to no end to have someone taking care of her. While she hated that she needed someone to care for her and that she was dealing with this pain, particularly at this moment, it was certainly more tolerable when someone was there to help her through it.

Gently lowering Cassie into the large tub, Adam waited until she was settled before turning the jets on low. The water level was perfect, and he turned off the spout and climbed in behind her so Cassie could relax against his chest. This was a first, and once they fitted themselves together, Adam found that it was quite a pleasant experience, one he wouldn't mind repeating when Cassie was feeling better.

They sat in the tub, letting the jets pulse over their bodies in silence. Adam rested his head next to Cassie's and simply enjoyed the sensation of having her in his arms. After several long minutes, he whispered, "How are you feeling?"

She sounded drowsy. "Mmm…better. This is as good as the heating pad. Can we sleep here?"

Adam chuckled. "We'd be pruney by morning."

"I don't have the strength to care," she murmured, shifting slightly. They returned to amicable silence, the sound of the water jets the only thing they could hear.

Some time later, Adam felt the water cooling and whispered Cassie's name. "I think it's time to pull the plug here." Cassie sat forward and Adam stood, the water cascading off of his muscular frame as he stepped from the tub, grabbed a fluffy towel from the heated rack, and wrapped it around himself before grabbing a second one for Cassie.

She stood, heedless of her own nakedness, and allowed Adam to wrap the plush towel around her and lift her from the tub. He placed her on her feet and dried her off before wrapping the towel snugly around her.

"Wait here," he said as he stepped away and walked over to his closet. In less than a minute, he had a cotton T-shirt in his hands. Without asking for permission, Adam loosened the towel and pulled the shirt over Cassie's head. "You'll be more comfortable sleeping in this" was all he said before taking her hand and leading her to the master bedroom.

Cassie stood next to the bed while Adam drew the blankets back and motioned for her to climb in. Obeying, feeling as if she were in a dream state, she snuggled into the cool sheets and watched as Adam removed the towel from around his hips and climbed in beside her. He turned off the light next to the bed and drew Cassie into his arms.

"Do you need anything else?" he whispered, kicking himself for not asking sooner.

"No, this is perfect." Her head rested on his shoulder as her arm wrapped around his middle and one of her silky thighs tangled with his. "Good night." Adam knew immediately that she was asleep.

If only sleep would claim him as quickly. The night had promised to be spectacular. Knowing that it would be this way made waiting that much harder. He wasn't selfish enough to press her; after witnessing her pain tonight, he berated himself for being such a bastard who had no sense of self-control.

The sound and feel of Cassie's soft breath against his chest were soothing, taming the beast within him. The last time he had held her while she slept they had been spooned together, her back to his chest. This position was much better.

Tomorrow would bring the end of their weekend,

and it felt like it was too soon. It would be three weeks before they would return. Adam thought of how long three weeks could seem. He knew it would be best if Cassie used all that time to recover. When he made love with her for the first time, he wanted it to be here, in this house, in this bed. Of that he was certain.

As a master planner, Adam began to formulate a plan of survival for the coming weeks. There was no way he could completely stay away from her, and yet being with her, whether for work or in a social setting, and not touching her would test the limits of his control.

There would be phone calls, both to discuss the upcoming retreat and for personal reasons; he was sure there would be a family event or two that he could find time to get involved in. Good Lord, his mother would be shocked.

Holding Cassie close, Adam smiled. While he didn't believe in forever, he was looking forward to whatever span of time he was going to have while being involved with Cassie.

He kissed the top of her head as sleep finally claimed him.

Chapter 9

THEY BEGAN THEIR RIDE HOME AFTER LUNCH, AND WHILE neither had encouraged or entertained the idea of engaging in the passion of the previous night, it was lurking in the backs of both their minds.

Cassie hated to leave the big, beautiful house but was comforted by the fact that she had accomplished, business-wise, what she needed to this weekend and she would be returning in three short weeks. As the road took them farther and farther away from the coast and closer to home, Cassie had a mental checklist going in her head of what she would need to do before returning.

Without her day planner, she couldn't be positive what else was scheduled for that weekend. Tomorrow, she would call their waitress from Friday night and make arrangements with her and then remember to touch base with her over the coming weeks.

The sound of her cell phone ringing startled her out of the peaceful, companionable silence. Looking at the phone, she saw that the caller was her father.

"Hey, Dad! How are you today?"

"Doin' good, sweetheart. How are you feeling?"

Cassie updated him on her health while not going into details about last night's setback. "I've got a follow-up appointment on Wednesday, but I think everything is healing as it should. Only time will tell."

"I'm glad, Cass, I really am. I want you never to have

to deal with those painful spells again." Cassie agreed. "Hey, are you up for dinner tomorrow night?"

She sighed lightheartedly. "What am I making?"

Stephen laughed. "Actually, um…Bev would like to cook dinner for the family." Cassie was stunned silent. While she knew that her father and Bev were going to be married, cooking had always been her responsibility, and she took it seriously. "Cass? You still there?"

"What? Oh, yes, yes…I'm still here. Sorry, my mind wandered. Actually, that sounds great. Are we eating at your house or hers?"

Sounding relieved that she wasn't upset, Stephen detailed that dinner would be at Bev's house and promised to email Cassie the directions. "So what time should I be there?" she asked.

"I don't know what your schedule is like tomorrow, but would six work?"

"That sounds great. Should I bring anything?" she asked, hopeful that she wouldn't totally be eliminated from the preparation of the meal.

"Actually, sweetheart, Bev is looking forward to doing the whole meal for everyone. I think she feels a little intimidated by you, so if you could—"

"It's okay, Dad. I get it. I am glad to come and be a guest. I'll see you tomorrow night at six." When Cassie placed her phone in her purse, she turned to look out the window and sighed.

"Everything okay?" Adam asked, concern lacing his voice.

Turning her head to him, she gave a small smile. "Family dinner tomorrow night at your mom's. I'm sure you'll get the call too."

He chuckled. "I doubt that."

"What? Why?"

"My mother and I don't normally *do* family dinners. I mean, she invited me to your father's that night mainly because they were making an announcement, but other than that, we don't socialize much."

"Well, that's sad, Adam. You guys are family, the only family you have, from what I can tell. You should spend time together."

"Cassandra, please…don't try to fix my relationship with my mother. It works for us both, and now, apparently, she'll have a whole new family to spend time with."

"Does that bother you?"

"Hell no." Actually, he wondered if Bev would call and invite him to come around more now that she was getting married. Would she want to include him in her new family?

He hoped not.

"It's not such a bad thing, you know. It's nice having people around you who care about you and who want to share in what's going on with your life and…" She stopped and sighed.

"So why the sigh? Clearly you enjoy the whole family get-together thing, so what's the problem?" Adam was curious.

Unable to help it, she let another sigh escape her lips. "There's no problem. It's that this is all new, you know? We all have our roles in the family, and they're changing."

"Ah, my mom is going to cook, isn't she?"

Cassie's head snapped toward Adam's. "How did you know?"

"If there is one thing I've learned about you, it's that you enjoy being the chef. You like the praise, and you thoroughly enjoy the whole process of preparation. Having Bev step in and take over sort of leaves you without a role."

"Very astute, Mr. Lawrence," she said with sarcasm, angry he had her pegged. "Maybe I'll actually get to relax and enjoy myself for once. Maybe I'll enjoy sitting back and letting someone else fret over the meal." She crossed her arms over her chest and pouted.

Adam found her adorable.

"Pouting doesn't suit you, Cassandra," he pointed out. "And fret? You never fret over anything, and believe me, if I know my mother, she is going to go overboard trying to impress you."

"She doesn't need to do that! Oh, gosh...I don't want there to be like a competition or anything! I—"

Adam took a hand off the steering wheel and reached for one of Cassie's. "Shh...it's all right, Cass, really. I don't think my mom is trying to have a competition with you. This is all new to her too. I don't think she ever dated anyone with kids, so she is trying to find her place in all this as well. Relax. Go tomorrow night, and enjoy having the night off."

Their fingers were linked together, and Cassie found his touch comforting. "Thanks. I know you're right. It feels weird. I never get to be the guest when I'm with my family. I'm more comfortable in the role of hired help."

Adam pulled his hand from hers, and if he weren't in the middle of a major highway, he would have slammed on the brakes. "What does that mean?" His tone suggested that he was appalled by her statement.

"What? The hired help?" Adam nodded. "When you know how to cook and people know that you own your own catering business, no one invites you for dinner where you don't do the cooking." The look on Adam's face showed that he was well and truly shocked. "It's not a big deal, Adam. I got used to it."

"So you never get to go anywhere and be a guest?"

"Nope. At least…" She stopped and thought for a moment. "Nope. If I get invited somewhere, I'm either bringing the meal or preparing it there."

"What about your friends? Or boyfriends?"

She chuckled at his outrage for her. "The business has been my main priority for quite some time, so there hasn't been a man in my life in a while. When there was, we would eat out mainly. As for friends? Well, most of my friends are married and having children now, and our schedules don't mesh much anymore."

Adam didn't see that as a bad thing; after all, he didn't socialize much with friends anymore, and he was fine with that. Looking at Cassie's face, however, he saw that it wasn't okay with her. And then he realized that it wasn't okay with him, either, because clearly he was no better than all the rest. Their relationship started as a business one, which meant it was about her cooking for him, but since then had he done anything to change that?

Sure, he'd brought her a pizza and taken her out to eat, but…hell, he did not like to think of himself as being like anybody else, and that meant he would have to treat Cassie as she'd never been treated before. Even if their relationship was brief, he wanted her to remember that he had cared enough to take better care of her and respect her time and feelings more than anyone else.

He let the subject drop, mainly because he feared that if he continued with it, his role in using her as the hired help would come up and he didn't want to focus on that right now. The remainder of the drive consisted of listening to music and discussing not much of anything; Adam's main focus was on not bringing up the subject of her family or his mom again for the time being.

When they arrived at Cassie's place, Adam parked and got out to retrieve her luggage. He waited while Cassie unlocked the door and followed her inside and up the stairs to her apartment. Had she not been recovering, he would have taken advantage of their location and made love to her there and spent the night. Since that wasn't an option, he settled for watching her go about putting her suitcase in her bedroom and checking her phone messages.

Sitting on the couch, Adam felt no hurry to leave. A few minutes later, Cassie joined him and handed him a glass of wine. "Thank you for a wonderful weekend. I can't wait to set up for your meetings."

Damn, he was hoping she'd be excited about being with him, but since last night, she hadn't made one mention of the intimacies they'd shared.

"I think it's going to be…" He didn't want to say "perfect" because Adam didn't believe in perfect if he wasn't the one doing the work, but he struggled for the right phrase.

"It's going to be great. Say it!" Cassie teased and took a sip of her drink. "I think I'll go down beforehand so I can make sure the place is clean and aired out, and I can have Debbie do a practice run so there's no awkwardness once everyone's there."

"Sounds good. Are you planning on driving down on Wednesday?"

"Actually, if it's all right with you, I think I'll head down Tuesday night. That way I can get up Wednesday and get things going. That will give me two full days of prep time before everyone arrives."

The wheels in Adam's mind started turning. He could arrange for some of his executives and VPs to handle things in the office so that he would be free to join Cassie at the beach and be alone with her before his meetings began. Adam didn't feel the need to let Cassie in on that bit of information; instead, he was opting for the element of surprise.

They sat quietly, as was becoming a habit, until Cassie turned to Adam and asked, "I think I have the makings of a meal in the kitchen. Would you like to stay for dinner?"

Here was his chance. It would be easy to let her do what she asked; he could sit here and relax and let her do what she enjoyed. But he wasn't prepared to let her. "I was thinking of getting some Chinese. We could stream a movie or something and hang out. It's been a long day; why don't you relax?"

His words startled her. He had essentially pampered her all weekend. She wasn't sure what to do with all this spare time and energy. "Really? Are you sure? It would be easier to go downstairs and whip something up."

Unable to help himself, Adam leaned forward and placed a gentle kiss on her nose. "Easier for whom?" Placing his glass on her coffee table, Adam stood and pulled his cell phone from his pocket. "What do you like?"

Cassie rattled off some of her personal favorites, and

together they decided on their orders. "Why don't you return your messages and get settled while I pick up the food?" Adam suggested.

Agreeing, Cassie watched him leave and wondered to herself what kind of a relationship she was going to end up having with Adam Lawrence.

Later that night, long after leaving the comfort of Cassie's apartment, Adam lay in his own bed and played over the events of the weekend in his mind. Seduction had been the plan, and while things didn't go exactly as he had hoped, the taste of what was to come had him hard. He knew that Cassie was a passionate woman, but he was not prepared for what she would be like in his bed.

The countdown was on until they were at the coast, and with any luck, she would be completely recovered and they could pick up where they left off. Adam had visions of having Cassie in every room of his home. A wicked grin crossed his face. Yes, by the time he arrived at the beach, he would be ready to take on such a quest.

Pushing the erotic images from his mind, he turned his attention to the more practical side of survival for now. His mother hadn't called to invite him for dinner, and while under normal circumstances he wouldn't be bothered by being excluded, knowing that Cassie would be there and he wouldn't didn't sit well with him. He made a mental note to call his mother in the morning and fish for an invitation.

Turning on his side and punching the pillow, Adam sighed as sleep eluded him.

At six o'clock sharp the next evening, Cassie stood on Bev's front porch. She felt naked without pots, pans, or at the very least a covered dish. She noticed that her siblings were already there; Katie had offered to drive with her, but Cassie had some bookkeeping to do that held her up a little. Ringing the bell, it was a bit of a shock to see her dad answering the door.

He gathered her into a big bear hug and kissed her cheek as he led her into the large eat-in kitchen where everyone was gathered. Cassie took in her surroundings and found that Bev's home was a lot like her child-hood one: large rooms that were comfortably furnished; bright, cheery walls; and a kitchen that could host large family gatherings. In truth, it felt like home.

Cassie walked around and kissed everyone hello, and when she got to Bev, the older woman embraced her tightly. "I hope that you don't mind that I wanted to cook tonight. I wanted to give you a bit of a break." Her smile was sincere, and Cassie couldn't help but smile with gratitude.

"Are you kidding? I've been looking forward to this all day!" She took the drink that Bev offered and went to sit at the table with her siblings, taking time to pick up Ella and snuggle her in her arms.

"Adam tells me that you're going to cater an event for him out in Manteo," Bev said as she chopped ingredients for their salad. Adam had spoken to his mom? After all his talk yesterday of them not being close? Well, maybe Bev had called him to invite him for dinner. She casu-ally looked around for any sign of him and then realized that everyone was looking to her for an answer.

"Oh, yes, we took a ride out to the house this

weekend. It's magnificent. I had the chance to talk to some local vendors, and I think Adam is going to be pleased with the results."

"As if he could be anything but," her father stated with a grin. "She looks good in your arms, Cass," he added. Cassie beamed at her father as she placed a soft kiss on Ella's cheek.

"She feels good in my arms, Dad." It was at that moment that Adam walked into the kitchen. He took in the smiling faces and the relaxed atmosphere and, for a moment, felt wildly out of place. Then he caught sight of Cassie with her niece in her arms, and his breath felt as if it were knocked out of him.

She looked positively serene, glowing with love as she held the small child, and Adam wasn't sure why the image affected him so much, but it did. He had to stop himself from staring and called out a greeting to his mother.

Dinner was boisterous with everyone talking at once about a myriad of different topics. Adam realized that this was how the Jacobs family operated, and while he still wasn't one hundred percent comfortable with it, he was unable to stop himself from joining in.

Matt was talking about a string of break-ins in a residential part of town, while Lauren was telling Bev about her college course load. Katie and Cassie were talking about the caterings they had coming up this weekend, while he and Stephen talked about business and Adam's upcoming travels.

All in all Adam found the whole thing pleasant, and the look of pure happiness on his mother's face told him that he'd made the right decision to be a part of this dinner.

"So, Cassie," Bev began, "tell us about your plans for the meeting Adam's holding at the beach."

Cassie looked nervously over at Adam in case he wanted to be the one to provide the details, but he smiled and nodded, and that was her cue. He realized that he enjoyed hearing her talk about her work, and she was so animated in her descriptions that even if Adam had never been to the house, he would have had a perfect picture in his mind of what she was describing.

"It sounds lovely," Bev said with a smile. "I always imagined that house being used for special events and big parties."

"I know what you mean. This is a small event. I could go wild with something a lot bigger. God knows there's enough space there for a large group. Oh! You and Dad should have your wedding there. It would be absolutely perfect! We could do flowers on the railings of the deck and lots and lots of candles all around… Oh, to see you coming down the stairs or maybe going down to the beach…it would be magical!" The words were out before Cassie could stop them, and soon Lauren and Katie were chiming in with questions and ideas, but Cassie could feel the tension coming from Adam's end of the table.

———〰———

Adam's sense of ease vanished, and he excused himself with claims of a call.

"Is everything all right?" Cassie had followed him to the porch.

He glared at her, that cold, hard stare that she'd seen him give dozens of times to his employees. "What could be wrong?" he snapped. "One weekend in my home, and you're already making plans for it yourself. Tell me, do you always make yourself at home that quickly, or is it just with me?"

Her eyes grew wide with shock. "Are you kidding me? She's your mother, for crying out loud, and it's her wedding! That's hardly planning something for me! How can you be so cold about this?"

"Cold? This has nothing to do with being cold, Cassandra. I simply don't appreciate you stepping in and offering up my home for parties without consulting me first. I hired you to plan an event for my company. If my mother wants to hire you to plan her wedding, then you two can discuss other venues or maybe talk to me privately before you start renting out space that isn't yours."

She looked as if he'd slapped her. Clearly, she had crossed a line, again, and he was not happy. Fine. Apparently, she was good enough to sleep with but not good enough to make suggestions for things that involved both their families. She made a mental note never to go there again.

Stiffening her spine, she nodded. "Fine, you're right. It was not my place to speak up."

It was the way she said *place* that got him. Their conversation yesterday about being the hired help rang out in his mind, and as much as he wanted to be pissed off at her for offering the house for a wedding, he felt like crap for making her feel like their weekend together meant nothing to him.

"Cassandra, look…"

She held up a hand to stop him. "No, really, let's

not go there right now. You made yourself abundantly clear." Turning, Cassie walked inside, firmly shutting the door behind her, leaving Adam alone in the darkness.

Chapter 10

CASSIE TOOK A FINAL LOOK AROUND HER KITCHEN AND picked up her checklist from the butcher-block island to make sure she had everything.

"Are you sure you still want to do this? Because I can go in your place." Katie was standing opposite Cassie, arms folded across her chest.

"It's going to be fine. I have a job to do, and as much as I am still ticked off at Adam for being…well, Adam, I am going to do that job and impress the hell out of those Europeans!"

In the two and a half weeks since that fateful night, Cassie had refused all of Adam's calls. She had gotten her information to Grace and managed to pick up the keys to the Manteo house while Adam was out of the office.

He had been relentless that first week in his attempts to talk to her. It had been painful at times and downright impossible at others to avoid him. He'd called, he'd sent flowers, and he'd shown up at her apartment late at night. Cassie refused to talk to him or answer the door. When the family had gotten together for dinner one night the previous week, he had shown up, but her family, while being polite to him, had rallied around her and made sure to keep her busy and unable to talk with him alone.

In this whole rotten situation, she felt the worst for Bev. After all, none of this was her fault; her son was a grown man who had control issues. Well, Cassie wasn't going to let that bother her. She had a job to do, and while it might be a bit awkward and uncomfortable to be with Adam in the house where they had nearly made love, Cassie knew she would be too busy with her job to pay much attention to him, and in turn, she hoped he would be too busy with his clients to focus any attention on her.

Walking around the work space, Cassie grabbed her sister and hugged her. "You are the best, you know that?" She kissed Kate on the cheek and smiled. "I appreciate how much everyone wants to fight this battle for me, but I am a professional, and I am going to do what I was hired to do."

"At least he didn't fire you this time."

"Yeah, thank God for small favors." Pulling her keys from her purse, Cassie took one final look around. "I think I've got everything that I need. Everything else is already there. Call me if you need anything. The Miller party—"

"Is a walk in the park, Cass. I can do a party of that size with my eyes closed. Go, get on the road, and enjoy the peace and solitude before Satan arrives."

"You have *got* to stop calling him that!" She laughed.

"I will when he stops acting like that."

"I guess we all never outgrow the rubber-and-glue scenario…" She kissed her sister one last time and walked out the door feeling confident and ready to take on the world.

The drive to Manteo was the perfect time for Cassie to clear her head and get mentally prepared for dealing with Adam. The only thing saving her was the fact that he wouldn't be arriving until Friday with the rest of the group. By that time, she should be able to handle seeing him. Actually, by that time, she'd be in full service mode, and she could make sure that every second of her time was spent doing something for his guests.

Her first inclination was to say *their guests*, but it was thinking like that that got her in trouble in the first place. Damn him! Damn *him* for ruining what was looking like a really decent relationship. Cassie was the first to admit that she didn't have the greatest taste in men, but that taste usually ran to picking men who were unmotivated and content to still live at home with their moms.

She had finally found someone who was confident, independent, and successful, and he ended up being a damn control freak. Wait…why was this a surprise to her? She knew this about Adam all along. As a matter of fact, if she were honest with herself, this was the exact reason she had quit on him a month ago! What was wrong with her? How could she have forgotten?

So now the blame lay fully at her own feet, and she didn't like it. He had seduced her with his kindness and sexy looks, and if her feelings were hurt, then it was her own fault. Well, there was a bitter pill to swallow.

No, she was not going to take all the responsibility for this. Adam needed to learn to not be so rude and to treat people with respect. Ha! Fat chance of that happening! Turning on some music, Cassie decided to wipe all thoughts of Adam out of her mind for the remainder of her drive. Checking the GPS, she saw that she still had two hours to go and decided to let her inner '80s child out, singing along to Bon Jovi for the next stretch of road.

The clock read six fifteen when Cassie pulled into

the driveway at Adam's house. There were a couple of lights on, and she stiffened for a minute but then realized that he must have them on a timer. She got out of the car, glared at the closed garage door, and wished that she had asked for the remote so she didn't have to walk up the steps to the front door with all her stuff; using the elevator would have been easier.

Deciding to grab her suitcase, she took the house key out of her purse and climbed the stairs; later she could open the garage door from the inside so she could haul her supplies up with ease in the elevator.

Several things hit her at once as she opened the door. First, there was music playing softly; second, something was cooking; and third, clearly she wasn't alone.

"Hello?" she nervously called out, refusing to walk any farther into the house and unsure what was going on.

Adam stepped into her field of vision, and she wanted to scream. Whether the scream was of frustration or anger or fear, she wasn't sure, but his early arrival had thrown a monkey wrench in her perfectly crafted plan of clearing her head.

"What are you doing here?" she demanded, hands on hips, eyes ablaze.

"It's my house," he stated simply. "How was your drive?" Adam walked toward her, took her suitcase from beside her, and moved it to the bottom of the staircase. When he noticed that she hadn't moved from her spot next to the entrance, he strode over, closed the door, and walked toward the kitchen.

If she wanted to scream a minute ago, she wanted to howl in rage now. How was her drive? *How was her drive?* That's all he had to say after showing up here unannounced after being such a jackass? How dare he! Cassie's first instinct was to turn around and flee, but if she knew anything about Adam Lawrence, she knew she'd be kissing this job goodbye, and she'd worked too hard to make it perfect to allow that to happen.

With no other choice, she sighed heavily and followed Adam into the kitchen. She stopped dead in her tracks at the sight before her. There were candles set along the breakfast bar, a fire roaring in the living room fireplace. Cassie could see steam coming from the grill outside, and under one of the heat lamps, a table set for two was covered in linen, with pillar candles as a centerpiece.

There were no words for what was going on in her mind. Adam was here and he had prepared a dinner for her. In all of her adult life, no man had ever taken the initiative and attempted to cook for her. She wasn't sure how to respond to this, what to say, how to act.

"I'm glad I timed this properly," Adam was saying as he poured them each a glass of wine. "I hope you didn't stop for something to eat on the way. I've got a couple of filets on the grill and picked up some crab cakes from that seafood market we saw last time." He looked around as if getting his bearings.

"I will admit that the salad is a kit I bought, so I'm sure it won't taste as good as yours, but my culinary skills are quite limited."

"What's going on, Adam?" Cassie knew that things had gone badly the last time they had been together, and while she was aware of the fact that Adam had tried to make it right, for him to go to this extreme seemed well out of character for him.

"I thought that was obvious, Cassandra. I've made

dinner for us. I figured you'd be hungry after a long drive."

"That's not what I meant, and you know it. We haven't spoken in weeks, and you weren't supposed to be here until Friday, so what's going on?"

He smiled. That was it—he smiled, put his glass down, and walked toward her. When he was standing directly in front of Cassie, he cupped her face and kissed her. Slowly, gently, luxuriating in the taste of her even when she wouldn't kiss him back.

Raising his head, Adam stared deeply into her eyes, the smile returning to his face. "I have to go check those steaks. They should be done." He walked away and went out to the grill. Cassie watched him remove the steaks and place them on a platter and then on the candlelit table. Next, he came inside and moved the rest of their meal outside.

Cassie followed and found that everything looked beautiful. Adam held out a chair for her, and Cassie sat and waited for him to do the same. She sipped at her wine, the cool evening breeze gently blowing her hair but the heat from the tall lamp keeping her warm. Anger simmered inside her, but she had enough curiosity in her to want to taste what he had prepared for her.

The hope was that the meal would be terrible and she could use that to fuel her bad feelings toward Adam, but after one bite of the tender filet, which melted in her mouth, she found that she couldn't use that excuse.

He was trying. There wasn't a doubt in Cassie's mind that Adam was well and truly trying to make things right. Her problem was that she was afraid to discuss what she was angry about because there was a very real possibility of them arguing some more and she knew that fighting with Adam never ended well for her.

"How's your steak?" he asked, concern and curiosity in his voice.

"Everything's delicious, Adam, thank you." Cassie returned her attention to the meal and refused to let herself look at him for any length of time because she knew if she did, all traces of anger would disappear. He seemed to have that effect on her, and right now she wanted nothing more than to be angry a little bit longer.

He had hurt her. Maybe not intentionally, but he had hurt her all the same. Cassie had come to accept that in her line of work she was going to meet wealthy and successful people who had a lot more money and power than she did, and that no matter how glamorous the atmosphere, no matter how posh the setting, she was always going to be the hired help. There had never been a time when it had bothered her like it had that night at Bev's house when Adam had made it so abundantly clear what her place was.

Thinking back, Cassie still couldn't see what the big deal was, and even if he wasn't that close with his mother, using this house that sat empty most of the year for her wedding should not have been such a big issue. But thinking about it, obsessing about it, was not going to help her right now. Right now she was here with Adam, sharing a meal and preparing to cater an important event for him.

She was hired to do a job.

There had been a momentary lapse in judgment on both their parts when they'd almost made love. Cassie knew that it had been a mistake; the only thing saving her pride at this point was that they hadn't slept together because otherwise she would have been mortified to have Adam speak to her as he had at Bev's that night. From this point on, she had to remember that he was the employer and she the employee. There would be no repeat of what had happened here last time.

Adam was watching Cassie intently, trying desperately to read her mind. She wouldn't look at him; she had used that technique on him before, ignoring him, and he didn't like it. What was she making such a big deal about? So he didn't want her taking it upon herself to offer up his house to people. That wasn't so unreasonable, was it? After all, it was his house, not hers. Spending one weekend here did not give her the right to invite other people.

True, the other people in question consisted of his own mother and her fiancé, but still, if anyone was going to offer out this home for a wedding, it would be him.

Only it wouldn't.

Adam had no desire to get sucked into all the wedding hoopla, and if Bev and Stephen were going to be married, well, they could make the arrangements themselves. Stephen probably expected him to foot the bill. Well, he would be sorely disappointed because Adam had no intention of shelling out anything for the wedding. If they were foolish enough to want to be married, they could carry the expense themselves.

Adam was scowling at the thought when Cassie finally lifted her head and looked at him. Adam noticed that she had finished her meal and was standing and clearing her place.

"Everything was delicious. Thank you, again."

Cassie turned and carried her plates into the house. Once the plates were rinsed and loaded in the dishwasher, she considered finishing the cleanup; after all, that was what she had been hired to do.

Looking around the kitchen, she saw that Adam had not made too big of a mess. She collected bowls and pans and loaded them into the dishwasher, and then wiped down all the countertops. That's what Adam saw her doing when he strode inside.

"What the hell are you doing?" he demanded, stopping short as he entered the kitchen, hands on hips.

Cassie looked at him as if she didn't understand the question. "What do you mean? I'm cleaning up."

"I can see that, Cassandra, I'm not an idiot. What I want to know is why you're cleaning up."

Confusion, plain and simple, showed all over her face. "There was a mess, I'm cleaning it up. I have to work in this kitchen for the next several days, and it needs to be clean in here. That's what you're paying me for."

Adam cursed under his breath. He had had it! He had planned this meal as a peace offering, but clearly Cassie wasn't ready to forgive and forget yet. Well, dammit, he was tired of waiting.

Cassie had turned from him and was rinsing something in the sink. Adam stormed up behind her, grabbed her upper arm, and spun her around. Her eyes were like fire when they met his, and although he hoped she would put up a struggle, she didn't. Cassie merely stared at him, daring him to prove her wrong.

"The job I hired you for doesn't start until Friday, so don't give me any of that crap about working. Dinner tonight had nothing to do with business, and you know it. Now, I have made multiple attempts to talk to you, and you have avoided me like the damn plague. I've had enough, dammit!"

He'd had enough? Cassie yanked her arm from his grasp. "Really? You've had enough? Well, too bad, Adam. You can't have everything your own way."

"Meaning what exactly?" His eyes narrowed to slits. He had a feeling what she had to say was going to raise his ire.

"Meaning that I refuse to be treated like your lover one minute and an employee the next. I thought that we'd shared something that weekend, and as soon as I did something that you didn't agree with, instead of talking to me privately about it or perhaps giving me the benefit of the doubt, you lashed out and reminded me of my place. So, if I had to choose which relationship with you I'd prefer, it's the business one. At least there I know exactly where I stand and have the option of whether I want to do business with you ever again. And, believe me, after this weekend, I think I'll be opting to *not* do business with you again."

Adam saw red. This was not going as he had planned. Cassie was supposed to be wowed by his gesture of a romantic dinner! By this point in the evening, he was sure that he would have her on the sofa or well on their way up to his bed. How the hell had it all gone so wrong so fast?

"What exactly is it that you want from me, Cassandra?" Unfortunately, she had already answered that question. Adam was unwilling to accept it.

"I want to do my job here and not be bothered by you.

I had planned on arriving here and having the place to myself to set up and prep, but your being here messed that up. As my employer, it's your prerogative to stay and oversee, I guess, but honestly, I wish you'd leave." The slight tremor in her voice unsettled Cassie. She had wanted to come off as strong and confident in her decision to not want Adam around. As she spoke, however, she felt nothing but turmoil.

How had she gotten this embroiled with this man in such a short time? They had never had conflicts like this before, and honestly, Cassie never fought with anyone the way she did with Adam. It was a side of herself that she wasn't enjoying very much. She wanted to do her job and be left alone. Her heart would heal. Eventually.

It was the slight catch in her voice that did it. In that moment, Adam realized what exactly he had done. In all his life, in all his dealings with people, Adam had said what was on his mind and never gave a thought to how it was received or how the other person felt.

Until now.

That little tremble while Cassie was trying to sound brave hit him like a ton of bricks. Adam realized that he had, indeed, hurt her. Even though, in the moment, that was his intent, seeing the results of that hurt caused an ache in his chest that was new to him. Maybe Cassie was the only person to feel this level of hurt at his hands, but Adam had a sinking sensation that wasn't the case. There were countless others he had treated with heartless disregard over the years; he would never know how his words had affected them.

Cassie's posture was rigid, her face one of cool disdain, but Adam would not let that stop him. If he was ever going to gain her forgiveness, if he was ever going to cleanse his very soul for what he had done to her, he had to knock down the wall that Cassie had around her and not stop until she knew how deeply sorry he was for hurting her.

Stepping forward, he ignored Cassie's retreat until her back was against the countertop, reached out, and gently cupped her face. Staring intently into those beautiful blue eyes, Adam leaned forward and rested his forehead against hers.

"I am sorry…so sorry, Cassandra, for hurting you." He placed a light kiss on her nose. "At the time, I didn't realize how hatefully I was behaving, and I am well and truly sorry for making you feel like you are nothing more to me than an employee. You are far from that to me."

Adam lifted his head and held Cassie's gaze. "I don't know how this happened, how we arrived at this place together after years of working together, but all I know is that I want to spend time with you. I want to get to know you." Skimming a hand along her cheek, Adam watched as Cassie's eyes drifted closed. "I want to kiss you and hold you. I want to take you upstairs to my bed and make love to you as I've wanted to for what seems like forever."

Cassie's eyes slowly fluttered open, and she trembled at the heat in Adam's eyes. "I am asking for your forgiveness, Cassandra. I *need* your forgiveness."

Adam's breath was warm on Cassie's face, and she desperately wanted to lean in and feel his mouth on hers and have his arms around her. She knew, though, that until she said she forgave him, Adam would respect her boundaries and not touch her. Which did she want more? Her pride or Adam?

Straining toward him, Cassie realized that with his apology, her pride was intact. For weeks she had dreamed about being in this house with him and finishing what they had started. If she didn't act now, if she didn't give in and take what she wanted, Cassie had no doubt that she would regret it for the rest of her life.

With a deep breath, she straightened slightly and whispered, "Yes, Adam, I forgive you." The last word barely left her mouth before Adam claimed her. His hands, which had been cupping her face, ran along her back and pulled her close. He was already aroused, and Cassie reveled in the hard length of him against her belly.

The madness claimed them as it had before and, now that Cassie knew how things could progress, made her want all the more. "Upstairs…" she panted. "Please…"

As much as it pained Adam to break contact with her delectable mouth, he released her long enough to swing her into his arms and up the stairs. "Elevator…" she whispered, hoping to encourage him to take the faster route, but he was already halfway up the first flight of stairs, taking them two at a time.

"Trust me, this is faster." True to his word, Adam had them in his suite faster than Cassie thought possible, and he wasn't remotely out of breath. He didn't release her until they were next to the bed, and then he placed her on the mattress and followed her, anxious for the full-body contact, even fully clothed.

Adam feasted on Cassie's mouth, her cheek, her throat. His hands shook with need as they roamed her body. He wanted this to last; he wanted to take his time and pleasure her in every way possible, not to make up for his callous behavior but simply for the sake of wanting to give her pleasure.

Cassie whispered his name. In response, Adam moved his hand to the hem of her T-shirt and lifted it up and over her head, exposing the blue lacy bra he swore matched her eyes. He had seen her naked before, and yet he was still stunned at how perfect she was. Slowly lifting a hand, he skimmed the smooth skin of her rib cage and up to cup one rounded breast, lifting slightly to force her nipple from the bra.

Once he could see it and see how tight and puckered it was for him, Adam lowered his head and first kissed it and then laved at it with his tongue before finally suckling from it. Cassie's back arched, and she cradled his head. It was an eerie sense of déjà vu, only this time Cassie knew that it wouldn't end with her climax or pain.

The thought of having Adam make love to her, having him inside her, had her clawing at Adam's shirt. She needed to feel skin; she wanted him naked. She wanted him as frenzied as she was. Adam released her breast long enough to pull his polo shirt over his head. Before returning his mouth to her, he unhooked the front clasp of her bra and pulled it from her body.

Leaning forward, their sighs mingled at the skin-on-skin contact. Adam's mouth returned to first one breast and then the other, and Cassie's head thrashed from side to side at the sensation. It was too much and yet not enough. She wanted to ask, beg, for his touch on other parts of her body but was, at the same time, reluctant to let Adam stop what he was doing.

Finally, when the tugging became too much, when

she wanted nothing more than to rip her jeans from her body, Cassie cried out his name, and Adam sensed what she wanted and readily obliged.

Cassie's jeans skimmed her legs, followed by her panties. Adam rested on his knees and simply looked at her. Had he ever felt this way? Had there ever been such rampant need crashing through him to the point that he felt he couldn't breathe without having a woman?

He felt it now.

Her arms were flung behind her head, and her legs parted, drawing his attention. Adam ran one rough hand up her leg from ankle to thigh before looking Cassie in the eye as he surged forward and touched her intimately. At the first touch of his fingers, Cassie cried out. By the time he circled and teased and inserted a second finger, her climax was upon her.

It was too soon, too much, too fast, but Cassie didn't care. She wanted this, needed this, and would do nothing to stop it. Crying out Adam's name over and over, she rode the wave of pleasure until she thought she could take no more.

In the distance, she felt Adam move and heard a tearing sound, and as her orgasm was about to subside, he entered her and had her soaring over the edge again. Hips pumping, Cassie reached up and wrapped her arms around Adam to pull him close; she wanted to kiss him, needed more than anything to feel his mouth on hers while she rode the crest.

Adam's tongue dueled with Cassie's as he stroked her deeply, mimicking the action of their loving. She was so incredibly tight wrapped around him, taking all of him until he could swear they would never be able to separate where one stopped and the other began. The sensations were intense as he rocked into her body, loving the feel of Cassie writhing beneath him.

Adam had known they'd be great together, but the reality of it was way better than the fantasy. Cassie moved her mouth from his and kissed his jaw, his throat, before settling on his chest and raining kisses across it. She flicked her tongue across one nipple, and Adam knew that his orgasm was imminent. He pumped, once, twice, harder, and suddenly it was upon him. Cassie cried out his name at that moment, and Adam knew that this experience was like nothing he'd ever felt before. His body stiffened as he emptied himself into her. Pulling him close, Cassie held tight as his body convulsed, loving the feel of him, relishing the hardness of muscle.

Adam rolled over and pulled Cassie with him, kissing the top of her head. "That was better than I'd thought possible," he whispered. "That was what I had hoped for the last time we were here." At the memory of their time in this bed, he stiffened.

"Are you okay? Did I hurt you?" His voice was laced with concern. It would have been horrible if he hurt her again, especially after what they had shared.

Cassie smiled and placed tiny kisses on his chest. "I'm fine, Adam. I knew this time would be different. The doctor told me that it would take a few weeks for me to recover. This time it was perfect." She pushed herself up so that she could look at his face. "Don't worry. I don't think it would be possible to feel any better than I do right now."

She was rewarded with a killer smile she wished he'd

use more often. Adam reached a hand out and smoothed the hair away from Cassie's face, loving the feel of it, the softness. "You are so beautiful, Cassandra, so damn beautiful." His hand roamed around and cupped her nape as he pulled her face toward his to kiss her. With his mouth lingering on hers, Adam wondered if it was too soon to have her again.

Cassie purred and rubbed and snuggled closer to him. "So…" she began, "you run your own business, you cook a decent steak, and you're not half-bad to look at…" She teased him with light kisses, and Adam found himself wanting to play along.

"Not half-bad, huh? Well, what if I told you that I also had a fabulous dessert planned for us?"

"You mean this wasn't it?"

"Oh, no…I'm smarter than that. And besides, that would have been way too obvious. No, I thought I was going to have to woo you a bit more, so I found the best dessert possible."

"Is there chocolate?"

"Baby, it's chocolate wrapped in chocolate and filled with chocolate."

"Okay, that upped your appearance factor…"

"Lucky me."

Cassie smiled wickedly. "Any chance of us eating dessert in that swimming pool of a tub you've got?"

Adam's eyes darkened with desire and the thoughts of the possibilities. "I think that could most definitely be arranged." He leaned in and kissed her, deeply, thoroughly. "Later…"

Chapter 11

CASSIE WAS BUSY SUPERVISING THE ARRIVAL OF RENTAL chairs and the setup of lights while Adam sat in the living room talking with Grace on the phone. He was only half-listening to his assistant; he was too enthralled with watching Cassie waltz around the deck as she assisted in all the commotion. He was having a hard time seeing how it was all going to come together, but Adam was confident that Cassie had everything under control.

Hell, the woman was an expert at being in control.

Adam thought of all the ways Cassie had been in control during the night and had to shift in his seat to accommodate the erection those images brought on. While he hadn't put into play his original fantasy of making love to her in every room of the house—yet—they had certainly made love in enough places that it would take Adam a long time before he could come into this house and not think of her.

Finishing his call with Grace with instructions for her to contact him as soon as their European clients arrived at the office on Thursday, Adam returned to watching Cassie. She was shouting orders to the electrician and moving and repositioning chairs that the crew from the rental company had set up. She was militant in her details, and Adam knew that it was only one of the reasons that he had used Cassie's company for the past two years. Every event she had ever done for him was executed exactly as he had wanted—something that was hard to find in any service industry, but Cassie seemed to know exactly how he wanted things and she listened to his needs.

That brought another smile and image to mind, and Adam knew he had to do something to get these work crews out of here soon so he and Cassie could be alone. Soon. Rising from the sofa, Adam walked out onto the deck and stood next to Cassie.

"How's it all going?" he asked, though all he wanted to hear was that the workmen were leaving.

"Great…" she said distractedly before turning her attention to the electrician. "Jerry, I don't want the lights so clustered together. I'm looking for a starry night, something twinkly, not stadium lighting." Cassie sighed with frustration and then turned to Adam. "Honestly, I would like someone, for once, to understand the difference between romantic lighting and highway lighting."

Adam chuckled. "Does it make a difference?"

Cassie looked at him wide-eyed. "Of course it makes a difference! If it didn't matter, I'd go to the store and grab some Christmas lights and throw them around! Geez, Adam." She took a couple of steps away, leaning over a railing to watch the progress of the lights being strung on the lower level. Nodding with approval, she returned her attention to Adam.

"I think it's important to create the right atmosphere. We're going for the whole 'enticing them with the beach' thing and eating outside to listen to the sounds of the waves crashing on the sand, and if you have a spotlight in your face, it sort of takes away from the appeal. Don't you think?"

She was so serious about twinkly lights, and all

Adam wanted to do was yell at everyone to leave his home immediately. Walking up to her, he leaned his face against hers and whispered, "I think that tonight, when it's good and dark outside, we'll turn off all the lights in the house and come out here and test out your lighting."

"Oh, really," she purred. "To what purpose?"

"To see if it all meets with my approval, of course." When she swatted playfully at Adam's arm, he added, "And to see how glorious you look naked under the twinkly lights."

Cassie sucked in a breath at his words. Twenty-four hours before, she couldn't have imagined the turn in their relationship. She had come here fully intending to stick to her guns and be all business.

She was so glad she had let that go! Too bad night was such a long way off. "I'll be looking forward to that." She kissed him lightly on the cheek and then turned to yell at Jerry for not spreading the lights out properly.

Adam wanted to be annoyed that she was working when he wanted to play, but he respected her work ethic, another reason they seemed to click. Resignation dawned, and Adam knew he would have to find something to do so Cassie could complete her own work without him distracting her.

He knew she needed to drive into town later on to confirm all her orders and do some shopping. He would accompany her, of course, and then perhaps when she was done shopping they could have an early dinner so they could simply play when they got home.

The idea had merit, and Adam smiled at his plan. Tonight he would like to take her skinny-dipping in the heated pool. After dessert in the tub last night—an image that would never have him looking at a bath the same way again—he couldn't wait to get Cassie naked and in the water again. True, their shared shower this morning had been adventurous, but his mind was made up about the pool.

Cassie was an incredible lover, responsive to his touch and not afraid to ask for what she wanted. She gave tirelessly, and she was exciting to be with. It wasn't often that he found a woman who met his needs in bed so completely or was as insatiable as he. Adam looked up at the sound of Cassie's laughter and thought of how well she truly did fit in here, in his world.

It was only a matter of time before Bev and Stephen married, and then they would be family. Adam knew that he was not the marrying kind, but he also felt a strange ache at the thought of a time when that was all Cassie would be, a distant relative he saw on holidays and at the occasional family get-together.

Eventually, this relationship would end, and he would move on, and so would Cassie. Adam imagined she would get married and have children someday, and... that thought did *not* sit well with him. How could he possibly sit around the Thanksgiving table and watch Cassie and her husband sharing a laugh or a kiss, knowing exactly what it was like to do those things with her?

He supposed it didn't matter because in the end, this relationship would be over and he would have to deal with it. Cassie came sprinting into the house and ran past him and up the stairs, her jean-clad legs taking the stairs two at a time. "Everything okay?" he yelled out.

Stopping on the stairs, she yelled to him, "No, it's all fine. I have some sketches for the layout that I need to get. It seems Jerry is more of a visual guy, and I can't seem to explain to him exactly what I'm going for. I'll be right down."

That was the difference between the two of them, he supposed. If he were out there dealing with Jerry the electrician, the man would have been fired by now. How hard could it be to string a set of damn lights? Cassie was being fair with the man, but if he didn't get his act together soon and finish up, Adam was going to step in and politely "suggest" that the man send someone who knew what they were doing if he wanted to get paid. Of course, Cassie would have a fit at that, so, watching as she sprinted past him with a poster board in her hand, Adam decided to go down to the lower level and play a game of pool to distract himself for a little while.

It took almost two hours, but finally, all the workmen were gone and Cassie strolled down to the game room where she found Adam. "It is done," she said as she dramatically dropped into a chair, put her head back, and closed her eyes. "What kind of an electrician whose specialty is working with the party rental people doesn't know how to string lights?"

"Did he finally figure it out?"

"No! I ended up doing it while I sent him to help with the torch lights." She let out a little growl of frustration. "I believe that the party rental people and the electrical company will be getting a letter of complaint from me when this weekend is over."

Adam wanted to argue with her that she should have fired the man and refused to pay, but this was her deal, and he was remembering to treat her not as an employee but as his lover.

With that thought in his mind, Adam took advantage of Cassie's position to put his cue stick quietly on the rack and then walk to her. Kneeling in front of her, Adam gently placed his hands on her knees and then ran them up her thighs. Cassie smiled but didn't lift her head or open her eyes.

"I think you've worked enough for today," he murmured, his hands on a quest to unbutton her blouse. "You deserve to take it easy the rest of the day."

Cassie moaned with delight as Adam released the last button and moved the fabric aside so he could cup her breasts. "Take it easy? I don't know about that. There's still a lot to do." Her words were raspy as she struggled for breath under Adam's masterful touch.

"Well, maybe I can help you to take a relaxing break then," he suggested.

Now Cassie raised her head. "If there is one thing I learned about you last night, it's that nothing we did was relaxing." That being said, Cassie leaned forward and initiated the kiss that she had been craving for hours. Adam let her take control, and he rose up slightly on his knees to bring them level with one another. She wrapped her arms around him, and when Adam banded his arms around her waist, he pulled Cassie to the floor with him.

Clothes were dispersed quickly, and as Cassie rose above him, poised to take him in, Adam knew without a doubt that he could never tire of this, of her. He made a promise to himself the moment she tightly wrapped her wet folds around him that he would no longer think or plan for tomorrow because he wanted to enjoy Cassie without the worry of when he would have to end it.

Chapter 12

AT ELEVEN SHARP FRIDAY MORNING, CASSIE SPOTTED THE limo pulling into the drive and was well into event planner mode. She had risen before Adam so she could get her work done without him tempting her back into bed. Looking around the main floor of the house, she was surprised that she had gotten everything done while spending so much time tangled around Adam!

Walking over to the intercom, she called to Adam in his office that his guests had arrived. While Adam went out to greet everyone, Cassie busied herself with placing platters of fruit and cheese and crackers on the breakfast bar. She wiped her hands with a cloth, straightened her apron, and ran to the bathroom mirror for a quick look at herself before anyone walked in.

There was a running checklist going through her mind; each of the bedrooms being used had been stocked with gift baskets that included chocolates, fragrances, cosmetics, and every essential the guests might need for the weekend, along with brochures on all the places Adam had booked for them. In each bathroom were spa robes and slippers, as well as champagne and small platters of fruit with gourmet cookies. As Cassie had left each room earlier, she couldn't help but be impressed by what Adam had done; his home now rivaled the most elite of spas.

Greetings were made as Adam introduced Cassie with no title other than "Cassandra," and she was relieved to find that all the guests spoke English, although each with a slightly different accent. Nigel and Camile Moreau were a lovely French couple; Martin and Elizabeth Chapin were in their thirties and very British. Finally, the slightly less British Max and Danielle Chamberlain. Cassie knew she'd like them the most. Both smiled brightly and focused on her during the introductions, and when they heard that Cassie would be preparing all the meals, Danielle almost pulled free of her husband to start talking recipes with her! The Chamberlains were the youngest of the three couples, and Cassie was relieved that she would have something in common with at least one of the women.

Within an hour, everyone had settled into their rooms, and Cassie was busy setting their lunch on the table she'd set on the deck. The weather was unseasonably warm for late October on the Carolina coast, and she was grateful for it. Adam did switch on two of the four heat lamps for good measure, and when the last of the food was on the table, Cassie held the door as Adam led the guests to their seats.

Seeing that everyone was settled, Cassie took one last glance outside and frowned. She knew she had set the table for seven but now spotted an empty chair—with a place setting—next to Adam. Turning to head into the kitchen, Cassie heard Adam excuse himself and walk toward her.

"Cassandra?"

She turned and saw him looking at her expectantly. "I know I set that table for seven, Adam. I didn't think I needed to interfere with your meeting," she whispered so the guests wouldn't overhear.

"And I told you that you were our hostess for the

weekend, and that means dining with us. Now please, Cassandra, our guests are waiting." He held out a hand and stared so intently at her that Cassie didn't have it in her to argue. She let herself be led to the table and apologized for the delay.

"I wanted to make sure I had remembered everything," she said lightly as the conversation started to buzz around her.

The meal started with an antipasto platter, followed by a cold tricolored tortellini salad with pesto, and finished with individual seafood quiches with a field greens salad on the side and freshly baked rolls. All in all, Cassie was pleased with the menu, and the praise that followed the meal reinforced that she had made all the right choices.

When Cassie stood to begin clearing, Adam excused himself and the executives—Nigel, Elizabeth, and Max—to talk business. The spouses all waved and said goodbye and yet stayed in their seats, content to listen to the waves and enjoy the scenery.

"Lunch was amazing, Cassandra," Danielle said when Cassie finally finished the cleanup and came out to the deck.

"Please, call me Cassie. Adam is the only one who insists on being so formal." All three nodded in understanding. "I'm glad you enjoyed it."

Danielle sighed and looked out at the water. "You must never tire of this view."

Cassie couldn't help but agree. "I've only been here twice, but honestly, if you are early risers, I highly recommend watching the sunrise. It is breathtaking."

"Is the house new, then, or you?" Martin Chapin asked.

The other two had the manners to look appalled at the statement, and Cassie could only hope that she could answer in a way that wouldn't raise anyone's ire. "I believe that Adam's had the house for a while. We've worked together for more than two years, and there's never been a need for me to come here before." That sounded good, didn't it?

Martin made a noncommittal sound, and before he could say anything else, both Camile and Danielle began questioning Cassie on the shops and spas that they would be visiting the next day. While Cassie answered everything with a smile she hoped reached her eyes, she couldn't help but wonder if playing hostess was such a good idea. Although two of the three were very pleasant and sociable, it was going to be harder to win over Martin Chapin, and doing so was completely out of her comfort zone.

It was only two in the afternoon, and Cassie cursed her own efficiency because there was nothing for her to do for at least the next three hours except to socialize. Deciding to forge ahead and deal with it, she stood and faced the group. "Our spa appointments aren't until tomorrow, but if anyone's up for a tour of the town and some light shopping, I would be happy to lead the way!"

Her tone was cheery and full of enthusiasm, and soon the four of them were walking out the door and piling into the Lexus SUV Adam had brought with him for such an outing. As part of their plans, Adam and Cassie had agreed that while he was in meetings, she should do whatever she needed to with the spouses and not disturb him. But part of her really needed to disturb him to ask how she was to handle the questions of their relationship, but she decided that Adam must trust her to do the right thing, so off she went.

Three hours later, Cassie felt as if she had run a marathon both mentally and physically. Luckily, by the time they arrived at the house, Debbie was already in the kitchen busily doing what needed to be done. Cassie could have kissed her.

The two female guests, each loaded with purchases, headed up to their rooms to relax for a couple of hours before dinner. Martin, who'd taken off on his own rambles in town, walked to the beach. Cassie pulled on her apron, clipped her hair back, and wished that she could do the same. She'd kill for a soak in the tub and maybe a nap before facing this group again but knew there was work to be done.

Adam found her sautéing fresh vegetables while Debbie set the table outside. "How was your afternoon?" he asked, leaning forward to smell what she was so easily tossing.

Cassie wanted desperately to say that all was wonderful, but something in her expression stopped Adam before she could speak. He leaned forward and turned off the burner. Taking the pan from her hand, he moved it to a cooler spot before calling out to Debbie to take over.

"Adam…I need to be…" He took her hand and pulled her from the kitchen, ignoring her protests. They took the elevator up to the master suite and didn't say a word until they were there.

Walking her over to the bed, he sat Cassie down and then stood and asked her the question again. "Truthfully, if you please…"

With a sigh of frustration, she glared at him. "Really,

Adam, I have a meal to prepare. I don't have time for this!"

"I say we do." He folded his arms across his chest, and in that moment Cassie knew there would be no swaying him. She'd do well to answer him and finish preparing dinner.

"It was fine. After you all went to the den to start your meeting, we sat and talked for a bit and then went shopping. Now we're back, they're all resting, and I'm cooking."

If there was one thing Adam had learned about Cassie, it was that she was always happy, except when she wasn't. And right now he knew she wasn't.

Saying nothing, he merely arched a brow at her and waited.

She hated when he did that! "Okay, fine. There was a moment after lunch when I was asked if the house was new or if I was, and it…well, it was awkward. I guess I didn't expect anyone to be so forward with their questions, that's all. And that's why I didn't want to play hostess. I don't want the questions, Adam!"

Adam sat beside her, gently laid her on the bed, and kissed her. "There, was that so hard?" he whispered, tracing one long finger along her jaw as he kissed her gently along the opposite cheek, down the slender column of her throat.

Humming a response, Cassie knew he didn't fully understand why she was upset but at the moment couldn't care less.

"Let me tell you a little something about our guests," he began in between kisses. "The Moreaus are old money, very respected. They have four kids and about a dozen grandkids already. The Chamberlains are the newlyweds of the group, and Max took over the company from Danielle's ailing father. He's eager to keep up her family's tradition in the company and yet make a name for himself. Danielle would rather they left the family business and lived on his family's farm. They're naive and young and desperate to start a family."

"The Chapins are part of an arranged marriage, a business merger. They have no children, nor do they want them. She'll eventually agree to have at least one because his father's will stipulates it. She's great at the business but does hold the reins tightly. I imagine she tells poor old Martin what to do most of the time, and he probably resents being relegated to the wives for the weekend."

Adam lifted his head and stared into Cassie's now-serene face. "He was the one who made the comment, wasn't he?"

Cassie nodded, and Adam rose and held out a hand to help her up from the bed. "Don't let him bother you, Cassandra. He's bitter." He pulled her along to the elevator door and pushed the button. Once inside, he backed her into the corner and kissed her thoroughly. "Don't let anyone take that sparkle out of your eyes ever again."

Before Cassie could respond, they were on the main floor. Adam strode away to start fixing drinks, and Cassie ran to the kitchen to put the finishing touches on what promised to be a spectacular meal.

Afterward, she mingled with the guests and had the opportunity to talk to the executives as well as the spouses.

—ww—

After breakfast the next morning, Cassie gathered the spouses together, and they headed into town for their spa appointments. She felt a little sheepish because Adam had handed her his gold card to use during their outing.

While in bed, he had asked her what she had purchased during the shopping spree earlier in the day since both wives had bragged about their findings. When she had confessed that she hadn't bought herself anything, Adam had frowned and asked why.

"Adam, I don't live in their league," she'd said simply. "I don't find joy in shopping for the sake of spending money. My business is too new for me to make frivolous purchases."

As Cassie was walking out the door on her way to chauffeur everyone to their spa appointments, Adam had pulled her aside, kissed her deeply, and placed the card in her hand with a demand that she be frivolous. His smile was wicked, and Cassie's mind raced with the possibilities in which they could both benefit from her frivolity. She smiled all the way to the spa.

Cassie and Danielle were in the same room for their hot-stone massages. When Adam had booked the packages, Cassie had thought he had merely taken care of the executive spouses, but she had been pleasantly surprised to find that he had booked all the treatments for her too. His generosity would most definitely be rewarded, she told herself.

Cassie was dreamily fantasizing about the night to come when Danielle cleared her throat. "Um…Cassie? Can I ask you something?"

"Sure…"

"Well, Max and I…well, we're doing what needs

to be done for the company, but I'm not...I don't know...I don't think I'm going to like being a corporate wife." She looked over at Cassie and asked, "Am I being selfish?"

"Being a corporate wife is not easy," Cassie began. "I mean, you'll be spending time apart, and even when you get to travel with Max, he'll be in meetings a lot."

Danielle leaned up slightly and smiled. With a sigh of relief, she said, "Exactly! I mean, we're newlyweds, we want to start a family, and it's not happening!"

Cassie chuckled. "Well, things don't always happen as we plan them. Getting pregnant is a funny thing." She shared the story of Katie's unplanned pregnancy. "Believe me, as much as we all love Ella and can't imagine our lives without her, I'm sure Katie wishes she had come along a little later when she was married."

"Do you want kids?"

A sad smile crept across Cassie's face. "Yes, I do. As a matter of fact, I had a procedure done to treat my endometriosis. If I didn't do something, I might not have been able to have kids. I'm hoping that it worked, but I won't know until I'm actively trying to have a baby."

"Does Adam want kids?"

Cassie's first response was a "hell no!" but she decided to keep that to herself. "I don't know, honestly, and our relationship is pretty new, so I don't think either of us is planning or thinking ahead along those lines."

Danielle laid her head down and sighed. "I want to be supportive of Max, I really do. I never thought he'd be that corporate guy, you know?"

"Maybe it's also that you never thought your dad would need someone to take over for him." She said the words gently, and when she looked at Danielle, she saw tears in her eyes.

"Yes," she whispered.

Their attendants came in before they could say any more, and the next few hours passed in a flurry of manicures, pedicures, and facials. Lunch was served to them compliments of the on-site restaurant, and while Cassie wasn't thrilled with the menu, no one else seemed to complain.

By the time they were done, Cassie honestly felt like a wet noodle. Her body was so relaxed and she felt so good that she wasn't ready to think about heading to the house and getting into work mode to prepare for dinner. They all climbed into the car, and Cassie decided she wanted to play a little bit more; with a check of her watch, she saw that she had a solid two hours before she had to be at the house.

"Anyone up for a little more shopping?"

With a car full of agreement, they headed to the mall, and Cassie found numerous frivolous items that would guarantee a proper thank-you to Adam for a perfect day.

Much, much later, sprawled across the king-size bed, Adam breathlessly whispered, "You're welcome."

Chapter 13

THEIR GUESTS WERE SCHEDULED TO LEAVE AFTER LUNCH, and as far as Cassie was concerned, the weekend was a huge success. She had served breakfast in the formal dining room, where she presented platters of homemade Belgian waffles with fresh fruit and also offered eggs Benedict to those requiring more protein.

Adam took the executives to his office on the lower level to finish negotiations while Cassie cleaned up and the spouses packed. She was taking a moment out on the deck to enjoy the peace when Danielle joined her.

"I want you to know, Cassie, that I appreciate all you did for everyone this weekend. Everything was wonderful."

"Thanks, Danielle. Are you all packed?"

She nodded. "I think Adam is very lucky to have you." She turned to Cassie as they both leaned over the rail of the deck observing the waves. "I mean it. I've seen a lot of corporate couples over the years, and while I know you didn't want to make a big deal about it, I think that you and Adam are perfect together."

Cassie bowed her head with dread. This was so not the conversation she wanted to be having. Danielle saw her dismay and went on to dispel it. "No, it's okay, Cassie. Really. Max has had some dealings with Adam in the past, and he cannot believe the change in him. It's because of you! I look at the two of you, the balance you have, and I think you make it look easy. You helped me to see that it can work."

"I didn't do anything—"

"No, you did, Cassie! Everything you said yesterday helped. Last night, while Max and I were in bed, we talked about our future, and for the first time, I feel like I can be the kind of wife he needs. The kind of wife that I know you'll make for Adam."

Lifting her head, Cassie stared at her. "Please, Danielle," Cassie started.

Danielle shook her head. "I have to admit that I didn't know what endometriosis was when we talked yesterday, but last night, I went online and looked it up. I'm so sorry you had to deal with that, and I think that when I get home, I may speak to my doctor because I have a lot of those symptoms. For all I know, that could be why we haven't gotten pregnant yet."

"I hope you get the help you need. I think you're going to make a wonderful mom."

Danielle smiled. "You will too, Cassie. I think you and Adam are going to realize what you have, and the next time I see you, you'll be married and hopefully on your way to having a baby."

There was no way to make Danielle understand that her relationship with Adam was more than likely going to end before it ever got to the point of marriage and babies. After all, who wanted to admit they were in a relationship that had an expiration date? It would be an odd conversation, to be sure, Cassie thought to herself. Desperate for something else to talk about, Cassie racked her brain for other topics but realized that, for

Danielle, these were the things she needed to say and that no one had to know about it.

Until she heard someone clear their throat.

Someone male.

Someone who, when she turned around, did not look happy.

"Oh, hello, Adam!" Danielle said as she walked toward him on her way inside. "Max and I had a fabulous weekend. I can't thank you enough for making this trip a veritable spa getaway for me. I really appreciate it." Then, in a very un-corporate-wife move, Danielle leaned in and kissed Adam on the cheek. "You and Cassie made this a very memorable trip for me, and thanks to Cassie, my greatest wish may soon come true."

She was oblivious to the tension on the deck as she walked inside, and Cassie could only stand rooted to the spot staring at Adam until she was sure they were alone.

"Are your meetings all done?" she asked cautiously.

He nodded tersely. "Yes. Everyone is packing up." Looking at his watch, he added, "Lunch is still scheduled for noon, isn't it?"

It was his tone. He had heard the conversation, and he was not happy about it. Cassie knew that tone of voice: cool and clipped. Adam was trying to be civil, but she knew he was deeply agitated by what he had heard and was annoyed to have to wait to discuss it.

"Yes, lunch is set for noon and will be more casual. I've got sandwiches and salads that we'll eat in the dining room. I've got dessert goody bags they can take with them for the ride to the airport."

"Very good" was all he said before turning from Cassie and walking into the house.

Have a baby with Cassie? That was only *part* of the conversation that had Adam's head spinning. What in the world had Cassie been telling these women? Granted, she seemed as baffled by Danielle's declarations as he was, but perhaps that was for his benefit. Adam raked a hand through his hair in frustration.

Dammit! He had no idea what Cassie had been discussing with the spouses all weekend, especially not after her initial run-in with Martin Chapin. He hadn't wanted to know what was being discussed, except now he felt like he was a fool for not.

While the cat was out of the bag on their relationship, Adam felt that they had been respectful and discreet in their time together in front of everyone. He couldn't deny that he found excuses to touch Cassie and that more than once he caught himself staring at her and, in turn, found one of his colleagues grinning at him, but it was his own damn business!

Sitting behind his desk, Adam replayed Cassie and Danielle's conversation in his mind. Sure, Cassie seemed to be emphatic about the two of them not being in love. Maybe a little too emphatic. Did she have any feelings for him? Was he the only one who felt anything? How pathetic would that make him? Here he was, Mr. Big-Time CEO who swore that he needed to have her to get her out of his system, and there was a great possibility the joke would be on him, and she would walk away without a second thought, and he'd be left behind broken.

No! He would not allow that to happen. He'd accomplished what he wanted to this weekend. His business expansion was on the right track; his negotiations went exactly as he had wanted them to and people would be talking about how Adam Lawrence did business and *want* to work with him.

And through it all, he had had the most sexually satisfying week of his life. Adam knew that days ago he had told himself not to think about ending things with Cassie and to live in the moment, but maybe that hadn't been such a good idea seeing now how people reacted to it. One weekend together, and there was speculation on them getting married and having children. That was so not in his plans, and he didn't need anyone trying to tell him how he should be living his life!

He heard voices up on the main level, and a glance at the clock told him it was almost noon. Another hour and everyone would be gone, and he'd have some time to be alone and think. The rental place would be coming by at three to collect its supplies, and Cassie had made arrangements for the cleaning crew to come in tomorrow after they had left.

Somewhere along the line they had talked about the possibility of staying tonight or going home, and Adam felt he had to get out of here and clear his head, to not be around Cassie and be influenced by her. If he was going to get a handle on this relationship and get to a place where he had total control, he had to get away from the temptation.

And Cassie was most definitely a temptation.

He thought about the night before, the sexy lingerie she had purchased for the specific purpose of him ripping it from her body. That image alone—Cassie stretching across his bed in red lace, begging him—made Adam shift in his seat to accommodate his arousal.

Damn her!

Cassie's laughter wafted to him, and Adam felt a stirring, not only of arousal but of something in the region of his chest. He rubbed his palm over the spot and sighed.

What harm could one more night bring?

Chapter 14

Two hours later, the house was fairly silent. After saying farewell to their group, Adam excused himself to go to the office to make calls and take care of emails. Cassie didn't argue mainly because she had work of her own to do in preparation of them leaving.

As she wiped down the granite countertops, she stopped to wonder at Danielle's words to her. She and Adam were involved, physically, but there was nothing about them, that she noticed anyway, that would make anyone believe they had a deep emotional relationship. They certainly didn't act like they were in love, did they?

She tossed the paper towels into the trash and went to unload the dishwasher. As she placed things in their proper places, Cassie couldn't help but realize that she liked it here. In this house. With this man. In this relationship. She wasn't foolish enough to think that Adam felt the same way, but Cassie prayed he wouldn't be cruel when it all ended.

And she had no doubt it would end. Adam would make sure of that.

Cassie longed to surprise him in his office, like she had in the days before his guests arrived. Looking around, she saw that everything was in order. With a secret smile, she kicked off her shoes and untied her apron. She walked quietly to the half bath and checked her reflection. Pleased that she looked okay, she was about to seek him out when the doorbell rang.

The party rental people had come to collect their supplies.

Waves of disappointment rolled over her, but Cassie knew that if she worked with the crew, the work would be done quickly.

If anyone noticed that Cassie was rushing them along, they chose to say nothing. If anyone picked up on her impatience with their attempt at small talk, they kept it to themselves. In less than an hour, Cassie was bidding them a good day and stopped short of slamming the door behind them while stripping.

Relax. Get a grip, she chanted to herself. It wasn't as if they had abstained from making love while they had people in the house; their lovemaking was more restricted than it had been in the days leading up to it. Cassie enjoyed the sexual, playful side of Adam, and her body was nearly quivering at the thought of being with him again.

Tiptoeing down the stairs, she looked around and saw that the door to his office was open. He was quiet, and when Cassie got to the door, she found Adam simply sitting and reading the newspaper.

"Hi," she said sweetly as she walked through the doorway.

"Hi, yourself. Was that the rental people I heard?"

"Mm-hmm," she said, walking around the side of his desk.

Adam put the paper down and looked at her quizzically. "Everything go okay?"

"Oh, yes. Everything went fine. It's all cleaned up, all

the supplies are gone, and I can say with great certainty that it is completely and utterly finished." Cassie pulled her shirt over her head, shook out her hair, and sat on Adam's desk directly in front of him.

It didn't take a rocket scientist to see where this was going, and Adam was willing to play along. "So… everybody's gone?"

"Yes." Cassie leaned forward so that her breasts were near Adam's face and unhooked her bra.

"And…we're all alone?"

She pulled the bra from her body and leaned on the desk as she dropped the scrap of silk and lace to the floor. "All alone."

Adam stood and looked at the glorious sight before him: Cassie, on his desk. Her breasts bared for him. His hands twitched with the need to touch her. But he waited. He liked the buildup of anticipation. "I was reading the paper…"

A throaty laugh escaped Cassie's throat before she could stop it. "I can lie here and wait until you're finished with it."

A grin spread across Adam's face because he could imagine her doing that. Slowly, teasingly, he began to lean over her. No part of his body touched hers, and Cassie felt her breathing grow ragged; her nipples tightened as they waited for Adam's touch. When she could feel the heat rolling off of his body, when there were mere inches between them, her control snapped.

One arm came up, snaked around Adam's neck, and pulled him toward her, her mouth meeting his in a kiss designed to make him insane. Papers fell to the floor, and a lamp crashed down after them as Adam climbed onto the desk, on top of Cassie, desperate for the contact. All thought of earlier discussions fled his mind. All he could think of was Cassie, of getting her naked, of having her wrapped around him, of the pleasure they would give and take.

"This is no good," he growled in her ear as he tried to find a position that worked for them both. Hastily, Adam stood. He grabbed Cassie's hand, yanked her from the desk, and threw her over his shoulder as she shrieked.

"Adam!"

He walked out of the office and to the game room and put Cassie on her feet next to the pool table. She never had a chance to say a word before Adam claimed her mouth again as he worked her pants off her body. His mouth trailed a path after her pants, and when Cassie's knees buckled, he lifted her onto the pool table and ripped another new pair of panties from her body.

Best money he'd ever spent.

Shoving his own clothes away, Adam couldn't wait any longer; it was too much—his need for her was too great. Foreplay was over. He entered her in one swift stroke that had Cassie bucking off the table and clutching at his shoulders. Their movements were frantic, frenzied. It was over way too soon, and as they both lay breathless and heaving, Adam stared at Cassie's flushed face and felt his heart drop to his knees.

She was beautiful. She was exciting and wild and represented everything that he had worked his whole life to avoid. Cassie smiled up at him and ran a limp hand over his chest. "Want me to get you that newspaper?" she asked.

Standing, Adam pulled away and held out a hand to

her. Taking it, Cassie stood before him, naked and weak. "I want you to come with me upstairs so we can finish this weekend out properly."

They scooped up their clothes, heedless of their nakedness as they rode the elevator up to his suite. Where in the game room there was wildness, here there was tenderness. Where before it had been fast-paced and frantic, now it was slow and sweet. Adam took his time memorizing every inch of Cassie's body, knowing that their time had to come to an end. He was beginning to need her too much, and Adam did not want to need anyone.

There was no thought to time or to reaching a climax; all Adam wanted was to go on touching, kissing, exploring, to bring Cassie to one peak after another. As she cried out his name, it was almost a sob. Adam knew that he would never be able to come to this house again. As much as he wasn't a commitment type of man, he finally found that he did have a heart, and it belonged to this woman.

He didn't want all that went with it.

It would be enough, the memories of this time. For a brief moment in his life, Adam Lawrence knew what it was like to love a woman and be loved in return. There was no doubt in his mind of Cassie's feelings for him. She might not have verbalized them, but they were there in everything she did, every move she made, in the way she touched him.

Rising above her, Adam stared deeply into her eyes, and it was all there for him to see. There were tears, and there was love. Cassie dreamily reached up and touched his face, whispered his name as he entered her. Her eyes closed briefly, but Adam pleaded for her to open them, to look at him, to watch him as he loved her.

"Yes," she whispered to him. "Love me."

With a slow thoroughness, with a patience that Adam didn't know he possessed, he loved her endlessly. With mouths, with hands, with entire bodies, they went on through the night with nothing but the light of the moon shining through the windows.

Sated and exhausted, they finally fell asleep as the first rays of the sun were coming through the clouds. Adam pulled Cassie close and kissed the top of her head as she turned toward him and ran a hand over his chest and a leg over his.

"I love you," she said, so quietly that Adam was almost unsure she'd said it.

It was both everything he wanted and everything he feared all in one. Too exhausted to think, he merely held her tight and let sleep claim him.

Chapter 15

NEITHER KNEW WHAT TO SAY WHEN THEY FINALLY AWOKE after noon. While Cassie was in no rush to get home, Adam most definitely needed to get to the office. Cassie prepared a light lunch for them, and once they had eaten and packed up their cars, she turned to Adam, desperate for something to say that wasn't the awkward small talk they'd been sharing all morning.

"Adam, I…" She looked at him and had to hide her disappointment when his face was expressionless, much like it used to be in their business dealings.

"The house closing staff are due this afternoon, aren't they?" he asked stiffly.

Cassie nodded.

"Good. When you get home, submit everything to Grace, and she'll take care of your check." He looked at his watch. "I have to go. Will you be okay driving home?" If there had been a hint of tenderness in his voice, Cassie would have been okay; she would have believed that last night had been real.

Tears clogged her throat as she nodded and turned away. She was reaching for the handle of her car door when Adam spun her around and claimed her mouth ruthlessly with his. The tenderness from last night was gone, and in its place was the kiss of a stranger, a kiss that signaled an end.

Without a word, Adam released her, walked to his

car, and sped away. Cassie stood where she was for some minutes, trying to compose herself. What had gone wrong? What had happened between dawn and now to make Adam change so drastically?

As if on autopilot, Cassie climbed into her car and made the three-hour drive home. She had no recollection of the scenery or of anything she saw along the way. Since it was a Monday, there was nobody waiting at the shop, and she was able to unload her car and settle into her apartment in relative peace and quiet. She'd had a magical week. She'd had a taste of what it was like to be in a relationship with someone who understood her and gave as much as he took.

With a mirthless laugh, Cassie swung her suitcase into her closet. She never thought she'd see the day when Adam Lawrence gave anything. But he had; throughout the week, he had given to her time and time again…and that's what hurt so much. Because in the end, his giving was all an act. He gave so that he could get, and Cassie most certainly gave to him—she gave him the perfect weekend for his clients, and that in turn was going to make him a lot of money.

It was all speculation, and deep down she knew it, but it helped her to keep from crumpling to the floor and crying to the point of pain. If she could make herself believe that Adam was the selfish bastard she had originally pegged him for, she would be all right. In time, she would forgive herself for being foolish and falling for his act, but for right now, it hurt too damn much.

Maybe it wasn't goodbye; maybe he was distracted. Maybe his mind was on getting to work; after all, he had been away for almost an entire week. Cassie had no idea what to think or what to allow herself to feel, and she wouldn't know until she saw Adam again.

Wiping the tears that were streaming down her face, she walked to the bathroom, washed up, and composed herself. There was no use in getting all worked up when she had no idea what there was to get worked up about.

The previous night had been like a dream, so full of passion like she'd never known. Perhaps Adam hadn't either. Maybe he didn't know what to do with what they had shared and it scared him. Cassie much preferred that scenario. Leaving the bathroom, she walked to the phone and decided to check in with her family. That normally made her feel better, and if she knew her family as well as she thought she did, she'd be sharing a meal with them within the hour.

Predictable was good.

Unless you were Adam Lawrence.

His life used to be predictable, and that was the way he liked it. Now it irritated the hell out of him. It was late Monday evening, and although less than twelve hours had passed since he had left Cassie, her face wouldn't leave his mind.

Her sleepy words stayed with him and made him uneasy. Damn, but he was being fickle. First, he was irritated because he thought she had no feelings for him, and now he was pissed because she did! *Make up your mind, Lawrence!*

Memories of the weekend flooded his mind: their lovemaking, their conversations. Not once during that entire time did it feel awkward or uncomfortable. Being without her made him feel that way, however.

Adam thought about the scene he'd witnessed when they were seeing the executives off. Cassie had been standing with the Chamberlains, and they were both beaming. Max Chamberlain had hugged Cassie, and Adam could tell that he was profusely thanking her, and then Danielle took a turn hugging her. He understood Danielle's enthusiasm, but why had Max felt the need to thank her?

Then there were the Chapins. As Cassie had walked over to say goodbye to them, he saw, unbelievably, Elizabeth Chapin smile and hug Cassie. He'd nearly fallen down the steps in shock. The woman who rarely cracked a smile or said a kind word to anyone actually hugged Cassie, and what was more, Cassie seemed genuinely pleased by the embrace.

She fit.

She fit into his life in every possible way. Looking back, Adam couldn't find it in himself to be angry over the initial disagreement they'd had. If it hadn't been for that moment, for that fight, they might not be where they were today. He might not have ever known what it was like to be with her, to know who she truly was. He might have lived his same, empty existence these past six weeks had it not been for that one fateful day.

How could he continue to hold a grudge against it?

Adam stood abruptly and looked at his watch. Dammit, it was too late to call or go over to Cassie's. Tomorrow was another day, and he'd have to wait. Knowing that he hated to fail at anything or to be wrong, Adam knew that waiting the night could only help him to see things more clearly. He was willing to take a chance with Cassie. He was willing to see if he could possibly have a relationship with her and see where it went.

He liked her; he trusted her.

He knew it was possible to love her.

One more check of his watch had him cursing his own timing. He was anxious to explain everything to Cassie, and after her declaration that morning, he knew she'd feel the same way as he did. He wanted to be wide awake and looking at her when she said it again.

Tomorrow couldn't come soon enough.

—⁓—

Unfortunately, tomorrow had other plans. When Adam arrived at the office, Grace was waiting with a stack of messages from his client in South America who was still having issues. Adam knew that he would have to go himself and fix the problem in person, but for the first time in his entire professional career, he wished there was someone else to do it for him.

Barking travel instructions at Grace as he packed up his briefcase, Adam made a mental note to call Cassie once he was in flight and on his way. With a swiftness he was known for, Adam had everything he needed packed and ready to go within the hour and the company jet waiting for him at RDU Airport. A driver brought him directly to the tarmac, and he shared a brief conversation with the pilot and flight attendant as they prepared to take off.

Knee-deep in paperwork and on his fifth call to South America to confirm his arrival and accommodations, Adam took a brief moment to call Cassie. He got her voicemail, and while he hated leaving messages, he was willing to make an exception.

"Hello, Cassandra, it's Adam…I am on my way to South America for a few days…I've got a difficult client I'm dealing with…but when I get back, I'd like to talk to you. You can reach me on my cell." He paused, unsure of himself and what to say. He hated having conversations with machines! "Anyway, I look forward to hearing from you. Bye."

Even to himself, Adam knew that he sounded awkward and uncomfortable. He was sure that he'd hear from Cassie at some point during the day, and if all went well, he'd be home within two to three days and he'd see her. The thought made him smile.

But best-laid plans and all that… It was almost a week before Adam returned home, and while he was gone, Cassie had tried to call him several times only to get his voicemail. By the time Adam was able to try and return her calls, it was always too late at night her time to call or he got her voicemail.

He was beyond frustrated.

It was Saturday evening when Adam finally found himself in Raleigh. Without bothering to stop at his home, he drove directly to Cassie's in hopes of finding her in.

The shop was dark, and there was no answer in her apartment. A look around the parking lot showed him that the catering van was gone, so she must be on a job. *Dammit!* Adam could have kicked himself for not calling first, but he had been so anxious to see her in person that he couldn't wait.

It was only after seven p.m., so he climbed into his

car and called his mother. Maybe she would have some idea of what kind of event Cassie was doing and when she could be expected to be done.

"Adam! How are you, sweetheart?" Bev gushed at the sound of her son's voice.

"Fine, Mother, fine. I just got back from six days in South America."

"Oh my! Is everything okay?"

Adam gave her the quick version of his week, sparing her the specifics. "Anyway, I was driving home from the airport and wanted to see how you were doing."

"We're all fine here. Stephen and I are watching Ella tonight because the girls had a big event. Katie said that we shouldn't expect to see her until around three a.m." She made a tsking sound. "They all work so hard, and I know it kills her to be away from Ella for so long."

A noncommittal sound came out as Adam waited to hear any news about Cassie. "The party is so big that Lauren is helping out. They are catering a wedding for two hundred people!"

Adam groaned with frustration. That meant that not only would he not be seeing Cassie tonight, but she was probably going to sleep all day tomorrow.

"Listen, Adam, while I have you on the phone, we're all going out to dinner Tuesday night. Nothing fancy, coming together to celebrate the end of Lauren's semester and some other family stuff. Would you like to join us?"

Normally, Adam would have avoided such a gathering like the plague, but if it meant being with Cassie and learning to be part of the family dynamic, then he was willing to give it a try.

Bev gave him all the information, and with promises of seeing each other Tuesday night, they hung up. Adam sat in the car staring at Cassie's building as if willing her to appear. Monday would have him swamped in the office from being away all week, and so with cursed luck, it would seem that the next time he would get to see her would be Tuesday night at this family dinner. Maybe he would call her and have Cassie meet him at his office on Tuesday and they could drive to dinner and go home together.

Starting the car and leaving the lot, Adam sighed with resignation and found himself wishing for Tuesday to arrive.

———

Cassie was nervous as she rode the elevator up to Adam's office. They had been playing phone tag ever since they'd left the beach, and although she took it as a positive sign that Adam was coming to a family dinner, she couldn't seem to shake the feeling that something was going to go wrong.

Grace smiled broadly when Cassie approached the desk. "Hey, Cass! Adam said to tell you that his meeting is running a bit long and that you should make yourself at home in his office."

Adam's assistant was nearly bouncing in her seat, and her eyes were bright with expectations. Cassie smiled at her. "Something on your mind, Grace?" she asked lightly.

"Who? Me? I'm wondering how all this family togetherness is working out."

With a chuckle, Cassie shook her head. "It's strange,

right? No matter how much time passes, I still cannot believe that my father is marrying Adam's mom. I mean, what are the odds of that happening?"

"Small world and all that."

"That's for sure. Anyway, we all adore Bev, and we're truly excited about the wedding…" She paused, and Grace could tell that Cassie was searching for the right thing to say.

"But it's still awkward because of Adam, right?" Grace supplied.

"Yes!" Cassie said, relieved that someone understood. "I think things are getting better, but sometimes he…well, you know how he is."

Grace nodded and smiled. "Yes, I certainly do." The phone on the desk rang, and Grace held up a slender finger to indicate to Cassie to wait for a moment while she took the call.

"Believe it or not, this call is for you."

"For me?" Disbelief laced her voice. "Who on earth would call me here?"

"It's Danielle Chamberlain."

A smile crept across Cassie's face as she held out her hand for the phone. Grace swatted it away. "Don't be ridiculous, you can take it in Adam's office."

Not wanting to keep Danielle waiting, Cassie walked into Adam's suite, tossed her purse onto the nearest surface, and walked around his desk as she picked up the phone. "Danielle?"

"Oh, Cassie, I'm so glad you were there! I was afraid that I'd have to make a dozen calls before I found you."

"Is everything okay? Are you all right?"

"Everything is beyond all right," Danielle said,

bursting with excitement. "I took your advice and went to see my doctor as soon as we got home from the trip."

"And?" Cassie prompted, praying that she was going to hear good news.

"We don't have to try to get pregnant because we already are!" The two women screeched with excitement, and Cassie felt a twinge of jealousy toward Danielle. She knew that now wasn't the right time for her to be pregnant, but at the same time, Cassie knew that she was anxious to have a family of her own.

"I wanted you to be one of the first to know. You were so wonderful to me that entire weekend, and you helped me put things into perspective. I don't have a lot of friends who understood what I was feeling."

"I'm so glad I was able to help, Danielle, really, and I'm so excited for you."

"What about you, Cassie? When are you and Adam going to get married and start a family?"

For a moment, Cassie was too stunned to speak. She had thought that she'd made herself clear on that last day about her and Adam's relationship. "Um, I don't think that's in the cards. Like I told you at the beach, our relationship isn't like that."

Danielle laughed. "Then you weren't seeing what the rest of us were seeing. You're in love with Adam! You've told him that, right?"

"No, I'm not in love with Adam, and—"

"You are, and wouldn't you love to have babies with him? Have you told him that?"

"The subject of a baby hasn't come up, and—"

Danielle was on a roll. "What are you waiting for? You're both crazy about one another!"

At that point, Cassie zoned out. She knew that her feelings for Adam were deep and they were real and that she was quite possibly already in love with him. But marriage and babies? Could they have that kind of a future together? Thinking on some of their previous conversations on the whole concept of love and marriage, she couldn't fathom Adam wanting any part of such a thing.

Danielle was still rambling on about all her baby plans, and Cassie made the appropriate comments when necessary. A quick glance at her watch told her she and Adam were going to be late for dinner with her family if she didn't get off the phone soon and go find Adam.

"Listen, Danielle, I hate to cut you short, but we're having dinner with my family tonight, and I've got to find Adam or we'll be late." Thank God she didn't have to lie, she thought.

"I understand. Oh, and Cassie? Please don't say anything yet to Adam about the baby. Max wants to do it."

"Believe me," Cassie stated with more than a little relief in her voice, "I will not be telling Adam about the baby." She quickly hung up and went to grab her purse as Adam walked into the office.

"Hey!" she said cheerily, the sight of him making her smile. "Is your meeting done?"

Adam stood in front of her, merely staring. "Adam?"

He cleared his throat. "Yes," he said gruffly. "Let me grab my jacket and we can go."

The walk to the car was relatively quiet. Cassie figured he was smoothing out from a tense meeting and was willing to let him unwind before meeting with everyone. She knew these get-togethers were new to him and a little overwhelming, so if he needed a few minutes of quiet, she was fine with that.

With fists tightly gripping the steering wheel, Adam drove toward the restaurant, his mind spinning. Was Cassie pregnant? He had only heard part of her conversation, and from what he did hear, that seemed to be the logical conclusion. When his meeting had let out and he'd returned to his office, Grace had notified him that Cassie was in his office on the phone. Out of consideration for her privacy, he'd waited until she was done. Unfortunately, her voice carried, and whomever it was she was speaking to, the talk was mainly about babies. He would have passed it off as a friend's pregnancy until he heard Cassie say that she wasn't going to tell him about it.

Why the hell would she keep that from him?

Glancing at Cassie, he felt his heart lurch. She was so damn beautiful that she made him ache. There had to be a way for him to find out if she was pregnant and why she was keeping it from him. But how? He could come out and ask her, but that might put her on the defensive and she'd deny it. He had to come up with a plan.

For tonight, he'd observe her, see how she behaved and how her family acted toward her. The thought of her keeping such a huge secret from him burned. He wanted to trust Cassie and believe that he'd misinterpreted what he'd heard, but Adam knew that trust was not his strong suit. If she thought that she'd keep his child from him and then demand money from him later on, she'd be in for a huge surprise! There would be no payout for having his baby. She could make her money some other way other than bargaining for what was rightfully his!

Hell, even in his own mind he sounded slightly deranged. Cassie had never asked him for anything; how could he possibly believe that she would do something so underhanded? She came from an honest family who worked hard for what they had. Adam was finally starting to see and respect that about them. The whole Jacobs family was made up of career-minded, good people. He was glad that his mother was going to be a part of such a group.

As they pulled into the parking lot of the Italian restaurant, Cassie turned to Adam and smiled. "I'm so glad you were able to join us tonight. I know family dinners aren't your thing, but tonight is a big night."

He was about to ask her why when the valet appeared and opened her door. Adam climbed out and rounded the hood of the car to join Cassie, and within minutes they were surrounded by her family's hearty greetings.

Over the next thirty minutes, they were seated and enjoying drinks while looking over the menus; the conversation never seemed to stop. He engaged in conversation about his recent trip to South America and saw both Cassie and his mother smile with pride. It all made him feel so good, but he couldn't shake the feeling that something was up. What had she meant about it being a big night? Would she announce her pregnancy here at the table in front of her whole family?

"So what do you think, Adam?" Cassie's father was looking at him expectantly across the table with a smile on his face. What had the man been talking about? "You're a businessman. Ever dabble in real estate?"

Before he could answer, another wave of conversation started to his left. He heard Lauren talking about trying to find a major company to take her on. She wanted to stay close to home right now, preferably in Raleigh, but the thought of soliciting strangers made her uneasy.

To his right, he heard Cassie and Katie talking about expanding CJ's: taking on a bigger staff and possibly adding a bakery to the business. The words around him became a loud buzzing in his head, and all he could hear clearly were Cassie's words from earlier: *"Believe me, I will not be telling Adam about the baby."*

He heard his name several more times; everyone was trying to engage him in one conversation or another, and they all seemed to be based upon wanting something from him: business advice, a job, perhaps money for expansion. Maybe that was her game: see if he would help her family and then tell him about the baby. Hell no, he thought. He was going to put a stop to this right now. Flattening the menu against the tabletop, he stood abruptly.

"Adam?" Cassie reached out and placed her hand on his arm. "Are you all right?"

Her touch burned, and he quickly pulled free of her. "All right?" he sneered. "No, I'm not all right, dammit! What the hell is going on here?" His eyes scanned the table, and he was met with nothing but confusion from six pairs of eyes.

With her voice no more than a whisper, Cassie reached out to him again. "Why don't you sit down?"

"I don't need to sit. I think I know what's going on." His gaze snapped to his mother's. "It always ends up like this, doesn't it? I almost thought that it was going to be different this time, that this family, these people, were going to be different. Clearly, I was wrong." There was an edge to his voice, and when he noted the fear in his mother's eyes, he almost apologized. Almost.

"Adam, please," Bev said, her voice trembling slightly. "Whatever it is that you're thinking, you're wrong."

"Am I?" he sneered. "You mean that I'm not being propositioned for a job or investments? Again? You'd think you'd have learned after the last time. It always comes to this—money. Well, I'll tell you what, I'm not interested in investing," he spat as he looked at Stephen. "Or hiring," he said to Lauren. "Or whatever it is you're cooking up," he said finally to Cassie. The look of utter devastation gave him pause, but then he remembered her words again, "*Believe me, I will not be telling Adam about the baby*," and knew that she was no different. She couldn't be trusted. His first assessment of her was the right one, and he was a fool to think otherwise.

Kicking the chair away from him, he strode from the table out of the restaurant and out of their lives.

Chapter 16

HOURS TURNED INTO DAYS, DAYS TURNED INTO WEEKS, AND yet it all had no meaning to Adam. He worked twenty hours a day, seven days a week, doing everything he could to erase the time he'd spent with Cassie and her family from his mind.

Unfortunately, it wasn't working.

Thanksgiving had come and gone without a word from his mother. That was something that had never happened in his entire life. After all the debacles with Bev's previous relationships, she had never forgotten Adam on a holiday—even if she was only able to call. Running a tired hand over his face, Adam sighed. Instead of being thankful that he was through with the Jacobs family, he had to be honest and admit that he missed them…and Bev. They had never gone for this long without speaking.

A quick glance at the calendar showed that it was a mere three weeks until Christmas. He tended to travel over Christmas, choosing to spend the holiday with strangers overseas than in his own home. This year that held no appeal. Adam contemplated picking up the phone and calling his mother—to check in and make sure she was okay—but shame kept him from making the call. At that moment, he saw the tears in her eyes once again and heard the tremble in her voice and didn't want to face the possibility of hearing it again on the other end of the phone.

Adam was shot out of his depressing thoughts as Grace walked through the office door with the day's mail. She tossed it on his desk with a snort of derision that was becoming her trademark these days. Apparently, she had heard about what had happened with Cassie and her family and had taken sides. Her displeasure with Adam was evident every time she looked at him. He was about to comment on how he was getting tired of her childish behavior when she turned and faced him.

"Stephen Jacobs is here to see you." It was as if she'd thrown down the gauntlet. One eyebrow arched, and she folded her arms across her middle as her expression dared Adam to refuse to see him.

Swallowing hard, he simply stared and said, "Show him in." He watched as Grace strode from the office. His mind raced with the thought of what Stephen Jacobs could have to say to him. Why now? After almost six weeks, why show up now? He didn't have to wait long because Stephen was a man with a purpose; he walked into Adam's office and directly up to his desk, where he tossed an oversized envelope down.

"Your mother doesn't know I'm here," he bluntly stated. "I'm not going to pretend to understand or excuse your behavior at our last meeting, but your mother and I are going to marry on Christmas Eve, and I know it would mean a lot if you were there." With that, Stephen turned and headed out of the office.

Adam jumped up from his chair. "Stephen, wait!" he called after him.

Stephen turned slowly and faced Adam, his expression guarded. "What do you want, Adam?"

Walking around his desk, Adam felt a sense of

desperation. "Is she okay? Is there anything I can do for the wedding?"

A small smile played across Stephen's face as he let out a pent-up breath. "Bev's fine. She misses you, and she's embarrassed by what happened, but other than that, I think all the wedding planning has kept her busy." He placed his hands in his trouser pockets and continued to stare at Adam. "We decided to have it at the house, nothing fancy, the family. All you need to do is show up."

While Adam knew that Stephen was trying to do the right thing, he had his doubts that he'd be welcomed by anyone at the event. "I don't think it would be such a good idea for me to come. I don't want to ruin your big day."

Stephen shook his head. "You don't get it, do you? Family forgives one another. You're Bev's son, and that makes you my family. Having you there would mean the world to her, and I want to do everything possible to make your mother happy. This isn't about you, Adam, this is about Bev."

"I know, I know," Adam said, raking a hand through his hair. "I'm trying to do the right thing here. Things got…awkward there at the end, and…well, I want everyone to be able to enjoy themselves, and I don't think my being there is going to make that possible."

"Nonsense," Stephen said, and he stepped forward and put a reassuring hand on Adam's shoulder. "Like I said, family forgives, and this isn't about you. We're getting together for a small wedding and some dinner."

Though the statement was meant to be reassuring, Adam recalled that he had made a debacle of every dinner he'd attended with the Jacobs family. Then

Adam remembered how excited his mother and Cassie had been when they talked about having the wedding at Adam's house on the beach. He cringed at the memory of how he'd killed their excitement with his selfishness and distrust. He didn't deserve anyone's forgiveness. "Why don't you have a seat and we'll talk about this?" he suggested.

The smile that spread across Stephen's face told Adam everything he needed to know.

—⁓—

"And you're sure he's not coming?" Cassie asked for the tenth time, as she put the finishing touches on the large, festive centerpiece on the dining room table.

"Oh my God," Lauren mumbled. "Please do not ask that question again." Placing the groceries in the refrigerator, she turned to Cassie. "We've been over this a million times. Dad invited Adam to the wedding. He declined. Instead, he offered the use of his beach house as a gift to Dad and Bev since he knew that Bev had expressed interest in having the wedding here."

"Still…don't you think it's odd that—"

"No!" both Katie and Lauren snapped.

With a sigh, Cassie took a look around, pleased with the progress that they'd made. It was two days before Christmas, and apparently Adam had even sprung for a decorator because when they had arrived earlier in the day, there were several elaborately decorated Christmas trees set up around the house and twinkly lights donning the exterior. There wasn't much else for them to do preparation-wise, so she tried to focus on the menu for the rest of their stay.

Lost in her own thoughts, she missed the look her two sisters exchanged. Soon Bev and Stephen arrived, followed by Matt.

"I think everyone is arriving today," Bev said, excitement in her voice. What was originally supposed to be the family had grown. Besides Cassie, her siblings, and the bride and groom, Bev's sister and brother-in-law were flying in, and Stephen's brother, Mark, was driving down for the festivities. Because the guest list was growing a bit and Cassie wanted to be able to relax, she had two of her servers who were going to be alone for the holidays come to stay with them. The extra hands were going to be a blessing on the day of the wedding.

With nine bedrooms, there was plenty of room for everyone without having to use the master suite. For some reason, Stephen and Bev had refused to use it, as had everyone else. Cassie had chosen one of the smaller bedrooms for herself, not allowing herself to go to the top floor. The memories were still too strong and hurt too much. Would she ever be over Adam? Would there come a day when she didn't think about him? Long for him? Ache for him?

Probably not going to happen while she was staying in his house, she thought miserably to herself. Dammit.

"We have one more surprise," Stephen said as he got everyone's attention. When all eyes were on his, he continued. "I didn't want to say anything until I was completely sure, but it looks like my sister Rose and her husband will be joining us for all the festivities too!" He hadn't seen his siblings in more than five years, so the fact that they were coming for his wedding was great news for everyone.

Silently, Cassie did the room count again. Okay, maybe Uncle Ed and Aunt Rose would take the master suite and she wouldn't have to worry. She didn't realize that she'd spoken the words out loud until Stephen commented, "Nonsense, you know your aunt, she hates to be higher than the second story. Fear of heights and all. Take the master suite, Cass, and be done with it, okay?" His tone was light, and Cassie was sure that he had no idea what he would be subjecting her to.

Over the course of the next two hours, all the guests arrived, and it was joyful chaos. Poor Matt got stuck with moving everyone's luggage all around the house, and the noise level was near deafening at times. Cassie looked at the time and saw that it was nearing four o'clock, and she instructed her servers to get the prepared snack trays out of the refrigerator and to put the lasagna that she'd made ahead of time into the oven so that they could all be eating dinner at five thirty.

When she felt that everything was under control, Cassie decided to face her demons and walked up the stairs to the master suite. As soon as her feet touched the plush carpeting, she felt her knees buckle. Forcing herself to keep moving, she shut the door and walked to the bathroom to freshen up.

So many memories assaulted her that she felt as if she were being smothered. Everywhere she looked she could see Adam, feel him. Every touch, every word played through her mind, and with a cry of despair, she stormed from the bathroom out onto the balcony and faced the cold winter air. She welcomed the frosty bite as she stared out at the ocean. There was a time when all she wanted was to be able to look out at this view anytime she wanted; now she knew that for the next several days it would make her sick.

With a fortifying breath, Cassie stepped back into the bedroom, closed the door to the balcony, and walked across the room, knowing that sleep was going to elude her tonight. At the doorway, she turned and looked at the bed. Like a flash of light, it hit her; she had told Adam that she loved him that last night they'd spent here. Was that what freaked him out? Was that why he had turned on her the way he had?

A lone tear rolled down her cheek. What did it matter? He was gone, refusing to come to his own mother's wedding so that he wouldn't have to see her. How was that for rejection? Wiping the stray tear away, Cassie walked out of the room and went to the kitchen to check on the meal.

As she suspected, no one seemed to have noticed her absence. A quick peek into the oven showed that the lasagna was cooking nicely and that her staff had the situation under control. She turned toward the refrigerator and was grabbing a bottle of water when someone came up behind her, placed a firm hand on her hip, and leaned against her.

She'd know that touch anywhere.

With a gasp of surprise, Cassie turned toward Adam's smiling face. "Sorry I'm late, darling. I didn't miss dinner, did I?" He kissed her lightly on the cheek and had to hold in a laugh at the expression on her face. She was surprised to see him; he wasn't sure if it was a good surprise or a bad one.

Cassie stared at Adam as if he was from another planet. What in the world was he doing here? Her entire family had promised her that he wasn't coming! A quick glance around the room showed no one other than herself to be surprised by his appearance. Taking a cautious step back, she asked, "What are you doing here?"

With an easy chuckle, he looked at Cassie and smiled, touching a finger lightly to her nose. "My mother's getting married. Where else would I be?"

Before Cassie could find the words to tell him exactly where she thought he should be, Adam was being welcomed by her traitorous family. She stood, mouth agape, as her brother shook his hand and welcomed him. Her father followed suit, and then both of her sisters walked over and hugged him! Blinking rapidly and wondering what on earth was going on, she almost choked as Katie handed Ella to Adam and he readily took the baby into his arms!

The room began to tilt and spin, and Cassie reached behind her to hold onto the counter to stay upright. It was like being in an episode of *The Twilight Zone*. Any minute she expected to pass out, but luckily one of her servers approached and had questions about the meal. Thankful for the distraction, Cassie busied herself. Unfortunately, time moved quickly, and before she knew it, she found herself seated next to Adam in the formal dining room and being served dinner.

Conversation rang out all around her, but all Cassie heard was her own heartbeat drumming in her ears. Adam hadn't said anything else to her since his initial comment, and she was thankful for his silence. She took a deep breath, reached for her glass of water, and took a long drink from it.

"Everything looks and smells wonderful, Cass," Matt said as he stood to toast the soon-to-be bride and groom.

Cassie was sure that his words were eloquent and wonderful, and she raised her glass at the appointed time but still couldn't focus fully on any of it. She could smell Adam's cologne, feel the heat of his body next to hers. Dear Lord, how on earth was she going to survive the next three days?

Dishes were being passed, and without touching a thing, Cassie found her plate full. Looking around in confusion as to how it all got there, she turned to find Adam smiling at her. "I hope you don't mind, but you were holding up the line." His tone was light and easy and very unlike she had ever heard him speak before. He looked so relaxed that Cassie found herself wanting to smile at him but couldn't seem to make her face cooperate.

"Um…thank you," she murmured and then turned her attention to her meal and began to eat. The food was like sawdust in her mouth, and she hoped she was the only one feeling that way. A look around the table showed her that everyone seemed to be enjoying the meal, so she let herself relax.

Once dinner was done and everything cleared away, people dispersed around the house. The men had taken over the game room, while the women sat around the fire in the living room talking about the wedding. Cassie stayed in the kitchen longer than was necessary and finally forced herself to relax.

A dessert buffet was put out, and everyone ate and visited some more. Before she knew it, people were starting to say their good nights and walking to their rooms. Now that Adam was here, Cassie figured she'd bunk in the game room with her servers. Not wanting to face Adam in the bedroom, she went up and began collecting her things. She was almost done when she turned to find him standing in the doorway.

"What are you doing?" he asked.

"I didn't realize that you'd be here, everyone said that you weren't coming." She cursed the tremor in her voice and was thankful that her hands were busy putting clothes in her suitcase so that he wouldn't notice them shaking as well. "I had no idea that so many relatives were going to be here, so I'm going to bunk down in the game room with the girls."

Cassie was waiting for Adam to play the role of the gentleman and tell her that it wasn't necessary for her to leave because he would, but he didn't. Instead, he walked into the room, sat on the bed, and removed his shoes. She stopped her packing and merely stared at him. Mild disappointment swamped her when he didn't make the offer to be the one to leave. When he stood to put his shoes away, Cassie went to the bathroom to collect the items she had placed in there earlier. When she came out, her suitcase was no longer on the bed. She found Adam emerging from the walk-in closet.

"Where's my suitcase?"

"In the closet." His response was said lightly as he walked to the bed and reclined against the pillows, his smile serene.

Many emotions were raging inside Cassie, but confusion won. "Why? It's been a long day, and I need my things."

"Amy and Madison are already camped out. All you'll do is wake them up, and they've got a lot of work to do over the next couple of days."

Sighing heavily because she hated having to talk to

him like he was a child, she said, "Be that as it may, I have to sleep somewhere."

"Sleep here."

Cassie looked at Adam as if he'd lost his mind. All her anguish and frustration from the past six weeks boiled to the surface. "Sleep here? What is wrong with you? You humiliate me—again, might I add—in front of my family, and then I don't hear from you for more than a month, and now you think you can waltz in here and ask me to sleep with you?" Realizing that the bedroom door was open and her voice was getting near a screech, she stormed over and shut it before rounding on him again.

"I'll admit that it's my fault that you assume that I'd want to. I mean, after all, you've done this in the past, and somehow I manage to keep ending up in bed with you. But not this time, Adam. I'll sleep out on the damn deck first!" Feeling confident that she had made her point, Cassie turned and headed for the closet to retrieve her luggage.

Her heart was pounding, and she was mumbling to herself about what kind of an idiot people must take her for when a shadow crossed the doorway.

"If you pick that up, I'm going to put it back."

Cassie stood straight. "I thought I made myself clear. I am not sharing a bed with you. You may have conned my family into welcoming you, but they don't know the real you. You act sincere, and then as soon as you get your way, you walk out. I'm not going there with you again, Adam," she said, her voice finally cracking. "I can't."

He stepped into the closet and took Cassie in his

arms. It felt so good to hold her again, and he was surprised that she didn't put up more of a fight; instead, she started to cry.

"Why couldn't you stay away?" she sobbed. "I don't understand why you need to be cruel."

Her words cut him deeply, and he placed a finger under her chin and forced her to look at him. "I'm not trying to be cruel, Cassandra," he said softly, "I realized I couldn't stay away. I missed you."

Disbelief marked her face, and Adam knew he had to come clean. "I had to be here. I couldn't lose you." His eyes scanned her face, the beautiful face that had been haunting him for weeks. Deciding to lay it all out on the table, he took a deep breath and said, "I know."

Eyebrows arched, Cassie leaned back and stared at him. "You know what?"

A small chuckle emerged because Adam knew that life with Cassie was never going to be boring. She was going to make him work for this. "I *know* about the baby."

She stepped out of his arms and nearly stumbled over her suitcase in her attempt to put some space between them. "What baby? What are you talking about?"

Now it was Adam's turn to be confused. "Our baby," he said simply, although there wasn't a lot of confidence behind the statement. "I heard you on the phone that day in my office. You're pregnant."

Cassie laughed out loud and stepped past him to get out of the closet. "I don't know what you thought you heard, Adam, but I am most definitely *not* pregnant. And what were you doing listening in on my conversation?"

Following her to the bedroom, Adam felt a slight

sense of panic at the turn in the conversation. "I wasn't intentionally listening to your conversation, you were in my office! Grace told me that you were on the phone, and I heard you talking about being pregnant and that you weren't going to tell me!"

"Is that why you freaked out in the restaurant? Rather than talking to me about what you *thought* you heard, you decided it would be better to rant and rave and say horrible things to me and my family?"

Adam pinched the bridge of his nose and took a deep breath to calm himself. This was not going the way he had planned. "Look, I will admit I behaved badly that night to everyone, and I have apologized to all of them for it…"

"Not to me," she stated.

"I was getting to that," he snapped, mentally counting to ten before he continued. "My feelings for you terrify me. I'd never felt for anyone what I feel for you. I don't trust easily, and there I was, willing to try, and then you announcing that you were pregnant but not wanting to ever tell me sort of flipped a switch. I am so sorry for the way I reacted, Cassandra, but I want you to know that I'm excited about the baby!"

With a mirthless laugh, Cassie sat on the edge of the bed. "Look, Adam, you completely misunderstood what you heard that day. I'm not pregnant."

"But on the phone…you said…"

"I was on the phone with Danielle Chamberlain, who actually *is* pregnant. She and Max are excited to become parents, but she didn't want me to tell you because Max wanted to do it himself. So I promised to keep silent. That's what you heard." Cassie sighed wearily, waiting for Adam's retreat.

"If you had simply asked me when you came into the office, I would have told you. Then we could have avoided all the ugliness that happened, and we could have ended our relationship differently," she said wearily.

Sitting beside her, Adam took her hand and stared at their connection. "What makes you think it would have ended?" he asked softly.

"I'm not stupid, Adam. I knew when we left here that you were having regrets and that it was only a matter of time. I figured that we would drift apart and try not to be awkward with each other when our parents married."

Sighing sadly, Cassie raised her head and looked at Adam. "So you're off the hook. I'm not pregnant. No one is trapping you. You don't have to be here, pretending to have a good time so that an angry mob won't come chasing after you over my honor or anything."

He was about to respond when there was a knock on the bedroom door. Stephen and Bev walked in, full of smiles. Adam and Cassie stood and faced them, both plastering smiles on their faces as they approached.

"We want you both to know how much we appreciate all that you've done to help with our wedding," Bev stated. "The house is so beautiful, Adam, and I love how it is like a Christmas wonderland everywhere I turn."

"It was my pleasure, Mom," he said gruffly. "You deserve to have a beautiful wedding."

She beamed at his words and then stepped forward to hug him. "It means the world to me that you're here to share it with me and to walk me down the aisle. Thank you."

She turned toward Cassie. "And you," she said,

hugging Cassie as well, "you have outdone yourself already with all the food and with all you've done with the preparations! I am the most relaxed bride in the world. Thank you."

"You are very welcome," Cassie said genuinely. "I want your wedding to be everything you want it to be so that you can start your lives together on a good note."

"That's my girl," Stephen said, taking a turn hugging Cassie. "You make me proud every day, Cass."

"Thanks, Dad."

"I know it's getting late, but we wanted to say how happy we are for the two of you. This wedding is more special because the two of you are back together." Cassie tried not to react to Bev's words and instead simply smiled and nodded, hugging the couple one last time before they left the room, shutting the door behind them.

"We're *back* together?" Cassie asked as soon as the door was shut. "You told your mother that we're back together? How did they even know we were together in the first place? I know I never told them that!" Her voice was nearing hysteria, and Adam reached out and placed his hands on her shoulders to try to calm her.

"I didn't technically *say* that we were together but that I was hopeful. You see, when I talked to everyone—"

Cassie threw Adam's hands from her shoulders. "When you talked to everyone? So you told my whole family that we were getting back together? And nobody questioned that or bothered to say anything to me?"

Adam was used to thinking quickly on his feet, but he had a feeling that no matter what he said, Cassie was still going to be upset. "I asked them not to upset you because of…well…" His eyes strayed to her stomach, and it took mere seconds for him to realize his mistake.

"You told them all that I was *pregnant*?"

"In all fairness, at the time it seemed to work in my favor. After all, how could they hate the father of your child, especially when I was stepping up to do the right thing?"

"Have you gone completely insane, Adam? You went behind my back and told my family something that, even if it was true, was none of their business! How could you do that?" Cassie demanded as she began to pace the length of the bedroom.

"Is that why everyone has been acting so weird toward me? Why I haven't done more than lift a dish without someone swooping in to help me?" She wasn't asking him the questions as much as putting together all the odd behavior of her family for the past couple of weeks. "That must be why Matt came and loaded the van for me and why Lauren has suddenly taken an interest in how I've been eating!" She turned to face him. "Did it ever once occur to you to come and talk to me first?"

Feeling cornered, Adam stared mutely at her for a moment. "I…it sort of just happened! Your father came to invite me to the wedding, and we talked, and I told him what I'd heard, and I promised to keep it to himself. Then I had to go see my mother and beg for her forgiveness, and then she asked about you, and it came out." He ran a hand through his hair. "By the time I got to your brother and sisters, it seemed a way to smooth things over with them."

Cassie stared at him in disbelief.

"Looking back, I can see how that was not the way I

should have gone, but what am I supposed to do? Tell me how to fix this, and I will." Walking toward her, Adam reached out. When Cassie flinched and moved out of his grasp, he felt as if all hope was lost. He waited what seemed like hours for her to speak again.

"In the midst of all this wedding hoopla, I now have to either upset our parents by telling them the truth or lie to them. Have I got that right?" she asked wearily.

"You don't have to lie, Cassandra. Give me another chance. No one will be thinking about the possibility of you being pregnant because they'll all be wrapped up in the wedding festivities. We'll deal with that issue after New Year's. Please say you'll give me another chance."

Cassie looked at him, desperately wanting to believe him and to give in and say yes. Unfortunately, she'd been down this road before and wasn't willing to take that chance with him again. Adam Lawrence had broken her heart, and the wound was too fresh for her to be willing to give him the opportunity to do it again.

A look at the clock showed it to be nearing midnight. She was so tired and wanted the day to end. "I can't do this with you now, Adam. I'm tired, and I'm confused, and the thought of facing everyone tomorrow knowing that they are all believing a lie…it's too much for me to deal with right now. I want to go to sleep." She walked past him and went to get her suitcase. Adam followed her into the closet.

"It's late, and you're tired. Please stay here tonight. I promise to be a perfect gentleman and keep my hands to myself. The bed is big enough for us to both sleep in it without ever touching." He saw the hesitation in her eyes, and it made him ache. "Please."

The slight nod of her head was all he needed. Carrying the suitcase out into the room, he placed it on the bench at the foot of the bed. Cassie opened it and grabbed a nightshirt and her toiletries and went into the bathroom. When she emerged a few minutes later, Adam was already in the bed, facing away from her with his bedside lamp off. She was thankful to not have to speak to him again.

She crawled into the bed, got comfortable under the blankets, and then lay on her side with her back to Adam, as close to the edge of the mattress as she could get without falling off. Turning off her bedside light, she let a small sigh escape. This was supposed to be a wonderful event; it was Christmas, and her father was getting married. In a matter of hours, all the joy that she had been feeling had been replaced with despair. How was she supposed to face her family in the morning?

Though Cassie longed for answers, her body longed for sleep even more. Morning would be here soon enough, and she hoped that by the time the sun came up, she'd have the answer to all her troubles.

Chapter 17

THE FIRST RAYS OF THE SUN WERE STARTING TO MAKE THEIR way across the bedroom. Cassie snuggled deeper into the blankets and sighed. She loved this bed. It didn't take long for her brain to engage and realize that she was pressed up against Adam from head to toe; their legs were tangled together, her head was on his chest, and his arms were wrapped around her. *Dammit!* she thought. He'd promised!

At the slight movement of her head, Adam knew she was awake and patiently waited to see what kind of response he would get. Reluctantly loosening his hold on her, he opened his eyes as he met her furious gaze.

"You promised," she hissed.

"Yes, I did," he said evenly.

"As if you weren't despicable enough, you had to try something cheap like this!" She sat up and pushed her hair from her eyes, sighing with frustration.

"Like what?"

Her head snapped toward him at his comment. "Like what? You told me that you would be a gentleman, and yet here we are, all tangled up together!"

Adam chuckled and sat up, adjusting the pillows behind him. "I hate to break it to you, Sweetheart, but check which side of the bed you're on."

Cassie's heart sank as she realized that Adam was exactly where he'd been last night when she'd come to bed. She was the one who had crossed the invisible line and over to enemy territory. "Oh."

Taking a chance, Adam reached out and gently pulled Cassie beside him against the pillows. She didn't resist, and if anything, she seemed to sigh and relax. She was the first to speak.

"I'm sorry."

Unable to resist, Adam wrapped an arm around her and kissed the top of her head. "It's okay," he said. "I've given you plenty of reasons to distrust me."

Cassie looked up at him and gave him a weak smile. "I don't want to go downstairs and face everyone. I don't know what to do."

"Then we'll stay up here all day and let them draw their own conclusions," he teased and gave an inward sigh of relief when Cassie's smile grew.

"I definitely don't want that," she said, nudging him with her elbow. "But, seriously, I don't know what I'm supposed to do. I don't want to lie to everyone. I've never lied to my father, and I'd hate to start now, right before his wedding."

Adam caressed her cheek and tilted her face up toward his. "The last time we were in this bed together, you said that you loved me." When Cassie went to protest, he placed a finger over her lips to silence her. "You were half-asleep, but you said it. It was the most wonderful and yet the most terrifying thing anyone had ever said to me, and I know that I reacted badly. This was never supposed to happen between us, and yet I can't begin to regret it. You turned my life upside down the day you quit in my office, and as angry as it made me at the time, I can't be sorry that it happened."

Removing his finger from her soft lips, Adam continued, "I can never apologize enough for all the ways I've hurt you, but I want you to know that not a day has gone by since that night in the restaurant that I haven't kicked myself for the way I treated you. You mean the world to me, and I don't want to imagine a life without you."

Everything in Cassie softened. In all the time she and Adam had spent together, this was the first time he had ever spoken of his feelings, and she knew by the sincerity in his eyes that this wasn't a game; it wasn't a means to an end.

"Don't go downstairs and lie to everyone, go downstairs with me, hand in hand, and celebrate."

A stray tear rolled down her cheek. "I want so badly to believe you…to believe *in* you, but I'm so scared. I don't think I can survive if you break my heart again."

Leaning forward, Adam kissed her gently on the lips. Pulling back, he stared into her eyes, hoping she'd read his true feelings there. "Cassandra, I love you. I've never said those words to anyone, and yet there are no other words to describe how I feel about you. My life has been so empty without you, and even though I know that there is no baby, I want that to be a temporary thing. I want to marry you, have babies with you, and have a life with you. Is it possible that you still love me?"

His words were Cassie's undoing. "Adam, I do love you. I tried not to, but I couldn't stop. Being here without you was so hard! Tell me again. Tell me that you love me."

"I love you. I'll tell you all day every day if that's what you want."

Wrapping a hand behind Adam's neck, Cassie pulled

him to her for the kiss that she'd been craving for weeks. They lay more comfortably on the bed as Adam kissed her like a starving man finally able to feast. In between kisses, he told Cassie how much she meant to him.

When they finally surfaced, Cassie was the first to speak. "As much as I want to stay right here in this bed with you, we have a full schedule of wedding preparations to attend to."

Reluctantly, he agreed. "So then you're feeling better about going downstairs and facing everyone?"

"Well, I'm not totally lying to them, but I dread the time when we do have to tell them that it was all a misunderstanding and I'm not pregnant. Hopefully, they'll all get a good laugh out of it."

"Or," he began, "we see what we can do to rectify that." A wicked grin crossed Adam's face as his hand skimmed over Cassie's cheek.

"A man with a plan…I like that."

*Keep reading for a sneak peek of the next
book in the Montgomery Brothers series*

Until *there was* Us

"DAMMIT," MEGAN MONTGOMERY CURSED AS SHE TRIED
to pull her phone from her bag and ended up nearly trip-
ping over her own two feet. She might be in a new city,
but she was the same old klutz she'd always been. The
airport was crowded, and she wasn't paying attention
to where she was going, and all in all, she felt like a
disaster. She murmured an apology to the people around
her before stepping aside to read her texts.

Her cousin Summer Reed was meeting her outside
baggage claim, and according to the text, she was cir-
cling the airport, trying to put her baby daughter to sleep.

Great.

The flight to Portland had been full, there had been
a crying baby behind Megan, and the last thing she
wanted was to be sitting near another crying baby—
even if she was incredibly adorable and related to her.
Ugh…her nerves were frayed. As if moving across the
country wasn't stressful enough, it had to get off to a
rocky start? She let out a breath and joined the throngs

of people again—careful to pay attention this time—and merged into the stream heading to the exit.

Fifteen minutes later she had her bags and was searching for Summer's red SUV. Spring in Portland was nicer than in Albany, Megan thought as she waited. She was practically bouncing on her toes as she watched the flow of cars. Her emotions were doing their own version of a tennis match, bouncing between being nervous and excited about this new adventure.

Leaving the job she'd had for the past three years hadn't been hard—especially since she knew from the beginning it had an end date—but opting to work for her cousin Zach on the other side of the country was definitely out of her comfort zone. Megan liked to keep things simple. Orderly. She had been settled in Albany and figured that even when her job ended, she'd find another in the same city.

That hadn't happened.

Instead, she had been handed an opportunity she'd always wanted but never thought she'd get—working within the family business.

It was crazy. After all, she *was* a Montgomery, and it shouldn't have been a big deal. The only problem was… she didn't understand finance, she wasn't particularly suave, and she didn't have the business savvy of the rest of her family. She was a computer girl—a techie—but she was really good at what she did!

Still, the planets seemed to have aligned perfectly for this job with Zach to open up just as she was in need of one. Who was she to question it? It was the perfect solution to her employment dilemma, and it was going to be a good thing for her to do something new.

No matter how terrifying it currently felt.

The sound of a horn broke Megan from her reverie, and she saw her cousin pulling up in front of her. With a big smile on her face, Megan waved to Summer and immediately loaded her bags into the hatch. With a shriek of excitement, Summer gave her a fierce hug.

"I am so glad you're here!" she cried. "I have been counting the days until I could see you and squeeze you and look at your face!"

Summer had always been the excitable one in the family. She had a heart of gold and a zest for life that Megan never quite understood, but she was hoping to have some of Summer's excitement rub off on her.

"Come on, come on, let's get you in the car! I want to hear all about your flight and how you're doing and if you're excited about starting work on Monday and—"

"Summer?"

"Hmm?"

"Breathe," Megan said with a smile.

With a nod, Summer walked around to the driver's side and climbed into the car. Megan did the same on the passenger side, but not before peeking into the rear seat at her niece—that sounded much better than "first cousin once removed."

"I have some super cute stuff for Amber in my suitcase," Megan said as she climbed in.

"You didn't have to do that. You already sent that precious crocheted baby blanket when she was born." Summer smiled and added, "It reminded me of the ones Nana used to make. Do you remember?"

Megan nodded. Nobody knew that her great-grandmother had taught her how to crochet when she was just a little girl, and she found it to be fascinating and relaxing. She had come home from Nana's one day with the most adorable, soft, cuddly baby blanket, and her father had scoffed at it, told her it was ugly, and mocked her desire to spend her time making things he considered frivolous. At first she had been heartbroken, and she stopped crocheting for a while, but the next time she was at her grandmother's, she got pulled in again to the comfort of the soft wool in her fingers, the pretty colors, the rhythm of stitching, and the gratification of seeing a ball of yarn turn into something beautiful. So she had continued her creations in private, making absolutely sure nobody knew about it. Crocheting was her secret hobby, and she donated all the baby blankets and clothing she made to local hospitals and women's shelters.

In the past several years, she hadn't had as much free time to indulge as she would have liked. Sometimes her fingers just itched. For an instant she considered confiding in Summer, but then she thought of her father's scorn and everyone laughing at her, and the moment passed. "So…how far are we from your house?"

"It's about an hour's drive," Summer said as they pulled away from the curb. "Amber's a good sleeper, so we can talk all we want without worrying about waking her up."

Was it wrong that Megan wanted to let out a sigh of relief and a hearty "hallelujah"?

She did sigh, but it was a happy one. They were on the road heading to Summer and Ethan's house, where she was going to be living for the foreseeable future in their guesthouse. Which reminded her…

"I feel bad about this," she began.

"About what?"

"You finally got your mom and everyone to go home, and now I'm moving in."

With a light laugh, Summer glanced at her briefly. "Are you kidding? This is going to be *way* more fun than having my mom here. You're the sister I never had! We're going to hang out together and work together and—"

Megan was about to respond when her phone rang. She smiled when she saw Gabriella's name on the screen. "I am in the car and on my way!" she said when she answered.

"Megan! We are so excited you're finally here! I wanted to ride with Summer, but things got hectic here, and then Zach was worried about me being in the car for so long, and…" She sighed. "I swear, you'd think I was an invalid the way he's carrying on."

"You're pregnant, and he's worried," Megan replied with a smile. "I think it's kind of sweet how he's so protective."

"It was sweet for the first two months when I was dealing with morning sickness. But we're nearly seven months in now, and I feel great, and he's making me crazy. Promise you'll distract him while you're here so I can at least go shopping by myself one day!" Gabriella said with a laugh.

"I promise. You say the word, and I'll keep him busy with codes and computer issues that will have his head spinning for days!"

"You have officially become my favorite person."

"I aim to please."

"Okay, so…it's going to take you about an hour to get to Summer's house," Gabriella explained, "and I'll meet you there."

"That sounds great! I'll see you then!" When Megan hung up, she felt a little more relaxed. This wasn't a move across the country where she didn't know anyone; she was going to be with family, and that made her smile.

With the phone still in her hand, she knew she needed to let her own family know she'd landed safely and was on her way to Summer's. Her mother had been overly anxious about this trip—and not in a weird I'm-going-to-miss-you way but in an I'm-very-excited-for-you one. Which was weird. For all the years she had been hounding Megan about moving closer to home, she was suddenly her number one cheerleader for moving to the other side of the country.

Definitely weird.

With a sigh because all she wanted was to close her eyes for a few minutes and unwind, she turned toward Summer. "Would you mind if I give my mom a quick call? I should have done it while I was waiting for my luggage, but…"

Summer laughed. "Go for it. I know my mother went a little crazy when I moved here and was on the phone with me constantly at first. So I understand."

With a quick nod, Megan hit Send on her mother's number and waited for her to answer.

"Are you there? Was your flight okay? Are you with Summer?" her mother said as a greeting.

Her anxious tone had Megan laughing softly. "Hi, Mom. Yes, I'm here, my flight was a little less than ideal, and I'm in the car with Summer and Amber right now."

"Oh, she brought Amber with her? How sweet! You'll have to send me some pictures!"

"We're in the car, Mom."

"I didn't mean right now," her mother said with a bit of a huff. "So you're there and you're on your way to Summer's, and…when are you going to start looking for an apartment?"

"Mom, we've talked about this. I'm only going to stay with them for a couple of weeks, and I thought it was okay for me to get here and relax for a few days before I had to spring into action."

"I'm just saying…you shouldn't rely on them for everything because they're already so busy with Amber and Summer going back to work, and…maybe you should ask them if they know of any vacant apartments near people they know. Plus, you'll need to make some friends of your own and maybe start socializing so—"

"You know what…our connection…bad…call you… weekend…"

It was childish, and she wasn't proud of it, but now was so not the time to deal with the whole lecture on her social life.

Beside her, Summer started to laugh, and Megan smacked her playfully on the arm.

"Megan? Megan, are you there?"

"Can't hear…go…soon!" And then she hung up and immediately turned her phone off.

Yeah, not her finest reaction to her mother, but her mind was spinning with too many other thoughts right now to add that to it.

Yes, she was living someplace new, was starting a new job, and was going to be meeting new people. And yes, it was a chance for a fresh start. None of this was news to Megan. Actually, she was looking forward to the opportunity. Her life in Albany had been…well…she was in a serious rut. She'd been working ten hours a day, six days a week, and the only people she'd socialized with were her coworkers.

Maybe socialized wasn't *quite* the right word. More like…saw them frequently…like whenever she came out of her office.

Which wasn't often.

Her muscles were starting to tense up again, and she forced herself to relax. This move was supposed to help her break out of her rut—force her to meet new people and be someone who didn't spend her entire life holed up in her office staring at a computer screen. All around her, people were meeting and having lives and falling in love and starting families. And as much as she argued how missing out didn't bother her, the truth was that it did.

Megan had always wanted to be the girl who had a ton of friends who went out for girls' nights and went away for weekends together. And then she wanted to meet a man and fall in love and have the kind of family she had grown up with.

Maybe it wasn't for everyone, but Megan wanted the American dream—it was a little outdated, and she'd learned to keep that ideal to herself because so many people felt like it wasn't something a modern woman should want. But she did. She really, really did. And the only way she was going to achieve it was to force herself to break out of her comfort zone and put herself out there—meet people. Go out. Date.

Sigh.

The last time she'd gone out on a date was…

Nothing was coming to mind.

"That can't be a good sign," she murmured.

"What's not a good sign is you talking to yourself when I'm sitting right here," Summer said. "Seriously, you can't let your mother stress you out like that."

"Easier said than done."

"Which part of the conversation did you in? The move? Finding a place of your own? Or the socializing?" When Megan gave her a quizzical look, Summer smiled. "Sorry, but your mom's voice carries."

"Oh." Okay, so this was exactly the kind of thing she wanted—a friend she could talk to when she was stressed out. "It was the socializing."

"I knew it!"

"Yeah, well…it was more the implication of what it entailed. It isn't just making friends, it's dating too."

"And that's a problem…why?"

"I've always been busy, and after my breakup with Colin, I didn't want to get involved with anyone."

"He was a major jerk, Megan. You should be relieved to be rid of him!"

"I am. I am. But…it wasn't easy to get over. Things were a little—"

"They were ugly and intense," Summer said. "I get it. But that was more than two years ago. You can't tell me you haven't dated since then."

"I've been busy." Unfortunately, she couldn't blame the lack of dating on her work schedule. It certainly didn't help, but it wasn't the real reason for her lack of interest.

It was Alex.